Go Around

Noyes excels at writing both romance and intrigue and it shows in this book. Her characters might as well be real they are so well-written. I'm a pretty big fan of second-chance love stories, and I love the way this one is done. You get the angst you expect from the two women trying to get past the pain of their separation and work their way back to being a couple in love. The outside forces that had a role in their breakup are still around and have to be dealt with. Add in a nasty bad guy (or guys) who are physically and psychologically stalking Elise and you get a tale full of danger, excitement, intrigue, and romance. I also love the Easter egg the author included for her book *Alone*. I actually laughed out loud at that little scene. E.J. Noyes' works always get my highest praise and recommendation, and this novel is no different. You really need to read this book.

-Betty H., *NetGalley*

In *Go Around*, E. J. Noyes has dipped her toes in the second chance romance pool and was masterful in blending angst, enduring love and suspense in it. The chemistry and dynamics between the pair were thick and palpable but what stood out for me throughout the book was the type of love everyone wished they had; fierce and protective, grounded in loyalty, passionate yet to be able to just be when you are with the other. Noyes also made Bennet, Avery's dog another highlight for me. He was the tension breaker and a giant darling.

-nutmeg, *NetGalley*

Pas de deux

Pas de deux doesn't disappoint: the writing is excellent, the pace is ideal, the characters are layered and, yes, relatable, including the secondary characters, from Caitlyn's groom Wren, to Addie's friend Teresa and, of course, Dewey the horse. One of the many things I loved in this book is the way the MCs deal with problems. They do this very adult and very rare-in-lesfic thing: they talk to each other. This book is proof that miscommunication isn't required for drama. Neither is a breakup. Well-fleshed characters with very human hang-ups bring all the angst and drama necessary. It's all the more interesting here as *Pas de deux* is part enemies-to-lovers romance, part second chance, depending on whose point of view is playing.

-Les Rêveur

This story is not the traditional enemies-to-lovers romance, and I love that. Noyes really puts emphasis on how skewed memories can become as you get older, and how an experience may appear different to another person who had the exact same one. Even if you are unfamiliar with dressage, Noyes' writing is still spot on and delivers the same compelling, fun, and intriguing story with loveable characters of both the two-legged and four-legged kind. This love letter to a sport she obviously has a passion for is so evident and I felt honored to have her share her passion with me and every reader who picks it up. If you love horses, enemies-to-lovers, or even just Noyes' stories in general, this one will definitely be a favorite on your list.

-The Lesbian Review

This romance hit two main tropes. For one main character this is a second chance romance, for the other character, this is an enemies to lovers romance. I loved the two different sides of how the character saw things and I think it gave the book a little zip that caught my attention from the beginning. I was very happy that while this was first person, the POV is actually from both main characters. It was perfect for this book especially since both mains can't even agree on their past. Seeing how each character thought and why, was the right choice for this romantic story. As long as you are a fan of horses, or at least are okay with them, then I would absolutely recommend this one. Noyes writes really well and makes smart choices so that is why she is one of the best.

-Lex Kent's Reviews, *goodreads*

Reaping the Benefits

The story is quite eccentric with its paranormal context but in fact is a pure romance at heart with a nice dose of humor. The book is written in third person, from the point of view of both protagonists, which is not common for Noyes, but it is executed perfectly. With all main elements done well, this makes an awesome read which I could easily recommend to all romance fans.

-Pin's Reviews, goodreads

I've read many love stories that entertain the idea of soul mates, but this one does something even more interesting. This one explores the depth of love and its ability to transcend death. This story plays with the idea that love has no limits or boundaries. Its exploration provides a unique setting for this heartfelt romantic tale. At its core it remains a romance. The love story between Jane and Morgan is tender and sweet. It's so cleverly and delightfully done; I've never read anything quite like it before. Noyes possesses the ability to see a story where others don't and turn that into something unique and captivating. She uses rich storytelling and engaging characters to enthrall and delight us.

It's fresh and original. It's everything you crave when you want to dig into a great romance. I highly recommend it.

-Deb M., NetGalley

I'm spectacularly smitten with Death, to be specific with E. J. Noyes' personification of death as Cici La Morte in this new and most wondrous book. Cici is not one of the main characters but she is the fulcrum about which the whole plot rotates. She simultaneously operates as a beautiful symbol of our fascination with the theme of death and loss, and as a comedic but wise Greek chorus guiding Morgan through the internal conflict threatening to tear her very soul apart. All of E. J. Noyes' previous books have had emotionally charged first-person narrative, so I was curious how her switch to writing in the third person would play out here, but it really works. Despite many lighthearted and genuinely funny moments I found that this book not only had E. J. Noyes' signature ability to make me cry, but also fascinating ideas and philosophies about grief, loss, and hope.

-Orlando J., NetGalley

If you're looking for a lesbian romance, but with a twist of something different, I recommend Reaping the Benefits. It's sweet, sexy, and fun.

-The Lesbian Review

If the Shoe Fits

When we pick up an E. J. Noyes book we expect intensity, characters with issues (circumstantial and/or internal), and a romance that builds believably. Considering this is *Ask, Tell* #3 we expected all of the above layered with epic seriousness. We were pleasantly surprised and totally floored by the humor in addition to what was already expected!

-*Best Lesfic Reviews*

Alone

E. J. Noyes is easily one of the most gifted writers pulling us into whatever world she creates making us live and feel every emotion with her characters. Definitely, loudly, vehemently recommended.

-Reviewer@Large, *NetGalley*

Alone is an absolutely stunning book. This book is not a 5-star, it is well above that. You don't see books like this one very often. Truly a treasure and one that will stay with you long after the final page.

-Tiff's Reviews, *goodreads*

There are only a handful of authors that I will drop everything to read as soon as a new book comes out, and Noyes is at the top of that list. It seems no matter what Noyes writes she doesn't disappoint. I will eagerly be waiting for whatever she writes next.

-Lex Kent's Reviews, *goodreads*

There are only a few books out there so compelling they seem to take control of you and force you to read them as quickly as possible. You can't put them down. You just want the world to go away and leave you alone until you can finish this story. *Alone* by E. J. Noyes is that book for me. This novel is absolutely wonderful.

-Betty H., *NetGalley*

Not only is this easily one of the best books of 2019, but it has worked its way onto my personal all-time top 10 list. There is not one formulaic thing going on, and it's "unputdownable."

-Karen C., *NetGalley*

I cannot give this anything more than five stars, but damn I wish I could. I would give it 15.

-Carolyn M., NetGalley

Ask Me Again

Not every story needs a sequel. *Ask, Tell* demanded it, and Noyes delivers in spectacular fashion. Sabine and Rebecca show us their fortitude and their strength in their love for each other...Thank you, Noyes, for giving us a great story, a great series, and amazing women that teach us the best things in life are worth fighting for.

There really is only one way to tell this story, and Noyes executes it perfectly. She gives us events from the first person perspective. However, she alternates each chapter between Sabine's point of view and Rebecca's point of view. You're able to get the full perspective of their inner feelings and turmoil they hide from one another. In addition, you're able to get the complete picture of the unconditional love Sabine and Rebecca have for each other. It's this little light of love that propels the reader to keep going and hope these women will finally reach the end of the darkness.

-The Lesbian Review

Gold

This is Noyes' third book, and her writing just keeps getting better and better with each release. She gives us such amazing characters that are easy for anyone to relate to. And she makes them so endearing that you can't help but want them to overcome the past and move forward toward their happily ever after.

-The Lesbian Review

This book is exactly the way I wish romance authors would get back to writing romance. This is what I want to read. If you are a Noyes fan, get this book. If you are a romance fan, get this book. I didn't even talk about the skiing... if you are a skiing fan, get this book.

-Lex Kent's Reviews, goodreads

Turbulence

Wow... and when I say 'wow' I mean... WOW. After the author's debut novel *Ask, Tell* got to my list of best books of 2017, I was wondering if that was just a fluke. Fortunately for us lesfic readers, now it's confirmed: E. J. Noyes CAN write. Not only that, she can write different genres... Written in first person from Isabelle's point of view, the reader gets into her headspace with all her insecurities, struggles, and character traits. Alongside Isabelle, we discover Audrey's personality, her life story and, most importantly, her feelings. Throughout the book, Ms. Noyes pushes us down a roller coaster of emotions as we accompany Isabelle in her journey of self-discovery. In the process, we laugh, suffer, and enjoy the ride.

-Gaby, *goodreads*

The entire story just flowed from the first page! E. J. Noyes did a superb job of bringing out Isabelle's and Audrey's personalities, faults, erratic emotions, and the burning passion they shared. The chemistry between both women was so palpable! I felt as though the writer drizzled every word she wrote with love, combustible desire, and intense longing.

-*The Lesbian Review*

Ask, Tell

This is a book with everything I love about top quality lesbian fiction: a fantastic romance between two wonderful women I can relate to, a location that really made me think again about something I thought I knew well, and brilliant pacing and scene-setting. I cannot recommend this novel highly enough.

-*Rainbow Book Reviews*

Noyes totally blew my mind from the first sentence. I went in timidly, and I came away awaiting her next release with bated breath. I really love how Noyes is able to get below the surface of the DADT legislation. She really captures the longing, the heartbreak, and especially the isolation that LGBTQ soldiers had to endure because the alternative was being deemed unfit to serve by their own government. I applaud Noyes for getting to the heart of the matter and giving a very important representation of what living and serving under this legislation truly meant for LGBTQ men and women of service.

-The Lesbian Review

E. J. Noyes was able to deliver on so many levels... This book is going to take you on a roller-coaster ride of ups and downs that you won't expect but it's so unbelievably worth it.

-Les Rêveur

Noyes clearly undertook a mammoth amount of research. I was totally engrossed. I'm not usually a reader of romance novels, but this one gripped me. The personal growth of the main character, the rich development of her fabulous best friend, Mitch, and the well-handled tension between Sabine and her love interest were all fantastic. This one definitely deserves five stars.

-CELEStial books Reviews

IF I DON'T ASK

Other Bella Books by E. J. Noyes

Ask, Tell
Turbulence
Gold
Ask Me Again
Alone
If the Shoe Fits
Reaping the Benefits
Pas de deux
Go Around

About the Author

E. J. Noyes is an Australian transplanted to New Zealand, which may be the awesomest thing to happen to her. She lives with her wife, a needy cat and too many plants (and is planning on getting more plants). When not indulging in her love of reading and writing, E. J. argues with her hair and pretends to be good at things.

IF I
DON'T
ASK

E. J. NOYES

BELLA
BOOKS
2022

Bella Books, Inc.
P.O. Box 10543
Tallahassee, FL 32302

Printed in the United States of America on acid-free paper.

First Edition - 2022

Editor: Cath Walker
Cover Designer: Kayla Mancuso

ISBN: 978-1-64247-391-9

PUBLISHER'S NOTE

Acknowledgments

Book Number Ten. I never thought I'd say (or more accurately, write) those words, but here we are. And what a way to bring it about, coming full circle back to my debut, *Ask, Tell*. This book has been in my brain from the moment I started to think *Ask, Tell* might actually be A Book, but it always felt a little like a silly, self-indulgent project. But with everything swirling around us, I just really needed to spend some time with fictional friends, and that's exactly what writing this book was like. I'm so fortunate that my readers love my fictional friends too.

With every book I produce, I feel I thank the same people over and over (and try to do it in a new and exciting way every time, so sorry if I repeat myself…), but I really do have the best small, tight-knit team around me, helping me make every book the best it can be.

Kate, even when you were dealing with all your stuff, you still found time for me and this book, and I will be eternally grateful for your thoughts and your support throughout the process.

Claire, I have some Faith…

Linda, Jessica, everyone at Bella – I still remember the morning I got that email telling me Bella Books wanted to publish *Ask, Tell*. I would never have imagined then that I'd find such an amazing publishing family. Thank you all for making the non-writing part of publishing work so easy.

Cath – double digits! I'll let you blow out the birthday candles for this one because you deserve all the cake. Thanks for being the best editor a gal could ask for. So much of editing is about trust, and I'm so grateful to have found an editor I trust completely, even when I know those (word) cuts are going to sting.

Pheebs. Heart emoji. In my very first book acknowledgments ever (back when you were partner, not wife), I said you've always felt like home to me. That sentiment has never been truer than during this past year. Home may have shifted, but what we share hasn't. I know you don't read my book acknowledgments, so maybe next book I'll just say "Ta, babe" and leave it at that…

Author's Note

The implementation (February 1994) and subsequent repeal (September 2011) of the United States Military policy *Don't Ask, Don't Tell* (DADT) plays an important role in LGBTQ+ history. As a blanket attempt to "fix" the problem of homosexuality in the military by pretending it was okay to be queer while serving—as long as you didn't tell anyone—DADT instead created a stifling environment for LGBTQ+ service personnel. They were still unable to serve openly and were subject to the same disciplinary action as they had been prior to the policy's implementation. DADT was a harmful, unnecessary policy that achieved nothing except discrimination and anguish, and continues to do so for those who served under it.

When my debut novel, *Ask, Tell*, was published in 2017, I never dreamed Sabine and Rebecca would become so cherished among the sapphic fiction community. I also never dreamed that I would write more than just that one book featuring two of my favorite leading ladies, yet here we are again, together, with their fourth—*If I Don't Ask*.

Written from Rebecca's point of view, *If I Don't Ask* holds everything I wish I could have included in *Ask, Tell*—if I'd had endless page space and a better knowledge of writing craft way back then. To those of you who have followed Sabine and Rebecca all the way from *Ask, Tell*—welcome back. And to everyone just joining them now—welcome.

CHAPTER ONE

FOB Atlantis Military Hospital, Paktika Province, Afghanistan
January, 2007

The phone ringing was a welcome distraction, dragging my thoughts away from my failure and the fact two members of the unit were going home early from deployment. I snatched up the handset and forced cheer I didn't feel into my, "LTC Rebecca Keane."

The quiet buzzing static and few seconds of delay indicated the call originated from the States, rather than another forward operating base. Finally, a familiar male voice came through. "Rebecca, Bill Linkfield. How are you?"

My forced cheer turned unforced. "Bill," I said warmly. "Good to hear from you. I'm doing well. They finally fixed the heating in my office, so things are looking up." January in Afghanistan—we were lucky to hit the midthirties during the day, and I'd been shivering through paperwork for the past week.

"Lucky you. Took them almost three weeks to fix my air-conditioning last time I was over there."

"I think I'd rather have no heat than no cooling."

"Same," he agreed. "Now I'm just calling with some good news. I have replacement surgeons for you, should be there late tomorrow."

I leaned into my chair, arching my back for a satisfying stretch. "Wonderful, thank you. What can you tell me about them?"

"Both general surgeons, trauma subspecialty." Bill paused, and his next words were steeped in apology. "And I'm sorry, but they're also fresh out of commissioned officer training. Yours is their first unit assignment. They'll stay with you and rotate out in July, then continue on as fully integrated members."

A shortened first deployment. Lucky people. I smiled at Bill's apologetic tone. "You should know by now that *fresh* is my favorite." I found genuine joy in teaching newly commissioned officers the ins and outs of how the Army operated in-theater overseas. "Thanks for getting me replacements so quickly."

"My pleasure. Hell of a thing to happen during your first deployment as an LTC."

"You're telling me." There was no malice or accusation in Bill's statement, so I had no anxiety about my relatively new promotion to lieutenant colonel. I glanced at the papers on my desk which would send two good and capable surgeons home. Adultery and pregnancy. A double whammy. "Here's hoping it never happens again."

"You had *The Talk* with the rest of them yet?" There was laughter in the question.

"I have. After we already had it before we left for this deployment. And again, it was like giving a sex talk to a group of middle-schoolers instead of a group of educated adults. A little snickering, lots of squirming and avoiding eye contact. I'm pretty sure they realized 'Please remember you're not supposed to be having sex with other people while you're on deployment' was related to Riley and Evans and their impending bundle of joy."

Bill grunted. "No matter how much you tell 'em, some of 'em can't be helped. Now their careers will suffer. Damned fools."

"I know, but I still think it's horrible. She seemed overjoyed to be pregnant and I'm happy for her in that regard. And not to mention she had *no* idea he's married. But the fact is he committed adultery, so he has to go, and she's pregnant, so she has to go. And even if I could overlook the fact she's not due to give birth for another five months, they still engaged in a handful of prohibited activities under General Order Number One and leaving them in the unit could be bad for morale. So now I have to integrate new members into an established team." I still wasn't sure that was any better for morale.

"If anyone can do it, Rebecca, you can," he said. There was a hint of cheerleader in his voice.

"Thanks for the vote of confidence."

"My pleasure. The helo is due at Atlantis around fourteen-hundred tomorrow, assuming there's no holdups."

There usually were holdups organizing a huge planeload of cargo and people to travel from the USA to Afghanistan. "Understood. And thanks again for getting me replacements so fast."

His laugh sounded almost devious. "Don't thank me yet. I have a feeling one of them is gonna grind your gears."

I'd yet to meet a subordinate that annoyed me to the point of frustration, and the thought that I'd have one now made me smile. "Oh? Which one?"

"Name's Fleischer. If type A, obsessive-compulsive perfectionists had an overlord, she'd be it."

I laughed at the visual. The unit was full of perfectionists—not a bad trait to have in Med Corps personnel. "Surely she can't be that bad."

"I don't think *bad* is the right adjective," he mused. "She's good, almost too good. I read her file from Officer Candidate School and she did everything perfectly. *Everything.* The OCS trainers said she made them feel like they were recruits who couldn't perform the most basic tasks."

My mirth melted away. "Is she insubordinate?" Perfectionism was fine, insubordination was not.

He hastened to backtrack. "Oh no, not at all. Model soldier and model surgeon too, according to everyone who's worked with her. Model everything. You might have to squash her down a little, put her in her place before she starts pushing against the way things are done."

I bristled at the insinuation that putting subordinates down "in their place" was the best way to make them realize how the Army worked. That didn't breed good leaders. It only bred contempt for the chain of command. I moderated my response. "I try not to squash anyone. But thanks for the heads-up."

"You're welcome. Their electronic files will be through soon and you can see for yourself." The sound of his hand slapping the desk carried through the line. "Right, I have a meeting to sleep through. I think you've got all you need. Let me know how they get on."

"Will do. And thanks again for your efficiency. It'll give me time to integrate them before things get busy."

Bill snorted a laugh. "Don't thank me yet, Rebecca. Stay in touch."

I returned to my paperwork and my feeling of having failed the team. Neither was pleasant. I rolled my shoulders, trying to push the unhelpful sensations aside. What had happened was over and done. I couldn't babysit the unit 24/7, and Riley and Evans were adults capable of making their own decisions, even if they were stupid ones. I'd just signed the forms authorizing their departure when an email pinged cheerfully into my inbox. Time to turn my focus from the old to the new.

I skimmed the body of the email and noted the names of my new team members. Captain Mitchell Boyd and Captain Sabine Fleischer, both thirty-three. Young, but their medical education and training were top-notch. As I read their files I noted not a single black mark. Not even a gray mark. They looked fit and healthy, and also like they'd been ripped from an Army recruitment brochure. Mitchell Boyd was All-American handsome—tanned, with a square jaw, piercing bright blue eyes and a nose that looked like it'd been broken in the past, but which only seemed to add to his rugged masculinity.

And then there was Sabine Fleischer... I stared for far longer than necessary. Her face was angular without being harsh, olive skin darkened by a tan, dark hair and eyes, cheekbones for days, and a laughing, sensual mouth that looked like it'd barely kept itself from smiling in her ID photograph. The longer I studied her, the more I became aware of a sensation I hadn't felt for well over a decade. A sensation I didn't want to feel.

Attraction.

Goddammit. I couldn't afford to feel that for *anyone*, especially not a fellow service member and *especially* not someone under my command. I could only hope her personality was as unappealing as her exterior was appealing. Maybe Bill would be right, and she'd grind my gears. I stared at the photograph again. There was something in that face that made me certain she wouldn't. Seriousness layered over the top of amusement layered over the top of an almost earnest, puppy-like expression. Sabine Fleischer looked like she'd turn herself inside out to perform a task perfectly and in exactly the way you wanted it done. Then ask you if she could do anything else for you. And smile the whole time.

I sighed and closed the email. She would do the opposite of grind my gears. I just knew it.

* * *

A little before 1500 the next day, the deep rotor sound of a Black Hawk announced the imminent arrival of my new team members.

Though I'd assigned Amy Peterson and Bobby Rodriguez—the two most outgoing, friendly personalities in the unit—to show Boyd and Fleischer around, they were nowhere in sight when I went to meet the transport.

The base was fairly quiet—or boring, depending on how you chose to look at it—and a helo that wasn't one of the Pave Hawks used by Pararescue who delivered our casualties had drawn the attention of half the FOB. People milled about, trying to seem like they just happened to be outside, moving from Point A to B, not like they wanted to catch a glimpse of the new arrivals. Welcome to Forward Operating Base Atlantis, Captains Boyd and Fleischer.

I strolled briskly through the cold, rotor-noisy air, noting they had already dragged their bags from the helo and set them down on the dusty, rocky ground away from the aircraft. Both looked as if they were waiting for someone to tell them what to do and where to go. As I walked closer, I sized them up. Mitchell Boyd would be easily six-one, if not more, and Sabine Fleischer looked to be a few inches taller than my five-five.

At my approach, they moved beside their bags and stood to attention. Almost in unison, they saluted and the moment I'd returned it, I smiled and raised my voice over the declining rotor noise. "At ease." I took my time to study them and tried not to let my gaze linger on Sabine Fleischer, whose dark eyes studied me with curious intensity. Her eye contact was unwavering, even as she blinked away the cold wind.

"Captain Boyd, Captain Fleischer. I'm Lieutenant Colonel Rebecca Keane, your new CO. Welcome to FOB Atlantis." I indicated the space with a sweeping arm. "We even turned on some balmy weather for your arrival."

That dragged smiles from them, though Sabine Fleischer immediately bit down on hers. As their ruddy cheeks attested, it was thirty-one degrees with a miserable wind whipping over from the west. After a quick glance to Boyd, she said, "Thank you, Colonel Keane. I think I speak for both of us when I say we're thrilled to be here. And the weather is…delightful," she added dryly. Her voice was unexpectedly deep and husky. It was also sensual, and sexy as hell. Of course it was, because why not throw everything at me at once?

Mitchell Boyd's Texan drawl agreed, "Sure is. Better than the freezin' rain at Bagram, ma'am."

I turned a genuinely amused smile on both of them. "Glad to oblige. Grab your kit and get inside out of the cold." I glanced at Peterson and

Rodriguez who'd just arrived with apologies for being late, citing a post-op check and paperwork. "Amy, show Fleischer around. Bobby, give Boyd the grand tour."

Bobby nodded, while Amy's answer was a cheerful, "Yes, ma'am." Then to Sabine, "Let me show you all the cool shit we have here, Bunkie." She lowered her voice but I still caught her murmured, "We are going to have some fucking fun together."

A flash of panic crossed Sabine's face before her mouth turned upward in an automatic smile. She nodded and turned that intense eye contact to Peterson. "Sure. Great."

I thought I understood her panic. Amy Peterson was…odd. Parisian-runway-model gorgeous, she could barely get a sentence out without an expletive and was one of those eternally fun-loving and cheerful optimists. Having that put in your face minutes after you'd arrived in a war-torn country for your first deployment would be a lot to take in. But Peterson was the perfect person to help someone acclimate, and being an equal-ranking surgeon should help foster a sense of camaraderie between the two women.

Mitchell tossed an easy smile at Sabine—interesting, and so noted—before he sauntered off with Bobby. According to their files they'd attended college and med school together, and followed the same basic Army career paths. It was logical they'd be friendly, but I'd need to keep an eye on things to make sure I didn't have another "Goodbye, two great surgeons" situation on my hands.

"Fleischer?"

She straightened immediately, arms rigid at her sides. But her voice was anything but rigid when she queried, "Yes, ma'am?"

"Come to my office once you're settled. Amy will show you where it is."

Another slightly alarmed look passed over her face before her expression slid back to neutrality, a hint of a smile playing about her mouth again. "Of course, ma'am."

"Very good." I turned and left first so I wouldn't be tempted to check her out as she walked away.

I'd expected Sabine to take a while to unpack, but within thirty minutes of her arrival I had a knock on my partially closed office door. "Yes?" I called.

The door opened slowly and Sabine appeared, throwing another salute which I quickly stood to return. Her smile was friendly, if a little uncertain. "Colonel Keane? Do you have time for me now?"

I gave her my friendly boss smile. "Fleischer, of course. Come on in and close the door behind you, please."

Without the cold wind stinging my eyes I could see her properly, and realized my previous two views of her—ID photo, and just before out on the landing pad—hadn't given me a real sense of her. Aside from her obvious attractiveness, everything screamed perfectionist, from her Army Combat Uniform, which despite the trip from D.C. was without a single wrinkle, to her hair in a neat bun, to the way she stood perfectly at attention. Sans her ACU cold-weather jacket, I noted she was lean and lithe like a gymnast.

I sat, moving my chair back slightly so I wouldn't appear quite so in-her-face when she was on the other side of my desk. "At ease, Sabine. Take a seat."

She wavered for a moment as if not sure of protocol, then lifted the chair so it wouldn't scrape and lowered herself gracefully. Still ramrod straight, she sat with her hands clasped together in her lap, everything except her eyes totally still. After a quick sweep of the room, those eyes strayed to my hands which rested on top of the desk. Specifically, she looked to my left hand and my grandmother's wedding band on my ring finger. The intensity of her gaze made me want to fidget and I laced my fingers together, moving one to cover the ring. "Are you settled in already?"

Her eyes widened. "Almost, ma'am. I've seen the barracks, rec space, and hospital facilities, but I decided to see you before I looked at the rest of the base. But…Peterson gives great tours," she added, almost earnestly, as if Amy had a promotion riding on how well she'd shown Sabine around, and Sabine wanted to be sure I knew she'd done a good job.

"Ah, that's good to know. I might have to promote her to official Welcome Wagon status. Though we don't get too many new kids on the block."

My banter seemed to have the intended effect, and she relaxed slightly. Slightly for Sabine Fleischer was a shoulder drop of a few millimeters. I watched her carefully, noting she didn't seem uptight so much as conscious of how she might appear to her new CO. There was something simmering under the surface and as I recalled her dry joke about the delightful weather, I wondered if the thing she was trying to hide was a ridiculous sense of humor. I pulled my hands from the table, and her occasional glances, and rested them on the arms of my chair. "What do you think of Atlantis so far?"

Sabine gestured at the vague space around us. "It's bigger than I imagined, and the facilities far nicer than I'd hoped for. I was worried we'd be sent to a tent town, and I'd have no idea of how things worked." From her expression it was clear that Sabine Fleischer didn't like not knowing how to do something. The smile fell away. "I apologize, ma'am. I didn't mean to imply those combat support hospitals, or the people working there, were somehow inferior, or…" The look she gave me was pure helplessness.

Though I would have loved to tease her, I decided instead to move right past it. There was time to ease her into team-teasing later. I smiled reassuringly. "I'm absolutely certain you would have risen to the occasion." The facilities at Atlantis weren't exactly five-star, but they were a little more stable and permanent than the tents and ISO containers that made up other FOBs. As well as our state-of-the art hospital facilities, we had private—albeit shared for lower ranks—rooms in the barracks instead of cots laid out in rows in a huge tent or building, a chow hall that churned out decent food, a recreation room large enough to accommodate the full off-shift, rudimentary sportsball facilities, our relaxation-time bonfire pit which was thankfully nowhere near the revolting waste burn pits, and then a whole lot of dirt enclosed by an eight-foot-tall razor-wire-topped chain-link fence. "Things *will* be different here than back home. I'm here to help you in any way you might need, and at any time."

"Thank you, ma'am." She leaned forward, almost as if she was about to share a confidence with me. "Do you have any tips for a deployment newbie? Peterson passed along a few helpful things but I feel like her perspective might be a little different to yours."

God, her voice. A ripple of excitement spread down my spine and I inhaled deeply before answering, "Sleep as much as you can, eat as much as you can, and try to remember that you can't control everything."

It was as if I'd just told her she wasn't allowed to breathe. Her jaw flexed, the side of her cheek sucking in and out like she was chewing the inside of it. So she was a control freak *and* a perfectionist, and both of those traits seemed to outshine any arrogance or ego, which was strange. In the course of my military career, I'd become very good at reading people, and it seemed arrogance and ego didn't burn at the forefront of Sabine Fleischer's personality. That, or she'd become adept at hiding those parts of herself.

"Thank you for that, Colonel Keane."

Satisfied she seemed to have taken what I'd said on board, I pulled out one of my pep talks. "Your team is your lifeline. Deployment can be difficult, especially your first when you're trying to learn the ropes *and* do your job. Lean on your team, let them lean on you. And you can all lean on me. My door is always open if you have any concerns."

"I appreciate that, ma'am. And I'll certainly come to you if I need anything."

"Good. I really do mean it." I paused to see if there was anything else, and when there wasn't, I offered her another smile and a, "Dismissed, Sabine. Can you please find Captain Boyd and ask him to come see me ASAP?"

Sabine rocketed to her feet, standing again with that perfect attention posture. I held back my smile, and added *intriguing* to my list, right underneath *gorgeous*. I could not wait to work a surgical case with her and see where she put all that perfectionism when things went south. She nodded. "Yes, ma'am. Thank you again for your advice."

When she turned around to leave, I dropped my eyes to my desk. Free of her intense gaze, I eased a little of the tight grip I'd been keeping on myself. A series of slow, deep breaths helped bring me back under control but lingering unease left me feeling on edge. Racing pulse, flutter of excitement in my stomach, undeniable interest in her? Check, check, check. The only rationalization for these reactions was desire, attraction. Unwanted at the best of times, but here and now and with…her? It was unacceptable.

Mitchell Boyd arrived in a flurry of charm, and by the time I'd finished with Mitch—as he'd asked to be called—it was time for afternoon rounds. I made myself coffee from the Keurig I kept hidden in my office and gathered my stethoscope and notebooks.

The meetings with the new team members suggested they'd both integrate well, and I allowed myself to set that concern aside to focus on what felt like an over-the-top worry. My "came out of nowhere to smack me in the face" attraction to Sabine Fleischer. What the heck was I supposed to do with that?

In my seventeen-year Army career I'd honed my poker face to the point that I even wore it in public outside my workplace, as had been pointed out to me numerous times by women I dated casually. It was such a habit that I never feared I'd slip up and reveal my most private thoughts. But despite my confidence in maintaining a neutral façade, this attraction to someone in the unit, to whom I would be close every single day, worried me. I was treading water in uncharted seas. If I allowed myself private thoughts about her, was it possible I'd slip up and give myself away out of mental familiarity? If I did, it would be disastrous.

I almost scoffed at myself. I was forty-one for Christ's sake, not some teenager mooning over a girl on the basketball team who I wanted to meet behind the bleachers for a make-out session. An attraction to a woman wasn't a new concept and I'd never had any problem ignoring such things before, so why should Sabine Fleischer be any different? I'd just do what I always did—put it in The Forgetting Place and move on with my life. For the first time in a very long time, that was the last thing I wanted to do.

CHAPTER TWO

By the time I'd finished with my official duties for the day and taken a barely warm and barely pressured shower, I'd almost forgotten Sabine Fleischer. Almost.

The chow hall was three-quarters full, the usual low hum of conversations echoing through the space as I glanced around for a spot where I wouldn't intrude. I missed being able to sit with a large group and talk and joke during mealtimes, but from the moment I was given my first leadership role, I'd decided I wouldn't insert myself into things that should be relaxing for the team, like meals, rec time and gym workouts. The only exception was football, but that was team-building and morale-boosting and we were all equals on the field. Or so we all pretended.

The distance between *Me* and *Them* was admittedly lonely and that weekly shared event away from surgery and reports and me being their boss was a lifeline. I loved my job, I loved leading a team. But I wished there wasn't such a disconnect between the ranks, albeit a necessary one.

I spotted Fleischer and Boyd at a table full of people in the middle of the room, and by all appearances everyone seemed to be getting along. I'd already had the feeling that both of them were fairly easy people to be with, but the relief at it being apparently true was a blessing. One less thing to worry about.

LTC Phil Burnett, the orthopod whose unit ran opposing shifts to mine, had claimed a space in the corner away from the food stations, and as I passed by, I indicated I'd be back to sit with him. Phil nodded, then leaned across to pull the chair opposite him forward to rest against the table edge. I smiled at his high-school action. It wasn't like anyone was going to take the seat, or likely any of the other seats at that table, except maybe some of the majors who occasionally socialized with us at mealtimes.

A new, but distinctive, voice rose above the cacophony. Sabine Fleischer's. By her tone, she was arguing about something but in a teasing, laughing way instead of being petulant and asshole-ish. I couldn't help myself, I looked. Mitch Boyd held an apple high in the air so she couldn't reach it unless she got up and started roughhousing, and she was poking his arm as if she could wear him down. The rest of the table laughed. Someone tossed their apple at Sabine and she nabbed it one-handed as it sailed toward her.

Sabine glanced up and caught my eye, also catching me watching her. Watching *them*. I raised my hands to shoulder height and clapped lightly in appreciation of her display of athleticism. She dipped her head, but not before I caught the pleasure flashing across her features. Boyd turned around, and his expression transformed to an easy smile. I offered him a friendly smile and a wave, which he returned. Just making sure my new team members were comfortable and settling in. Nothing more.

I loaded my plate with shepherd's pie and salad, and nabbed a bottle of room-temperature water. God, I missed cooking. I missed food that had more than a pinch of seasoning. I missed planning meals for friends and slow trips through grocery aisles. I missed reading restaurant menus.

I knew what a logistical nightmare supplying FOBs with *any* item could be, and with the added cultural challenges of our host country making some things near-impossible to obtain, we were lucky we were served the fresh-ish, mostly high-quality meals we were. And also lucky that something was available to eat from the chow hall at all hours, even if it was only leftovers or a sandwich made by sympathetic kitchen staff.

The staff did their best with what they had, and I was sure they knew the old adage of "An Army Marches on its Stomach." And I'd certainly eaten worse on deployments. But just once I wanted something with a flavor that wasn't somewhere along the spectrum of bland. The moment I'd slept off my flights after returning home from this deployment, I'd be loading up on ingredients for meals to fill my freezer. And buying a good single malt. A rich, full-bodied red. A light, fruity white. I allowed myself a brief mope for the food and drinks I missed.

After shaking an unhealthy amount of salt, and pepper, over my meal I threaded my way through the tables and chairs back to Phil. "Evening. Mind some company?"

Phil offered me his usual sweet smile. "Rebecca, I'll never say no to sharing a meal with you." He affected an exaggerated pout. "I'm going to miss my food companion if things heat up again and we're both flat-out busy. I'm also going to miss leisurely sit-down meals."

I pulled a hot-sauce packet from my pocket and squeezed it over my shepherd's pie, attempting to add some flavor to a meal that catered to the lowest common tastebud denominator of the personnel at the FOB. "Same. Maybe if we ask nicely, they'll just…stop fighting for the rest of the year, not just slow down over winter?"

Phil nodded thoughtfully as he chewed. "Great idea. Why haven't we thought of that before?"

"Beats me."

"How're your newbies?" He gestured behind me, across the room to where they were seated. They'd quieted down a little but it was clear from the noise behind me that they were all enjoying their social time. As they should.

"Seem to be doing fine, though they're yet to get their hands bloody." Which wasn't always a bad thing in our circumstances. "I wouldn't pick them as surgeons if I didn't know it. They're both obviously intelligent but from what I've seen of them I get a sense they're laidback, goofy almost?"

Phil used his fork to gesture at the subjects of our conversation. "Better than so arrogant that there's no space for anyone but them in the room." He stretched and spread his arms out to indicate the space around us. "Why do you think I'm still here instead of making my fortune doing joint replacements? I couldn't stand the personalities I'd have surrounding me all day, every day. I think the Army has a way of keeping the assholes under control." His eyebrows bounced. "Until those assholes climb the ladder and get to be in charge of us."

Laughing, I agreed, "That's true."

Phil tore open a dinner roll and, after smearing a foil pat of butter on his bread, began wiping gravy from his plate. "How're you doing?"

I almost choked in surprise at his unexpected question. "Me? I'm fine. Why do you ask?"

"Just checking in after the Riley and Evans debacle."

"Ah, right, yes. That." Lowering my voice I admitted, "I'm upset for them and that they could have ruined their careers. Frustrated too, I guess. And also wondering if I'm totally blind to what's going on under my nose." I shrugged. "But otherwise I'm okay. Thanks for checking in."

"Anytime. You know we can't know everything that goes on around here, especially if they're doing their damnedest to hide it." He gave me a knowing look. "You remember when someone made moonshine a couple years back?"

"I remember it all too well." It was amazing what you could do with fruit, fruit juice, sugar, and bread. In the interest of thoroughness, the other COs and I had had a small taste before we disposed of it. It wasn't horrible, if you didn't mind searing your throat and intestines with alcohol. "Reminded me of some of the shenanigans we used to get up to in the Balkans." I opened my water bottle. "It's just…I feel like I failed two good surgeons by not realizing they were involved. Maybe I could have stopped it. But I suppose if I want to choose the glass-half-full option, now I have the opportunity to work with two new surgeons who could both be amazing assets to the unit."

"I'd go with that. Sometimes fresh blood helps." He pushed his plate to the side. "Speaking of things they try to hide, I hear it's intake stakes this week. Want me to get my *agent* to place a bet on your behalf?"

"Sure. Are you going in too?" The Med Corps ran all sorts of under-the-table betting pools, wagering money or Commissary supplies. They'd bet on things like most intakes for the day, whether we'd get T-Rations or A-Rations this week, how many days it'd take to fill the burn pits after they'd been cleared. And when we got home, there'd be one for when and where we'd deploy again. I'd won that one once, fair and square, without any insider CO knowledge.

Phil feigned indignance. "Damned straight I am. Winning gives me permission to buy extra Snickers without my wife realizing how much chocolate I'm eating."

"If you want a Snickers, all you need to do is ask me and I'll buy you one. Put me in for twenty and a trauma intake, uh…day after tomorrow day shift."

"You shithead," he said good-naturedly, "why are you tempting fate?"

"No temptation, just logic. Have you seen the mission board?"

"I have and I'm choosing to believe everything's going to go perfectly and maybe even that this is the mission that gets this whole thing wrapped up and I can go home in time for my grandson's birth and watch him grow up without having to leave again."

"Nice optimism."

"You mean delusion," Phil said dryly. "Even I know it." He rolled his eyes as he pushed back his chair. "Enjoy your relaxing evening. I'm off to stare at my pile of paperwork."

"See you in the morning." I put my head down and concentrated on finishing my meal and trying to ignore the intoxicating sound of Sabine Fleischer's laughter.

In my experience, supplying fast and reliable Internet was way down the list of important things the higher-ups thought to provide troops on a forward operating base. And in my opinion, it was a mistake, especially now when digital communication was the way of the people. With so many clambering to check emails and video call with loved ones, the service usually fell over and played dead.

Thankfully the work systems had a dedicated service which saved me *some* frustration. But I refused to pay extortionate rates to set up a personal Internet service outside the wi-fi provided by the Army for personal use, and thus was relegated to the slower-than-dial-up speeds for checking my non-work emails. I knew some of my colleagues used the better "official" Internet for their personal emails and video calls, but I wanted no trace of my personal life on an official Army laptop where anyone might find it. It was unlikely, but my paranoia about my private life had been part of my professional life for so long that I didn't think I'd ever shake the feeling of someone finding out my secrets.

The Internet was generally better in the more open common areas, but I didn't feel like being out and exposed, and had sequestered myself in my modest quarters, sitting with my legs outstretched on my bed instead of at the small desk. Finally the damned thing started unrolling, or rather staggering and stuttering, emails down the screen and I began skimming through them. Along with the usual spam that seemed to filter through my filters despite my best efforts, there was an email from my best and oldest friend, Linda.

Subject: *Grocery Order*
Hey you.

Hope you're surviving over there. I miss you. But I sent a parcel with snacks and supplies today (made friends with a super cute but way too young taco joint manager and they've been hoarding hot sauce for me for you).

Nothing much to report from here, except one VERY important thing. I met someone in my pottery class. I want to set you two up for a date when you get back. It'll be worth your time, pinky promise. They're cute, fun, sweet, and LOVE blue-eyed blondes, especially ones with adorable dimples. Hint hint. And hint some more.

Let me know what you think. And let me know when my parcel arrives so I can prepare myself for the praise you're going to heap upon me.

Take care of yourself. Video or IM chat soon?

L

As always, Linda was careful to avoid specifics and pronouns, and I loved her for her care. I hated this constant subterfuge. I hit Reply and waited for cyberspace to catch up so I could type out my response.

Subject: Re: Grocery Order

Linda,

You're amazing. I'll be watching eagerly for my parcel – your timing is impeccable as usual, I'm running low on hot sauce. Please marry the taco place manager, age be damned.

Everything's fine here, we're not busy which is nice. But we're coming into warmer months so I expect things to get hectic soon. Not so nice.

Does your pottery person not care about anything other than the fact I'm a blonde with blue eyes and dimples? Things like my personality or interests or anything like that? You know, the <u>important</u> things… Given you know my feelings on the matter, you should be able to guess my response but thanks for going out of your way to try and set me up with someone.

I'll attempt a video call at our usual time next week. Attempt…

Miss you too.

Rebecca

I read Linda's email again, smiling at her audacity. She, of all people, should know I didn't date. We had had a very short relationship almost eighteen years ago, not long after my long-term relationship broke down and just before I joined the Army. After a month of amazing sex, but realizing we didn't work as a couple, we decided to just become very good friends. Good friends who, if Linda wasn't seeing anyone, occasionally slept together when I came home from a deployment. My "buffer into finding a girlfriend," Linda called it. She was the only woman who hadn't faded into oblivion upon learning that I would be away for close to a year at a time and that dating me was like dating a ghost.

But I didn't want to date. I just wanted something easy, like the casual and shallow dinner and sex relationships I'd cultivated during the periods between deployments. Still, I had to admit I gained very little out of my "romance routine," if it could even be called that. It felt selfish and self-serving to keep women at arm's length after bringing them close enough for me to consider being their bedmate.

After my last few deployments I'd had a slow-moving sensation I'd categorized as apathy, where I couldn't even be bothered meeting up with friends of friends, women from dating sites, or leaving home to meet women in bars. And after a night of soul-searching on my couch, aided by six fingers of McCallan over an hour, I'd concluded that I didn't want these short-term and mostly meaningless relationships anymore.

But…I also didn't want to commit myself to someone and end up in exactly the same position I'd found myself two decades ago. And I didn't want to be alone. Maybe I had no idea what I really wanted. Maybe my work situation, with *Don't Ask, Don't Tell* butting into everything, made it too hard for me to have a personal life. It was one thing to keep part of myself hidden. It was another, unfair, thing entirely to ask a partner to pretend they didn't exist because I couldn't be out and proud at work.

Maybe I was just doing what I'd always done—making excuses to hide the fact that at my core, I felt I wasn't capable of commitment. After all, a fear of commitment, of being tied to a situation I didn't want, was the thing that started my Army career. I'd run away then, and years later, I was still doing it.

But that was the safest thing for me. For everyone.

CHAPTER THREE

While everyone streamed in for our morning briefing, I looked over my notes and occasionally glanced up to see who I was still waiting on. My two new team members had taken seats in the front row, almost center, which meant Sabine's intently attentive face was directly in front of me. I'd hardly seen them yesterday for their second day at Atlantis, and assumed it had been as easy as their first.

After going through the usual operational items, I moved on to listening to the team's weekly grievances which mostly related to the shitty Internet, sparse Commissary supplies, having to drink goat's or powdered milk instead of their two-percent, and annoying equipment malfunctions around the FOB.

I tried to placate them in a way that wasn't condescending, because they'd all known what to expect when they'd joined the military, and compared to some combat units, we lived in luxury. "I know you're frustrated by these things and I'm sorry. I'm also sure you all know how difficult it can be getting supplies in, and when we're working with and supporting local suppliers we sometimes have to be flexible. Most of the gripes you've inboxed me about equipment requisitions are in the works. In the meantime, we'll do what we do best. Which is?"

A mumbling of agreement filled the space before a chorus of, "We make it work."

Smiling, I agreed, "Exactly. What about some gratitudes?"

Thankfully the mood changed immediately. Overwhelmingly, our weekly flag football games came first, then the additional gaming console and television in the rec room, the expanded bonfire pit, a fresh shipment of scrubs, and finally the surf 'n' turf—steak and shrimp—the chow hall served every Wednesday night.

Sabine remained silent except for the occasional murmur of agreement or low, amused laugh, and had been staring at me the whole meeting like she was trying to absorb what I said through her eyes. Because she watched me so intently, I couldn't avoid those dark eyes. And every time we made eye contact, even the most fleeting, I felt a strange thrill of excitement before an immediate sense of self-ridicule at my girlish reaction.

"Before you're dismissed, a heads up." I tried not to let my focus linger on Sabine, who'd immediately straightened at those words, her pen at the ready. "I think our quiet period might be coming to an end."

I waited for the collective groan to die down and held up placating hands. "I know, I know. But we're not here to play video games, work on our tan, or repaint the rec room, though you've done a great job with it. As I'm sure your ears have been telling you, coalition forces are still running their combat operations here in the Eastern Provinces. They're winding things up but I expect that if there are casualties, we'll be seeing them here, given our proximity to the action. Sleep and eat when you can so you're at your sharpest when you need to be. When *I* need you to be." I made sure to smile at all of them. "Dismissed. Take care of yourselves and each other."

I caught Sabine's eye as she left, and after a wide-eyed look of surprise, she flashed me an almost-nervous lopsided smile then rushed to catch up to Amy who was telling a very interested Mitch about surf 'n' turf and how sometimes we got lobster too. I wasted time collecting my things to keep myself from staring after Sabine's departing figure. Though she'd said nothing to me in the past hour, the intensity of her focus made me feel as if I'd just had a long personal conversation with her.

After breakfast I wandered across to the hospital to check on the few post-operative cases we had, which were all humanitarian—non-combatant civilians with issues like hernias and appendicitis. When the hospital was quiet like this I often had a disconcerting sense of unease, knowing the hammer would fall at any moment and probably land on my toe. We rarely had steady flows of trauma events; it was either so busy it would have been stressful if we weren't trained for such things, or so quiet it was almost boring.

While walking back from the post-op recovery ward, I heard a male Texan drawl float from around the corner. The moment I realized what he'd said, I stopped dead. Mitch Boyd had asked quietly, "Whaddya think of our new boss?"

I honestly didn't make a habit of eavesdropping, but I often overheard a conversation simply because people hadn't realized I was there. Continuing around the corner now would cause Mitch and whoever he was talking to—given his question and his friend circle, it had to be Sabine—embarrassment, so I decided to wait and do some unofficial reconnaissance in the name of unit morale. If I didn't know there was a problem, I couldn't fix it, right?

Sabine answered, almost as quietly as Mitch had asked his question, "I think she's brilliant. Not an asshole, which is a bonus. And she's just got this...*vibe* about her, like she knows exactly what she's doing and that you can trust her to make the right calls, to keep you safe. I think it's her voice. She's so calm and confident, intelligent and cultured-sounding."

He laughed. "Oh, really?" The words were drawn out teasingly.

The sound of a slap on flesh was Sabine's answer.

Mitch's laughter was louder this time. "Just because someone sounds intelligent and cultured, that doesn't mean they are."

"Well, that's not a problem with you, is it, Mitch?"

A low chuckle. "I only pretend to sound like a dumb hick so you'll feel smarter, Sabs."

"Surrre." I could hear the eye roll in that one word. Then a pause, and a quiet, almost accusatory question from Sabine. "You don't like her?"

"I absolutely do like her. Maybe not as much as you do, but I like her plenty for only knowing her a coupla days. But let's see what we think by end of deployment, huh? And once we've worked a case with her? Maybe she's a total surgical asshole."

"Sure, end of deployment," Sabine mused. "I really don't think she'll be a surgical asshole."

"Why not?"

"Have you ever met a surgical asshole who wasn't an asshole the rest of the time?"

"Good point," he mumbled.

Sabine's tone lightened, almost as if she'd decided she'd won some unspoken argument and it was time to move on. "You checked out the prep room yet?"

"Yeah. Well-stocked, and with all scrub sizes so thank fuck I don't have to go askin' round for the tall-muscled-man size. But the color of those scrubs will wash me out somethin' fierce." A touch of camp had crept into his tone. Now that was interesting. Joking, or something else…?

Sabine laughed. "Yeah, but did you see they've also got camo scrubs? Between those and working emergency traumas in our ACU, we'll never see each other in the OR."

"Marco," he said dryly.

Sabine's answer was a giggling, "Polo." They laughed together before Sabine spoke again. "Come to the chow hall with me? I'm still trying to figure out what time of day the best food is."

"Darlin', I don't think there's any best time of day for food on deployment."

Their footsteps faded, but I waited before I followed. And for the first time in my life, I pondered the sound of my own voice. I'd walked barely ten steps when the incoming casualty line, which was linked to multiple phones throughout all buildings to ensure someone could always answer, started up on the wall near the pre-op prep room. I snatched up the phone, noting I'd just won a bet, albeit not an enjoyable one. "LTC Rebecca Keane. We're available for intake."

As I listened, I jotted down shorthand notes on the pad that lived perpetually in my breast pocket. Single casualty, GSW torso, ETA less than five minutes. As I ended the call I punched a button on the wall beside the phone to trigger the call of "Attention on the FOB," which echoed through the halls of the hospital and across the grounds outside, making me feel as if I were surrounded by people cupping their hands around their mouths to shout those words at me. Both Fleischer and Boyd came skidding back, jostling each other before they spotted me and screeched to a halt.

Their simultaneous, "Ma'am" was both a greeting and an apology.

"Congratulations, you're first to report. I only need one assist for now, so rock-paper-scissors or whatever you need to do to figure out who's scrubbing in with me. And do it in the next five seconds, please." There would be plenty of time to familiarize myself with how they worked, and me plus one would suffice for this trauma.

An unspoken message seemed to pass between them before Sabine stepped forward. "I'm ready, ma'am."

"Good. Now, it only sounds like small-team trauma, with a single casualty, but I still want you on standby, Mitch. Watch the intake procedure, get familiar with it so when it's your turn next you know exactly what you're doing."

He nodded. "Absolutely. Yes, ma'am."

With a mix of excitement, anticipation, and nonchalance, the rest of the team came rushing into the room. I smiled at them. "Too slow. I have Fleischer. I need you, Bobby, for anesthesia, and also Nurse Team B, please. Everyone else, you're still on standby in case things get messy or they decide to bring us more."

A chorus of agreement filled the space and everyone surplus to needs drifted away to resume whatever they'd been doing. As I quickly pulled on my cloth scrub cap and tied it, I told Sabine, "If you can do it in under two minutes, get changed into scrubs for surgery now, otherwise we go in as we are. Assessment PPE over the top." To Mitch I said, "Grab yourself some PPE just in case it's messy while you're observing."

Mitch hovered unobtrusively as the Combat Pararescuemen—PJs—rushed a stretcher carrying a man wearing only his underwear through the doors. His torso was one gigantic bruise and I had an immediate sense of what had happened. "Thank you, take him right into the first bay, please. Sabine, clinical exam STAT."

She stood opposite me as we ran through a quick, targeted clinical exam. I percussed his thorax, tapping, feeling and listening for signs of internal hemorrhage. The moment I took my hands away, Sabine had the probe on his belly.

"What do you see?" I asked.

"Nasty liver lac, belly full of blood." Sabine looked up at me, her solid eye contact almost pleading, as if she feared I might disagree. She turned the screen toward me.

After a quick glance at the screen, I raised my eyes to hers. "I agree. Okay, let's go." To the rest of the hovering surgical team I said, "Prep laparotomy trays please."

Sarah, the lead nurse from Team B rushed away to scrub and relay the message to prep the instrument trays we needed. Sabine and I followed the casualty to the OR. I peeled off my gloves and disposable PPE and began a quick surgical scrub, desperate to get in and stop the hemorrhage. As Sabine lathered her hands with a surgical scrub sponge she asked, "How did this happen? He was wearing body armor? There's no penetrating injury, so it has to be blunt force trauma, but how?" Her voice rose in disbelief with every question.

"We're seeing it more and more with hard body armor, especially when it gets between a person and a high-caliber projectile. The hard plates distort and transfer the ballistic energy into the torso. So instead of a penetrating wound, we're getting blunt force trauma." I glanced sideways at her. "*Always* consider BABT in a casualty who's presented without penetrating injury after collecting a projectile in the vest. Especially with this telltale bruising."

"Behind armor blunt trauma. Yes, ma'am."

I rinsed my hands and shook them out. "Okay, let's go."

She was right behind me as we rushed into the room to slip into sterile gowns, gloves, and protective eyewear, before positioning herself for a laparotomy. Bobby spoke up from by the anesthetic machine. "Already under for you, Fleischer. Once you've worked with me, you'll never want another anesthesiologist. I'm the best."

As soon as I'd started my midline incision, Sabine spoke. In a light, conversational tone that felt incongruous with how fast we needed to move, she responded to Bobby. "Whether you're the best or not is yet to be seen. But you're certainly one of the most egotistical, which is saying something…"

I held back my laugh. Everyone else, including Bobby, let theirs free.

Frowning, I announced, "There's a bucket of blood in here. I'm going to need suction and an Everest of laps in here, please. Suction. More, more. Thank you." Sabine was right with me, almost ahead of me, with everything I asked for. I used my finger to confirm my visual assessment. "Grade four liver laceration right posterior-inferior, IVC is intact, right hepatic vein is…yes, it's lacerated. Get him whole blood right now. Sabine, what are we doing?"

As she applied lap pads to control the hemorrhage, Sabine rushed out, "I can't see any other source of bleeding. It's just that lac on the right lobe compromising the right hepatic vein. Inflow vascular control with Pringle maneuver, then parenchymal and vascular repair with sutures."

"You don't want to resect?"

"I—" She tilted her head side to side as if having discourse with herself, and after a moment said, "No, ma'am. I'm confident we can repair it without resection."

"Good. Let's get it done. And quickly."

Sabine placed the clamp with quick efficiency. She was obviously both fast and effective, and I was excited to see someone who had both skill and apparently no desire to steamroll their partner. I was impressed. Confident, clean, quick. Sabine was one of those surgeons who seemed to know intuitively what her co-surgeon needed and how best to verbalize what she herself wanted in a way that didn't come across as short-tempered or arrogant.

Every member of the team, from surgeons to anesthesiologists to nurses, was highly skilled. But there were more than a few egos which I knew chafed under the immovable nature of chain of command. Hopefully Sabine and Mitch would slot into the OR as easily as they had outside it, because I did not need any more dramas in the unit.

Every now and then I'd ask her something and she'd respond instantly, and correctly. There was nothing to do other than smile my encouragement and agreement then observe her doing what she obviously did best. Once we'd completed, checked, and closed, I looked up to find her watching me. "Nicely done, Fleischer."

"Thank you, ma'am." Her eyes brightened. "I…guess he's going to live-r." Pink spread around the edges of her mask to her ears and neck. Her eyes suggested she couldn't believe she'd just said such a thing.

I pressed my lips together to keep myself from guffawing at the hilariously awful dad-joke that'd just come out of her mouth. A deep breath helped settle the laughter bubbling in my chest and I managed an almost-steady, "Yes. I guess he is."

The rest of the room erupted into good-natured hysterics. Sabine raised a hand in acknowledgment. "Thank you, thank you, I'll be here all week." She looked as if she wanted firstly for me to forget every word, and secondly to vaporize into thin air so she could disappear. She was utterly adorable.

Outside the OR, Sabine joined me at the sink. She wilted. "I'm sorry, ma'am. I've said some stupid things before but that's right up there. I promise I do have a modicum of intelligence in my head." She grinned wryly. "Unfortunately, there also seems to be a weird, jokey ten-year-old kid in there too."

I really wanted to see more of the jokey kid. "Don't worry about it, Sabine. Keeping your sense of humor is always beneficial, both here during your deployments and when you get back to D.C. and into working full-time at Walter Reed," I said, shaking water from my hands. "Very early on I had a CO tell me that if you can't laugh about things while you're deployed, you'll probably cry."

She stepped back so I could reach the paper towel dispenser on the wall, but in the limited space near the sinks there was barely enough room for me to reach without touching her, even though she was pressed to the wall. If she was bothered by me being *this close* to accidentally brushing against her arm, she gave no indication. "Is that the advice you'd pass along to me too, ma'am?"

The way she looked at me made me feel totally exposed, as if she'd reached into my mind and was gently searching my thoughts. I was grateful she couldn't actually search my thoughts because I'd just had a sudden and unexpected mental image of kissing her. Maybe it was her almost-innocent, eyebrows-raised expression, as if she trusted me to be truthful and keep her safe in this unsafe place. Or maybe it was just that she was so damned attractive and I was so damned lonely. Regardless of the reason, it played out so clearly in my mind's eye. The moment of pause right before mutual attraction is acknowledged. That second pause to be sure. Then the kiss. I could almost feel the soft warmth of her lips, her hands sliding through my hair and cupping the back of my head, her fingers gliding over my neck.

The rush of heat wasn't unexpected, and I forced myself to keep looking at her instead of averting my gaze away from the discomfort of my attraction to a subordinate, *and* the fact I'd just had a very clear and very enjoyable mental image of kissing her. I pushed my fingertips hard into my palms, and when it didn't help erase the image I pressed the pads of my thumb and forefinger together, rubbing them back and forth.

Aunt Thérèse used to call the gesture "Rebecca's Reset," noting how I'd started doing it after my parents died. Every time my *tante* saw it, she'd bundle me up into a hug, smother my forehead in kisses, then make me an omelet whether I was hungry or not. Rebecca's Reset was a habit I'd never broken, though every time I became aware of it, I reasoned I could be dealing with my emotional discomfort in an unhealthy way instead of just self-soothing.

After a slow, settling breath I said, "Among other snippets of advice, yes. Though sometimes, I think crying is the only thing that'll help." I balled the paper towel and attempted a three-pointer.

When my throw missed, Sabine laughed and bent to retrieve the bundle. "I'll remember that." Instead of trying to re-create my attempted basketball shot, she carefully disposed of the paper towel, then smiled at me like she'd handed in an assignment for extra credit. Goddammit, she was so cute. And definitely not in the young person handing in an assignment way, but in the gorgeous adult with an appealing and fun personality way.

"Enjoy the rest of your day, Sabine. And again, great work today. I'm glad you've joined the unit." After realizing that sounded close to favoritism, I added, "Both you and Boyd."

She dipped her head. "Thank you, ma'am. It was fun. And great working with you."

As much as I tried to ignore it, the disconcerting sensation flooding my body made it hard to concentrate. It was lust. Pure and simple. Thankfully lust was just a chemical response that I could learn to ignore. But my mind kept wandering back to my imaginary kiss, and then to my reaction. Had I given myself away? I was sure I hadn't, just as I was sure of another thing…

I was so screwed.

* * *

The halls in the living quarters were never entirely quiet, and the constant sound of people moving to and from the bathrooms, or making calls to loved ones back home, or coming and going from the hospital provided comforting background noise. Before I joined the Army I'd always considered myself a lover of solitude. But a few weeks on my first deployment had cured me of that. Or perhaps more accurately, taught me to deal with never-silence.

The second time I heard the different shuffling of footsteps outside my door, I went to investigate. Given how well I knew the team, down to their usual sleep habits and their nighttime footwear, my feeling was the person doing midnight laps was one of the new team members.

I spotted a lithe shape walking down the hall away from me. Sabine. Instead of being in its usual tight bun, her hair was drawn up into a loose ponytail. It was longer than I'd thought, probably just past shoulder length, and I thought of how much I'd like to run my fingers through it, feel the sleek softness of her hair gliding over my naked skin.

"Fleischer?"

Sabine stopped immediately. Her shoulders dropped, fingers played against her thighs. She thought she was in trouble. She turned, and at my gesture to come closer, closed the gap between us. Her smile was a little forced, but not fake. "Good evening, Colonel Keane."

I pulled my door mostly closed so she couldn't see into my room. "More like good morning, wouldn't you say?" I smiled to soften the words when I noticed her panicked expression. "Do you make a habit of wandering the halls in the small hours?"

Sabine's forehead crumpled. "I…well, it's only my third night here, ma'am, so no, I don't make a habit of it. I just can't sleep tonight."

"Peterson's snoring?"

She laughed quietly. "There is that, but I have earplugs in case it gets too loud. I think I'm a little hyped after today's surgery."

I propped myself against the wall. "How so? Is that usual?"

Her mouth quirked and she leaned slightly closer. "I don't think anything's usual here, ma'am, but no, I don't usually have issues sleeping. I think it's just going over everything, wanting to be sure I did everything as I should have."

"You did," I assured her.

"Thank you. I—" Her frown creased the space between her dark, arched eyebrows. "And I keep thinking about the BABT. Wondering what we can do about that. If there's anything we can do from a medical perspective."

"You're thinking of a career change? From surgeon to armorer?"

Her expression blanked for a moment until it seemed to register that I was teasing. She laughed, then apparently realized how loud it was and pressed the side of her forefinger against her mouth as if shushing herself. "No, ma'am. Though if I did my first project would be female-friendly vests so we wouldn't have anatomically incorrect plates jamming us in the chest and armpits and hips. I was thinking more about care in the field, if we could train medics to be more aware of BABT as a possible clinical diagnosis, maybe how to stabilize or even treat this sort of injury in the field so it's not so dire when they reach us."

As she tried to put form to her words, they tumbled out and around each other, like her brain had thought of what she wanted to say ten seconds ago and she was trying to go back and retrieve the thoughts. I got the sense Sabine was always ten steps ahead of everyone, including her own brain. And then there were her hands. I had to force myself to not look, which was no small task given they were dominating the space. The more she spoke, the more runaway her thoughts seemed, the more she gestured to emphasize her words. Watching her talk was mesmerizing and I had to focus on the fact we were having a two-way conversation instead of just studying the fascinating nuances of her.

I nodded, slowly, giving myself time to gather my response. "That's an interesting idea, and a great one. But knowing the system as I do, it'd likely take years to get close to implementing any change to care protocols in the field. Then there's the aspect of getting the training to all our medics. No small feat."

Her face fell. "Oh. That's a good point, Colonel Keane. It was just a thought," she added quickly.

"It's a very good one. But nothing in the Army comes quickly and the powers-that-be have a habit of implementing policies without considering the greater good." And sometimes ignoring policies that would benefit the greater good…

"Yes, I'm aware." It was said carefully, almost knowingly.

That one sentence begged me to ask her what she meant, but there was nuance there I didn't want to delve into. Or rather, I wanted to delve into it, but it wasn't safe. I redirected us back to the medical conversation. "But if you wanted to put something forward, perhaps do some research and find case studies, then I'd support that."

Sabine's face turned contrite. "Oh, no. I mean that sounds amazing, ma'am, and I'd love to research it. But I don't want to rock any boats. I just want to fulfill my obligation and learn as much as I can and then quietly separate from the Army."

"Not a lifer then?"

This smile was heartbreakingly resigned, and if I wasn't so conditioned to hiding my feelings I might have reacted to it, reached to touch her, comfort her. "Much to my father's disappointment, no," she said.

"Military family?"

"Yes, ma'am. My father and his brothers, my grandfather and great-grandfather all served. World Wars One and Two, and Vietnam."

I wanted to ask her more, to have her open up to me about why she'd joined the Army simply because of family tradition if she didn't have her heart in it. I knew a decent percentage of boots-on-the-ground personnel joined out of feeling a family obligation but having her, a surgeon, join up simply because her family boasted generations of military service didn't compute. I wanted nothing more in that moment, at 12:43 a.m., to sit down with her and learn everything I could about her. To talk with her like we were regular people just getting to know one another. Instead, I smiled wearily. "Try to get some sleep, Sabine."

Her return smile was knowing. "Yes, ma'am, I will. Just…one more lap."

CHAPTER FOUR

The integration of Sabine and Mitch had been seamless, and a week in they were already acting like they'd been with us for years. I'd seen them regularly socializing outside of mealtimes, nobody had come to me with any "anonymous" complaints, and both of them were top-notch surgeons with excellent work ethics. But now it was time to assess the most important thing about them.

How good they were at flag football.

Everyone on base seemed to have one main sports love, and while I had no objection to football (thanks to my aunt's unwavering support of the Philadelphia Eagles), I still sat at the lower end of the fan scale—unlike Bobby Rodriguez who seemed as if he wanted to stick his head into a gas oven when his beloved Chicago Bears lost. But joining in with the weekly football games was a great opportunity to bond with everyone. And perhaps most importantly, it let me shed my leadership mantle and just enjoy fresh air, exercise, and time with people as a regular member of the crowd.

I knew some of our players weren't all that interested in the game and only filled spots so we could have full teams, so if we could get two capable and willing bodies, we could release those long-suffering participants. I considered recruiting Bobby to recruit Sabine and

Mitch, but when I saw both of them in the weight room, I popped my head in. Sabine swung from where she'd been lying on the bench press with Mitch spotting her, and jumped to her feet. "Colonel Keane. Do you need the room?"

Initially, I'd suspected they might be in a relationship—they were almost always together during free time, and not just in a "we're both new and clinging to each other" way—but the more I watched them, the more I realized they were just very good friends. They treated each other like a favorite sibling instead of lovers trying to pretend they weren't lovers. "Not at all. Are you two in for a game of flag football? I'm sure you've both heard about the weekly game."

They both nodded vigorously, but it was Sabine who answered enthusiastically, "Yes, ma'am."

I twisted my watch around from where it'd relocated to the underside of my wrist. "Excellent. We'll rally in the rec room in five minutes to make sure we've got enough for teams."

"Sounds perfect. I meant great. I mean...good. Ma'am. Sounds good. We'll be there." With every rambling word, her voice rose and her cheeks reddened. And beside her, Mitch was utterly still, with lips pressed tightly together.

There was nothing for me to do except offer a contained, "Very good then," and leave them before I burst out laughing. As I walked away I heard Mitch's unintelligible teasing and the indignant tone of Sabine's reply.

When I stepped into the recreation room five minutes later, everyone focused on me, to the hilarious *tock-tock-tock* soundtrack of a dropped ping-pong ball. "Football time, team! Everyone in full winter ACU, please, including gloves. I need all hands in perfect working order, not frostbitten to heck."

Sabine spoke up, though it wasn't directed at me, or anyone apparently, more like she was musing to herself. "The likelihood of frostbite is low today. Temperature is above freezing, with low windchill and we'll be playing a vigorous football game and keeping warm."

I raised my eyebrows at her and she looked down at her feet and mumbled, "Gloves are a great idea." After a pause, she looked up again and held eye contact with me as she apologized. "Sorry, Colonel Keane."

I nodded my acceptance of her apology, then returned to the important task at hand. "Gear up! Team selection is out on the field in ten minutes. Last one out there has to drop off all the laundry after our next trauma."

That moved them faster than anything could. The base laundry, in some inexplicable idiocy of FOB planning, was on the opposite side of the base from the hospital and barracks. It was annoying enough to take your own laundry there but not wanting to carry bags of everyone else's dirty, sweaty, bloody scrubs was an excellent motivator to get them hustling.

And hustle they did. In a clump of bodies pushing at each other, they jogged onto the field where I'd been waiting, admiring the clear skies and enjoying the sun warming my skin. Bobby Rodriguez arrived last, doing a vague impersonation of a powerwalk and carrying the mesh bag of team flag belts and vests, and a couple of footballs. I'd bought the vests and belts myself before this deployment after hearing one-too-many complaints about the old rags we'd tuck into our belt loops to use for flags, but Bobby acted like they were a personal gift from me to him and took custody of the whole kit after each game. He took such good care of the gear that I left him to it.

I did my best carnival announcer impersonation, spreading my arms wide. "Aaaand it's laundry-man Rodriguezzzzz."

Bobby shrugged, fixing us all with a beaming, smug smile. "Y'all work so hard standing up for hours, doing all that slicing and suturing and suctioning while I'm just sitting on my ass, busting that ass keeping the patient alive. Thought I'd give everyone a break and do laundry service this week." He bent to pick up a small rock next to the paint line he'd carefully marked out that morning, as he did every morning of football gameday to ensure we had a "real" playing field.

Amy used both fists to lightly punch each of his biceps. "You're my hero."

Bobby fluttered his eyelashes. "Peterson, I'm everyone's hero."

I did a quick headcount and confirmed we had enough bodies for a seven-a-side game. As I looked around at the assembly I tried to decide if I wanted Sabine on my team, or the other team. If she was on my team I wouldn't have to worry about touching her. But if she was on my team, it would make it a lot harder for me to sneakily watch her. I really shouldn't be watching her, sneakily or otherwise.

Major David Conway, one of Phil's surgeons, was our official referee and also responsible for deciding the make-up of the teams. Team selection was a highly delicate process of him drawing names out of an old mayonnaise bucket we'd repurposed from the kitchen. I ended up on Green Team with both Sabine and Mitch, as well as Amy, Bobby, nurse Sarah, and one of my surgeons, John Auger. As we fitted our flag vests over our bulky winter ACU jackets I checked in with the new members of the unit. "Sabine, do you have a preferred position?"

"No, ma'am. Wherever you want me is fine. I—" Her eyebrows came together. "I'm pretty fast."

"Noted. How about you, Mitch?"

"My favorite position is the one where I'm callin' the shots." His smile was cocky, yet amazingly, somehow lacked arrogance.

I laughed. "Also noted. I'll let Bobby, Captain Football himself, decide."

Sabine nodded while Mitch tugged the brim of his cap. "Yes, ma'am." Neither his words or demeanor had an ounce of flirtation or disrespect, more just his natural affable charm which I suspected he couldn't turn off even if he tried.

If I weren't immune to such masculine charms, I'd probably have a crush on the man. Half the population of Atlantis probably did already. Maybe Phil and I needed to gather everyone for another "no sex while deployed" talk. And maybe we should add a little note about the no-no's of relationships across ranks, because while I didn't have a crush on Mitch, I certainly had my eye on the *other* new member of the team.

I immediately admonished myself. Goddammit, Rebecca, she's not available, she's not allowed, and she's not someone deserving of your ridiculous objectification. I stepped back to give myself some space and let Bobby give Sabine and Mitch the rundown of the rules of our friendly-not-so-friendly game, which we'd adapted to our mix and match style of swapping teams to keep things fresh. As Bobby blathered and assigned positions, I pretended to check the Velcro fastenings of the flags at my waist, using the time to shift my focus and settle my unease about my afore-noticed ridiculous objectification.

Bobby broke me out of my head with a respectful, "Ready, Colonel Keane?"

I looked up, smiling brightly. "Absolutely." We didn't have side captains as such, and I definitely wouldn't have wanted to insert myself as one in a recreational game, but I usually gave my team a pep talk prior to play—mostly because I *really* hated losing and wanted to infuse them with all the confidence and morale I possibly could. "Right, team. Let's run like there's one brownie in the chow hall and everyone's trying to get it."

That earned a round of laughter. I peered around the circle, catching everyone's eye, and noted Sabine's gaze. It was…not reverent exactly, but definitely awestruck, which unfortunately added a point to my *oh so cute* column. I shook the thought out of my head. Time for football.

Within the first few offensive plays it was clear that Sabine wasn't lying when she'd said she was fast. I'd always considered myself a sneaky and speedy receiver but she far outshone me, and it became increasingly difficult to concentrate on what I was doing instead of watching her sprint upfield with the smooth grace of a cheetah.

And it also became abundantly clear that both of my new surgeons, despite obviously being best friends off the field, acted like mortal enemies when they were on it. And they were on the same team. I dreaded to think what they would be like if they were on opposing teams. At every mistake or missed opportunity, the pair of them bickered at one another like siblings. Worse than. They cheered and pep-talked the other members of our side, but it was like they only had dagger eyes for each other. Shit-talking during football games was natural. But only ever directed to the other team. This was just bizarre.

After Sabine missed a wide throw from Mitch, he stalked over to her. "Christ, Sabine. Do you even know how to catch a football?"

She raised her chin, staring him down—no mean feat considering he was six inches taller. "I do. Do you know how to throw one? Because from where I was, the ball wasn't coming anywhere near me."

"Because you weren't where I told you to be."

"If I went where you *told* me to, Mr. Self-appointed Captain of the Team, I'd have been flagged in two seconds." She extended her arms and spun a full three-sixty degrees. "Read the play, Mitch!"

"I'll give you something to read," he muttered.

I set my hands on my hips, trying my damnedest not to reveal how amusing I found the whole thing. "Are you two about done? Can we play some football now, or has our weekly fun game somehow turned into a bickering competition?"

They both whipped around to face me. Sabine looked utterly mortified. "Yes, ma'am. Sorry, ma'am." Her mortification melted into a smile lifting the edges of her mouth. "Out of curiosity, between Mitch and me, who do you think would win this hypothetical bickering competition?"

"At this stage, it's a dead tie," I said dryly.

Her barely there smile turned delighted. "I'll take it."

I nodded and moved back to my position on the line, at the other end from her. For now, everyone seemed to be on the amused side of the scale as they watched the newest people on the base go at each other like they were professional anti-cheerleaders. But it could easily tip from amusing the team to affecting morale. If the team didn't get a chance to enjoy themselves, forget about all the shit going on around us and blow off steam, then all that steam built until the pressure exploded. Part of my job was ensuring things like that didn't happen.

I tried to keep my eyes on the plays and players around me, but that inevitably meant I had to look at Sabine. And almost every time I looked to her, I'd catch her watching me. I decided it was because she'd probably never had a CO interact with her during rec time. But she seemed to be suffering a particularly intense bout of consternation about it.

When we huddled to discuss our next play, Sabine leaned over to peer at Mitch. She pulled her buff higher so it covered her mouth and nose but I still heard her clearly, and if his expression was anything to go by, so did Mitch when she drawled, "Are you throwing the ball to me, or the opposition this time?"

Mitch's look was withering. "Know what? I think I might make this next play a pass to Colonel Keane here. Give myself a minute of respite from your bellyachin'." He turned a winning smile on me. "Assuming that's okay with you, ma'am?"

"Fine with me," I said. "Let's do it."

Mitch's pass was a good one, and I zigzagged my way forward ten yards before I ran into a wall of Red Team and was flagged. I threw the ball to Amy who sent it onward. The ball made its way through most of the hands on our team until it reached Sabine who tossed it back to Mitch. "Nice catch," she said when he snatched it from the air in one hand. "Better than your passes."

His smile was saccharine sweet. "Thanks. What was it that general attending said our first day?" Mitch pretended to mull it over. "Hmm, that's right. He said mine were the best set o'hands he'd seen in a good long while. Best set o'hands," he repeated, digging it in.

I spoke instead of Sabine. "That's a fine compliment, Mitch. Maybe you can use that best set of hands you've got there to throw the ball and help us win the game?" I'd intended to sound encouraging but with all the shit-talking flying around, it came out as slightly condescending.

Mitch chuckled and nodded. "Yes, ma'am."

And Sabine… Her mouth fell open. She coughed out a laugh before she turned away and crouched down to fiddle with her boot laces. Her shoulders shook with silent laughter, the sounds of her guffaws muffled behind her gloves.

"Nice to see you find it all so funny, Sabs," Mitch drawled.

She straightened up. "Oh no, Mitch. Just remembering something I read on the Internet this morning."

"The Internet was down this morning. Again."

"Maybe I read it yesterday morning then," she said airily as she jogged over to get set for our next play.

"It was down yesterday morning too, Sabine," I commented.

Mirth was plain in her eyes. "So it was, ma'am."

By halftime, despite playing a fierce and scrappy game of reasonably solid defense and passable offense, my team was down and looking unlikely to recover unless we found a miracle. Both Sabine and I had caught passes from Mitch and managed to gain some yards but we just couldn't capitalize. After another wide throw from Mitch, Sabine held her hands up, twinkling her fingers. "These are my hands, Mitch. Maybe a better set than yours. This is where you need to throw the ball, not at my damned feet, which, skilled as they are—cannot catch."

"Then put your hands in the spot they're supposed to be."

And so it continued until the moment Conway blew the final whistle, and it was like every ounce of competitiveness and vitriol was sucked out of them and replaced with teasing passive-aggression. Sabine punched Mitch's pectoral and she did not pull it. Her smile was fake as fake could be as she slow-clapped him. "Great job. We would have almost won it if not for your bad calls and shitty throws."

His smile was equally disdainful. "Thanks, Sabs. Maybe next time we'll get 'em. If you can learn what a football play is, that is."

"Check your emails," she shot back. "I'm sending you a video. Subject, How to Play Football."

"Check yours. There'll be a How to be a Cheerleader video."

She stepped up to him, eyes narrowing as she got right up in his face. "Are you saying I should be on the sidelines instead of on the field?"

"I'm not *not* saying it."

"Don't forget, I've seen you in a skirt. You look great, prime cheerleader material. Probably better than me."

Big, burly Mitch Boyd in a skirt. That was an interesting visual. I cut in before he could come back at her again. "Fleischer, Boyd, a word?"

They looked at each other, both of them wearing a *What have you done now?* expression. I moved a few yards away and they followed. They stood at loose attention before me and Sabine braved a, "What can we help you with, ma'am? If this is about what I said about frostbite conditions before the game, I apologize. Sometimes my brain and mouth don't connect. You were absolutely right to make us wear gloves."

I nodded my acknowledgment but didn't say anything further about her second apology. Instead, I asked them both, "You two are friends, yes?"

This time Mitch got in first. "Yes, ma'am. The best. Ever since our first day of premed."

"Hmm. Do you always try to kill one another when you're teaming up during friendly sports games? Or is it just something in the air here that's making you act like mortal enemies?"

Sabine's eyes widened. "Oh. Uh, it's just that…we're…competitive. And he's so bossy, nobody can do a thing right on his team. I don't like being treated like a kid who can't follow instructions." She added a hasty, "Ma'am."

Mitch's indignant outrage at being called bossy was comical, but Sabine wasn't wrong—he'd been running the team, overruling everything, from the moment Bobby had first tossed him the ball. He hastened to defend himself. "I may be bossy sometimes when I've got a football in my hands, Colonel Keane, but Sabine is stubborn as heck and doesn't listen to good sense. Simple as that."

And Mitch wasn't wrong either. "I see. Well, henceforth, the pair of you can either learn to play together or you can be on separate teams forevermore." I smiled benevolently. "Your bickering isn't good for morale, or my migraines."

They exchanged a slow look, but were smiling. Mitch turned that smile on me. "Might be best to keep us separated, ma'am."

"Separated it is. From now on, you two can sit out while we draw whose team we'll be on." Being held up as examples of "how not to bond" might get them to figure it out. If either of them were bothered by my ruling, they didn't show it.

Sabine nodded decisively. "Sounds like a good plan."

I waved everyone else over. "Okay, from now on, Boyd and Fleischer will be separated for team games. Instead of our names, we can all draw either *Mitch* or *Sabine* from the mayo bucket and that will decide the teams. Any objections?"

There were no objections, only a great deal of laughter. From Mitch and Sabine included. At least they were good sports about the whole thing, which had been a gamble I'd thankfully won. "Good game, everyone. You're all dismissed. Cool down properly, and refuel. I'll see you all later. Enjoy the rest of your day."

Mitch gave Sabine a friendly side-on hug then jogged away to catch up to Bobby and John. Amy slung her arm around Sabine's shoulders and as they walked away she blurted, "That was fucking magnificent."

"I'm so mortified," Sabine groaned.

"Don't be." Amy guffawed. "You've taught us all new comebacks for when we're fighting with our siblings."

Sabine's response was muffled, but the laughter wasn't. The sound of her mirth made me feel as if I'd just had a dose of serotonin. Time to go cool myself down too. Maybe a clichéd cold shower would do the trick. As I stared after Sabine, I decided it probably wouldn't help one damned bit.

CHAPTER FIVE

By almost three months after Sabine and Mitch's arrival at Atlantis, I had a solid sense of who they were and how they worked best and their professional weaknesses, which I'd been helping them strengthen. *Gently* in Sabine's case because she was prone to take anything suggesting she hadn't succeeded absolutely as a complete failure. She had a healthy self-confidence and the expected surgeon's arrogance, but it was balanced by her desperate desire to do everything perfectly, which sometimes made her seem insecure. An interesting and intriguing combination.

She was an interesting and intriguing combination.

Professionally, she was everything I could have asked for in a surgeon, and then some. She had undeniable talent, but also an innate ability to navigate traumas with a team that made her seem almost telepathic. Sabine was always the first person after every trauma to get her paperwork to me, and her notes were not only legible but detailed.

And personally... I tried not to notice, but given the close proximity on base, and my persistent interest, I couldn't help myself. She was incredibly routine-oriented, right down to her breakfast. She'd wait for fresh batches of powdered milk which, unlike most who used it for cereal, she put in her coffee—always two of the small catering-size mugs. Most of us drank coffee like it was a hot potato, chugging it as quickly as we could after ignoring any additions, or hastily utilizing the chemical-tasting creamers and sugar. Not Sabine.

She was out on the dirt running track every day to get in at least five miles, even if it was interrupted by work or weather and she had to stagger her miles across a few sessions. She read every free chance she got, always the same three books: a historical non-fiction about Ancient Rome, or German versions of Nietzsche and a falling-apart Kafka. After Googling the titles I realized those two were Nietzsche's *On the Genealogy of Morality* and Kafka's *The Metamorphosis*.

I'd rarely seen her less-than-immaculate, as if she spent half her free time starching her uniforms and spraying her hair to keep it in place. Her obvious focus on adhering to uniform standards made my mind wander to places it shouldn't, because I couldn't help wondering what she might look like out of uniform and not-so-immaculate. My imagination frequently took an unplanned trip, thinking of Sabine rumpled in tangled sheets. Hair loose and spread across the pillow. Tanned skin flushed and slick with sweat. Breasts rising and falling as she tried to catch her breath after I'd enjoyed myself between her thighs.

The erotic-tinted thoughts were obviously a dead giveaway as to my feelings, and the more I noticed about her, the more I accepted noticing these things was a sure sign I was seriously attracted to her. Attraction on its own was fine. But this went beyond simple attraction.

I realized, with some dread, that I liked her, plain and simple. And *like* was so dangerous. It would worm its way under my skin, become part of me, catch me unawares at the worst time and trip me up. I made a mental note to unpack these feelings more deeply at some stage. But in the meantime, I'd let thoughts come freely in case the answer suddenly hit me in the head. And my free thoughts always circled back to the same thing.

Loneliness.

It was the most logical explanation. Despite being surrounded by people, I was lonely. So, was this attachment just that I was desperate for genuine friendship with someone who had an appealing personality, and it was warping into me thinking beyond friendship because she also had appealing everything else? Or was it that Sabine was someone with whom I could imagine myself in a relationship, and I was doing just that in a safe way because I knew she was so unavailable? And unavailable was safe. There was no danger in fantasy. Or…was it simply a genuine attraction that didn't need any deep or meaningful unpacking because it was what it was?

But it *did* need to be unpacked and addressed. It needed to be
figured out and then put away because by its very nature and my very
situation, I needed to know why her, why this, why now? Because if I
didn't understand it, I wouldn't be able to control it. I wouldn't be able
to contain it. And I needed to contain it. Everything in my life was
contained neatly in its proper place. Work. My sexuality. My, admittedly
few, historical romantic relationships back home. My friendships, both
personal and professional. A Venn diagram where certain things could
never intersect. Like work and romantic relationships. Especially not a
romantic work relationship with someone under my command. Huge
no way, no how, even without the added same-sex complication of
Don't Ask, Don't Tell. Unfortunately, having figured out a little of the
why didn't tell me what I should do about the *how*...

I made a quick stop by the wards to check everything was okay,
everyone was stable and comfortable, and the transfers of recovering
casualties to Landstuhl, Germany were on schedule, then strolled
across the base toward the chow hall for lunch. By all accounts it was a
beautiful early-spring day. Warm without baking. Light wind winding
its way around the buildings. A few wispy clouds streaking across the
cerulean sky. I paused by the machinery shed and raised my face to
the sun, absorbing some Vitamin D and enjoying my few moments of
peaceful sunshine. Peaceful was a relative term. The base was its usual
noisy self, and today we had the added bonus of the rumbling distant
sound of helos echoing through the valley.

I spotted Sabine eating lunch with a small group. Murphy's Law
of unworkable attractions meant I noticed her everywhere. Sabine
held the table's attention as she relayed a story, her hands moving
emphatically through the air. She glanced up as I passed by and smiled
at me. "Ma'am." Her smile was friendly, but also tinged with something
extra. Something that sent a shudder over my skin.

The rest of the table followed suit with their greetings and after
I'd responded, I kept moving, leaving them to eat their lunch without
their CO hovering over them. While I stood by the sandwich station,
waiting for the major in front of me to decide if he wanted an Italian or
chicken salad sandwich, I heard Sabine's laugh, loud and unashamed.
She laughed as if laughter was fuel for her, and that distinctive deep,
husky mirth made my breath catch.

Two almost simultaneous thoughts came to me—a pitiful middle-
school-ish wish that it had been me, something I'd said or done that
she'd found worthy of her amusement, and then the realization that
those exact thoughts were not only childish but absurd. Though I

could be friendly, I wasn't her friend. I was her boss. It was time I remembered how to act like one.

* * *

The last thing I expected to see when I walked into the shower block to wash off my run was Sabine wearing nothing but a towel. I paused just inside the doorway and peered around to see who else was there. Nobody. Goddammit.

Having only the two of us in this small space where we'd both be naked, albeit in shower cubicles, felt too intimate. Sabine looked up from where she was bent over trying to extract a new laundry bag from the stash on the bottom shelf. One hand moved to yank the fabric down over the tops of her thighs, the other covered the towel tucked between her breasts, as if she feared it might spontaneously undo itself.

Sabine straightened with comical slowness, her expression a mix of shock and embarrassment, with a tinge of horrified. "Colonel Keane. I'm sorry. I'm just…I…got puked on," she said quickly, as if trying to explain why she wasn't dressed in a public place, even if it was the shower block where such a thing was expected. "Went right through to the skin."

"Oh. Lucky you."

"Mmm." She looked me up and down and then averted her eyes as if she'd just realized that she'd checked me out, even if it had been unintentional. "Amy's bringing my things," she murmured to the floor. "I just had to get those clothes off ASAP."

"Ah. Are you a sympathetic vomiter?" I set my shower bag and fresh clothes on one of the shelves.

"Not at all. It's just gross to be covered in puke." Sabine raised both hands, palms up. "Mitch on the other hand? Total emetophobe."

The thought made me smile. I didn't know anyone who enjoyed vomit, but someone who'd been through med school and a surgical residency being afraid of it was an amusing thought. Mitch Boyd must have some serious goal-focus to move past that phobia. "Interesting. So if I spot him sprinting away I should look for someone who's about to vomit?"

"Yes, ma'am. He's an excellent indicator of potential puke. He'll break land-speed records to get away from it."

"I'll keep that in mind." I unlaced my boots and pushed my feet into flip-flops, very purposely keeping my eyes to myself. I'd already seen the smooth expanse of limbs, the way her hair fell straight as a sheet of obsidian, except for the crinkles where she'd had it restrained in a bun all day, and the small, neat swell of breasts and cleavage into which she'd tucked the end of her towel.

Even with my back to her, I sensed her watching me or trying not to. I often felt or witnessed that from her, her curious gaze settling upon me or a quick glance away when she'd been caught. I understood it, having had similar curiosity about my commanding officers when I was fresh into my Army career and wondering about them as people instead of this mysterious and all-knowing leader they appeared to be. Now I knew there was nothing mysterious or all-knowing about commanding officers. We were just people with hobbies, likes and dislikes, thoughts and desires the same as everyone else.

Desires.

I gathered my things, slipped into a shower cubicle, and locked the plywood door. Safely out of sight, I leaned against the wall and took a few moments to recenter myself. This was going to become an issue if I didn't get control of myself. I knew I *could* control myself—I'd worked with masses of attractive women over my career, though had never felt the immediate pull that I did to Sabine Fleischer. Singularly, I mused to myself, her physicality or personality would have attracted me. But combined? I felt helpless. I rarely felt helpless, and it was the one emotion I'd always found hard to overcome.

I set Sabine aside to focus on showering and getting away as quickly as I could. Midway through shampooing my hair, Amy's voice echoed through the small shower block. "Fleischer? Yo! You still in here?"

Sabine's voice rose over the sound of my unsatisfyingly warm and weak shower. "Yeah, I'm in the cubicle on the end." After a quick pause she added, "So is Colonel Keane." A strangled choking sound emanated from Sabine's direction. "I mean, she's in here." Her voice strained upward as if she'd just realized that trying to explain was only making it hilariously worse. I tried not to laugh as she kept trying to dig herself free. "I mean, she's not in *here* here with me but she's here in the shower block. Having a shower. In her own cubicle." There was a thud of some body part hitting the cubicle wall.

Amy snorted. "Thanks for the overly complex explanation." She raised her voice to greet me with a cheerful, "Hello, Colonel Keane."

I took a moment to make sure I wasn't going to sound like a goat being strangled before answering, "Hello, Amy."

"Coming over the top, Sabs." A plastic bag rustled and thudded.

"Thanks," Sabine muttered.

"FYI, I saw the kitchen staff making pizza, so you'd better not be late for dinner again because I'm not saving you any."

Sabine's indignant exasperation was comical. "I won't be late. And I was only late that one time because I was finishing up op notes which I thought was more important than getting a good seat at dinner."

Amy's sigh was overexaggerated. "You need to adjust your priorities, Fleischer. We're not in Kansas anymore. There's always time for paperwork, but there's not always time to get the good food." She paused and a tinge of realization crept into her voice as a slow and careful enunciation. "Not that doing paperwork and getting it to your boss right away isn't *super* important I mean. Ma'am."

"Right," I agreed dryly.

"Great," was Amy's cheerful response. "I'll just go now and...do some paperwork. Catch you later, Sabine. Goodbye, Colonel Keane."

"Bye, Amy. Enjoy the rest of your day."

Sabine cleared her throat. I heard a few garbled noises, as if she was practicing talking, before she raised her voice to be heard over both our showers. Her voice dripped mortification. "I'm so sorry about that, ma'am. My brain is clearly not engaged. I didn't mean to imply that—"

I shut off my shower and cut her off before she could dig herself in deeper, though the implication of us in a shower cubicle together had made my skin heat more than the pitiful showerhead had. I made myself laugh, feigning mirth when all I wanted was to let my brain carry the fantasy of us in a shower together to its sensuous climax. "I know. Don't worry about it, Sabine." I had to clench my thighs together to stop them trembling, and kept my eyes on the water persistently dripping from the showerhead.

If I closed my eyes, I'd picture letting myself into her shower stall, running my hands over her sleek, slippery body. Dropping to my knees. The musky scent and taste of her. I'd imagine her hands roughly pushing my face against her wet heat, guiding me to how she most wanted my tongue and lips to work against her clitoris. I'd be able to hear the sounds she'd make as she came and then the sounds I'd make when she pulled me to my feet, spun me around and pressed me against the wall so she could finger-fuck me.

I drew in a shaky breath and let it out slowly, hoping to settle the overwhelming arousal burning through my body. Well done, Rebecca. Imagining what you'd imagine if you *could* imagine it really wasn't the best idea.

There was a long pause, then Sabine's shower shut off too. "Yes, ma'am."

I concentrated on dressing quickly, not wanting to be in the shower block a moment longer than necessary. "Have a good day," I rushed out, and almost sprinted from the block. As I walked back to my quarters to drop off my shower kit, I tried to ignore the arousal still surging around my body. Goddammit. The mental image was still so arousing, I thought about locking my door to take care of it. With the steady throb between my thighs it would probably take barely a moment.

But just as quickly, I grew anxious. Were my private fantasies predatory? Disrespectful? I was in a position of power over her, yes, but nothing about my attraction would eventuate so there would be no coercion, no threat to her career—if I'd been so inclined, which of course I wasn't. I would *never* act on my thoughts, obviously, and therefore she wouldn't even know. But it was so inappropriate for me to think of her like that. I had a job—to lead her through her Army career. And if I couldn't do that job because I was attracted to her, then I had no business being in a position of leadership.

I dabbed a light amount of perfume at my wrists and neck—frivolous, but one of the few things I used to help me feel normal—then left my room to go hide in my office until I didn't feel like I was going to drool at Sabine if I saw her. I knew she'd just had a verbal slip. But the fact she'd become so flustered over it felt telling, as if she'd revealed something and regretted it. Or maybe it was that the idea of it was so foreign to her that she'd flipped out.

Or…maybe I was just projecting my own thoughts into the situation and adding a whopping dose of wishful thinking. I now understood perfectly how Riley and Evans had gotten into their pregnancy predicament. Deployments were damned hard. People got lonely, missed physical affection, acted unthinkingly.

But it wasn't allowed and not just because I was Sabine's boss and she was in a relationship—as evidenced by some video calls I'd overheard. The *Don't Ask, Don't Tell* policy had all of us muzzled, and not just the LGBT members of the United States Armed Forces. I knew, despite the plain gold band on my left ring finger, that my peers suspected I didn't really have a husband who I just didn't talk about. When we'd discuss significant others, I'd always pass off my turn to share. And then came the awkward silence, the knowing looks, and sometimes someone would mutter, "Fuckin' DADT" before we'd move on to another topic, and I'd try not to think about how unfair it was that I couldn't even agree with them because it would give me away. It would give me away for a secret that everyone already seemed to know.

Fucking DADT indeed. This was what those implementing such policies didn't understand—people knew and overwhelmingly, nobody cared. Nobody cared, except for never being able to be fully truthful or even relaxed around those we trusted to have our backs. Not quite the successful policy they'd hoped for…

After dinner with Phil I retired to my room for an instant-messaging chat with Linda. The Internet had been intermittently good and I decided to take my chances in my room rather than risk anyone seeing my screen which, knowing Linda, would have a not-safe-for-work conversation on it. After removing my boots I sat on my bed, leaning against the wall. When I opened up the messaging system, there was already a message waiting for me.

LKelly: I'm here, you there?

RKeane: I'm here. Sorry, waylaid by…you know, things. How're you?

It took a few minutes for her response to arrive, by which time I'd moved so I was lying in bed with my head at the foot to get the best signal.

LKelly: Hey, sorry, got bored waiting and went for a snack. I do know about your waylaying. I'm good. You??

RKeane: Same.

After a moment I added a second message.

RKeane: Good but a little discombobulated too.

LKelly: I love that word. Why's that?

RKeane: Not really sure. It's been an odd few weeks, work-wise, things feel a little unsettled around here moving back into busy time. Maybe just feeling lonely? Or lonelier would be more accurate.

There was no way in hell I was going to admit in actual typed words that I was fantasizing about someone in the unit. That would have to wait for an actual face-to-face conversation with Linda. In a few months I could sit down with her and maybe try to work through this attraction.

LKelly: Do I need to send you some more erotica? Maybe some women in uniform stuff?

Women in uniform. Women like Sabine Fleischer. That was probably the last thing I needed, though I seemed to be doing just fine conjuring up mental images of her all on my own. Mostly *out* of uniform.

RKeane: The last bunch of stories were just fine, thank you. More than fine. I'm still getting some good mileage out of them.

*LKelly: *lol* What about some porn? I know a great lesbian site that's for women, no creepy made for men angles. I could get a membership and download some for you? Send it on a hard drive?*

RKeane: Tempting, but probably not a great idea in case I forget to plug in my headphones properly and the whole base gets an earful of my masturbatory material.

Not to mention being sent pornography from friend or family was technically a no-go. Long gone were the days of tittie mags hidden in the mail. I was sure most everyone here had external hard drives full of porn, but I couldn't get over the fear of someone finding my self-service stash. I felt worried enough about keeping literature with an obvious lesbian theme on my personal laptop. Erotica videos featuring two women was a complete no-go, as much as I would have enjoyed some genuine lesbian scenes.

LKelly: Maybe someone will overhear and come knocking on your door for a little "dalliance" and help you get rid of some of that loneliness. It's not like you're a nun…

The image from earlier in the shower came flooding back, bringing with it a fresh surge of arousal that made my skin heat. God, it was like I was fifteen all over again and just discovering I liked girls.

RKeane: No I'm not, but so many rules against it. And besides, I've got you to help me with that. *smile*

LKelly: And help I will.

My pager chimed with a post-op report. Nothing urgent. But I had a sudden unpleasant sensation that I couldn't continue this conversation. Everything I typed and everything I read made me think of Sabine.

RKeane: Sorry I have to go. I've just been paged.

It wasn't a lie, obviously, but I didn't need to respond to the page. I just wanted an excuse to get away from a conversation heading in a direction I had no desire to go.

LKelly: No problem. Talk soon. MYLY.

Miss You, Love You. She really was the best friend. Supportive and kind, compassionate and understanding, and receptive to everything I offered her in return.

RKeane: MYLY too. Talk soon.

I closed my laptop and for a moment, just lay there staring at my closed door. What I really wanted was to do something about the mental image that refused to leave my brain, to lie naked in bed as I imagined Sabine underneath me, on top of me. I wanted to think about the taste of her, exactly what sounds she'd make as I slicked my tongue through her labia, closed my lips around her clitoris. I rolled onto my back and had just worked my belt loose when the uncomfortable truth hit me again, like the proverbial lightning bolt from the sky.

I *really* couldn't do this, as much as I wanted to drag my fingers over my clitoris and climax imagining it was Sabine's tongue. Masturbating while thinking about a *subordinate* really wasn't right. My hands shook as I fastened my belt, made sure my tee was tucked in, and pulled my boots back on. Time to go for a walk outside or around the wards. Anywhere but here where I was alone with thoughts that were becoming dangerous.

CHAPTER SIX

Although it was before sunrise, the base already hummed with noise and movement. In mid-June, the early mornings offered some respite from the intense heat, and a lot of people squeezed in their runs or gym workouts in the dawn light. As I walked across the base to the side furthest from the mountain range to the west, I exchanged pleasantries with a few of them, relieved when nobody seemed inclined to engage in a long conversation.

A few benches constructed from wooden shipping pallets were laid out in a semicircle, set ten feet inside the fence. I stood beside the bonfire pit to wait for the sun to rise and slowly illuminate the FOB, before it would slink over the ground and climb up the mountains to my left. The air was pleasantly warm and in the dim light the sky appeared cloud free, promising a beautiful day.

I'd been watching the horizon for a few minutes when I sensed someone approaching from my periphery. Turning to face the interloper, and readying myself to deal with some crisis or another, I was surprised to see Sabine instead of Phil or one of the majors. Not an interloper at all. She paused, as if checking whether she was allowed to come closer. I pivoted to face her, unsurprised to find myself already smiling. Once I'd returned her sharp salute, I said, "Morning, Sabine."

"Good morning, Colonel Keane. Apologies for disturbing your quiet time. I thought you were Amy." Sabine moved up to stand beside me, a foot away, with hands behind her back.

Given Amy Peterson was four inches taller than me, I wasn't sure how Sabine had mistaken us. But she seemed guileless so I let it be. "It's fine. And it's a shame to not share the sunrise." I glanced at the horizon, then my watch. "In about three minutes, it'll be stunning."

She squared her shoulders as if bracing herself for the view. "Do you come out here to watch the sunrise often?"

"Almost every day, on every one of my deployments since I joined the Army, unless the weather or an emergency makes it impossible." I laughed quietly. "It's less pleasant when the weather's bad, but I think it's worth a slightly early wake-up and being occasionally cold or wet."

"I think I see that," she said.

I turned away from the blossoming sunrise to look at her and caught her watching me. Her expression was a mix of curiosity and something that looked an awful lot like admiration. Though, the light *was* dim and I could be mistaken. "I found early on that having one consistent thing in my day helped with all the other inconsistencies."

Sabine's laugh was rich and full of genuine mirth. "Inconsistencies. Yes, ma'am. I admit I've been struggling with those. I...like my routines."

I bit down on my smile at her self-deprecating understatement. "I think we all do. But it's how you learn to deal with those inconsistencies that'll shape you as a surgeon, especially if you're working in emergency or trauma medicine. When we're back at Walter Reed and you're performing routine, scheduled procedures, it'll be easier."

She nodded slowly, thoughtfully. "I think I'm getting better with the not knowing what'll happen day-to-day."

"I think you are too," I agreed. The shift in light dragged my focus from her, almost reluctantly back toward the approaching sunrise. "Here it comes," I murmured.

We stood quietly side by side, not touching but close enough that I felt an almost electric tingle tightening my skin. If it were any other situation and we were outside our work relationship, I might have made a joking comment about how she was like a semiconductor. And I suddenly wanted that—for us to be not here, to be not stuck in this work relationship, to be free to say what I wanted—to be real so badly that it almost stole my breath.

"Oh wow," she whispered. "I can't believe I've been missing out on this and now it's almost time to leave."

It took me a few moments to compose myself enough to answer. "There's always tomorrow, and the day after that, and the deployment after this." Though it felt a little trite, I added, "That's the beauty of a sunrise. There'll always be another one."

As she slowly moved her head to take in the scene, Sabine mused, "That's true." She paused as her focus rested on me. "I'll try to come out to see some more sunrises, but if I don't manage to, then at least I got this one."

She'd been here for five months, and in just under a month we'd be rotating out and going back to D.C. Now was as good a time as any for a check-in. "How've you found your first deployment, Sabine? Anything you'd like to share with me? Anything that's been concerning or bothering you? You don't need to be stoic here."

Her smile was immediate, illuminating the dim light. "I promised on my first day that I'd come see you if I had a problem."

"That you did."

She paused just a moment too long. "There's nothing bothering me, ma'am. This deployment has been an incredible experience, but…I have to admit I'm excited to go home."

"Mmm, I can understand that. Being away for so long can be difficult. But, and I know this sounds like a recruitment advertisement, we're doing essential and important work here. Work that not everyone can do. You should be proud of that and proud of your contribution."

Sabine nodded. "Yes, we are. And yes, ma'am, I am." She paused, her forehead furrowing. The low dawn light cast shadows across her face, accentuating the arching curves of her cheekbones and the smooth lines of her nose and jaw. "I'd imagine it's hard for your… husband to watch you deploy repeatedly. He must worry about you." Her voice went up an octave at the end, as if she'd been nervous about saying it. It was borderline too personal a comment, but I let it slide in favor of trying to dig a little deeper into her.

"This is our job, Sabine. And hopefully our spouses and partners understand that, if not accept it." The fact she believed my unspoken lie was both heartening and heartbreaking. The heartbreaking was ridiculous. Why would I be upset over her thinking I was married, and to a man? Because I had some ridiculous subconscious delusion that involved us becoming more than…this. A foolish thought, especially from pragmatist me.

She was quiet for a while, as if weighing up how to respond. "I'm not sure my—mine does understand or accept it. Or ever will."

"I'm sorry to hear that. Being away from home is hard, being away for as long as we are, where we are, doing what we do? It's even more difficult if you don't have a solid support system back home."

She laughed warmly. "I do have a solid support system back home, ma'am. My sister and my parents."

"That's good. And also so important." I took one last long look at the sunrise before accepting it was time for me to go inside and begin my day. But first... I turned to Sabine. "A piece of advice? I know we're all desperate to get home, but try to enjoy the rest of your time here. The Army always gives you something, whether it's something you thought you wanted or not. Take whatever a deployment offers you, good and bad, and turn it into something you can use for the rest of your life. Trust me, anything you can learn, even if it's something as simple as the fact everything you'll eat on deployment tastes better with hot sauce, is something worth knowing."

She laughed. "I will, Colonel Keane. Thank you."

Colonel Keane. I'd never minded being addressed by my rank but for some reason, from her mouth, it bothered me. I wasn't sure if it was the reinforcement of the distance between us, or the way she somehow made *Colonel* and *ma'am* seem like a soft endearment. I fought the urge to touch her, balling my hands into fists. "I should get inside. Don't stay out here too long. You'll miss out on breakfast."

"You sound like Amy." She leaned slightly closer, still smiling. "I won't. I'm just going to take another few minutes to enjoy the view." She paused, the smile wavering a little as if she was considering what to say. "I hope you have a great day, ma'am."

"You too." I tried to sound as pleasantly neutral as I would responding to that sentiment from anyone, but I knew I sounded too warm. Too inviting. It was time to move, away from her and away from my own inability to be professional. I walked a fine line with the whole unit—being the boss and leader, but also being approachable and friendly enough that they trusted me and would come to me if they needed help or had any issues that might compromise the unit or casualty care. But I knew I was teetering on the wrong side of the line with Sabine.

"What the hell are you doing, Rebecca?" I murmured to myself. "What are you thinking?"

Unfortunately, I still had no answer.

After a relatively quiet day, except for a straightforward hernia repair for one of the locals that we'd had scheduled for almost a week, I double-checked the mission board and the recovery ward and deemed everything stable enough that I could spend the afternoon playing golf. "Playing golf" was a generous term for a FOB in Afghanistan. In addition to a few rough putting holes in concrete-hard ground that refused to remain pebble free no matter how frequently we swept it, we had a long mound of dirt that we used as the tee-off for our "driving range" to send golf balls toward the mountains.

We paid some of the local kids to collect any golf balls that made it over the wire and leave them lined up at the gate for us to reuse. Lined up, not left in a bucket or pile because the disgusting reality of our situation was that we had to be suspicious even of kids. And the balls were a certain brand and all marked in such a way that it'd be easy to see if someone had cut them open to tamper with them and create an explosive device. Fun things were not always fun.

I'd spent almost half an hour whacking balls in a futile attempt to wallop out some of my tension—not work, but personal—and had yet to find any sort of Zen. Phil had left after five minutes, declaring his golf swing was AWOL and he wasn't going to do his mental health such a disservice by landing all his shots inside the fence.

With every ball I sent down the range, I went over and over everything I'd been trying to make sense of for the past five months. But I found no solution. Was I deluded? Honestly, how real could my attraction to Sabine be? It really was probably nothing more than a physical attraction, brought about by the fact I was lonely and hadn't had a long-term romantic relationship for almost two decades.

Short term and oh-so-casual relationships? Absolutely. But I'd deliberately avoided giving all of myself for a very long time. Maybe some subconscious part of myself thought it was time to try again and had latched onto the first person it thought might be suitable, despite how ridiculously unsuitable she was. So, all I had to do was figure out if it was just a physical attraction, or something deeper. Once I knew for sure, I could formulate a plan for getting over it.

I almost laughed at that. I'd been telling myself I needed to get over it for months now, and had made no real effort. I'd always been most honest with myself, and now was no different. I'd made no real effort—despite the confusion and disgust in myself—because I liked this feeling. Being attracted to someone felt amazing, and in this place you had to grab *amazing* every chance you could.

I used the tee pliers to work my broken tee out of the hole and pressed in a new one. I'd just set the ball down when I heard the laughing, joking approach of two people. Sabine and Mitch. Perfect.

They each dropped some cash into the lockbox with GREEN FEES painted on the front that we kept chained to the rack of drivers and putters. The money was used to pay for the golf ball return service and everyone on the base was generous with their donations. Mitch nodded his greeting, while Sabine pulled her sunglasses off and gave me a friendly, "Afternoon, Colonel Keane. I assume anyone's allowed to play this course? Or could we get a visitor's pass?"

"Mitch, Sabine. Good afternoon. And of course everyone's welcome. No memberships or golf handicaps here." I mentally patted myself on the back for my tone, steady and perfectly balanced between friendly and I'm-your-boss.

Sabine shaded her eyes with her hand as she peered down the driving range. "Sounds good to us, ma'am." She turned to me with a wry smile. "Though, I think this might be one of the rougher courses I've ever played on."

Laughing, I agreed, "Probably." I used my driver to point at the rack of golf clubs as I told her, "I think we've got a couple of left-handed drivers and putters around here."

"It's fine, but thank you. I golf and shoot right-handed." Her smile came with a small eye roll. "The drawback of being the only leftie in the family when your dad's trying to teach you things with his equipment." She shrugged and fumbled in the bucket of wooden tees, handing one to Mitch. "I could have unlearned it when I got old enough to buy my own things but it was muscle memory by then so I didn't see the point."

Mitch leaned around her to talk to me. "What she means to say, ma'am, is that she enjoys showing off her superior coordination and ambidextrousness."

Sabine raised an eyebrow at him then bent to try and press her tee into the hard-packed dirt. She exhaled a frustrated grunt. "Do they steamroll the grounds around here to make them deliberately impenetrable?"

Mitch chuckled. "Not so superior with your coordination now, huh, Spaghetti-o? Lemme try."

Before he could try to ram his tee into the ground, and inevitably snap it, I said, "Hold on a moment. Try this." I collected the tee-hole punch—a small, metal, mushroom-shaped device with a short stem the width of a tee, and a finger loop welded to one side of the mushroom top—from the equipment shelves. "We had to get a special tool fabricated, because we kept breaking all the tees trying to get them into the ground."

Sabine didn't move when I stepped up beside her, and I debated just handing the punch to her and telling her to have a go at it. But, teach by doing and all that. My hip lightly brushed her thigh as I bent down, and she stepped hastily to the side. It'd been the most innocent touch, far less than what happened during surgery when we jostled for space, but she'd obviously been spooked by something.

I was far from spooked.

I used my foot on the domed top of the punch to push a shallow hole into the dirt, then hooked a finger in the loop and pulled the tool out. "Voilà! One pre-punched tee hole. You can use the ready-made holes from other people of course, but the wind tends to blow dirt into them to cover them up pretty quickly. And there's pliers over there for when you inevitably break a tee off and it gets stuck." I held the punch out between her and Mitch, and Sabine took it from me, using just her forefinger to hook the small loop.

She studied the object like it was some mind-blowing invention. "Thank you, ma'am." She passed it to Mitch who quickly punched a hole, set his tee, and then pocketed the punch.

I pounced on him. "You'll be sure to put that back when you're done, won't you? Otherwise you'll have a bunch of angry golfers after you."

"Of course, ma'am. Just keepin' it here ready to use. I learned my lesson about stealing when I was in the fourth grade."

Stealing hearts probably. Sabine's arrival had shot my focus and I took a few moments to settle myself before driving the ball downrange. It landed well short of the fence, hampered by the backdraft and my lack of concentration.

Sabine's question to her friend was laced with beatific helpfulness. "Need some tips, Mitch? Like…how to actually hit the ball?"

"Wouldya get off my case for just one thing today, Sabs? I'm dyin' here. Not everyone is as naturally gifted as you at every goddamn thing they turn their hand to, nor do we all have a golf handicap in the single digits," he said sarcastically, but with a solid dose of fondness too.

Before Sabine could speak up, I chimed in, deadpan, "I think she has a point. You're a surgeon, Mitch. Golfing should absolutely be part of your skillset. We all need one instance in our life when someone comes to get us from a round of golf so we can go save a life. What else would we talk about at award dinners?"

He grinned. "I think I'll save that for the fancy guys, ma'am. Those plastics and neuros and cardios need the glory, not me. I'm just happy bein' out here, saving lives quietly, you know?"

"You're such a hero," Sabine said, but unlike their usual competitive jibes, it was kind and affectionate.

Mitch tipped an imaginary cowboy hat at her. Sabine swung and slogged the ball solidly over the wire. Mitch clobbered the dirt instead. At the dull thud of club hitting ground, Sabine drawled, "C'mon, Mitch. You hit the ball, not the dirt underneath it."

After mumbling something to himself, Mitch hit his golf ball over the fence too, sending it farther than Sabine's. "In your face," he muttered at her.

Sabine let the handle of her driver rest against her hip and curled both hands into cylinders which she brought to her eyes, as if pretending to have binoculars. "Nice. Now you just have to do that every time."

"Smartass." He glanced down at his feet. "Dammit, I broke the tee. You know what? I'm just gonna go practice my puttin'."

"Practice a lot. I'm a respected member of the golf club and if you think I'm taking you golfing when we get home, think again. Unless you can figure out how not to damage the fairways and greens with your trip-worthy divots in the next three weeks."

Instead of answering, Mitch collected the two halves of his broken tee then moved away to swap his driver for a putter, leaving Sabine and me alone. After landing another ball short of the fence, I turned to her. "Just out of curiosity, what *is* your golf handicap, Sabine?"

She sent her ball over the wire again and after a decisive nod, turned to me. "Lowest I ever reached was twenty-one, but I don't get to play much now so I stopped keeping track. Not *that* good, ma'am. Best round I ever shot was an eighty-one but there were *a lot* of lucky shots that day."

I whistled through my teeth. "Wow. I might keep my best score and my golf handicap to myself." I was somewhere between a casual golfer and a complete novice.

Thankfully she didn't ask for numbers. Instead, she laughed then glanced at Mitch, who was swearing his way around the putting "green," before turning her attention back to me. "I'm great at teeing off, not so great at the other stuff like chipping and putting and all that. So I'm good at long drives, and then everything else is just cross-my-fingers lucky shots."

"Ah. You prefer just slogging the ball instead of intricate, trigonometrical putting?" She was obviously athletic, but my assessment of her was more brain than body and I would have thought working out angles and speeds and forces would appeal to her.

"Kind of, yeah. Or it's what I practiced the most as a kid." At my querying eyebrows, she elaborated, "My dad's a dairy farmer, so I grew up with plenty of space. Anyway, I'd take a bucket of golf balls out into one of the empty pastures and just hit the balls from one end to the other whenever I was upset about something." Sabine lightly pressed the head of her golf club into the dirt as if pressing down divots. "School, friends, teen angst, that kind of stuff. Putting and chipping and all those other shots aren't very good for working out frustrations, so I never really got good at those. But I practiced my long drives a *lot*."

She'd shared something that felt so incredibly personal about her younger self and things she'd struggled with, that I almost didn't know how to respond. "Did it help?" I asked.

Sabine laughed. "With my golf swing, or all those things that felt like end-of-the-world problems as a teenager?"

After a short pause I said, "Both."

She glanced at something over my shoulder, her mouth twisting as she thoughtfully chewed the inside of her cheek. Sabine turned her focus back to me, and the moment her gaze landed on me it softened into an expression that almost made me forget to breathe. It was hopeful and intimate, yet respectful, as if she was desperate to tell me something personal but didn't dare. After an eternal pause she murmured, "Yes, ma'am. I think it did."

That quiet response had an edge to it, something that felt inviting, almost tentatively flirtatious. If I'd met her in a bar, I would have known exactly how to come back at her with an answering openness, a reciprocal flirtation. But here…it couldn't really be that. Could it?

Even though I took a slow steadying breath, my voice still caught on my answer. "I'm pleased to hear that, Sabine." It was time for me to go before the electricity coursing around my body sparked and caught fire. "I think I've had enough for today. I'll leave you both to it." I stowed my driver and turned to walk away, then paused and turned back. "Boyd, Fleischer?"

Mitch rushed to stand by Sabine and they stood with hands by their sides, staring right at me. Or in Sabine's case—like she was staring right into me.

I made sure to look at both of them and not let my gaze linger on her. "Enjoy your last few weeks of deployment. It's been wonderful having both of you join the team and I'm excited to continue working with you when we get back to D.C."

"Thank you, ma'am," they answered together. Mitch looked as pleased as anyone would when their boss told them they'd done a good job. Sabine looked like I'd just told her she was in the running for a Nobel Prize. She raised her golf club as if in salute. "I think I speak for both Mitch and me when I thank you for your leadership during our first deployment. It's been an amazing experience and we're both excited for the rest of our assignment with you."

I smiled at her toast-worthy speech. "Indeed. As am I." Excited, and also dreading it. But not for any reason anyone might understand. "Enjoy your afternoon."

The rest of their assignment with me. I did some mental math. I knew from her file that Sabine obtained her medical degree using the Army Health Professions Scholarship Program, which meant she was contracted to seven years of active duty with the Army. She'd be working under my command stateside at Walter Reed and then for any of our unit's deployments for six and a half more years. There was no way to get away from her, to get away from my desire. The only thing I could do was to figure out how I was to survive all that time working with her.

CHAPTER SEVEN

Washington D.C.
July 2007

I took a quick tour around my one-bedroom studio apartment in Upper Northwest D.C. Despite Linda's best care, most of the potted plants on my balcony were barely hanging on to life, and the rest I had to pronounce deceased. This was as much a part of my deployment cycle as leaving and returning. During my time stateside, I grew new plants and nurtured them until my small, precious balcony was overflowing with healthy greenery. Then while I was away, they'd die. Despite mourning my plants, the familiar inevitability of their demise was somehow comforting.

Though Linda had a brown thumb, she was otherwise excellent at getting my apartment ready for me. She'd turned on my fridge and stocked it with a few essentials, cracked open windows to air the space, and washed some clothes and linens so I didn't have to sleep with musty smelling sheets.

Everything looked exactly as I'd left it over ten months ago—fifteen-years-ago-modern and sparsely furnished, with photographs and art on every wall that wasn't taken up with overflowing bookshelves. My apartment had never felt like home; it was just a place I lived. A place that never changed, but every time I returned from a deployment, *I* felt changed. A little older, a little wiser, a little more jaded, and a lot more worn down.

Even more draining was the unsettling, underlying sensation of wanting change in my personal life, of wanting something more concrete. Some*one* more concrete. I couldn't recall the last time I'd felt that, and the fact my attraction to Sabine had reignited a most basic desire was both thrilling and terrifying.

Satisfied everything was fine, I turned my attention to my most pressing needs. Shower. Sleep. Scotch. Sex. I sent a quick text, a simple *I'm back*. Within ten minutes I had a phone call. Though I knew who it was, I still answered with, "Rebecca Keane."

Linda sounded as if she'd just won a lottery fortune. "Goddammit, Rebecca. It's good to hear your voice for real, not video-call distorted aaaand now we're disconnected."

My throat felt tight with emotion, knowing my friend was now just a few miles away instead of many thousands. "You too."

"When did you get home?"

"Just walked in the door fifteen minutes ago."

"And texting me was the first thing you did. I'm touched. Let me guess. You want your car?"

"Guessed it in one." Every deployment, as well as being a plant-mom, Linda kept my car in her garage and would turn it over periodically.

There was a pause before a quietly hopeful, "Is there anything else you want?"

"Yes," I said simply.

"Me too," Linda murmured. "I'm not seeing anyone at the moment, so…" She let the insinuation hang between us. "How desperate are you?"

"For my car or for the first orgasm that I didn't give myself in ages?"

She laughed. "Both."

"Quite, but I've also been traveling for over twenty-four hours and look, smell, and feel exactly like that."

"Then why don't I bring the car around tomorrow afternoon? And, just because I like you, I'll pay for some takeout for dinner, *and* bring a fresh supply of orgasms."

Thank god for uncomplicated friends-slash-casual-sex friends. "Sounds perfect. Thank you."

"Ohhh, you will be thanking me." The smile in her voice came through the phone. "Get some sleep, Rebecca. Because I'm going to keep you awake tomorrow night."

"That's the kind of insomnia I can get on board with. Sure beats emergencies or being kept awake by constant indirect-fire sirens."

She huffed out another laugh, told me she'd be round about three p.m., and we said our goodbyes. I dragged my bags into the bedroom and unpacked everything onto the floor by my bed. Bed. It looked so tempting and I only just managed to stop myself from collapsing onto it and sprawling out on the large, comfortable mattress. Only the fact I was grimy from travel stopped me. I stripped out of my clothes and dropped them onto the laundry pile.

As usual, my hot water spluttered to life before it started blasting, and I stepped into the spray, blissfully hot and gushing out. Glorious. Good showers—consistently hot and full-pressured—were one of the things high on the list of things I missed. A bath would have sent me into a fully blissed-out state but there was barely enough room for the shower, sink and toilet, let alone a bathtub.

As I scrubbed my skin, I again considered moving into a bigger apartment or even buying a house. Making a home. And as I always did, I decided it wasn't worth it—I was hardly here when I was in the city and my job always had the threat of relocation, hence my reluctance to purchase instead of renting. And renting was my safety net; easier to pack up and run away if I ever needed to. So I'd take my showers and dream of long, soaking baths.

My thoughts drifted to the unit and their homecomings. Above everything else I hoped they were enjoying time with family and friends and starting the process of coming down. This transition time into reintegration was critical to help them reset and recharge before we'd be deployed again, likely in around a year. And though I'd been trying desperately not to, my thoughts turned to Sabine. Or most specifically—the time we'd been in the shower block together.

In the privacy of my home, and starved of physical touch for so long, my conviction to not treat Sabine like some masturbatory fantasy fell away. If I wanted to, I *could* let the fantasy sprint as far as I wanted it to. And it did… It ran right out of control until my arousal beat insistently between my thighs. I slid a hand over my breasts, gently pinched my nipples, ran my palms over my belly until I couldn't stand the torment any longer. I tried to be gentle, to tease my climax out with light and careful touches against my clitoris. But the mental image of Sabine kneeling between my thighs as water cascaded over us made *light and careful* nearly impossible.

Abruptly and unwantedly my fantasy turned into unpleasant realism. Sabine Fleischer had a partner. And right now, she would probably be reconnecting with that partner. The sense of disappointment that replaced my arousal was also unwanted but a much-needed wake-up call. We had work therapists, one of whom was a very good friend of mine and also serving silenced under DADT. But I couldn't put this burden on him. And I couldn't tell any other work therapists that I was attracted to a subordinate, even if I didn't disclose that I was a lesbian. I hadn't seen my personal therapist in years, but maybe it was time to make an appointment and try to work through this mental roundabout before I deployed again.

I quickly finished my shower, pulled on a pair of sweatpants and a long-sleeved tee and did what any single person with no immediate family would do their first night home—poured a glass of wine and settled on my couch to watch television until I nodded off. I woke with a stiff neck and dragged myself into my bed. Alone.

After a solid eight hours of sleep I spent the morning meandering around the apartment, tidying and organizing, and making grocery lists. Once Linda had delivered my car I was going to restock and then I'd cook myself an extravagant feast for no other reason than to enjoy the act of cooking and the resulting freezer leftovers.

A little after three p.m., Linda knocked before using her key. After setting the key and a bottle of McCallan on the sideboard, she enfolded me into a warm hug. I held her tightly, absorbing the sensation of my first real intimate physical contact in far too long, pressing my face into her shoulder. She smelled, as always, of sandalwood and I inhaled the comforting scent. She took my face in both her hands and planted a smacking kiss on my mouth. "Goddamn, how is it every time you go away for work, you come back even more gorgeous than before?"

"My body loves stress, apparently. Thinks it's good for the skin."

Laughing, she turned me around and when we faced each other again, she nodded appreciatively. "And everything else, apparently." Linda grabbed the bottle. "Now, what do you want first? Bed or booze?"

I took a few moments to think. Before Linda arrived I would have said a slow glass of scotch and conversation unrelated to work was exactly what I needed. But now she was here, my other more basic need came to the forefront. I ran my palms over her breasts and down her belly. "Bed," I murmured. "It's been too long."

We helped each other out of our clothing with the ease and familiarity of lovers who'd been here before and were completely comfortable with each other. Our foreplay was just as familiar, each of us knowing exactly what the other needed. She kissed my nipples before she slowly kissed her way down my belly until she was nestled between my spread legs. The wet warmth of her mouth made me twitch, and I let myself relax into her caresses.

My arousal was insistent, yet felt distant somehow, as if it and I weren't on the same page. The sensation had nothing to do with Linda's expert touch and the soft glide of her tongue over my most sensitive places. She touched me with the easy confidence of someone who, after years of this casual sexual relationship cemented by our solid friendship, knew exactly what I liked. And I absolutely liked it. But despite that, my climax hovered just out of reach and I couldn't catch it.

Linda popped up from between my thighs where she'd been giving me some very enjoyable oral sex. She kissed my hip and gently wiped her mouth on my skin. Ever perceptive, she asked, "Would you like me to do something else?" There was zero accusation in her question.

A sliver of embarrassment made my cheeks heat. I raised myself up, propping my elbows behind myself so I could look at her. "No! No, it's not…Shit. This sounds like a cliché, but it's me, not you. I'm just not—"

Linda's smile was mischievous. "In the orgasm zone?"

I huffed out an audible breath. "Right. That." I reached down and took her hand. "What you're doing feels amazing, as it always does, it's just my brain isn't cooperating."

"What're you thinking about?" She stroked lightly up and down my inner thigh.

"What you're doing. How good it feels. How much I want to come." I laughed. "And I *really* want to come. I've been waiting months for this and now I'm just…not working as I should be."

Linda kissed and licked her way across my belly, hmming as she went. When she looked up again, she was grinning. She bit my hip lightly, teasingly. "Maybe it's time to be less present. Change that movie playing in your head to something a little more climax-inducing."

I carefully extricated myself and slid down to sit beside her. I leaned against her side and stroked my fingertips up and down her spine. "I don't know, it feels wrong to think about something else, some*one* else when it's you with me here now."

"Rebecca, it's me. You don't need to pretend. We both know what this is and I'm not going to be offended if you're thinking about someone else while I'm fucking you. The bedroom is a judgment-free zone, remember?"

Not that I'd ever needed a lover's permission, but knowing there were no expectations except "pleasure however we come by it" was still comforting. I kissed her bare shoulder. "I know, but I feel bad about…not being fully present."

"It really doesn't bother me. I'm happy knowing it's the sensation I'm providing that's helping whatever sexy image is playing in your head." She winked. "You should know my ego isn't in the room. I'm just happy to help out around the edges." Linda rolled onto her back, pulling me on top of her. Her hands roamed my back, nails lightly scratching before she cupped my ass and pulled me until I straddled her thigh. She rocked me back and forth, pressing her leg firmly against my clitoris.

The pressure felt incredible and I leaned forward to brace myself with hands on the bed beside her shoulders, relaxing my hips to let her guide me. My arousal slowly returned and I closed my eyes and let my fantasies run free. And again, and unsurprisingly, they ran directly to the place I'd been avoiding. It began as a clear imagining of Sabine underneath me, her fingers slipping over my clitoris and gliding inside me, and I rocked my hips into the sensation.

Linda rolled me onto my back, and after putting her mouth on my nipples, gently biting tender flesh, she kissed and licked and sucked her way down my torso and pushed my knees apart. I could hear Sabine's murmured, "Do you want me to fuck you? May I put my mouth on you?" and my breathless answer of, "Yes, oh god, yes!" right before a warm tongue slid through my arousal. As her tongue made its way languorously around my clitoris, long fingers slipped into my heat. She was gentle at first before she increased her speed, fucking me harder and faster until I was gasping with every stroke.

The visual running freely through my head flipped quickly, and instead of Sabine fucking me, it was me fucking her. My mouth and hands explored her body and I reveled in my discoveries. Small firm breasts with tight nipples. Smooth tanned skin, tangy with sweat. Long graceful limbs. Musky arousal and responsive clitoris. Sabine's voice was as clear in my head as it was in person, begging me to lick her, to fuck her, to let her come. The thought of fucking her quickly turned my previously ambivalent arousal into something so overwhelming I could barely focus.

My legs quivered as my climax built into something I could no longer control, and I orgasmed with the image of being nestled between Sabine's spread thighs, my hands on her breasts and her hand roughly gripping my hair as she cried out her pleasure. I could almost taste her arousal and feel her sweat-slick skin under my palms. The sensation was unlike any climax I'd ever experienced—a deep, full-body spread of heat shuddering through me. When I opened my eyes, I was almost surprised to find myself staring up at my own ceiling.

I lay still as the heat that had flooded my body dissipated, leaving me feeling weak and boneless. Linda slipped from between my thighs and moved to lie beside me. When I gently cupped her breast and played my thumb over her nipple, she put her hand on top of mine. "Give me a minute to catch my breath."

I gently pinched. "Are you getting old?"

Chuckling, she kissed me. "No. You're just insatiable as always, and wore me right out." Linda slid out of bed. "Back in a minute."

I watched as she walked out of the room, noting she seemed... smaller. Before she'd changed careers to become a personal trainer, she'd worked as a gym teacher for high schoolers. A self-confessed gym junkie ever since I'd known her, she seemed like she'd lost some muscle tone, and the faint outline of ribs on her back was new. I made a mental note to ask if she'd been sick, remembering when she had mono in our second year of friendship and had turned into a shadow of herself.

Within minutes she came back with two very generous glasses of the McCallan. After handing one to me, she clinked her glass against mine. "Here's to you being back on my doorstep again."

"Cheers." The scotch was smooth, with the perfect amount of burn, and after savoring the mouthful, I drank another.

After sipping her own drink, Linda casually asked, "So...who is she?"

"Who is who?"

"The woman who just gave you what sounded like the most spectacular orgasm, with my help."

"Oh." I fought down a blush. A *blush*. I did not blush. "It's not important," I hedged.

"Oh my fucking god, Rebecca!" She slapped the back of her fingers against my skin. "You're utterly impossible. You're really going to keep this from me?"

"It's stupid and it's ridiculous and it is so not like me to be hung up like this. So yes, I think I will keep it from you." At least until I knew what I was doing, or more accurately—what I wasn't doing.

"No," Linda agreed. "It's not like you at all. Which tells me it's not stupid and ridiculous." Her expression softened. "And I can tell by the look on your face that you're dying to talk about it."

After so many months of holding on to this feeling, I was. Linda was not only a safe place for sex, but for all my secrets, and I knew they'd be okay with her. But…I still didn't feel quite ready to release my thoughts into the world where they'd exist in actual time and space instead of just in my consciousness. Carefully holding my glass aloft, I squirmed up to lean against my pile of pillows. "I have a huge problem."

"Like, a 'my credit card was declined' kind of problem or something more personal?"

"Personal. But also like a 'I don't want to ruin the mood with my problem right now' problem."

My friend knew exactly when to push and when to back away. She draped her leg over my thigh and with light fingertips, drew patterns on my skin. "Will it be a problem you'll want to *ruin* some other moment with eventually?"

"Yes, I think so." There was no way I could go on like this without unpacking things. It was one thing to do mental gymnastics myself, but I really needed a completely objective opinion from the most nonjudgmental person I knew. Just not right now when I was enjoying time with my friend.

Linda bent down and kissed my shoulder. "Well, when you're ready to talk about it, you know I'll be here."

CHAPTER EIGHT

As soon as the unit came back after our three weeks of post-deployment block leave, we were thrown right back into the thick of it. I could never decide if I preferred the work in a nice stateside hospital, or the work on deployment. There was something undeniably joyful about the civilized feeling of going home to my own bed, having a glass of wine or delicious single malt if I wanted to, seeing friends, and eating food that felt like love instead of a lukewarm friendship.

But deployment was when I felt most like a leader, the person they relied on to guide them through abnormal and sometimes frightening times, felt most like I was truly making a difference, as clichéd as that sounded. And that incredible feeling balanced out the not-so-great aspects of being away from home working in a warzone for almost a year at a time.

Time also moved differently between working in the States and on deployment—a living example of Einstein's theory of relativity—which made weighing the pros and cons even more difficult. The comfort and relative ease of my US duty station had time rushing past, almost like I'd sit at my desk to deal with some of my never-diminishing paperwork, then look up to find a month had passed. Being away on deployments tended to drag time out, a phenomenon I'd always found interesting because there was rarely a lack of excitement even if it was just in the background.

But regardless of the passage of time, there was always one constant—I had an important job to do. While on leave I'd snuck into work a few times to tidy my office and had emailed the team, wishing them an enjoyable and restful break and reminding them of our meeting time our first day back. I had casual debriefing drinks with Phil as we usually did, and did things that brought me pleasure—tending to my new plants, cooking, going to restaurants and bars and movies, being with Linda. An added bonus was that separation from Sabine Fleischer's constant presence made me feel as if I'd loosened a too-tight piece of clothing.

Unfortunately, I couldn't stay away from her forever, and I'd thought of strategies to help manage my attraction. So far my options were: balancing my time with her on my surgical team rotation, figuring out when she and Mitch used the gym and ate meals and avoiding those areas at those times, and trying like heck not to be caught alone with her. Solid strategies and also a totally normal plan for dealing with a subordinate…

As a ranking officer, I'd managed to snag a base parking permit, but because I loathed D.C.'s traffic, I preferred to take the bus each day. I wasn't the only person based at Walter Reed who preferred public transport to the traffic or roulette of parking if you didn't have a pass, and usually by the time the bus got to work, I was sitting in a sea of Med Corps personnel.

I stared mindlessly out the window as the bus traveled through the city, refamiliarizing myself with the sights. As we pulled up to a stop about ten minutes from base, I spotted Sabine waiting under the bus shelter. She stood ramrod straight with her backpack squarely on both shoulders, looking like a kid excited for her first day at school. Oh goddammit. The free seat next to me felt like a gigantic flashing beacon, just begging her to sit there. Sabine strode up the aisle, faltering when she saw me. She offered me a polite nod and a genuine, if not slightly alarmed, smile then walked right past and sat in the row behind me and across the aisle.

I tried to relax, but for the rest of the bus ride, I felt her gaze on the back of my neck like a caress and had to consciously resist looking around at her. The second the bus pulled up at our stop, I gathered my backpack and briefcase, hoping to exit in front of her and make my escape. But Sabine was already on her feet, her eyes fixed on me when

I reflexively glanced back at her. She smiled and indicated I should go ahead, so I slipped into the exiting stream.

Option One: Walk away quickly, looking very busy and important and unapproachable. But I didn't think I could fake the unapproachable.

Option Two: Find someone to talk to so I looked unavailable. But there was nobody around me, aside from Sabine, that I could nab for a quick conversation.

Option Three: Grow up and deal with it. I had years more of this, and performing mental gymnastics whenever I was near her was juvenile and not a solution to my dilemma.

In the end, Sabine solved the problem for me as she fell in beside me and offered a politely neutral, "Good morning, Colonel Keane."

The sound of her voice was exactly as it had been in all my thoughts about her these past few weeks and sent the same thrill shooting down my spine. I chanced a look at her and found nothing except casual interest in her expression; gone was that look I'd come to expect from her in Afghanistan. Its absence was surprisingly disappointing. "Good morning, Sabine. Did you enjoy your leave?"

"Yes, ma'am, I did," she said, an extra note of brightness in her voice. "I'm rested and ready to get back to work."

"I'm very glad to hear it."

We walked silently for a minute before she tentatively queried, "And how about yours, ma'am?"

Oh it was wonderful, Sabine. I had sex with someone and couldn't climax—until I imagined it was you and me in bed and then I came harder than I think I ever have with a partner before. I tried to reconcile why I'm so attracted to you and couldn't, and then I tried to tell myself that I shouldn't be attracted to you, but I still just can't help myself. And most nights, I think about you in a way that's not entirely appropriate for a commanding officer to be thinking about a subordinate.

I tilted my head to catch her eye as we walked, and said calmly, "It was restorative, thank you for asking."

Ten feet in front of us, Amy slid out of a station wagon with a handsome African-American man behind the wheel. She blew a kiss to the small child strapped into the backseat, then another one to presumably her husband, before turning and almost running right into Sabine and me. Saved by the Peterson. Her smile was the brilliant one of someone seeing their friends for the first time after summer break. "Good morning, Colonel Keane. Morning, Sabine."

Sabine nodded hello but deferred to me for a response.

"Good morning, Amy. How was your break?"

"I have a two-year-old, ma'am, and he hadn't seen me in ten months," she said as if that explained exactly how her break was. "So, it was both wonderful and very, very tiring."

Kids. What an utter mystery. I laughed in a way I hoped sounded supportive and didn't convey my relief that I hadn't had a misbehaving child to deal with. "Ah. I see."

She nodded decisively as she waved with both hands at the child being driven away. "So if you happen to see me hanging around well after I'm supposed to be home, that's why. I'm hiding and taking some me time."

Sabine muffled her snorted laugh and pulled open the door. She stepped back to let first me then Amy inside the building. When I turned back to look at them, I accidentally caught Sabine's eye and quickly moved to look from one to the other. "I'll remember that." I fought against the urge to clear the discomfort sitting in my throat. "I'll see you both for our first team meeting at oh-nine hundred?"

Their response was a simultaneous, "Yes, ma'am," which left me with nothing to do but slink away to my office.

* * *

As it turned out, my concern about forced proximity to Sabine was completely baseless. It was as if the moment she landed on home soil, a switch had been thrown and instead of interacting with me like I was someone she wanted to know better, she treated me as the rest of the team did—friendly, yet deferential and respectful.

I rarely caught her looking at me if I happened to glance at her during team meetings, briefings, surgeries, or when we'd see each other in the halls or wards or the lunch and recreation rooms. And most noticeably, she never caught my bus again. It made it easier for me to put my feelings on simmer instead of constantly ready to boil over. The change in her attitude was both welcome and yet, also felt like validation. Because me noticing the change meant I hadn't been imagining her behavior at Atlantis.

I could find only one explanation—that she'd latched on to her CO during her first real deployment and hadn't quite known how to interact with me, and had maybe been struck with a small dose of hero worship. And now she was back with a partner to go home to every night. So perhaps my attraction wasn't really real and I'd just been responding to her energy somehow. Perhaps without that energy coming at me, my feelings would wither and die on the vine. Or perhaps, the most likely explanation was that I was engaging in a healthy bout of hopeless wishful thinking about my inappropriate feelings.

Days turned to weeks and then months, and my attraction to Sabine didn't exactly wither and die, but it did slink away. My workdays were full of mostly routine surgery and deployment-readiness checks and preps—attending endless briefings, making sure our emergency medicine was up to scratch and the team's mental and physical health was collectively as good as it could be, collating equipment lists and medical supplies requisitions. We ran trauma drills both in the comfort of the surgical wing and also outside on the lawns in all weather conditions, mixed with other units to play flag football and soccer, and I made sure to have my usual Jigsaw Puzzle Tuesdays and Cake Fridays.

And despite promising myself I was going to see my therapist, I didn't.

Phil and I had both snuck into the deployment betting pool and I was just waiting for our call-up. The email came after four months, informing me that we would deploy again "on or around" November 15th, 2008. Sixteen months at home—not bad. This time we'd be going to Khost Province on the eastern border of Afghanistan and to one of the newer hospital FOBs for a twelve-month rotation. An extra four months at home for an extra two months on top of our usual deployment stint. I'd take it.

I'd lost a hundred bucks in the betting pool but only by the skin of my teeth—I'd picked Khost Province for a twelve-month deployment, but I'd thought they'd mobilize us sooner. I sent out a page telling the team to meet me in our briefing room at 1500, stretched the tension from my body, then pushed back my chair to finally take a break for lunch.

The lunchroom was partially full, with people spread out in small groups. Then there was Sabine sitting hunched over the jigsaw puzzle table, a half-eaten salad by her left elbow. I could see that even though I'd only put it out half an hour ago, the border and a few small sections were in place. As I passed by, I took a peek. This one was admittedly one of my crueler offerings—a thousand-piece Where's Waldo? puzzle.

Sabine's forehead was creased in concentration as she sorted the pieces into piles. Watching how people did jigsaw puzzles was one of my favorite pastimes, and I'd noticed their approach usually matched their personalities. Mitch Boyd was reckless, fitting together pieces he thought *might* match and usually failing. Amy Peterson was impatient, finishing small sections—usually a corner edge—before giving up. Bobby Rodriguez was careful but quick and usually had most of the edge done before anyone else. Sabine was methodical, sorting everything into matching colors and then shapes before she even put two pieces together. Having such diversity coming at a jigsaw puzzle was an excellent way to foster teamwork and adaptability.

I paused on the opposite side of the table. "How's it coming along?"

Sabine's head snapped up, eyes widening as she took me in. "Slowly. This one is brutal, ma'am," she commented.

"Wait until I bring in the three-thousand piece one that's just a sheet of black."

"I think I might be on vacation that week," Sabine deadpanned.

Her dry tone made me laugh. "That would be a shame."

She fiddled with a double-wing piece. "Are all of the puzzles yours, ma'am?" At my nod of assent she said, "I didn't know you liked jigsaw puzzles." It was almost wondrous, like this portion of my private life she'd been allowed to access was special somehow.

"I do. It's one of my relaxation hobbies." I decided to give her another small piece of my private life. "Alongside cooking. Most of these puzzles are ones I've done but I've been collecting some new ones at thrift stores too, so expect missing pieces in those."

She looked as if she'd been slapped. "I—but how can you complete a jigsaw puzzle if you don't have all the pieces? I've had that happen twice and I had to go buy a whole new one."

Her admission was unsurprising. "I suppose technically you can't *complete* it, but does that really matter? It's only a few pieces from thousands."

For a moment she seemed to forget the neutrality she'd been throwing at me for the past four months, and flashed me a smile that made her eyes and nose crease. "I feel like we might be traveling on different wavelengths, Colonel Keane. Missing jigsaw puzzle pieces might *actually* be my definition of torture."

And I forgot my resolution to set aside my emotional attachment to her. "Maybe we are on different wavelengths. Maybe not."

Sabine's response was an immediate smile, brilliant and warm. Then just as quickly, it fell from her face like she'd remembered something unpleasant. It made my insides twist with discomfort and I wondered what exactly I'd said to cause this reaction.

Or maybe…not everything is about you, Rebecca.

Perhaps this had nothing to do with me at all and was simply Sabine. Maybe *this* was the real Sabine Fleischer. I dismissed the thought. This person didn't seem as comfortable as the person with whom I'd been deployed. Faking her personality while in Afghanistan was more than anyone could manage. No, this Sabine was forcing herself to be someone she wasn't, at least in front of me. I gave her my best friendly-boss smile. "I'll leave you to it, Sabine. Good luck with Waldo."

Her shoulders dropped and I caught the rush of air in her relieved exhalation. "Thank you, ma'am. I'll need it."

I backtracked and left the lunchroom, suddenly aware that being in the same room with her, even if I wasn't close, wasn't a good idea now. Was this going to be the next six years of my life? Constantly aware of her feelings and trying to be sensitive to them? No, I couldn't do that. I had many responsibilities as a CO, including supporting and nurturing those under my command. But I wasn't about to change my leadership style just because she had some issue to which I wasn't privy. Of course I wouldn't be nasty or do anything to hold her back, but I wasn't going to tiptoe around her.

Yet here I was, doing just that, walking away to ease the discomfort between us. Sure, I could have turned around and gone back to the lunchroom instead of my office to eat my sandwich, but that would have drawn attention to myself. And I'd spent seventeen years avoiding drawing attention to myself. Just this one time, I told myself.

I was a few minutes late to the briefing room and everyone was already assembled. One thing Sabine hadn't changed was her front-and-center position at every meeting, with Mitch to her right. She, like everyone else, looked up as I entered. That quick glance was attentive, before it slid back into neutrality. I set my laptop, folders, and the papers on the table facing the rows of chairs.

"Sorry to keep you waiting, team. Just making sure I had all the information I needed before we got started." I peered around the room, briefly catching everyone's eyes. Nobody seemed alarmed or at all concerned, though I suspected they suspected the reason for this last-minute meeting.

I handed John Auger a stack of photocopied information sheets, each one ten stapled pages, and after taking one, he passed the stack along to start the chain reaction of distribution. There was no reason to delay, and as the information sheets made their way around, I said, "I received our next deployment orders today."

The passing of papers paused for a second, then resumed as if I hadn't spoken.

"As you'll notice on page two, we leave on or around November fifteenth, next year. We report to FOB Invicta in Khost Province, Afghanistan for a twelve-month rotation out of country." I smiled at the few who were looking at me instead of the sheets of paper. "It's a newer FOB and I've been told the facilities are quite nice. By FOB standards," I added dryly.

That earned me a few low chuckles.

"Everything you need to know for now is in your briefing document, and as you know we'll be spending the next twelve months preparing ourselves professionally, personally, physically, and psychologically. I'll learn more in the coming months, but if there's anything you'd like to discuss in the meantime, you all know where my office is, and that includes your families if they have anything they'd like to talk about. Any questions for now?"

There was a chorus of head shakes and, "No, ma'am," so I wound up the meeting.

"Take the time to read through everything and think about how you're going to best use this time to prepare yourselves. And I'll be here with you every step of that preparation. I'm so proud to work alongside you all, and I'm eager to get back to where we're needed and help those who need us. Dismissed."

Chair legs scraped as everyone stood, then rearranged the chairs back into neat lines. I received some nods, a lot of smiles and one or two despondent looks to which I returned my best sympathetic-but-realistic smile. I leaned against the table and watched them all exit, with Sabine tailing the group. Just before she walked through the door she paused and glanced back at me. She met my eyes for the briefest of moments before turning around again and leaving me staring after her.

CHAPTER NINE

Having Linda, completely separate from work, had been an absolute godsend. We had dinner or drinks at least once a week, and thankfully she hadn't pushed me about the whole "fantasizing about someone else" thing, nor had she probed for more information about who it actually was. Until October when she turned up on my doorstep with ingredients for dinner, a bottle of champagne, and *that* look that said she was done not knowing my dirty little secret. To her credit, she waited until after we'd eaten the seared salmon with creamy white wine and caper sauce I'd prepared, before she came at me with her questions.

"Are you ever going to tell me what was going on that night we slept together?" We hadn't had sex since, because one time when I got back was usually just how we worked, and she'd started seeing someone exclusively not long after that.

I raised my eyebrows. "We both had amazing orgasms and drank a very nice scotch and talked for hours and I slept better than I had in months. The End."

"You're so fucking funny," she said dryly. "I meant, and I know you know what I meant, that *problem* you mentioned."

"Right. That."

"Is it still a problem?"

"It is." I drank a sacrilegiously large gulp of champagne in a feeble attempt to settle my sudden nerves.

"So," she prompted me, with a gentle arm prod, "what kind of problem is it?"

I paused, debating not answering. The problem had kind of maybe sort of gone away. Or more accurately, had faded. But it still lingered in the background. I sighed. "It's an 'I'm attracted to a woman who's my subordinate' kind of problem. And also a 'She's in a relationship so even if it were possible, it's totally impossible' kind of problem."

"Oh." Linda nodded slowly. "Fuck. That's not allowed, right?"

"Yes, *fuck* about sums it up. And no, it's not allowed. Even for heterosexual couples it would be problematic because of the chain of command. It's ridiculous, right, this whole attraction? Tell me it's ridiculous. Tell me *I'm* ridiculous."

Linda's expression was carefully noncommittal which I knew meant she didn't agree and was going to throw a bucketful of support at me regardless. "What makes it ridiculous?"

I threw my hands up, narrowly avoiding spilling my drink. "Everything! Where should I start? I don't know if she's into women. I don't know for sure that she's interested in me or just naturally a friendly and interested person, which she absolutely is. But who cares about any of that because firstly, again, she's in a relationship; secondly, I'm her commanding officer; and thirdly, there's the marvel that's *Don't Ask, Don't Tell*. So it's all just..." I searched desperately for an adequate word, but the only one I could find was, "Fucked. It's just fucked."

"Fucked indeed," Linda agreed. "Soo..." she mused. "How against the rules is it exactly? What rank is she?" Thankfully, thanks to our friendship, she had a vague idea of Army workings and I wouldn't need to explain every detail of commissioned and enlisted and chains of command.

"Could be career-ending for both of us if anyone found out. She's a captain, but that doesn't matter. I'm her direct superior. It's basically one big dead end. But again, it's just childish, wishful thinking on my part."

"Ah. So it'll be unrequited crushing for the rest of time?"

"It's more than just a crush." I couldn't help annoyance seeping into my tone. Linda calling it a crush implied she thought it just a silly, passing thing. It was so much more than that, which made the sting of knowing it would never eventuate hurt even more.

"What is it then?"

"Possibility." I sighed. "It's unrecognized possibility. I don't know, maybe it's not exactly *her* so much as that idea of wanting to be with someone again, being excited by that attraction. But of course I'd choose someone so far out of reach even if DADT didn't exist. It's me sabotaging myself before anything could even happen, yet again."

She coughed out a laugh. "Sabotage? What the fuck?"

"Come on, Linda. You know I sabotage relationships. I did it with Clare because it wasn't what I wanted with my life. So instead of being mature about it, I just ran away from it all without even trying to negotiate how our life might look like if I stayed."

"That's *one* relationship, and you had a perfectly valid reason to end it too. It was going to a place you didn't want to go. Had never wanted to go."

I rarely let myself think about my last long-term relationship, of the feeling of being trapped and maneuvered into a situation I didn't want. Because whenever I did, the overwhelming emotional trauma made me feel as if I'd been cut and left bleeding. The self-doubt was smothering. Because what if my problem wasn't that I'd irrationally panicked that Clare's domestic dreams and her own unrelenting career ambitions might push me off my course and end with me being a baking housewife instead of a surgeon, but that I had commitment issues?

I raised a forefinger. "Right, one relationship that I ended nineteen years ago. And since then, how many serious, lasting relationships have I had?" When she didn't answer, I pointed out what she already knew. "None. Except for you which isn't even a relationship. Just brief dating then a lasting friendship and sporadic sex."

"And you think what exactly? That you haven't had a relationship since Clare because you're…stopping anything before it can even get off the ground?"

"Mhmm, that's right."

"Orrr maybe, could it be that with your ridiculously busy life and the fact you spend so much time in other countries and in a job that actively discourages same-sex relationships, you just haven't met anyone to share your life with?"

"Maybe…" I stared into my champagne, wishing the answers were there. "I'm lonely. So fucking lonely." I gripped her hand, squeezing. "I know how that sounds and I'm not trying to make you feel like shit or make you feel like you don't matter, because you do. You really do. You're my tether to normality when I'm in places that aren't normal. Your friendship makes me feel almost normal. But…" I faltered, unsure of how to express what I felt, not sure if I even knew what I felt.

"But it's not enough. This isn't enough." She gently raised my chin to kiss my forehead. "I know."

"I don't even know how to explain it. I don't want a relationship, but I don't want to be alone anymore. But this thing I feel for her is so…so…pointless. But I just can't make myself let go of this ridiculous infatuation or attraction or whatever it is."

"Talk it out with me. What is it about her specifically that's caught your eye?"

I huffed out a humorless laugh. "I think it would take less time for me to explain what about her *hasn't*. She is basically the polar opposite of every other woman I've dated. Aside from the intelligent and kind and compassionate and all those standard good qualities that you know are nonnegotiable for me."

"How so?"

I paused, trying to frame my answer in a way that captured my feelings. "She's fun and goofy, irreverent without being disrespectful but like it's more for her own amusement. So type A she should be annoying but instead she's careful and exacting and always seeking to help and please and be better. She's kind and thoughtful, compassionate, intelligent and watchful, funnily offbeat. And, she's fucking gorgeous. Cheekbones for days. The darkest eyes, thick hair so dark it's almost black and it has no curl, so it's like this sleek curtain. And her mouth…"

Linda smirked. "Wow. You're a smitten little kitten."

After a long pause, I admitted a defeated, "Yes, I really am. And I think it's going to break me because I don't know what to do. I'm so tired. I'm so worn down. And I'm worried one day I'll slip up and give myself away."

She took my hand between both of hers, using her thumbs to stroke my skin. "I know you are, hon. I'm sorry I can't do anything more to help you."

I curled my fingers into hers. "I know you would if you could. It's just so…like I can't even explain it sometimes and that feeling of being alone and wanting something is even worse when I'm away. And here's this person right there in front of me who's like a sick joke from the universe. Here's everything you want, someone incredible and interesting and smart and beautiful, but you can only look and never touch, even if she was single and available and interested."

"The universe is an asshole."

"That it is," I agreed.

Linda studied me intently. "What else is there? I feel like there's more you want to talk about."

"I think I'm trying to figure out whether or not I'm completely crazy. It's not like I have finely tuned attraction gaydar but it's not completely uncalibrated either. I just always get the feeling that there's *more*, like she's holding something back every time we have a conversation. I don't know if it's just her, or it's something she wants to say but feels she can't? If I could remove work from the equation then I'd have said with certainty that something's there." I made a musing sound when I thought back over the cool normality of the last fifteen months. "Or, I should say there was, back then."

My friend's face crumpled as she tried to work through my waffling. "*Then* as in deployment?"

"Mhmm. And now, since we've been back, I feel like she's consciously distancing herself from me. And I don't know why. Or if it's even happening, or if it's my stupid imagination."

Linda made a swirling motion with her forefinger. "Scroll back up. She's in a relationship, right?"

"As far as I know, yes she still is."

"Hmm," Linda mused, nodding to herself. "Seems to me like a bit of while the cat's away, the mice play. Or…while the cat's away the cat plays. So when she's away from her significant other maybe she finds it easier to be open with you, but now she's home and going home to them every night, she's been smacked in the face with a hefty dose of realism."

I thought it over for a minute. "I don't get that cheating vibe, though. Like I don't think cheating is in her personality at all. She's just not that kind of person."

"Ah yes, because cheaters always announce themselves," Linda deadpanned.

"No, but she's *so* black and white, as in this is the right way to do things and this is the wrong way. She joined the Army because she comes from a military family and felt it was her obligation. I don't think she'd do anything she thought was immoral, even if it were allowed, while she was in a relationship. And of course I wouldn't want that either. It's just…*is* she thinking about something? Was she? It sure as heck felt like it to me. And I think that uncertainty is part of what's driving me nuts."

Linda topped up both our glasses, mine a little more than hers. "Do you think thinking about someone else is cheating?"

I honestly didn't know. "I think it depends on how invested you are in those thoughts, what your personal feelings about infidelity are, where those lines lie for you and your partner. I think I'd lean toward no, thinking isn't cheating." After an indulgent sip of champagne, I added, "I feel like if you're fully invested in your relationship and are getting what you need from it then you wouldn't be thinking about another person, or actively engaging in any form of cheating, physical or just thinking. But I've never been in the situation as the cheater or the cheatee, so I'm really not sure. What do you think?"

She shrugged. "I think it depends on how much emotional investment the thinker allocates to it. Like, don't most people have silly fantasies about someone else even when they're in a relationship? Because they know it's a fantasy. So if they're just thinking about another person's personality and how they enjoy being with them and maybe fantasizing about sleeping with them as an abstract kind of thought, then I don't think it's cheating. But if there's an emotional aspect to those thoughts and fantasies, and the thinking about another person is affecting your relationship negatively or causes a breakup, then yeah, I'd say that's a no-go." She laughed and raised her glass to me. "Look, I know you better than anyone, Rebecca, and I know no matter the situation you would never knowingly cause another person pain, physical or emotional."

"Thank you." I curled my legs underneath myself and leaned into the arm of the couch. "I can't shake the feeling that I'm being predatory in some way. That I should be more respectful of her because she's just an unknowing participant in my fantasies. I think the work situation is making me feel more guilty than I would if she was just any other woman I was attracted to, but maybe couldn't be with because of their commitment or whatever."

Linda lowered her voice to fake-menace. "Have you cornered her in the hallway and forced yourself on her? Are you holding her back or putting her forward at work because of how you feel?"

I laughed at the absurdity of those notions. "No, of course not."

"Then no, I don't think you're being predatory, even in your thoughts."

"Well I'm being *something*."

"Horny," she supplied helpfully.

"Maybe. I've never felt like this before."

"I'm wounded," she deadpanned.

"You know what I mean." I stretched out my leg and used my toes to poke her arm.

Linda laughed, lightly tickling my sole. "I think you're overthinking a simple attraction. I get that the work situation complicates it, but unrequited attractions happen all the time, all around the world. You're special, but you're not a special snowflake for this one. So you'll just have to learn how to get over it and get over her. What's that saying? The best way to get over someone…"

"Is to get under someone else," I finished. "Tried that for this situation. Made it worse. Or perhaps more accurately, it didn't resolve a damned thing."

"You tried it once! With me! And that was over a year ago. That's not exactly *trying*."

"I'm not going to go out and find myself someone to sleep with in the hope I forget about Sabine. Not to mention I'm leaving again soon, so it's not fair on me or this hypothetical woman when I'll be gone in twenty-two days."

"True…" Linda agreed. She quirked an eyebrow. "And finally we have a name. Sabine, huh? Hot."

"Trust me, her name is the least hot thing about her." I allowed myself a few indulgent thoughts before moving on. "Maybe I should conduct a little experiment over there and see if she's different again while we're deployed, from the way she was last time and the way she's been at home."

"Good call. Pretend it's a science or psych experiment or something. Getting clinical is a surefire way to take all the sexiness out of it. Write a research paper: 'Does she only flirt with you when you're overseas?'"

"A case study of real or imagined flirtation during sixteen months working stateside versus twelve months deployed? I'm sure journals will be clamoring to publish it. Maybe I'll get a paper in *Nature*."

"Right." Linda's grin faded and she exhaled a frustrated grunt. "I fucking *hate* how little time they let you stay home before they send you away again."

It could be worse really—some of the combat units had full-year deployments and were allowed even less time back home before redeploying. "I know. But I'll be home again before you know it, so we can pause this conversation and pick it right back up then." Because nothing would change. I mentally added "Unpack the emotional toll of months of hidden sexual desire" to my coming-home list, right underneath "Rescue my balcony garden from Linda's *care*."

"Can't wait. So what are you gonna do about it in the meantime? Your crush on Sabine that is."

I laughed dryly. "Absolutely nothing. That's all I can do. I'm going to put it into The Forgetting Place with everything else I can't let myself think about." Or try to. I'd basically proven that it was already a lost cause.

As if she'd read my mind, Linda singsonged, "Good luck with that."

"Yeah…"

"How long will you keep it in The Forgetting Place?"

My voice felt tight when I said, "About five more years."

"Fuck," Linda breathed. "That's…not going to be fun."

"Not at all." I forced a smile. "Good thing I'm an expert at keeping things in The Forgetting Place."

"Maybe too much of an expert sometimes," Linda commented with a raised eyebrow.

"What else would you have me do? Risk everything in my life and hers just on a whim and a hunch?"

"I want you to live a life that makes you happy," she said seriously, far too seriously for her.

"I'd like that too, and I'm trying. But until things change with *Don't Ask, Don't Tell*, or I change careers, I'm going to be stuck with satisfied." Satisfied was okay. I'd had satisfied for years now and I was surviving. I just had to survive a little longer, working beside Sabine while trying to ignore the attraction so strong and so unworkable that it made my chest ache.

No problem.

CHAPTER TEN

FOB Invicta Military Hospital, Khost Province, Afghanistan
April, 2009

Deploying to a new FOB was equal parts exciting and confusing, and it was my responsibility to manage it for both me and the team. I enjoyed the challenge of us working together as we learned to operate in a new setting, but the flipsides came from both bureaucracy and boots on the ground. Things were never laid out in the same way from one FOB to the next, things would be broken or barely working and inevitably, despite instructions to the contrary and basic good manners, the previous occupants would undoubtedly leave things more shambolic than I liked.

Forward Operating Base Invicta may have been a newer base when we'd received our orders but when we'd arrived five months ago it was showing signs of use. The hospital facilities had everything we could ever want or need. But it had taken us months to get things sorted and cleaned to a standard I wanted, and there was still hospital equipment that remained unfixed. Like the damned paper towel dispenser in the scrub room that stuck no matter how many times anyone fiddled with it, got a screwdriver into the mechanism in an attempt to loosen it, or hit it in frustration.

The FOB was set in a secured area in a miles-wide valley between two mountain ranges in the east of the country, on the Afghanistan-

Pakistan border. The mountains enclosing us had received a dusting of snow at the start of the year but now in the middle of a pleasant spring, that snow was long gone, revealing the stark rocky structures underneath. Beautiful. The gullies through the mountains provided interesting and variable texture and some days when I was so tired that I could barely think, I'd go out as the sun set on another day and watch the shadows slide down the mountainside. The sound of the razor-wire-topped chain-link fence clinking in the wind provided a soothing background, letting me forget all my underlying worries to focus on the present.

I'd managed to find a comfortable place balancing my job and my attraction to Sabine, which had eased but hadn't gone away despite my best efforts to pretend like I didn't ache to touch her every time she was close. The variability of my days made it easier to focus on other things and unless I was near her or alone in my room at night, I rarely thought about her that way.

Within weeks of us landing at Invicta, she'd relaxed back into the Sabine Fleischer I'd known when I'd first met her almost two years earlier at Atlantis. Instead of cool, she was warm. Instead of avoiding me, she seemed to find me in hallways or during rounds. And instead of making me feel like I was imagining how she acted toward me, her demeanor reinforced that whether she knew it or not, the way she sometimes spoke to me and looked at me made me certain she thought something more than just *Commanding Officer*.

So it seemed Linda had been right—and would be delighted to hear it—that Sabine's apparent soft flirtatiousness was likely due to her relaxing while being away from her relationship back home. It wasn't the first time I'd seen it—cough-cough Riley and Evans—but I'd never had it directed at me until Sabine. I dragged my mind back to that conversation with Linda. ...*if you're fully invested in your relationship and are getting what you need from it then you wouldn't be thinking about another person...* I played those words over and over in my head until they'd settled some of my feeling of possibly being an unwitting other woman.

I probably should have spoken to Sabine and told her that I'd been picking up on some things that perhaps weren't entirely appropriate, but I still wasn't sure I wasn't just projecting my own desires onto her. For me to say anything would imply something about myself *and* about her. And I wasn't in the habit of asking. Or telling.

I knew my reasoning was feeble, but I kept rationalizing it as harmless. Because if I didn't, then I was afraid I might lose the one thing in this place that made me feel good. And I couldn't think of anything worse…

* * *

We had had a horrible few weeks, with bad outcomes layered over bad outcomes, and nobody seemed immune to the demoralization. In an attempt to boost morale, I turned to some of my tried-and-true things—a few marshmallow-toasting bonfires after dinner, and a movie night where *The Princess Bride* won as the movie of choice by three votes over *Alien*. I tried to keep our football game light and fun and made sure everyone knew I was available 24/7.

The team came to talk with me about how they felt hopeless in the face of constant traumas and how they were struggling with missing families and friends—not at all unusual in our circumstances, especially not six months into a twelve-month deployment—and thankfully they all seemed to gain something meaningful from the visit. And then there was Bobby Rodriguez who came to talk with me about the Chicago Bears. Probably because everyone else was sick of hearing him talk about the NFL, and my invitation to come chat meant I was a captive audience. My admission that I was actually more of a baseball fan earned me an aghast look and hopefully a reprieve from hearing Bears team stats for a few months.

Overall, everyone seemed to be coping as well as could be expected and I relaxed a little when I realized the team wasn't about to implode under the stress. We'd been here before and we'd be here again; it was up to me to help everyone through these shitty times as best I could. I kept a slightly closer eye on Sabine because I knew how she operated and that she would be struggling with feeling personal failure despite circumstances beyond everyone's control. *And* because she was one of the few who hadn't come to talk with me, which hadn't surprised me in the slightest. She seemed to be doing okay—relatively speaking—and I knew she had a solid support system in Mitch and Amy, so I didn't chase her up.

I'd just rounded a corner by the post-op recovery room when a body came flying along the corridor. Before I could do anything, we collided at top speed. Sabine. The sudden inadvertent tackle threw me completely off balance and I reached behind myself for something to grab, finding nothing. Sabine's momentum propelled us both back into the wall and something that felt suspiciously like an elbow hit me in the stomach. The way we landed had Sabine pressed full length against me, pushing me up against the wall. With both of us wearing only our undershirts, I could feel every line and curve of her body against mine.

If I wasn't struggling to breathe around my spasming diaphragm, I might have taken a moment to unpack the way that felt and how it mirrored a fantasy, or two, that I'd had. She gripped my upper arms, either for her own balance or to keep me from toppling, and her hands on my bare arms sent goose bumps racing along my skin. Our gazes locked. I was sure my face probably mirrored hers, which was shocked, but quickly and also surprisingly, morphed into shocked with touch of desire.

I doubted she even knew she was looking at me like she'd just found me in a club, willing and ready to go home with someone, and that look combined with my sudden winding brought a surge of panic as I tried to draw a breath.

Sabine's tongue flashed along her lower lip then disappeared again before her lips parted like she was about to speak. But she didn't. Suddenly desperate to get away from this temptation, I tried to move but was sandwiched between the wall and Sabine. As if recognizing what I was trying to do, Sabine took a half-step backward, leaving a wall of air between us. But she kept hold of my arms. The lingering sensation of how her body felt had rendered me unable to speak.

For once, Sabine was unusually inarticulate. "Colonel Keane, I…I'm…so, uh, um. Sorry. I'm so sorry. I shouldn't have been running. Especially not around corners. I'm sorry. Are you all right?" Her dark eyes were wide with panic.

The whole incident couldn't have lasted more than a few seconds but it felt like a torturous eternity. I pressed a hand underneath my breasts, trying to calm my breathing enough to speak without wheezing. "Only dying a little. Where's the fire?" I finally managed to cough out.

"I'm late for a video call and I'm trying to avoid the you're-late-again drama at home." Her face contorted into something that looked like embarrassment. "Sorry, that was an overshare. I'm so *so* sorry I ran into you. Are you all right, ma'am?" she repeated, this time a little hoarsely.

"I'm fine. Thank you for checking." Fine except for the fact she was still holding on to me, and underneath the lingering and awful sensation of being winded, my body hummed with adrenaline and the faint hint of arousal.

As if she'd realized that exact same thing, Sabine dropped my arms like they were two sticks of dynamite. She moved as if she was going to brush down my tee sleeves to uncrumple them, before her arms fell back to her sides. She was still so close I could have counted each of the freckles sprinkled over her nose and cheeks. If I didn't move away, I was going to do quite possibly the stupidest and most dangerous thing I'd ever done in my life. I was going to kiss her.

With my hands behind me, I sidestepped along the wall until I'd put a few feet between us. Only when I was a safe distance from her did I turn and face her again. I could have said a hundred things, each one of which I would have regretted, so instead I said, "I'll let you go for your call. Enjoy your time with your…family, Sabine."

Her expression fell before she hastily regained control of her face. "Yes, Colonel Keane. I will. Sorry again." After I nodded my dismissal, she turned sharply and powerwalked down the hall.

I stared after her, watching the quick, confident steps and the roll of her hips, until I realized how obvious I was being and forced my eyes to the floor. Phil's quiet, "Rebecca?" startled me out of my stupor.

"Yes?" I shook the fog from my brain and tried again. "Phil, sorry. How are you?"

"Better than you it seems. You look like you've just had a call that we've got a whole platoon of casualties coming in."

Forcing a smile I assured him, "No no, nothing like that. Just spaced out for a moment." I glanced around. "Perhaps the middle of the corridor wasn't the best place for that."

"Ah. So nothing's wrong then?"

"Not at all," I lied. My heartbeat hammered out *liar, liar, liar*.

He pressed his palm to his chest, feigning over-the-top relief. "Phew. I've finished my paperwork and I just got to a really good part in my novel. Working my off-shift is not on my agenda for today."

For lack of anything else to say, I managed, "Your leisure time is safe for now."

"Thank you, deployment deities." Phil offered me a warm smile. "I'll leave you to your thinking."

Once he was out of sight, I leaned back against the wall and held both hands to my stomach, trying desperately to settle myself. The sensation of Sabine's body against mine, her warm soft hands on my bare skin lingered like a pleasant dream. It was so easy to let my body think of it as something other than an accident.

My breathlessness had nothing to do with my having been winded. Try as I might, I couldn't shake the sensation that I'd seen real desire in her eyes. Desire I'd never seen before. But she was attached and even if she was single, we were serving in a military under *Don't Ask, Don't Tell*, and she was my subordinate and—

Fuck.

I was so fucked.

CHAPTER ELEVEN

I woke before dawn after just a few hours of uneasy sleep, quietly dressed and slipped outside. The FOB had spotlights to illuminate the entire base if needed, but unless we were actively expecting a transport, we tended to operate fairly dark to keep ourselves as low-profile as possible. By now I could easily find my way around outside in the near-darkness.

The sound of the fence clinking in the wind provided an eerie background noise in the predawn light, making me feel as if I was walking myself into my very own horror-movie basement. I strolled across the flat area we used for football and soccer until I was by the bench where people often came for some quiet time. I was early for the sunrise, even by my standards, so I sat on the bench with my arm slung over the back to wait for the first rays of the sun.

Objectively, the sunrises and sunsets at Invicta sat firmly in my top three of all my deployments, even on mornings like this one when I was so tired I felt barely functional. Maybe even more so on mornings like this where a beautiful sunrise to start my day was exactly what I needed to ease my physical and emotional fatigue.

The sound of someone walking over the gravelly dirt drew my attention from the shadowed mountain range and its impending show. Sabine's silhouette was both a welcome arrival and an alarming intrusion when my guard was low. I stood to avoid the awkward angle of trying to squint up at her in the dim light.

"Good morning, Sabine." I was conscious of my tone. It was as friendly as any CO should be when talking to a member of their team, but there was also a softness to it, an unconscious, almost inviting, warmth.

She sounded pleased as she answered, "Good morning, ma'am." At this early hour, her voice seemed even rougher with just-woken gravel, and I wondered what it would be like to wake up beside her and hear that roughness every morning. She moved beside me, standing about two feet away with her hands loosely behind her back.

"I'm surprised to see you here. Couldn't sleep?"

Her laugh was low and with a touch of self-deprecation in the underlying *ahhhaa*. "I tried very hard to take your advice from last deployment about the power of watching a beautiful sunrise to start every day, but I'm sure you've noticed that I failed. Miserably. I thought it about time I tried again."

I had indeed noticed, though to me it was less of a failure and more me thinking that she simply wasn't interested in something that was my private joy. "It's not for everyone," I said, careful now to keep my tone even.

"Oh, no, ma'am. I love a good sunrise as much as the next person. But then I also took your advice about sleeping as much as I could which kind of knocked sunrises off the to-do list."

I could imagine her agonizing over her choice. "Well...I suppose if I had to choose waking up before dawn or being well-rested to get the best out of myself, I'd probably say being well-rested is the better choice. Unless you're reenergized by sunrises?"

"No, I wouldn't say I am. Are you, ma'am?"

I glanced at the lightening sky, the hints of pinky-red and dusty orange. "I think I am, yes."

"Why?" she asked quietly, and I heard her genuine interest.

"It's a brand-new day. Anything can happen."

"I think I read that on an inspirational greeting card once," she said dryly.

I raised my eyebrows at her and answered just as dryly, "Where do you think I got that answer from?"

Sabine's laughter cut through the still, quiet morning. "So that's where all your motivational speeches and inspirational messages come from? Greeting cards? Here I was just thinking you had a knack for inspiring your team."

She was so delighted by her own joke that I decided to play along. "It's all a ruse," I said conspiratorially.

"It's a very good one." Though there was still humor in it, her voice lowered to something more intimate. "You've certainly inspired me."

The quiet nuance sent a shiver over my skin and I fought to moderate my response. "Then it's working."

"Mmm," was the only thing she said before turning away again.

We stood quietly together, her obviously waiting for the sunrise and me trying to refocus my thoughts after that hint of invitation in her voice. Her obvious relaxation and good humor made me decide to check in with her. "How're you doing, Sabine? We've had a pretty rough few weeks. Rough few months really." I didn't want to point out that she was the only person with whom I hadn't had a conversation, even a roundabout one, about the string of bad outcomes we'd suffered as a team. "Is there anything you feel like talking about with me?"

Her posture changed immediately. She wasn't exactly defensive but she stiffened into discomfort. Ordinarily I wouldn't have pushed but given the team's collective downer I needed to do my best to help everyone into a place where they felt better about it. Or at least to a place where they'd managed to put it aside. I didn't feel she was in either of those places. I remained silent, waiting for her to answer, even with just a simple no, she didn't feel like talking.

It took her a minute before she uttered a quiet, "I'm okay, ma'am. It's part of the job, isn't it?"

"It is, but just because it's part of the job doesn't mean it's easy or that you have to just grit your teeth and push through. It's okay to struggle and to let people help you. It's okay to find things hard professionally or personally. And…it's also perfectly okay to feel nothing about things like the weeks we just had." I leaned forward slightly, trying to catch her gaze, which was doggedly fixed on the mountain range. "But I think you do feel something about it."

Every time a patient of Sabine's didn't make it, she seemed to take it as a personal slap in the face instead of just accepting that this was the way things are during war. Nobody liked losing patients, whether it was a member of the coalition forces, one of the contractors working with the coalition, or an Afghan national. Everyone else seemed able to set that disappointment aside, or at least place it somewhere where it wasn't affecting them. But not her. She put it somewhere and held on to it, and I watched it eat at her.

She exhaled loudly. "I feel…mad. Mad that this has happened and mad that I couldn't do better."

I wanted to comfort her and let her know that it would be okay. But that was not going to help her. Or me. "Sabine, this isn't a test you've failed. None of us could have done better."

"I know that, ma'am," she shot back. Her eyebrows arched, as if the thing I'd suggested was ludicrous.

"Yes. And I also know they teach us how to deal with patients dying, but it's not that easy. I've been doing this a while, Sabine, and I'm afraid it doesn't change. I've seen it in Bosnia, Iraq, and now Afghanistan, and I learned very early on that you just can't fix everyone. And that is *awful*. But if you let it eat you up instead of finding a way to move past it or put it somewhere it's not going to bother you, then you won't be useful to the next person who's relying on you." I paused a moment to see that she was still with me. "Do you understand what I'm saying?"

"Yes, ma'am. I know. I'm trying." It came out quietly, almost tentatively, and the disconnect between her resolute expression and the almost needy assertion was jarring. She looked away and I followed her gaze back to the mountains, where the sunrise had snuck up on us. Sabine huffed out a breath. "Dang, we missed it."

She was clearly done discussing her feelings, and I moved past it with her. "Remember, that's the best thing about sunrises. There'll always be another one tomorrow." I choked out a laugh at my ridiculous cliché. "I read that in a book of leadership quotes."

"Really?"

"No. I'm just teasing. But it's true. There's always another chance if you miss it today. Beautiful things happen every day if you pause and take a moment to find them. And we haven't *really* missed it." I gestured toward the mountain range, where the clouds were taking on the pastels of the sunrise. "Just the very start, and it's still going to be spectacular today."

"Then maybe I'll see you here tomorrow morning. I don't like doing things only partway." Her voice softened, grew intimate. "I want to experience all of it."

I glanced over at her, stunned by the image in front of me. Even if I weren't enamored with her, I still would have been utterly captivated. And if I were an artist, this would be how I would paint her—face softly lit by the dawn palette, eyes bright with curiosity. I only just held back my, "I'd like that" and instead smiled and said, "If it's anything like this morning, it'll be a great start to your day for sure."

Sabine held my gaze and I almost buckled under its intensity. "I know it will be," she murmured.

I took an unconscious step backward, unsure what to do with what she'd just offered me. After a moment I realized there was nothing I could do with it. Not here. "I'd best get in and start my day."

"Will you be joining the soccer game this afternoon, ma'am?"

"I'll be there, yes. Work permitting," I added as an unnecessary caveat.

What sounded a lot like pleasure colored her tone. "Then I might see you there."

My voice caught on my response. "Yes, you might."

Despite being a newer addition to our sports roster, the soccer games still drew a good group of players and spectators. And as with the football, those who weren't playing dragged seating out to line the sidelines to watch and return wayward balls. There were a few free spaces, one of them beside Sabine, and after a brief internal debate I decided I was mature enough to sit next to her. She seemed surprised when I asked, "Can I steal this seat?"

"Of course, ma'am."

After I settled on the world's most uncomfortable waffle-patterned milk crate, I asked, "You don't like soccer?" I indicated the game and then her. I'd have expected someone with her team spirit and athleticism to be at the front of the line to join in.

"Oh no, I like it a whole lot, played through high school and a little in college. But seems I'm not really needed." She gestured to Mitch, standing with his arms stretched up to hold on to the wooden crossbeam of the makeshift goal while he watched the play at the other end of the field. "And there's only so much shit-talking I can take during my relaxing rec time. And from here, I can heckle him and he's got nothing to come back at me with." The edges of her mouth turned down a little. "Except maybe a cheerleader jibe."

I laughed. "I see." I pushed aside the image of her in a skimpy cheerleader uniform.

She glanced at me. "How about you, ma'am? Why aren't you playing?" The questions were almost shy.

"Two left soccer feet, I'm afraid. I'm fine just sprinting up the field holding a football, but every time I try to dribble a soccer ball, I trip myself. Not helpful to myself or the team. And I like my knees ungrazed and my wrists unbroken."

Her finely arched eyebrows rose in surprise. "Really? I can't imagine that. I've always thought you were very athletic." She bit the inside of her cheek and after a pause added a hasty, "I mean, when we're playing football that is."

I ignored the fact that she'd obviously been watching me, and leaned slightly closer, lowering my voice. "It's an illusion. But don't tell anyone. I have an image to maintain with the unit of being good at everything."

"Your secret's safe with me, ma'am." She paused, smiled. "Another ruse?"

"You could say that."

We both turned back to the game just in time to watch John Augur expertly threading his way through the defense to pummel a ball past Mitch's outstretched arms. While John's team celebrated, Mitch picked himself up and dusted himself off. Sabine cupped her hands around her mouth to carry her criticism. "As goalkeeper, you're supposed to keep the ball *out* of your goal, Mitch, not escort it in and invite it to stay for dinner!"

Mitch spun around, double middle fingers already raised. The moment he spotted me next to Sabine, his hands dropped like they weighed a thousand pounds. He raised one hand in apology then turned his back to us. Or probably more accurately, to Sabine. She laughed loudly. "Ha! That was worth the crap he'll give me later." The laughter faded. "I—my apologies, ma'am. I'm quite certain those double birds were directed at me and absolutely not at you. He's probably dying inside right now."

"Undoubtedly," I said dryly. "Given the less-than-friendly discourse you two engage in during football matches, I'm *quite* certain he meant them for you."

She shifted on her milk crate so she could face me. "It's just for fun, really. He's my best friend and it kind of developed in med school as a way to blow off steam and vent in a safe space. But it's not serious," she said earnestly.

"I know." I paused and debated if I should tell her what I was thinking. "It's actually quite amusing to watch you two go at each other like you're mortal enemies on the field and then walk off the field like the game never happened and you're best friends again. But, I have to be careful and consider the effect on the whole unit. You understand that's why we made our *Keep Sabine and Mitch Separate* rule, right?"

Her smile was brilliant. "Absolutely, ma'am." The smile turned mischievous. "I like it. Makes it even better when his team loses. I can really go after him for it."

Laughing, I agreed, "And I'm sure you do just that."

Amy popped up on the other side of Sabine. "Afternoon, Colonel Keane."

"Hi, Amy."

She snapped open a camp chair and sat down. "Ahoy, Sabs. Who's winning?"

Sabine shuffled her crate so she wasn't jammed right up against her roommate's chair, which had the unfortunate side effect of putting her closer to me. "Not Mitch and that's all I care about."

"You're such a bitch," Amy laughed.

Sabine shrugged. "If wanting your bossy, competitive best friend taken down a few pegs is being a bitch, then yes, I'm a bitch."

"Right, that's exactly my point."

With Amy here, I felt a little like a third wheel and decided to extricate myself. Not to mention having Sabine's thigh now mere inches from mine made me all too aware of how much I wanted to slide my hand onto her leg, have her take my hand as it rested there. I stood and made my goodbyes. "Well, I guess that's about as much procrastination as I can justify for today. Enjoy your afternoon, ladies."

Both of them rose slightly from their seats. "You too, ma'am," Sabine said. Her words were without nuance, but there was undeniable disappointment on her face.

I forced myself to walk slowly across the base back to my office, though I wanted to sprint away from her, from my mental slip. One mental slip in a sea of mental slips. I still wondered if she even knew she was doing it, being so lightly flirtatious and easy with me, or if it was just her. But I'd seen how she interacted with other superiors and detected none of the easy familiarity, the thing I would call tentative flirting if we were in any other situation. I knew her well enough to know that Sabine Fleischer was not manipulative, so I could discard her behavior as currying favor for professional gain.

Which left only one conclusion. Whether or not she knew she was doing it, Sabine had been flirting with me. Not deeply. Not overtly. But it was there. That knowledge didn't give me as much relief as I would have expected, because so many things were wrong. Her romantic relationship. Our work relationship. The fact that if anyone saw her doing it, they might report her which would drag me into it, and I didn't know how good my poker face would be when asked about it.

So it was there, and what could I do about it? Hold on to my childish wish that there was something more than mutual respect between us, and just...wait and hope for better, different times. But hope was *such* a dangerous thing. Especially for someone like me.

CHAPTER TWELVE

After dealing with the occupants of an MRAP that had been crippled by chain-IEDs—Mine-Resistant Ambush Protected vehicles only went so far against multiple Improvised Explosive Devices—then swarmed by insurgents, I didn't think the day could get any worse. I mentally punched myself in the arm. Way to start the jinx, Rebecca. I'd dismissed everyone to have some downtime, but within forty-five minutes I'd received another incoming call. I groaned as I pressed the button to send out the "Attention on the FOB" message to drag everyone back in. I'd barely had time to drink a cup of coffee and eat a muffin, and hoped they were all ready for more hours in surgery.

I'd been told it was a squad who'd walked into a cluster of IEDs and that we had one upper and four lower involuntary amputations among three casualties. Bad odds for one of them. I pushed through the door connecting the prep area to our surgical unit and found everyone assembled and in the middle of changing back into scrubs. "We have three incoming, ETA five minutes. IED. Four lower amps, one upper. Blast trauma. We'll know more when they arrive."

There were no verbal acknowledgments but I saw it in their nods, their eye contact. I fiddled with my cap. Sabine appeared to be in la-la land and aside from a lingering look as I entered, had been preoccupied at her locker.

"Captain Fleischer?"

She spun around immediately, looking at me with widened eyes, as if indicating she was really *really* listening to me now. "Ma'am?"

I held her gaze. "You, Auger and Rodriguez take casualty A with Thorne for ortho. Landon and Boyd, on casualty B with Stanton for anesthesia and Maxwell for ortho. Peterson, Bennett, Hadley, you're with me on C. Nurse teams A, B, C, your assignments are with the casualties as alphabetically assigned." I finally paused to catch my breath. "I know we've already had a long and tiring day, but I also *know* you've got a little more in you. I trust you and I believe in you. You all know the drill. Nice and steady, no mistakes." My eyes caught on Sabine as I swept them around, trying to gauge the emotion of the room. Aside from Sabine's eyes widening again as if I'd just caught her watching porn during work hours, everyone seemed as solid as they could be given the hectic day we'd already had.

The surgery itself was unremarkable—yet another involuntary lower limb amputation and associated trauma from the upward effects of the blast. There was little we could do but control bleeding, confirm organs were uncompromised, and tidy the stump to leave it in the best possible condition to accept a prosthesis. Though as I pushed out of the room, I felt the same usual sense of bittersweet satisfaction.

What we did here mattered but in the back of my mind was always the knowledge that what came after, when I'd waved goodbye and wished them luck, would likely be one of the most difficult periods of their lives. I set that thought in its appropriate compartment. If I dwelled on the injustice and unfairness then I'd fall down a rabbit hole and never find my way out.

Sabine was already out of surgery and at the far end of the sink, bouncing and jiggling as if she needed to pee. I knew the feeling, and her pee dance, which still looked carefully choreographed, made me smile. In an act of frustration I recognized well, she yanked at the paper towel dispenser. "Piece of shit equipment," she mumbled.

Sabine apparently hadn't realized I was right beside her and when I cleared my throat, she started. Avoiding the broken dispenser, I just shook the water off my hands.

She tidied her posture and raised her chin, her eyes saying far more than her tired, husky, "Ma'am."

"Initial surgical report, Captain?" My unintentional crispness reflected my own need to get the details fast so I could race to the bathroom. And maybe a little armor to protect myself.

Her tongue flashed along her lower lip before she carefully enunciated, like a teen giving a report in front of class, "Casualty is on his way to recovery, Colonel. Nate attended to the amputations and we've left the sites open. We'll watch for infection, then tidy up more when we're more certain about viability. John and I repaired damage to liver and large intestine. There was a small amount of bleeding, but we were able to contain it. I expect no issues."

"Very good. I expect the written by tomorrow."

She seemed aghast that I'd even mentioned it. "Of course, ma'am." Her inhalation was shallow before her careful, quiet, "Have there been any issues with my other surgeries or reports from this week, Colonel?"

I stared but tried not to. She looked like I'd just told her the assignment she'd handed in was all wrong, and her consternation was utterly adorable. "No, Sabine. Why would there be?"

"No reason, ma'am, I just thought..." She fumbled through her response and after clearing her throat she quietly said, "I just wanted to make sure everything was in order, ma'am. You seemed disappointed in me, in my outcome from this morning."

I adopted my most patient smile, when all I wanted to do was hug her and kiss the confusion from her face. "Disappointed? I was, yes. *For* you, not *in* you, Sabine. Everything is fine."

This exhalation was the opposite of her shallow inhalation, like she was pushing out all her anxiety with it. "Thank you, ma'am."

I folded my scrub cap in half and tucked it into a pocket ready for laundering. "Enjoy the rest of your day." I nodded my dismissal and exited the small room.

Sabine's, "You too, Colonel" followed me.

I allowed my thoughts to linger on her just for the short powerwalk to the bathrooms, because little snippets of my infatuation were easy to manage and provided a welcome distraction. If someone had told me two years ago that a confident, yet desperate for a superior's approval, type A surgeon would have my insides twisted up in knots for those two years, I would have laughed at them. But every time she looked at me like my opinion was the only one she cared about, like she wanted me to tell her more, *be* more, I felt less like LTC Rebecca Keane. I felt like plain old Rebecca. And I liked it.

After spending an hour with paperwork, half an hour trying to loosen tension with a run, and then lingering over dinner, my shift was done and I felt it safe to take a shower. I'd just finished dabbing perfume at my pulse points when I was paged with an update to go to post-op recovery and check on my patient, still unconscious hours after he should be conscious.

I'd been through my notes, spoken with Amy, checked scans and vitals and had a reasonable idea of why someone who should have woken hours ago, hadn't. As I was readying to talk to the nurses about ordering a cranial CT and continued monitoring, I spotted Sabine in the recovery ward, having what appeared to be a one-sided conversation with a recovering trauma casualty. She tucked a chart under her arm and strode along the space between beds toward the door. Never miss the opportunity for a second opinion, a teachable moment, or…a few seconds alone with her. I waved my chart at her. "Fleischer, a word?"

Sabine stopped instantly, turning to face me. She tried to hide it, but a flash of pleasure colored her features before she smoothed her expression to calmly attentive. "Of course, Colonel."

I walked away, gesturing for her to follow me to the nurses' station. Sabine stopped by my side, watching me expectantly as I flipped open the chart and moved closer so she could read it. "I wanted your opinion on something, Sabine."

She tucked her chart folder under her arm and leaned in to stare at the one I held out. "Yes, ma'am?"

I glanced at her, conscious of our proximity yet unable to move away without being conspicuous or removing the chart from her easy study. "He's in recovery but still unconscious and showing vastly decreased brain activity."

She frowned, exhaling a barely audible, "Hmmmph" as if verbalizing her thought processes ticking along. "He didn't present as neurologically impaired?" she asked, running her forefinger over the lines of my handwriting before raising her eyes to mine.

I stared at her hand, studied the length of her fingers and her short, neat nails. "No, completely responsive on arrival."

"Head CT?"

A good call, and also the most obvious, as well as an EEG. I gave her an encouraging smile, hoping she might look outside this box of obviousness. "I'm waiting for it but I thought you might have an idea."

"All I can think of is PCS, ma'am." Post-concussive syndrome. Another good call, and likely the correct one. The resulting shock waves from IED blasts cause more than obvious physical damage. She held her hands out, gesturing as if imagining working through the problem. "We had that case last month…but he wasn't symptomatic until a day or so post-op." Sabine peered at the chart again. "I'm sorry, that's all I can think of." Then as if recognizing she'd been narrating her words with her hands, she dropped them to her sides.

"Thank you, Captain. That was my thought too. I'm pleased to know we're on the same page," I said with unintentional softness.

Her eyes went wide and she gaped for a moment before responding with a rough, "Yes, ma'am. I'm sorry I don't have more for you." Sabine moved a step away from me, but I didn't sense any discomfort in the movement. I sensed the same feeling that lingered in myself. Distrust. That if I remained close, I'd touch her. I wasn't allowed to touch her. Not now, not later, not ever.

Uneasy, I moved backward, straightening my posture so I wasn't leaning into her. "As you were." I snapped the chart closed and walked off before she could say anything more.

Before *I* could say anything more...

* * *

I'd just hung up on the call about an incoming gallbladder emergency when I realized with glee I could do it laparoscopically. Exciting times. Novelty was rare around here and I took every chance I could get, and was sure someone else would enjoy the chance to perform a laparoscopic cholecystectomy. Most of the team were sleeping or enjoying some time with the gaming consoles, pool and ping-pong tables in the rec room, so I went stalking through the chow hall in search of another pair of hands.

There was a smattering of people eating a late breakfast, and sitting alone in a corner of the room, with toast and her book, was Sabine. I contemplated just walking out and doing the procedure myself, but this was skills development and she deserved my ongoing support with that. When I stood beside her for almost thirty seconds without her noticing, I marveled at the intensity of her focus. Eating peanut butter toast and reading her Kafka, she was apparently in a bubble of self-contained pleasure.

Sabine turned a well-loved page with a PB-smeared finger and once she'd wiped it off the page and licked her finger, I quietly said, "Captain Fleischer."

She dropped her toast and book with a thud, and spun around. Her expression was comically panicked as she squirmed and twisted on the seat and eventually stood, pressed back against the table. She was still chewing as she saluted—unnecessarily—and after a few seconds I caught the forced swallow. Her eyes scrunched and I could almost feel the sensation she was experiencing. Carb chest, noun: When you're forced to choke down carbs as fast as you can before you're called for another surgery and the food forms a painful concrete lump in your esophagus.

Sabine's response was a tight, hoarse, "Colonel Keane. Good morning."

I studied her, trying not to smile at her expression. "Do you need some liquid to wash that down, Sabine?"

She swallowed forcibly again, before her words almost wheezed out. "I would appreciate a moment for that, ma'am. Please excuse me." Turning away from me, she picked up her coffee. If I knew her, and I did, it'd be lukewarm by now.

"Take your time, Captain."

She drained the mug then ran her thumb around her lips. That slow movement of her thumb kicked my pulse up for a few beats. "I apologize, Colonel. I wasn't expecting company. How may I help you?"

She still had a tiny smear of peanut butter at the edge of her mouth and all I could think about was licking it off. My smile felt forced, too wide. "I need you, Sabine."

Her eyebrows shot up as her voice pitched down. "Ma'am?"

"We've just had a sergeant come in who needs his gallbladder removed." I brought my thumb and forefinger a quarter of an inch apart. "This close to rupture. I want you to assist me with the laparoscopic chole."

Her mouth fell into an O. "That sounds very interesting, Colonel. I appreciate the opportunity."

"We're just waiting on a room to be prepped, so you have time to finish your breakfast." I glanced at her book, the same German-language copy of *The Metamorphosis* that she'd had on her first deployment. "Fifteen minutes?"

"Yes, ma'am." She snatched up the book and the rest of her breakfast and after waiting for my nod of dismissal, rushed away.

The patient was prepped and I'd almost finished my scrub when Sabine stepped up to the sink. Along with excitement, tension radiated from her like heatwaves and I could hear the low mumble as she talked to herself. It was easy to guess why. She hadn't done many laparoscopic procedures, because you couldn't fix what we usually did here with a laparoscope. I rinsed my hands. "Are you ready, Sabine?"

She turned her head toward me, her eyes bright with anticipation and maybe a touch of fear. "Just running over the procedure again, ma'am."

"I'll be right there helping you. I know the scopes can be awkward if you're not used to them, but it really does help get them back out there faster." I bumped the faucet with my elbow and shook my hands.

Sabine's face was serious, but her voice betrayed her excitement. "I know, and I'm excited to have the chance to brush up on my skills, Colonel."

"You're lucky, once upon a time we had to do it the old-fashioned way. Then the year before your first tour we had an unusually high number of incarcerated hernias, angry gallbladders and appendixes. That's when I wrote a thorough report on the benefits of laparoscopy and our requisition was approved." I smiled, remembering how I'd felt like a kid at Christmas when I'd finally had a win for a large equipment requisition. Now most of the FOB hospitals were equipped for laparoscopic procedures.

Her return smile was visible in her eyes. "Sounds like you were very persuasive, ma'am."

She had no idea just how persuasive I could be. Still smiling, I backed through the door to the OR. "See you in there."

I'd just finishing placing the trocars when Sabine stepped up beside me. She was adorably clumsy with the instruments, trying to manipulate them while watching the surgical field via a monitor. Her determination and consternation at not acing a procedure was clear but she kept at it, her focus intently on me as I alternately guided her or left her to work it out on her own.

To make things even more interesting, a combat mission was occurring close by, and along with the regular Indirect Fire Sirens—which we had to ignore because we were in surgery—every few minutes, the floor vibrated as an explosion echoed through the valley. As Sabine struggled to position her instruments for the final steps, I decided it was time for me to intervene. I shuffled closer, aware of the exact moment my hip brushed against her thigh. "Change your angle slightly, Sabine." She moved the scope in the opposite direction and I laughed. "No, no. Here, go in like…this." The easiest way would be for me to guide her, and I placed my hand over hers, helping her to make minor pitch adjustments. It took just a few seconds for her to get the feel for it with my guidance, and I reluctantly pulled my hands away to let her finish. "Excellent. There. Now clip, cut, and dissect."

She quickly placed the clips, cut the artery and bile duct then dissected the gallbladder away.

Flawless. "Perfect. Now bag and remove."

I thought I caught a small squeak of excitement from her as she removed the gallbladder, and had to refrain from commenting on it.

"Looks good. Let's close up." I peered at her, waiting to see if she had anything to add.

She caught my eye. "Yes, ma'am. I agree."

I read over the op notes before signing my name, murmuring my thanks to Sarah, and passing the chart to Sabine. Sabine must have speed-read the notes because she was at the door and holding it open for me just as I was about to push through.

I waved my hand under the automatic soap dispenser. "Would have taken courage to hide the pain from that gallbladder as long as he did." Soldiers were such ridiculously macho idiots sometimes.

"Yes, indeed it would have." She pointed at the dispenser. "Excuse me. Apologies, ma'am," she murmured when she tried to reach across me in the tiny scrub space.

I was stuck between the sink, the wall, the dispenser, and her, and I was all too aware of her proximity and my body's automatic response to it. Heat spread over my skin a moment before goose bumps, and an unmistakable surge of excitement made my stomach flutter. I fought to keep my voice from betraying me. "Excellent surgery, Captain." I yanked out a wad of paper towel which I offered to Sabine before pulling more out to dry my hands.

"Thank you." She paused as the floor vibrated again. "…Colonel." She raised her shoulders, hunching her neck down into them as if trying to suppress a shudder.

"Are you okay, Sabine?" I asked quietly.

She looked up from where she'd been staring at the ground. "Yes, ma'am. Perfectly all right." She couldn't have sounded less convincing if she tried.

I smiled sympathetically. "Just think, if you can do a lap chole with the floor vibrating under your feet, you can do one anywhere." I leaned against the sink. "Make sure you put it on your résumé." Smiling, I wondered if she'd pick up on my teasing and if it would help relax her.

Sabine's voice lowered and her tone changed to almost sensual, inviting, as she asked, "May I use you as a reference for this particular skill listing, ma'am?"

Jesus. Oh Christ. I really had just heard that. I was *not* imagining things and this was *not* me projecting onto her. Now my insides twisted simultaneously with anxiety and excitement and I forced myself to smile and laugh at her joking answer, seductive as it was. "Of course, Sabine. I'll make sure I'm effusive, should anyone ever ask." I tossed my paper towel in the trash, thankful it landed and I didn't have to move closer to her to retrieve it. "I'll see you later."

She returned my smile and her expression was utterly guileless. She didn't even know what she was doing, or if she did she was excellent at pretending she didn't. "Thank you, Colonel. Have a pleasant afternoon."

I managed a calm, "And you."

The IF siren hadn't let up, but after so many years of hearing them and gauging the sound of artillery, I knew when I needed to hide and when, like now, I could just be cautious but still go outside. As I pushed out into the hot August air, I could hear distant gunfire coming from somewhere outside the FOB. Good, more work, more distractions. No, no, not good. I didn't want someone to be critically injured just so I had something to do to take my mind off Sabine. Because now, having confirmed that she obviously felt something beyond just me being her boss, I had a new problem.

But what was I supposed to do? Send her home? Transfer her to someone else's unit? Betray her trust and ruin her career? Because she'd be investigated for homosexual conduct if I even *hinted* that I thought she was borderline being a little too familiar with me. Should I discipline her for something that just felt like she was touching the line instead of actually crossing it? The line that I'd been touching too, so hell, I'd have to put my hand up for an investigation as well, not to mention other disciplinary action because once I admitted that I'd suspected she was being perhaps overly friendly from her first deployment it would be all downhill, and I'd have to admit that I'd been just as friendly with her. I didn't really think "I just couldn't help myself" was going to help me any in the discipline department.

I cared about her and I didn't want her to suffer because of something that, really, was harmless. I had never felt so weak in my life. No matter what I did, I had to do *something* because this situation was quickly becoming impossible. As much as I hated it, the only way I could think of to get her to realize what she was doing, or stop doing it, was to push her away. Subtly of course, but I needed to do it and hope she caught the message. Because I really couldn't live like this for much longer. I couldn't control what she did or said, but I could control myself.

I had to, for both our sakes.

CHAPTER THIRTEEN

Linda texting me instead of her usual email or instant message wasn't entirely out of character, but the fact it was after midnight in D.C. was. She was probably at a bar and wanted my opinion on someone she was thinking of taking home. A quick glance at the message told me I was wrong.

I really need to see your face. Will that horrible internet work long enough for a video call? The sooner the better.

Sure. I'll call you before I go in for dinner when it's a more civilized time for you?

Earlier if you can? It's important. Sorry, I know you're working.

I need to do rounds and some urgent discharge paperwork, so give me an hour, hour and a half? Maybe two… I'll text to make sure you're still awake.

I will be. Talk to you then. I love you.

You too xo

I'd finished my rounds and discharge paperwork and was sneaking back to my room to call Linda when I heard a raised voice from down the hall. It didn't sound like a heated-but-friendly match on a gaming console, or even just someone frustrated with their game. It sounded like an argument. Brilliant. Sighing, I rolled my shoulders and prepared myself for mediation.

As I walked closer I realized it wasn't an argument, but one angry voice coming from the phone cubicles. And I'd been so focused on breaking up an argument that I hadn't realized who it was. Sabine. I'd never heard this tone from her. From around the corner, her voice echoed through the empty hallway and I took a moment to be sure I was hearing what I thought I was hearing—an argument, her distress, her resignation, then her fury. Sabine almost choked, gasping as she shouted, "Fuck you, Victoria. Fuck! You! You fucking adulterous, animal-stealing cunt!"

Wow.

The sharp sound of plastic slamming against plastic was quickly followed by loud clattering. I didn't think Sabine had seen me, but I saw her. She leaned against the wall, bent forward at the waist, with her hands cupped over her mouth. The only way to describe her expression was shocked, almost murderous, and it was so unexpected on her usually serene or attentive or laughing face that I decided I wouldn't go to her to make sure she was okay as I'd intended. That expression made it clear she didn't want to talk to anyone, probably least of all her boss. She turned away and picked up the phone again, and I slipped back around the corner out of sight.

It took about five seconds to put all the pieces of this puzzle together. I'd heard the end of a breakup conversation. *Victoria.* A breakup conversation between two women. A pang of empathy welled up in my chest and as I walked away, the realization sunk in. She'd just broken up with her partner. She'd just broken up with *a woman.* A dozen emotions surged.

For her? Sadness, pity, sympathy.

For myself? Hope. Pointless, disgusting hope.

Disgusting summed it up perfectly. You are disgusting, Rebecca. Alongside my self-recrimination, a new worry pushed itself forward. I'd clearly heard what she'd said, and the obvious fact that she'd just broken up with her apparently female partner. And if I'd heard it, who else might have?

I had to trust that nobody would ask, but I also needed to prepare myself for damage control. A quick glance into the nearby rooms found them empty. For some reason, and I wasn't going to question the grace of the universe, but everyone seemed to be in the hospital, their rooms, or outside, and it seemed nobody had heard her telephone conversation. She was beyond lucky that it'd been me instead of someone less sympathetic to what had just happened.

As it turned out, someone had heard it, but not fully, as I discovered during my quick stop to grab coffee. Two of Phil's surgeons were strolling down the hallway in front of me, having a quiet but not-quiet-enough conversation, and it was easy to pick up who it was about.

"She just broke up with some guy, sounded like he was cheating on her? I think she threw a chair or something. Or that's what it sounded like from outside."

Some guy. Well, I supposed, if the cat had to be out of the bag at least it had been misidentified.

"Breakup rage. *Nice.* She's the last person I'd have expected rage from." A knowing laugh. "But I thought she was with Mitch? Fuck, I mean, poor Sabine but hello, Boyd."

"Nah, they're just best friends."

"Ladies," I called after them. "A moment of your time, please?"

They both froze and turned around. "Colonel Keane. Good morning."

"Good morning." I adopted my friendliest and most patient smile, aiming for honey, not vinegar. "I'm all for a good bout of gossip but perhaps, given the sensitive nature of this particular piece, it might be prudent to let Fleischer have her moment of grief without the whole base watching her and comparing notes?"

Their expressions told me the chain was already well underway, likely as a game of Telephone. Goddammit, it didn't take long for things to get around and then get out of hand. Given it was about five minutes after I'd overheard Sabine and it was already *some guy*, not *some girl*, I thought she might have just had the luckiest break of her life.

"Yes, ma'am. Of course."

I indicated they should carry on and watched them scurry off, undoubtedly to continue their conversation. Shit, speaking of… I still needed to call Linda. I considered putting it off so I could find Sabine and see if she was okay, relatively speaking, or check if she needed anything from me—a tight, comforting hug was high on my fantasy list—but given Linda's insistence, I decided I could spare her five minutes, even if it was just to tell her to her face that I really didn't have five minutes to spare.

As I made my way to the barracks, I sent a text to let her know I was just about to call and received a *Yay* in response.

"Hi, and sorry," I said as soon as the video connected. "I've got a forest fire here that I'm trying to put out. I'm going to have to run again in a few minutes." I fixed my wonky, hastily put-in earphones.

She nodded quickly. "Oh, okay."

"What's up? Lady problems?" I finally took a moment to look at my friend and was stunned by what I saw. Though I'd seen her a few weeks ago in a video call, as she appeared now on my laptop screen, Linda looked exhausted to the point of illness, with dark rings nestled under her eyes, her face hollow, hair flat and lifeless. I frowned. "Did you get two extra jobs? Or has some woman been running you ragged in the bedroom?"

Linda's normally bright voice was dull. "Rebecca. I—" Her words caught into hoarseness. "Damn you look good." Her appearance had already alerted me to the fact something was up, and her voice confirmed it.

"You don't," I said flatly, trying to ignore the stirrings of uneasiness. "What's going on?"

She didn't hesitate, or mince words. I almost wished she had because it might have given me some time to process before she said, "I have cancer, Rebecca. Advanced stage three pancreatic cancer. It's started spreading right through me and it's going to kill me." She held up both hands, palms toward the camera. "Please don't cry. You know it sets me off and I don't want to spend the rest of my life crying. I've spent all afternoon and night trying to figure out how to tell you, trying to get the guts to just come out and say it and I'm sorry, I know you're working but..." She shrugged. "So yeah. That's it."

I clenched my molars to hold back my tears, but failed utterly at keeping my voice steady. "Okay okay. No tears. I, uh...I don't even know what to say. I want to ask all the medical questions but I know you'll just tell me to shut the fuck up." Advanced stage three metastatic pancreatic cancer. Terminal. Fast.

Linda snorted out a laugh. "That I will." Her mirth faded. "I have doctors, and what I really need from you right now is for you to be a friend, not a doctor."

I nodded, inhaling slowly in a futile attempt to calm down. "I can do that. I'll be the best fucking friend you've ever had."

"Thank you." She blew me a kiss.

"Why are you dying?" I blurted. "It's not fair." Despite my age and emotional maturity, my medical degree, my years of experience with death, I sounded like a child.

Linda's expression softened. "Honey, the Nationals not winning isn't fair. Not getting a run of green lights the whole way home isn't fair. Some asshole getting the last bit of shrimp at the buffet isn't fair. This is just...life. Happens to the best of us. And the worst too, apparently." There was a touch of sadness in the smile. "But, I do have some good news."

"Then please, for the love of all that's good, give it to me."

The hint of sadness I'd detected disappeared completely, turning to incongruous delight. Her delight made sense when she blurted, "I'm getting married!"

That was as much of a bombshell as her cancer diagnosis, and thankfully nowhere near as heartbreaking. "Oh my god. Congratulations!" Linda dealt in humor, so I forced my devastation aside for a moment. "Jesus. Cancer, dying, getting married. Way to drop a bunch of bombs at once. You couldn't have trickle-fed me some of that information to let it soak in a little? Or even told me that you were seeing someone that was serious enough you'd considered marriage?"

"Figured it'd be easiest to just do it all in one call. And it's all happened so fast, like literally in the last few days. I'm just trying to figure out what to do from here."

"Good point." I set aside the banter to focus on her health issues. I almost didn't want to ask, but I had to. The question caught in my throat as I asked it. "How long do you have?"

Linda didn't flinch, didn't waver. "Nine months. Give or take."

I felt like vomiting. My best friend would be dead in nine months, likely less. "Did you know you were sick?" I recalled she'd seemed thinner, tired when we'd said goodbye before I left for this deployment, but I never thought… "Have you had any treatment at all? God no, of course you haven't, you just found out. Okay, so what's your oncologist say? What's the plan? Chemoradiation, palliative surgery? How's your pain, are you—"

"Rebecca." She cut me off and made a zip-it motion over her lips. And despite the fact I'd broken the rule of not asking about it, she still answered me. "I didn't feel great but I didn't realize how not great I was. Just thought I was a little run-down. And don't even start with your 'I should have seen it' bullshit. I can see it on your face, plain as day. You couldn't have seen it, you couldn't have known. It's been in me for years they say." She held up a hand to pause the conversation. Her coughing fit lasted for almost fifteen seconds, and it took another thirty for her to stop wheezing and start breathing somewhat normally again. "And no treatment. I don't want to spend my last days feeling even sicker from chemotherapy or radiation or recovering from surgery when it's just going to delay the inevitable. I've decided to live my life while I still can. Carpe diem and all that. I've learned life really is too short and that's not just something you say when you want an excuse to do something dumb or reckless."

I almost spluttered out my incredulity. "Are you serious? Delaying the inevitable? That *delay* could be the difference between living a few months and living *years*."

"Don't doctor me now, please." Her expression fell to pleading. "I just need to work through this my own way. I know that's hard for you but it's how I need to do it. Friend, not physician, remember?"

I bit back everything I knew would be hurtful to her, all my anger that she wasn't even going to try to give herself more time, and nodded. "Okay. Friend it is. But please note my very strong objection."

Her shoulders dropped. "It's noted. And thank you. Now, back to my marriage." A less-than-subtle way to get me off her case... "So I'm getting married to a woman I love and who I would have married anyway. We're just moving the timeline up. I know what it's like in your job and I know you're deployed but if there's *any* chance you could be there, stand up with me, it would mean the world to me. And I also know it's short notice, and I would love to wait until you get home in November but I'm not sure I'll be here, or able to travel then." She exhaled a shaky breath. "All my research tells me doctors who give the terminal prognosis are usually optimistic. So I'm going to go with five or six months, just to average it out."

I had to stop myself agreeing with her on her life expectancy self-estimate. It wasn't helpful now. I put my emotions in the box where I kept every unhelpful thing in my life. "Are you going to tell me anything about her? Even a name? Is this the woman you were dating when I was home last?"

Linda's face contorted to confusion. "Her? Oh, god no. And we weren't dating, technically, just sleeping together. My...*fiancée*'s name is Michelle. Do you remember the pottery class woman I mentioned who I wanted to set you up with? Shit...it was your last deployment, right?"

I dragged my mind back. "The one who likes blue-eyed blondes and didn't care about anything aside from that?"

She chuckled. "That's the one. A few months after I told her you'd politely declined me pushing you two together for a date, she disappeared from class. Then just turned up again suddenly about nine months ago. I joked I'd never try to set her up with anyone again in case she did another year-long disappearing act. Then I asked her out."

"And she gave up her one important and immovable thing of blonde and blue for a hazel-eyed brunette? Wow. You must be great in bed," I deadpanned.

"You know it. And now I realize that even if you'd said yes to dating her, it wouldn't have worked because if she likes me, she wouldn't have liked you."

"That's very true. Why didn't you tell me you'd started dating someone and that it was this serious? We share everything."

Linda shifted uneasily. "Because it felt a little like rubbing it in your face, especially while you're stuck there in a relationship black hole. And with that…other issue."

That other issue which was growing rapidly more problematic for me every day. That other issue which was nothing compared to the fact my best friend was dying. "I really appreciate your thoughtfulness, but I'm a big girl and I can handle knowing my friend is in love."

"I'll remember that. Speaking of that other issue, how is your sexy captain?"

I gaped. "Are you kidding me? You really want to talk about *that* right now?"

"Of course I do. I want to talk about everything while I can."

"It's…complicated." I almost said, "We can talk about it when I get home" when I realized she might not be alive when I got back from deployment. I lowered my voice. "She's as confounding as ever, and based on a telephone call I overheard about twenty minutes ago, now single." I felt revolting for talking about this in the face of the news I'd just received, but also for discussing it with someone outside of work. But Linda was a safe space and I needed that more than anything. A safe space. And she was dying.

"Holeeee shit. Oh my god. I mean, so sad for her about the breakup, but also…" Her voice rose hopefully with her unsaid *you know*.

"But also nothing," I said flatly.

Linda ignored me. "Question. Do you guys get like, breakup leave or something? A few weeks where you can go home and have a little micro meltdown and cry and burn photos and smash plates and collect everything that's been dumped on the sidewalk and figure shit out, like where you're going to live now?"

"Unfortunately not."

"Shame. Sometimes that's exactly what's needed."

"Right. I, uh…shit, I can't think about that right now, looking at you. I want to think about you. Do you have anything booked for your ceremony? I mean, how are you working it all?" Given same-sex marriage wasn't legal in D.C., I assumed they were going to one of the few states where it was, or more likely—out of the country.

"We're doing it in Canada. It'd be nice to be able to get married in the state I live in, but you know, why let us queers have rights, right? So fuck this country, period, I'm giving my marriage money to Canada. May as well get some usage out of my passport before I die." She smiled shakily. "Again, I know it's a longshot but if there's any way you could make it, Rebecca, I'd be so grateful to have you by my side. I know how hard it would be and they probably won't let you leave, but if you can, please try?"

"I want to be by your side. Send me the details and the dates and I'll see what I can do. I'll do everything I can," I promised.

"Thank you." Linda's smile seemed a little more solid, as if telling me had pulled a weight from her chest. She exhaled. "Okay, I'm about to crash. I'm so sorry to dump this on you and run, but—"

"It's fine. I get it." I forced down my grief. "Just let me know the plans and I'll see if I can wrangle it."

She smiled her brilliant, charming smile, and it broke my heart just a little. "I'll get Michelle to email you the details right now. I love you."

"Love you too."

I stared at the blank screen for a good minute before closing my laptop and pushing it aside. Everything I'd just been told swam around my head, but none of it touched the sides and stuck. I knew these facts for certain: Linda was dying, she was getting married, I might not ever see her in person again. Everything else was white noise, irrelevant, unimportant.

It was time to call in a favor. Luckily, I had one up my sleeve.

CHAPTER FOURTEEN

A Master of Compartmentalization.

My Aunt Thérèse had first called me that when I was five and a half, not long after my parents died. Or so she'd told me when she'd mentioned it again when I was seven, then nine…twelve…thirteen… sixteen. I didn't remember her calling me that the first time. I didn't remember anything really except for knowing that I'd never see Mommy and Daddy ever again and that if I thought about it, it made me feel like I wanted to stand in the street so a car would hit me and I could go wherever my parents were. So, as much as I could, I tried not to think about it.

I didn't know what she actually meant until she explained it to me when I was older, and she was right—I was adept at compartmentalizing things. It was a necessary skill and one I was grateful that I'd somehow managed to master, but it came with a price. One can't keep the lid on a pressure cooker forever. Sometimes, you have to let the tension ease a little or else it comes out when you least expect, or want, it to. But there was nowhere I could let it out here and I feared the day I was no longer able to keep everything inside.

After checking the wedding details in the email from Michelle via Linda's account and speaking with Phil, I locked my office door and took a few calming breaths. Goddammit, I still had Sabine and her personal issue to deal with. But she was going to have to wait until I didn't feel like I was about to crumble. I sat with my eyes closed for a few minutes, consciously relaxing my breathing, and when I no longer felt like throwing my stapler at the wall, I called Colonel Donna Linwood.

"Rebecca. I was just thinking last week that I'd forgotten to send you a birthday care package. I'm so sorry. How are you?" Her gentle alto voice was usually calming, but now I felt anything but soothed.

"Honestly? I've been better. And it's not just about adding another tally mark to my age. I need to call in that favor you owe me, please." At one of our leadership functions, Donna had ignored the "Never eat the seafood at a buffet" rule, and I'd stepped in to give her speech for her while she'd spent the night in the ladies' room. Then I'd driven her home, and cleaned vomit out of my car after she missed the bucket the cleaning staff had lent her.

There was amusement in Donna's tone. "I was starting to think you'd forgotten about that. What is it that you need?"

"I need to take a week of leave, stateside. It's an emergency. Phil Burnett has already agreed to cover me while I'm gone and I'll be fully contactable should any need arise, which it shouldn't."

"You don't have any immediate family that qualifies you for emergency leave." The words were matter-of-fact, but not cruel.

I smiled at her obvious statement. "No, I don't. But only a few people in the Army know that." I was gambling that our friendship was as solid as I'd thought it was all these years, because I knew what I was asking was a big one, and not setting a good example for the unit if they found out I was going home for what would essentially be bereavement leave, but not for a close family member. "My friend has terminal pancreatic cancer and she wants to get married before she dies. She's my only close friend, basically the only family I have now my aunt is gone, and if we wait until I'm finished with this deployment, she'll likely be dead."

Linda dead. I couldn't picture it. What would I do without her solid presence? Who was going to make me laugh when I felt like crying, or tell me I was being a fool when I couldn't see the obvious solution to my problems?

"I see," Donna said carefully. "And you taking some emergency leave is the only solution?"

"The other solution is I'm not there and she dies before I see her get married or even see her in person ever again. But I don't like that solution. I don't want to beg, but I've never utilized my leave to its full extent and I'm asking for your help. Because I'll be OCONUS, in Canada, I don't think it's appropriate to approve my own leave." Even if I was CONUS—within the Continental United States—I'd probably still feel odd about it because this wasn't ordinary leave.

"Why do you need to go to Canada?" There was no censure in her voice, only curiosity.

"Because our country won't allow someone like her to get married anywhere she wants within its borders," I said neutrally. I didn't need to elaborate. Donna was as affected by DADT as I was.

"Okay, send it through to me. I'll make sure it happens and nobody who doesn't need to see it will, so there'll be no questions from those who shouldn't ask questions."

I held on to my relieved rush of air. "Thank you. I appreciate it."

"You're welcome." Laptop keys sounded in the background of Donna's casual, "I assume you've been keeping up with the news?"

I knew exactly what she was referring to. The whispers about Congress repealing *Don't Ask, Don't Tell* were a welcome change from the usual bombardment of unpleasant news. "I did indeed. Exciting times."

"Mmm, yes they are. Yolanda tells me she's looking forward to attending leadership functions, hanging off my arm and being a hot wife, end quote."

"Kingsley's going to choke on his tongue."

"Let him. Ridiculous homophobic fool." Her tone softened. "Best of luck with your friend, Rebecca. She's lucky to have someone like you who'll drop everything and break rules to make her happy."

"Oh that's me, all right," I drawled. "A regular bad-girl rule breaker." As soon as I'd said that, I thought of all the other rules I'd considered breaking. Or if I wanted to be technical and utterly truthful—*was* breaking by letting the familiarity between Sabine and I run as far as it had.

Donna laughed with me. "I remember that time you took a pen from a leadership forum. You're a terrible influence."

"It was an accident. I had to write some notes and completely forgot I'd put it in my pocket."

"It was a two-thousand-dollar Mont Blanc fountain pen," she said flatly.

"Which I returned as soon as I realized. I am a model citizen and a model leader." The lie felt sour in the face of everything I'd been thinking about Sabine. Sabine. Goddammit to hell, I still had to deal with that problem.

Donna's voice softened to fondness. "Yes, you are. Your team is beyond lucky to have you."

My laugh felt like dust. "You know, sometimes I'm not so sure."

Since ending my call with Donna, I'd been staring at my pile of paperwork, my thoughts pinging between Linda and Sabine without landing on anything concrete about either. Linda's news had left me feeling pulled completely apart, despite my managing to accept it. On a superficial professional level, at least. Personally, I didn't think it had penetrated my skin. I'd almost decided to give up and go spend time in the weight room to burn off some energy when a knock on my office door provided some much-needed distraction. I quietly cleared my throat, hoping I wouldn't sound as emotional as I felt. "Come in."

Mitch poked his head inside, his distress evident. Pressing the door closed, he stood rigidly in front of my desk. "Ma'am, I wonder if you might be able to help me with a problem. Sabine," he added before I could ask.

"Help you how exactly, Mitch?"

His fingers curled into loose fists as if he was only just restraining his emotion. "She's out there runnin' around in this godawful heat like a damned fool and she'll give herself heatstroke if she's not careful. I tried to get her to come in, but she ignored me."

"I see. And she can't ignore me, can she." It was a statement, not a question, because we both knew the answer.

"Exactly." His mouth quirked into an almost-smile, but his apparent enjoyment of the fact his friend was about to get a dose of discipline, however mild, was overwhelmed by his obvious worry.

"Why is she out running now? She already got her five miles in this morning before the temperature picked up." I pressed my lips together, all too aware that I'd just given away how much I watched her. I was sure I knew why she was running herself into the ground, but having Mitch confirm my suspicion would make my job a whole lot easier.

"She…received some bad news from home."

Very diplomatically put. He was a good friend indeed. "I see. And I suppose me asking if she's all right would be an idiotic question, given she's out running herself ragged because of said news?"

"Yes, ma'am, that would be correct," he murmured. "And no, I don't believe she is all right. At all." Mitch sagged for a moment before regaining control of his anguish.

"Okay, I'll go out and talk to her. How long has she been out there?"

"By my calculation? Close to an hour."

Jesus. It was any wonder she hadn't killed herself. I stood up right away. "Okay, I'll go now." My concern for her butted up against my anger that she could do something so reckless. After a detour to the chow hall for a cold bottle of water, I pushed outside. It was just before 1100 and the late-morning summer heat was like a slap in the face with a blast of air from an oven.

Across the grounds, Sabine was a small dot shuffling around the running track. Shuffling was exactly right—she wasn't running, she was barely moving. But she was still doggedly making her way around the dirt circuit. And I wondered what her goal was exactly. Was she trying to run until she passed out, maybe hoping to force herself into a few moments of mental respite? Was she punishing herself for something? Or was she just so utterly unable to process what she'd experienced that she wasn't thinking at all?

By the time she came around the side of the running track closest to the buildings, I was still too far away and couldn't stop her before she'd add another lap to her tally. After sidestepping a pile of vomit on the long side of the track, I walked diagonally to intercept her. Sabine, having apparently realized that she had to stop because her CO was there, dropped abruptly to a walk about fifty yards away. She moved slowly toward me with her hands on the small of her back, and even from this distance I could see the exaggerated movement of her chest and shoulders as she tried to get air into her lungs.

I forced myself to appear relaxed, because confrontation wasn't going to help. Sabine came to attention in front of me, gasping noisily. Her face was bright red and her sopping-wet tee stuck to her torso. "Good morning, Colonel." She ran her tongue over her teeth.

I looked her over, rationalizing that her being drenched in sweat meant she was yet to reach heatstroke stage. A tiny plus in a sea of minuses. I kept my tone light as I held out the water to her. "Captain Fleischer, may I inquire what you're doing out here running around in this heat?"

Sabine took the bottle from me. "Thank you, ma'am. I—" Her forehead wrinkled for a moment. "I'm trying to acclimate for my New York Marathon training." It was said completely straight-faced before she gulped down some water.

My lips twitched with the effort of keeping my smile at bay. She was such a facetious shithead sometimes. "They run that in fall, not summer," I said evenly, taking a step closer. "I don't think it's comparable to current conditions."

Her mouth opened and closed again, as if she realized she'd been caught in her funny lie. I pulled off my sunglasses and caught her eyes. Sabine, sans sunglasses, squinted and blinked hard in the bright light. She seemed to want something from me, though I wasn't sure if it was reassurance or reprimand. "Sabine, I cannot think of anything or anyone who is worth a dose of heat exhaustion. Go inside, get to the showers and cool down. That's an order." As soon as I spoke, I realized I'd given away that I knew what had happened, but I didn't think she'd noticed. She seemed spaced-out which wasn't unusual given what had happened, but *was* concerning for someone like Sabine who was always sharp and focused, even when she was messing around with friends. I made a note to check on her again once she'd cooled off.

Her mouth opened again, and for a moment she looked like she was going to rebut that she was totally fine, despite the fact she'd literally run herself into the ground. Instead, she muttered, "Yes, ma'am."

I nodded, unable to say what I really wanted to. I wanted to tell her how sorry I was. I wanted to tell her not to ever put herself in a situation like this again where she could have killed herself or at the very least, made herself seriously unwell. I wanted to hold her tight, soothe her and tell her that she would be okay, even if everything felt as if it was falling apart right now.

She didn't move and the moment of understanding that passed between us felt so thick I almost reached out to grab it. I tried not to look pitying, because she didn't deserve that, as much as I couldn't help feeling it for her. I just…felt so sorry for her. Breakups were awful, and from what I'd gathered it was a long-term relationship, which made it even worse. Being dumped from an ocean away would be utterly devastating, especially if what I'd pieced together was true and her partner had cheated on her. But there was nothing more I could do, and nothing more I could say.

I spun around and strode away, dragging in deep gulps of air. What I really needed was to talk to Linda and try to unpack this new batch of feelings. But Linda had pancreatic cancer and less than a year to live, and for just one perfect breathtaking second I'd forgotten that. Would it be like that until the end? Moments of seeming normality until one day I'd realize she wasn't there.

I didn't recall much about my feelings as a child after my parents died—everything felt fuzzy-edged, as if I was watching it through a thick veil hiding me from the truth—but I did remember once or twice coming home from school and thinking that I'd show them my art. And then I'd remember I couldn't.

I hid in my office, alternating between staring at paperwork, thinking about Linda, and wondering how I could best help Sabine with her breakup. Or if I even needed to help her. My empathetic, compassionate side said I absolutely needed to offer my support, even if she chose not to take it. The best way would have been as a supportive friend, but that was obviously not an option.

Then there was my other problem, the one where my best friend had terminal cancer and apparently wasn't going to do anything about it except accept it. Because no matter how I tried, I couldn't turn off my physician brain which said the same thing as my friend brain: I could have longer with her if she'd just...try. That made me uncomfortable because Linda's life was her own to do as she pleased, but I wanted so much more than it seemed we'd have.

So I went back to pondering Sabine, which for now was marginally less painful than pondering Linda. Yet again, Linda's words slid to the forefront.

...go home and have a little micro meltdown and figure shit out...

She was right, maybe that was exactly what Sabine needed right now. But could I just throw away the rules because she meant more to me than my other team members? Objectively, she had the time available, and technically she would be eligible to take some CONUS leave, given the length of this deployment. It was a stretch, but not one that would make me uncomfortable reaching for, especially given her circumstances. I'd been lucky in all my years of leadership never to encounter this situation and didn't really know how to deal with it aside from my usual offering of support for anyone in the team who was having an issue. But that didn't feel like enough here.

She was obviously struggling and not thinking clearly. If I left her here to fester, instead of sending her home to deal with it, it might escalate and affect my whole team. Of course, that was assuming she even wanted or needed to go home. But I could offer her the option. I checked the leave schedule for the next month, noting everyone who'd applied for a few days' recharge of Rest and Recreation leave in Qatar. If I was going to give Sabine time stateside, it would have to be when I had as full a roster as possible to maintain operational strength. There would be space just after my latest rotation of R&R'ers returned. I stared at the dates. If she took that leave, the backend of her vacation would overlap with the start of my time at home with Linda.

I set that thought, and all its implications, aside.

Given she was on the second-team roster this week—not needed unless there was a large-scale event that required all hands—I'd expected to have to search the grounds for her, but found her and Mitch in the barracks, tucked around a corner in a semi-private space. I spotted the end of their hug, relieved that she had comfort of some sort. But he was leaving this afternoon for his R&R, and then she would have no one...

"Captains."

They separated and came to attention, their greeting a simultaneous, "Ma'am."

I nodded at them both before focusing my attention on Sabine. "Fleischer, I'd like to see you in my office, please. Oh-nine-hundred tomorrow."

Her forehead crinkled, and at my expectant stare she finally answered, "Of course, Colonel."

"As you were." I continued past them, conscious of eyes on my back as I walked away.

I'd barely made it to my office when the incoming call for a triple-GSW came in, ETA six minutes. Just enough time to change into scrubs, always my preference instead of dirtying my limited supply of uniforms, and by now I had it down to changing in under ninety seconds. The incoming-casualty alert and associated call for all on-shift personnel followed me back to the hospital.

As I stepped into the prep room after completing my casualty assessment, I spotted someone who wasn't supposed to be there and almost stumbled. "Fleischer, you're not supposed to be on shift."

Sabine paused then shook her head. "No, ma'am, but Boyd thought..." She smiled fleetingly and forcibly. "I thought perhaps you might need some extra hands."

I studied her, trying to work out what exactly was going on. It was clear from her expression that being here wasn't really her idea. But a win right now might be something helpful to her, boost her morale, and from what I'd assessed, it should be a fairly straightforward trauma. "I'd like you to assist me. Peterson!" Amy jumped up and came right over, her hands still working at containing escaped hair. "How long is it since you slept?" I asked before she had a chance to say anything.

Her face scrunched as she pondered my question. The fact she had to think about it told me it'd been far too long. Finally she admitted, "Uh, twenty...seven hours? Ma'am."

"You're off. Get some rest."

"Yes, Colonel. Thank you." Amy shrugged at Sabine, then walked out, whistling the *M*A*S*H* theme.

Sabine looked away.

I was finishing my scrub when she stepped in beside me to begin hers. She still needed a briefing on the case so I took my time and filled her in on the PFC on the table. I sensed she *was* taking it in on some cerebral level, but she seemed absent. And all I got in response was a blank, "Yes, ma'am. Understood." She was here, but she also wasn't, not as deeply engaged as she was usually.

I had a rare flash of doubt that I'd made a bad call. Maybe this wasn't a good idea. But it was too late to swap her out now. I was capable of performing a GSW trauma on my own with surgical-nurse assistance. I'd just hold Sabine's hand if she needed it.

I took my time rinsing my hands while I waged war with what I wanted to say versus what I should say. Before I could stop myself, I whispered, "I'm very sorry to hear of your relationship breakup." I wanted to say so much more, to offer her some comfort at a time where she was obviously struggling, to tell her she could always come talk to me as a friend, that she should take care of herself, that I cared about her.

But I couldn't say any of that because I wasn't allowed to. And even if I was, I knew I wouldn't be able to hide my hope. Before Sabine could respond, I turned away, shook my hands off and pushed backward into the OR. As I dried my hands on sterile towels, I chanced a look back through the glass panel to the sinks. She was watching me, her expression so intense and unguarded that I felt stripped bare.

I turned away.

CHAPTER FIFTEEN

I'd just opened a book in what I knew would be a useless attempt to distract myself to sleep when an instant message alert pinged on my laptop. I crab-crawled to the end of the bed where the device was charging and pushed the screen fully open. I hadn't expected it to be anyone but Linda, but it was odd that she was instant messaging me now, after we'd spoken earlier.

LKelly: You awake?

RKeane: No.

LKelly: Lol. Dearest friend, I need you to tell me about your Captain. And yes, I know I have other things to think about right now but if I don't keep trying to feel normal then I'm going to go insane.

The idea that she was *still* obsessed with this, despite everything going on in her life, made me laugh. I resisted the urge to ask how she was—I'd spoken to her less than thirteen hours earlier—and decided to go with the flow. Friend, not doctor, right? Still, I couldn't shake the discomfort that I shouldn't be pretending her health issues weren't there, even as she was asking me to basically do just that.

RKeane: Where should I even start?

LKelly: I already know all the boring and sad stuff about how it's not allowed and blah blah so tell me all the juicy stuff.

RKeane: The juicy stuff where even if I set the work portion of it aside, I feel disgusting for feeling this way about someone who's just been dumped from thousands of miles away?

It took some time for Linda's response to land, after the typing indicator arrived and disappeared a few times.

LKelly: Yeah, that juicy stuff. I don't think feelings and thoughts are disgusting. If you broke them up just by thinking about it then yeah, that's gross.

A line of smiling emojis appeared.

LKelly: DID you break them up through pure force of will and thought power?

RKeane: Very funny. Nothing juicy, but... There WAS a weird moment between us. A bunch of weird moments if I think about it. Before they broke up though. I'm innocent.

LKelly: Spill it.

I tapped my fingertips on the keyboard, trying to decide how exactly to explain it.

RKeane: Kind of unintentionally from me but I'm sure she recognized it. It wasn't real flirting like a conscious effort to indicate interest but for a moment I forgot where we were and there was definitely an attraction vibe. I feel like it's getting harder and harder to keep it all inside. Definitely leaking out. Which sounds gross. You know what I mean.

LKelly: I do. Was she freaked out?

RKeane: Maybe? But I don't know if it was because of that or just the unexpectedness of it all. And I'd literally just decided I was done with all of this shit. Like REALLY done and that it was time to pull out Ice Rebecca. Cool and calm but never frosty. And it would all just freeze over and melt away with the spring and I'd never have to worry about this ever again.

LKelly: Surrre you were. You do know that Ice Rebecca isn't actually a thing, you just think it is. You don't have it in you to be an ice queen. And your metaphor is weird.

RKeane: You're not helping.

LKelly: Sorry, didn't know I was supposed to. I'm just here for the gossip. Ordinarily I'd say go for it, especially with my newfound carpe diem life. But with all the Army rules career stuff you mentioned, all I'm going to say is — be careful. I don't want to see YOU or someone you obviously care about getting hurt.

RKeane: Me either. So how do I get over this? What am I supposed to do? Because now instead of pushing her away, all I want to do is pull her close and make sure she's okay.

There was no answer.

Goddamn you, Internet. Or at least, I hoped it was the Internet.

* * *

I slept fitfully, which on top of my usual semi-insomnia had left me feeling like I was walking around with a head full of cotton wool. There was also an email waiting from Linda, in her typical blunt and unselfish style. I knew that involving herself in my not-relationship woes made her happy for some inexplicable reason and I decided if she wanted to distract herself from her health issues with my Sabine Saga then I'd play along.

So fucking sorry, I have no idea how but I fell asleep in the middle of our conversation last night. I blame cancer. Think I might blame that every time I'm an asshole from now on. I don't know what you should do, but whatever you do it has to be something you can live with for the rest of your life. Think about it. LYMY.

Something I could live with for the rest of my life…

I had no idea what that could be. Deep down I knew that cutting this attraction off at its base was the moral thing, the legal thing, the right thing by the institution to which I'd offered my professional life. But that was *not* going to make me happy. Could I live with knowing I'd always walked the straight, narrow line, pushing happiness off to the side every time it blocked my path? Was the sacrifice worth it? If I was honest, I didn't really think so.

Because *what if?* That was the thing that kept dragging me back over and over, even though every time I came back all I saw was one obstacle or another from me, the Army, Sabine, or my uncertainty about her feelings. It was that dangerous hope, a tiny thing pulling on my sleeve and whispering, "But…what if it could happen one day?" The mental gymnastics had sent me so far ahead of myself that everything in the here and now felt hazy and unclear.

Right at 0900, there was a soft knock on the closed door of my office. Despite everything, it seemed Sabine hadn't lost her knack for to-the-second punctuality. "Come in, Captain," I called.

The door slowly swung open and Sabine slipped inside. She wasn't quite able to mask her dread, but her salute was a sharp snap that I could have videoed to show new recruits, and she added a faux-cheerful, "Good morning, ma'am."

I suppressed my smile at her faked enthusiasm as I rose from my chair to return her salute. "Close the door, please."

Sabine's face fell but she did as I'd asked and when she turned around again I indicated she should take a seat opposite me. Discomfort seeped from her every pore, and I gave her my most calming and reassuring smile. Other than the fatigue she was trying to hide, she seemed okay. Relatively speaking.

From the edge of my vision I saw her looking around my small office, which was basically a plywood box with room enough for my desk, a full wall of filing cabinets, assorted necessary electronics, and my sneaky Keurig coffee maker. The only personalization I ever allocated to any of my field offices were copies of my degrees, some college academic awards and military commendations. No photographs, no paintings or portraits. Nothing that might give me away.

Sabine removed her hands from the arms of the chair and rested them in her lap as she stared at some point on my desk. For the first time since I'd known her, her face seemed devoid of all emotion. I flipped open her personnel file, skimming details I already knew by heart. I looked up at her. "How are you, Captain?"

Her tongue flashed along her lower lip. "I'm very well, thank you, Colonel."

I searched her gaze, unsure of what I was looking for. "If you need to talk about anything, I'm always available, Sabine." Knowing her as I did, I knew she'd need to be pushed to take up my offer.

"Thank you, ma'am. I appreciate that." Her shoulders dropped fractionally with relief, but she looked anything but appreciative.

She looked like she was about to melt into a puddle and I decided to spare her any further anguish, and get right to my point. "Sabine, at my discretion, I've decided you're able to take some R and R."

Her expression changed instantly to surprised confusion. Both eyebrows moved into her thinking face and she quietly cleared her throat. "Oh? I wasn't aware I was able to take leave now, ma'am."

"As I said, it's at my discretion. Technically, you're eligible." I smiled patiently. "Of course, it's your decision but a little time off-base might be helpful." I tried to make it seem like a suggestion, rather than an order, even though I absolutely thought it in her best interest. "How about two weeks? Departing three days after Captain Boyd returns would be the soonest I can allow it." Given Mitch was currently in Qatar, she'd be leaving in seven days. And I'd be leaving in eighteen…

The thoughts flashing through her mind flashed in her eyes, though her face remained almost expressionless. I could see her battling with herself, weighing every pro and con of going home now versus staying here. After twenty seconds of silence, Sabine leaned forward slightly and I wondered if she was about to tell me no-fucking-thank-you. I kept eye contact with her, willing her to see that this could be a good thing, and trying to keep my own thoughts and that tiny possibility from coloring my influence.

Instead of declining as I'd been almost certain she'd do, Sabine blurted loudly, "That would be…nice. Thank you, Colonel."

I tried not to let my relief show. Not only would this hopefully be what she needed, but it would give me a little over two weeks of separation from her. If I stayed away when we were both stateside at the same time, that is. If…

Sabine sat quietly while I brought up the relevant form and began filling it in. "Will you be at your home address?"

"Yes, and no doubt also in Ohio with my family, ma'am," she said, her voice hoarser than usual.

Family. Good. Support was just what she needed. Asking her about her family would be the natural progression for this conversation, but it was also leading and the last thing I needed was to be led somewhere off this path. I checked her file, noting next of kin and typing rapidly to fill in the fields. After quickly checking all the details, I hit Print and passed the form and a pen across my desk to her. "I'll put this through right away, Sabine."

"Thank you, Colonel."

She took her time reading the form, then added her signature and the date in her usual careful penmanship. She spun the paper around and slid it back toward me. Our fingers brushed. It didn't send a rush of heat or goose bumps up my arm, but it did make me think of her fingers lightly brushing over other parts of my skin.

I signed the form and slid it into my priority filing tray. "Is there anything else I can help you with, Sabine?" I hoped if I kept offering, maybe one day she'd take it.

"Actually, there is, ma'am. I need to change some personal details. Specifically, my Record of Emergency Data."

The form designating who was notified in the event of death or an incident, and also detailing the breakdown of beneficiaries for our death gratuity. I raised a surprised eyebrow. If that didn't confirm she'd broken up with her partner, nothing would. "Of course. No AOP change?" Arrears of Pay was any money due to us when we died after retiring from the Army, and had nominated beneficiaries that might also need changing if she was changing her RED.

"No, ma'am," she said instantly.

I spun around to face my bank of filing cabinets and went to the one in the far corner, rummaging through it until I found what I needed. Sabine shot to her feet at my approach and took the pages I offered, her head bowed while she flipped through them as if studying the words might bring her the answers she sought.

I remained where I was, close enough to see the finer laugh lines at the edges of her eyes. "There's very little I don't know about what is happening around here, Sabine. I would like to reiterate that my door is always open if you need a confidant."

Sabine's head snapped up at that. She held eye contact, and the desperation in hers was raw. She *wanted* to talk about it, needed to. But I sensed that she truly didn't actually know how to verbalize what she felt. After a long pause she blurted, "Thank you, ma'am. It was just a bit unexpected."

I studied her, wondering if she'd elaborate. "It often is," I said as evenly as I could. I needed to be careful that I didn't give away how much I knew, or worse—give away my feelings.

Sabine's face wavered between caution and openness. "I would have preferred to know it was happening, rather than being bombed from across the world. Metaphorically speaking, ma'am," she clarified.

I leaned back against my desk, resting my clasped hands against my thighs. She was the most fascinating woman I'd ever met, simultaneously open while keeping herself closed. Assured and competent, yet also lacking confidence in some things. Mature, but also childishly playful. "Do you think being prepared would have made a difference to the way you're feeling now, Sabine?"

Her eyebrows rose in surprise. "Yes, ma'am. I could have formulated a strategy, or even gotten in first." There was the slightest hint of arrogance in the statement, but the words were what caught my focus. *Gotten in first.* Was she implying that her relationship hadn't been peaches and cream for a while now? More importantly—why did that even matter to me? Because maybe it would make me feel less uncomfortable about how she'd been interacting with me, knowing she might have emotionally checked out of that relationship before I ever came into her life.

"So, your pride is also hurt," I said, a little more bluntly than I meant to. "I'm surprised. I've never considered you egotistical." Professionally egotistical, sure, but not personally.

Her backpedal was so fast she almost tripped over her words. "I'm not! I mean, I don't think I am. At least no more than anyone else, ma'am."

True enough. I tilted my head in acknowledgment, and mused a quiet sound that made it clear we didn't have to continue with a subject that was making her uncomfortable, and wasn't going to move us forward. "I'll see you later this afternoon?" Our weekly team meeting where I'd not only have to work through our usual agenda, but also watch carefully for any signs that gossip might still be swirling around.

Her teeth grazed her lower lip. "Yes, ma'am."

"Very good." I pushed off my desk, catching myself before I was propelled right into her. "Think about what I said. Dismissed, Captain."

"Thank you, Colonel." She saluted and once I'd returned it she spun sharply on her heel and left my office, closing the door with the softest click.

I sank back into my chair and leaned forward until my forehead rested on Sabine's file. I would have stayed there trying to dissect our conversation for who-knows-how-long if not for an email alert on my work laptop. My request for a spot on a Space-A flight back to D.C. had been approved, and my transport to Bagram to board that flight confirmed. Given my rank, I was sure they'd put me on the first and thankfully most convenient Space Available slot as soon as I arrived at Bagram, instead of juggling me around like most others. One problem sorted.

Now to address everything else I had on my plate. First up, team meeting agenda.

Aside from being the last to arrive, I noted that after agreeing to take leave, Sabine seemed a little more like herself. Some of the tension had relaxed out of her shoulders and the lines at the edges of her mouth seemed smoother. Either she was coping relatively okay, or pretending she was. I dismissed that second thought. Sabine was many things, but burdened with false bravado she was not. She was so full of emotion and expression, and though she *could* mask what she felt, some of it always slipped out.

After the meeting I lodged her leave, RED, and AOP forms as priority and spent an unnecessarily long time distracting myself with patients. Though I knew I'd be in for a no-hot-water experience, I waited until after dinner when the bulk of the base had showered. The cold water felt refreshing as it rained—or more accurately, dribbled—down on me, and I stood as long as I dared without feeling like I was wasting water. Something about a steady stream of water over my head always shook my thoughts loose.

The timing of Sabine's trip home overlapping with mine was just a coincidence. Nothing more. I'd made the call that she needed to get home soon. And she couldn't go before Mitch returned. My trip was immovable because of Linda and Michelle's wedding. Just a coincidence. Nothing more.

After two chapters of my book, checking my emails and messages in case Linda needed something, another chapter of my book and then a short erotica story from the collection Linda had provided, I still hadn't fallen asleep. And I was now sleeplessly exhausted, and a little aroused. I knew one surefire way to help myself relax, but even after so many deployments I'd never been able to shake the discomfort of masturbating with someone sleeping on the other side of a thin wall, and people who called me their boss all around me.

Still... I was beyond tired, stressed, and upset about a swarm of challenges. Maybe a climax-induced sleep was exactly what I needed. Unbidden, the image that had run merrily through my brain when I'd been with Linda returned—me and Sabine engaged in sweaty, intense, sensual sex.

Arousal shuddered over my skin and the immediate pulse of need had me pressing my thighs together to draw out the sensation. It was the kind of arousal I knew would reward me generously if I could hold off, draw myself out. But it was so intense that I wanted to touch myself right then and make myself climax. I brushed a hand over my breast, teased my nipple through the fabric of my tank, continued down my stomach, lightly stroked the bare skin above the waistband of my pajama pants.

I was a second away from pushing my pajamas down my thighs when I heard the distinctive sound of Sabine trying to walk quietly through the halls, which in her case was a kind of Ugg-clad shuffling. I pressed the button to illuminate my watch. 2:07 a.m. Jesus, Sabine. Apparently my assessment of her *coping okay* was way off the mark. I'd heard her shuffle past my door last night right as I'd been falling asleep, and assumed she was ducking out to the bathroom. Now I knew she'd been pacing. Based on her predilection for both anxiety-related insomnia and an inability to be still when she was stressed or upset, her wandering now could only mean one thing. She was anxious, stressed, or upset. Or all three.

Now that I knew she was out in the halls instead of in her room on the other side of the building, a sleep-inducing orgasm was totally off the table. I rolled over and closed my eyes again, trying to relax and ignore the arousal that hadn't gotten the message that it was going to be ignored tonight.

The faint shuffle of Sabine approaching again increased my concern. I slid out of bed, flicked on the light and opened the door, peering down the hall. She was about ten feet from my door, walking zombie-like, as if she'd allocated no thought to this activity except *move*. "Captain Fleischer," I said, loud enough to catch her attention, but quiet enough to not wake sleeping personnel.

Like a cat burglar caught in the act, she stopped dead and turned around slowly. I leaned out of my bedroom doorway, conscious that I was in pajamas and braless. As she slowly walked back toward me, my tired-eyed focus on her wavered and I grabbed my glasses from the bedside table. "This is the second night in a row you've been walking the hallways instead of sleeping, Sabine." Well done, Rebecca, you sound like a stalker. I cleared my throat and tried to explain myself. "The footwear you insist on wearing as slippers make a very distinctive sound when you're pacing the hallways." I stared at her Uggs. "This is also the second time this morning you've walked past my doorway." And not the first or even second time I'd caught her stress-insomnia pacing.

Sabine raised both hands, palms up. "I apologize for disturbing you, Colonel," she said, her voice a low murmur.

Oh, she was disturbing me, but not in the way she thought. "Have you been to sick bay to get something to help you sleep, Sabine?"

"No, ma'am."

I slid my glasses off and rubbed my eyes. Despite how I felt about her, Sabine Fleischer was quite possibly one of the most frustrating people I'd ever been assigned. I'd never met someone so focused on others' care while being so willfully, resistantly ignorant to her own. "Perhaps you should consider it."

"I will, Colonel. Consider it, I mean." It was said quickly, an automatic reaction that I doubted she'd follow through on.

"Good, now please go back and try to sleep."

"Yes, ma'am. Just another lap." She flashed me a cheerful, slightly forced smile and made a swirling motion with her forefinger.

I tried to adopt a jokingly serious tone. "If I hear you go past my door again, I'm going to force you down the hallway and lock you in your room."

Her lips twitched. "Yes, Colonel."

I stepped back into my room and closed the door between us. Only when I was sure she was gone did I collapse against the wall. I doubted I was going to be sleeping tonight either.

CHAPTER SIXTEEN

After catching Sabine in the throes of stress-insomnia, I'd been wavering on whether or not I should intervene. She clearly needed help, but what kind and from whom was uncertain. But when she had a meltdown during our flag football game after dropping a pass for a touchdown, my decision was made for me. It was clear that if Sabine was sleeping at all, it was minimal, and I knew from sneaky peeks during mealtimes that she was barely eating. It hurt me that she was suffering so much and clearly unable to manage, but at the same time I had to balance that care I had for her as a human…a woman, with my responsibilities as a commanding officer.

But before I could formulate an intervention strategy, the day went to shit. A stable casualty decided to be unstable with what turned out to be reactive postoperative hemorrhage and we'd had to go back to the OR. I'd barely finished washing my hands when the loud ring of yet another incoming patient call started up. I rushed to answer it. Single incoming, GSW left arm and multiple rounds taken in the torso, thankfully stopped by his ballistic plates. Not so thankfully, I was already imagining what we'd find. I sent John and Sabine out to meet the Pararescue team so I could assign OR teams and chug down a bottle of water before I collapsed with dehydration in the middle of surgery.

As I rushed up the hall, the casualty was rushed through the doors in a flurry of activity, including CPR. That was not on the menu. The PJ squeezing the resuscitator blurted, "He literally just arrested, right as we were getting him out."

"Gotta be BABT," John babbled excitedly. An odd thing to be excited about, but fatigue adrenaline was a strange beast. "Tamponade?"

Sabine's forehead wrinkled and she mouthed the word. Tamponade.

I moved past her, brushing along her side as I declared, "I'm leading this one. Sabine, take over compressions. John, get on the bag." All she had to do were chest compressions, simple and rhythmical, something she could do in her sleep. Even if she wasn't sleeping. My focus narrowed to the trauma but I was still aware of everything swirling around me. Sabine climbed onto the stretcher to straddle the casualty and once the PJ had finished his cycle, she confirmed lack of pulse and rhythm and began her compressions. Even if I hadn't been told he'd taken rounds in the vest as well as in the bicep, it was obvious from the furious bruising on his left pectoral region, spreading down over his abdomen. BABT strikes again.

Over the sound of the clinical exam and stats, I could hear Sabine's ragged breathing as she performed compressions. Her expression was vacant, and she was muttering something to herself under her breath. But it didn't sound like anything I needed to hear so I tuned it out.

"Okay, let's move." As we rushed through the halls, I kept throwing out instructions. "Bobby, I want him under by the time I'm at the sink."

He grinned cockily. "Yes, ma'am."

"Sabine, once he's intubated, I want you scrubbed and back in there assisting me. Remember the BABT case we had your first deployment?" It was a long shot, but maybe reminding her of something we'd done before, the first surgery we'd every performed together might snap her out of…whatever this was.

She nodded dumbly, shaking sweat from her chin to drip onto the man's face. I had to leave her to get sterile and I rushed through my scrub, conscious of the rapidly winding clock and the slim window we had to get in and repair. I glanced up from my scrub in time to see Sabine cease compressions, do a vitals check, and mumble a single word before she resumed her compressions. Asystole. I was going to have to get in there, no more messing around.

As I was gowned and gloved, I glanced at the images which showed pericardial effusion and abdominal fluid. Blood. "He's been down for almost six minutes. We're doing a lateral thoracotomy." If I wasn't dealing with BABT and potentially ruptured who-knows-what in there, I would have just done a pericardiocentesis to relieve the tamponade. "Get trays ready, please. Kathy, take over compressions. Sabine, go scrub."

Sabine transferred compressions to Kathy and climbed off the man's legs, shaking her arms out the moment she landed on the floor. I heard her voice catch before she almost-whispered, "What's his name?"

For a second, everyone went utterly still. No word, no sound.

My scalpel paused. "Daniels."

Her relief was palpable. I met her gaze and knew all my concern was in mine. "Do you need to be relieved, Sabine?"

"No, ma'am." A quiet, husky response but she seemed genuine enough.

"Okay, good. Get scrubbed, STAT."

My thoracotomy was quick and not entirely neat. From his position behind me, Bobby mused, "Sucks when the thing that's supposed to save you is what might kill you."

Of all the ridiculous things to say. "Not the time for speculation, Bobby," I said quietly. I could have slapped him. I incised the pericardium, suctioned blood and clots to provide some visualization, and searched for obvious cardiac trauma. I found none.

"Nice sensitivity, Rodriguez," Sabine snapped.

It was like being in a locker room of bickering teens. I pulled out my command voice. "Focus everyone." I steadied my tone and added calmly, "This is not good. Fleischer, you've handled BABT with me before. Hurry up, please."

Though she'd been out and scrubbed, and was now dressed and surgically sterile, she didn't move. She didn't say a word, just kept staring at the man on the table front of me. The man whose heart was not beating. I slipped my hand in again and began open cardiac massage. Sabine still didn't move, and I lost my grip on my frustration. "Sabine! I need you over here right now."

She looked right at me. "He's been shot in the arm too. Why hasn't anyone done anything about it?"

John almost choked on his incredulity. "No shit. We've got bigger issues here."

"Fleischer!" The word came out more sharply than I'd intended but she seemed to be spiraling into something and my previous attempts to get her attention had failed.

Thankfully something in my tone seemed to register and she looked up from where she'd been staring at her feet. "Yes?"

"Please step out."

"Pardon me, ma'am?" Sabine's voice was so husky and rough with her unchecked emotion that it was almost breaking.

My attention was on the man whose dying heart I had in my hand and I didn't look at her when I said, "Leave the OR. You're relieved." I knew what I'd just done to her, knew that perhaps I'd made things worse for her. But my priority was patient care, even as that knowing voice at the back of my head murmured this was a lost cause. I had one chance to repair this trauma. I could repair Sabine's fragility later.

After almost half a minute I heard the snap and rip as she stripped off her gloves and gown, the thudding whoosh of the door. But I couldn't look at her, even as I wanted to. "John, get in here right now and control this hemorrhage. I can't even tell where it's coming from with all this blood…spleen, liver, just find it and stop it."

From the corner of my eye I saw Sabine on the other side of the glass, watching us. Our eyes met and a flash of annoyance and frustration and upset sped through me. I jerked my chin toward the main door, indicating in no uncertain terms that she was to leave as I'd told her to do. Her mouth fell open. And then she was gone.

Even with the internal bleeding somewhat controlled and every life-saving measure we threw at him, we were unable to resuscitate, and I left the room with an unusual feeling of anger on top of my usual disappointment. It wasn't Sabine's fault—his prognosis was always very poor—but the fact she'd frozen so spectacularly was indicative of a problem far deeper than I'd imagined. And I hadn't seen what was right there. Sabine was unraveling, as if she was pulling at threads here and there and breaking them off. Little things at a time, not enough to make her fall completely apart, just enough to make her unstable.

I'd avoided pushing at her too much because I didn't want to insert myself into a personal matter that I'd expected her to overcome with the help of her friends here and her family back home. It was clear that I needed to intervene now, and that I should have done so days ago. I'd screwed up and let her spiral further than she should have because my better judgment had been clouded by my sensitivity to her unique needs. But I could fix that now.

I found Amy in the rec room playing chess with Conway. Kicking his ass at chess more accurately. "Peterson, a word?"

She stood immediately. "Of course, ma'am." To Conway she said, "You got lucky, sir."

Amy followed me out and around a corner where we would have some privacy. She stood impassively, clearly curious but just as clearly not concerned she was about to be disciplined. "What can I help you with, ma'am?"

"Do you know where Sabine is?"

"No, I don't." The pause before she answered, and her slow, careful tone suggested she knew what had happened. "I haven't seen her since before that trauma alarm."

So she was hiding, which made me even more concerned. I resisted the urge to slump against the wall and rub the fatigue from my eyes. "Amy…you have permission to speak freely. What's going on? I know she's struggling, but it's now abundantly clear that it's more serious than I'd thought. Can you shed any light for me?"

Peterson didn't hesitate, and despite her forthrightness, it was obvious she was upset. I didn't know if she was upset that I'd pushed her into telling on her friend and roommate, or upset because Sabine's mental and physical health had declined to barely functioning. "She's not sleeping, or if she is, it's not in our room. She's hardly eating, or if she is—I'm not seeing it. I've tried to help her, tried to be there as a friend so she can talk but it's like she's just got this barrier up. I don't think it's intentional, but it's there. I even offered to sign off on something to help her sleep, but she said she didn't want it, that it made her groggy. Like…groggier than not sleeping? Whenever I wake up during the night, she's not there and pardon my French, ma'am, but she looks like fucking shit."

Amy's assessment confirmed what I'd observed, and the truth of what I'd just heard made me feel like I'd dived into an ice-cold pool. I only just suppressed my shudder. "Thank you. Can you find her, please, and have her come to my office immediately."

Her eyes widened. "Yes, ma'am. Will do. Right away."

She turned to walk away and I called her back. "Amy?"

"Ma'am?"

"Thank you for your honesty. You did the right thing."

Amy nodded and I left her to go run the errand for me while I ran an errand of my own. I was going to have to do something I didn't want to, but it was something I felt necessary for Sabine's wellbeing. She'd probably despise me for it, for my insistence and my involvement. I almost didn't care. She'd refused help when it'd been offered in good faith from a friend and medical professional. Sabine wasn't stupid, but she clearly wasn't thinking clearly right now. And now it was on me to think for her until she could do so herself.

I stopped by the dispensary to fill the script I'd hastily scribbled out in my office. While I waited, I leaned against the wall and wondered if this really was the right course of action, if I was doing the right thing. Questioning myself was rare. Doubting myself was even rarer. But now I had the uneasy feeling that this could change the dynamic between us forever and jeopardize all the trust she'd placed in me so far.

The dispensary nurse interrupted my runaway thoughts. "Colonel Keane?"

"Mm? Yes, sorry." I made myself smile as I took the bottle from her and signed for the pills. "I must be a million miles away. Thank you."

The faint rattle of pills in my pocket as I walked back to my office gave me the answer. This was the right thing for Sabine. She needed help, and her continuing as she had been was a danger not only to patient care and team cohesion, but to herself. I could help her and if it came to it, I'd wear whatever anger or frustration or distrust she wanted to throw at me as a consequence of doing what was best for her.

The knock on my open door wasn't a surprise, but its promptness was. I'd expected it to take Amy a good half hour to find Sabine. When I glanced up, she threw a sharp salute. "Good afternoon, Colonel." Sabine's hair was obviously wet, and though in its usual bun, was as unruly as I'd ever seen it.

I rose from my chair and returned her salute. "Come in, Sabine. Close the door please."

She pushed it closed, then gave it another nudge as if ensuring it was properly secured. She moved quickly to stand in front of my desk at rigid attention, her gaze fixed on the wall behind me.

"At ease," I said as I lowered myself down into my chair. I almost invited her to sit but considering this was technically part-disciplinary meeting, I left her to stand with her hands behind her back. And I hated it. I hated feeling like I'd failed her. I hated feeling like I had to hurt her in order to help her. And I hated this feeling of just wanting to hug her, of wanting to hold her in the hope that it might ease some of her struggle.

I turned my pen over and over, trying to find the right words. Death wasn't a new phenomenon to any of us, but for some reason I cared about how she'd react. Everything about her from her body language to her expression screamed distress, panic, fear. Eventually, I went with a simple, "We were unable to resuscitate."

She exhaled an audibly shaky breath.

I raised my eyes to meet hers, stunned by their pure, raw panic. I'd never seen an expression like it, not from her. It was almost like I'd just given her the worst news of her life, which considering the horrible news she'd received less than a week ago, was saying something. "Is there anything you'd like to say, Captain? Do you understand why I asked you to leave?"

Sabine nodded, her mouth working open and closed before she croaked, "I—" And that was all that came out of her mouth. She nodded again.

I frowned, still turning the pen over in my fingers. "Sabine…I'm concerned about you, as are other people on this base." *Concerned* barely touched the surface of what I felt right now, but it felt like the softest way to tell her I was so worried for her I could hardly think of what to do.

For some reason, she kept staring at my left hand and the intensity of her focus made me self-conscious, because the only thing that could be drawing her attention there was my fake wedding band. I opened my drawer and pulled out the bottle of pills I'd had dispensed, along with Sabine's medical file.

I set the bottle on the desk and opened her file, using the time to collect my thoughts before passing the script for seven zolpidem— Ambien—ten milligrams across the desk to her. "Peterson told me she offered to write a script for something to assist you with your insomnia. And you refused." She gave me no clue as to how she'd taken this revelation.

Until she answered me. She looked and sounded as if she was barely managing to hold on to her indignation. "Colonel, with all respect due, I didn't ask for this."

"I know, Sabine. But you will take one now and go back to your room immediately. Peterson will keep an eye on you. You're also cleared for one day of sick leave tomorrow, confined to barracks."

"And if I decline?" After a brief pause she added, "Ma'am."

"Then I will have to give you a written reprimand, Captain. You may consider this an oral admonishment." I paused, and gentled my tone a little. "Sabine, please stop arguing. You're exhausted, stressed, and you need to sleep. Part of my job is ensuring that people under my command are fit and able to fulfill their duties. Anything less compromises the unit and casualty care. You're struggling." I had to bite back my emotion. "Please, let me help you."

A nerve twitched in her eyelid and she blinked hard as if that might stop the spasm. But she said nothing. She didn't acknowledge me at all except for that intense, knowing, fearful stare. I pushed the file forward. "Sign this for me, please."

She stared at the page where I'd marked her down for one day of sick leave tomorrow. I'd left it deliberately ambiguous, simply noted as "personal." After a long, silent moment, Sabine pulled the pen from her breast pocket and signed her file. I took the folder back and placed it carefully in my out tray. "Have you been to see Psych, Captain?"

The pause told me she was considering being evasive, but she answered with, "No, Colonel."

"I think you should. I believe talking would help."

Her response was instantaneous. "Are you going to force me to do that too, ma'am?" Her eyes fluttered closed for a few moments before she opened them wide. Now on top of all the other emotions that had passed over her face, she also looked mortified. "I...I'm very sorry, Colonel Keane. That was rude of me."

Yes, it was, but I decided to give her this free pass, and ignored her tone. "No, Sabine, I'm not going to force you." I smiled in an attempt to soften the mood. "Not yet." I filled a paper cup from the water cooler wedged into the corner of my office. After shaking a single Ambien from the bottle, I held it out on my palm. Sabine pinched it carefully from my hand and after accepting the water from me, swallowed it. I offered a wry smile, hoping again that some levity might ease the tension in the room. "Do I have to check under your tongue?"

She crumpled the paper cup. "Of course not, ma'am."

"Good. Now get going. I'll see you tomorrow afternoon, or later." I capped the bottle of pills and passed it to her.

Sabine shoved it roughly into her pocket. "Thank you, Colonel." She blinked hard as the nerve in her eyelid began jittering again.

I nodded and sat behind my desk. There was nothing more I could say to her, nothing to soften what I'd done. She left my office without another word, shutting the door behind her. I leaned back into my chair and closed my eyes, trying to wrangle my thoughts and emotions. I'd done the right thing for both Sabine and the unit. But trying to balance my feelings—my need to care for her as someone I had feelings for, and as a member of the team—had proven far more difficult than I'd thought. This is why they don't allow the thing you're thinking of, Rebecca. Because you can't be objective. You left this too late because you didn't want to hurt her feelings.

But...I *could* be objective. I'd just proven that to myself. I'd acted in the best interests of the unit, even though I knew it would hurt her. And an unintended bonus side effect of her being confined to barracks tomorrow while she hopefully slept and regained some equilibrium was that I wouldn't see her. Maybe I could regain some of my own equilibrium.

CHAPTER SEVENTEEN

Amy seemed to relish her new role as Sabine Spy, as she'd called it when I'd explained Sabine had taken ten milligrams of zolpidem and should probably be checked on periodically.

"Will do, ma'am," was Amy's cheerful response. Then she'd paused and added a more serious, "Thank you, Colonel Keane, for uh... helping her."

As I'd instructed, Sabine had remained confined to barracks for the whole next day and I didn't see her at all until dinnertime where she'd sat surrounded by friends, wisecracking and seeming more like herself. Or at least on her way back to herself. It made me feel slightly better about what I'd done.

The day after her enforced rest day, Sabine had found me in my office and offered me a sincere apology for her behavior. Her openness and giving me this so freely had felt like a small win. And then she'd looked at me in that way she had, like she was trying to see inside me, trying to feel what I was feeling, that I'd panicked. And yet, despite my reiterating that my door was always open for her, she still hadn't said anything. Maybe she never would. Maybe the apology was her version of spilling her emotional guts. And I would have to be satisfied with that.

With Mitch having arrived back from his R&R that morning I felt even better about Sabine, and in my mental triage I moved her from red down to yellow, expecting green in another few days when she'd be back in the States with her family. She obviously wasn't miraculously better, but she'd rested, eaten, and her best friend and main support system had returned which meant I finally felt as if I didn't have to watch over her constantly to ensure she was safe.

An unscheduled video call from Linda had me shoving my paperwork aside to answer. The moment she came into view, Linda raised both hands to the sky. "Miracle! I took a punt and actually caught you!" She brushed her shoulders off as if congratulating herself.

I pushed my panic down. "Is everything okay? Are you okay?"

She scoffed, "Rebecca, do I look okay?"

I stared at her more closely. "Well…yes, you do actually. Considering."

"Exactly. Because I am okay. Considering. Can't a person call their friend just to say hi, tell them they love them and that they mean the world to them?"

"Of course they can. Let me guess? Carpe diem?"

She winked. "You know it, baby."

Though my office was reasonably soundproof, I still lowered my voice. "I love you too. You know that, right?"

"Of course I do." Linda grinned. "Right, now that's out in the open, I'll let you get back to saving lives."

"That's really all you called for?"

"It is. And now I can tick it off my dying list—regularly let people know how much they mean to me."

Her words triggered a niggle at the back of my subconscious, but I couldn't quite pin it down. "That's a good plan. I'll try to do that more often too. Talk soon?"

"You know it." She blew me a kiss and ended the call, leaving me feeling both warmed and slightly dumbfounded at the short interruption.

The niggle came into sharp focus as Linda's casual, "Regularly let people know how much they mean to me" looped back into my mind.

The idea was so sudden, and so ridiculous, that I almost dismissed it outright. But it refused to go away, digging down like a stubborn weed. By the time I'd finished my paperwork for the afternoon, it'd grown too big to ignore and too big to pull out. And when I spotted Sabine over at the corner bench speaking with Mitch it was too perfect and too private an opportunity to ignore.

The late afternoon sun cast long shadows down the mountains and across the dirt, the sky that perfect dusky pink as we approached sunset each evening. Mitch left Sabine on the bench and came toward me. "Afternoon, Colonel Keane." He gestured behind himself. "You here to try and get her to talk about her feelings?"

I laughed quietly. "Something like that."

"Well then, I wish you the very best of luck. Enjoy your evening, ma'am."

"You too, Mitch."

Sabine stood at my approach and when I got close enough to catch the hopefulness on her face, she saluted. "Colonel Keane, good afternoon."

I returned her salute. "Captain Fleischer, good afternoon to you too." The moment Sabine's hand fell, I lowered myself to the bench and indicated she should take a seat. She did, settling herself a foot from me. After a moment, she subtly shuffled slightly farther away.

"How are you?" I asked quietly.

She didn't hesitate. "I'm well, thank you, ma'am."

I paused, weighing up what I wanted to say. And as each of my thoughts ordered themselves, Linda's words about letting people know their value to you kept shoving to the forefront. I inhaled slowly, and decided to begin with something less in-her-face. "Sabine, you know I'm required to ensure you're fit for work physically, but also emotionally." I turned slightly on the bench so I was facing her, rather than blocking her with my body language. I didn't want to block her, I wanted to let her in. "I would like to believe in the two deployments we've worked together that you think enough of me to talk to me if you had any issues. But so far you have not, even at my invitation." I leaned back into the bench and crossed my legs.

Her eyebrows rose in surprise. "I do, ma'am. I mean, I think highly of you, but…I'm not certain I know what you're saying?" The more she spoke, the slower her words became.

Their carefulness made me sure she knew exactly what I was saying but she was either too aware of everything that stood between us, or was too afraid to break rank to be truthful with me. I smiled patiently. "I know you know I'm aware of your relationship breakdown. You may or may not be aware that I also know some of the details involved with it."

She frowned and I almost laughed at the comical expression of childish frustration—eyebrows jammed downward, nose wrinkled. "If I may ask, Colonel? How do you know?"

"The same way I know everything, Sabine." I leaned as close as I dared and flashed a conspiratorial smile, lowering my voice as I told her, "People gossip. Nobody else knows specifics, if you're concerned, Sabine." I glanced around, even though I knew we were alone, and said something dangerous. "But, certain things are…*obvious* to people who know what those things are."

She stiffened, and for a moment I wondered if I'd said too much. But as quickly as the tension appeared, it flowed out of her as if it had been nothing more than surprise at what I'd implied. I peered past the fence to watch the approaching sunset, before turning back to Sabine. "I think we both know military life can make relationships difficult to maintain. After the recent upheaval in your life, and other incidents, I just wanted to touch base with you." The implication of what I'd almost implied and what I felt I was about to imply made my skin prickle.

"I appreciate that, ma'am. I'm fine." Sabine offered a wonky smile, before averting her gaze to peer down at her booted feet, scuffing in the dirt.

We sat without speaking for a few moments, and I used the quiet to contemplate exactly how to tell her what I wanted to tell her. I couldn't elaborate and explain about Linda, about how the imminent death of my friend had made me want to change the way I approached some things in my life, but I could come at it in a roundabout way. "The nature of our job, having bad outcomes, these things can sometimes make us reevaluate what's important to us. The people who are important to us."

Her teeth grazed her lower lip as she nodded, smiling a slightly lopsided smile as if she was giving me the correct answer to a quiz question. "My mom always tells me to let people know what they mean to you, while you can. You just never know when it'll be over, do you, ma'am?"

Seemed Sabine's mother and Linda both lived by the same ideology. I smiled. "I think that's a fine principle to abide by," I agreed, feeling my smile fading as the reality of what I was about to admit hit me. "Sabine, I want you to know I value you enormously as a colleague." I faltered, warring with myself, but in the end I just couldn't hold it in. "However, beyond what I've just said, I also care about you a great deal." My mouth fell open but thankfully I closed it again before I went any further.

Her gaze fell to my lips, and her expression turned almost… hungry. It was so obvious that she was thinking the same thing as me—

that I wanted to kiss her so badly that I could almost taste her, feel her skin under my fingertips. I even leaned forward slightly, anticipating it, wanting it, before I came to my senses and moved back again. My heart hammered with both anticipation and the fear of what felt so close and so forbidden. I had no idea what to do, what to say, what to think.

Sabine spluttered a moment before articulating a hoarse, "Thank you, ma'am." Her eyes fluttered closed. "I mean, I'm…fond of you too," she mumbled. She opened her eyes and gave me a look of utter helplessness. "What I meant to say is I care about you too, Colonel." It was a near-whisper, and I didn't know if she was afraid of someone hearing it, or if she was afraid to let herself hear it aloud.

I moved to touch her then but instead of resting my hand on her thigh as I'd wanted, I put it firmly on my own. I pressed the tip of my thumb and forefinger together, sliding them hard against each other, hoping desperately to stop this overwhelming sense of my life running away from me. I couldn't stop looking at her, but thankfully the overriding thought was that I needed to move this conversation in a different direction or I was going to do something that would get us both fired. Or worse. "I notice you still haven't seen Psych."

Sabine's cheeks puffed with the force of her exhalation. "I had considered it, ma'am."

Considered it and obviously decided not to. "Then why haven't you been?"

Her mouth twitched. "I didn't want to lie by omission, Colonel…"

Goddammit, I hadn't even considered that. I smiled, tilting my head in concession. "Understandable, but it is my strong recommendation that you attend."

Now her mouth twisted and I knew she was chewing the inside of her cheek, probably trying to think of a way to squirm out of talking about her feelings.

"Don't argue, Sabine," I said, trying to keep my tone playful.

"Yes, ma'am."

I uncrossed then recrossed my legs, shifting myself so I wasn't so close to her. "You may find it will help. I'm confident you'll find a workaround for sharing the things you need to, but not things you don't want to." Or she would just omit everything, including why she was there, or flat out lie.

She mused a quiet sound, before her mouth twisted with a quick pang of anguish. She blurted, "My…my pets are gone. Taken out of state and I, uh, didn't even get to see them, and I can't do anything about it because I'm here."

My heart sank for her. She was obviously still struggling to accept and understand *why*, and was latching onto the small details she couldn't control, the things that had been taken from her. "I can imagine it must be very difficult for you to accept. Being helpless is an awful feeling," I said tenderly.

Sabine nodded, her teeth buried in her lower lip. I'd been where she was right now, feeling so utterly lost that I had no idea if I'd ever find myself again. But I did. And then I kept finding more of myself. And she would too, eventually. I cleared my throat and exhaled a long breath. "Sabine, when I was nineteen, I became involved with someone. It was the start of my first real relationship." She didn't say anything, but her eyebrows shot up in surprise.

I continued, "It was all-consuming, as I'm sure you're aware things can be when you're that age. We were together all through most of our premed, then medical school and into residency where I went into surgery and...*they* went on to be a physician." I glanced at her, wondering if she'd picked up on the meaning of that neutral pronoun.

The widening of her eyes told me she had. But she said nothing.

"Anyway, the long and short of it is the relationship ended during my residency. After so much time spent defining myself by the fact I was with this person and having molded myself around the concept of being in a couple, I was lost. Completely and utterly adrift, even though I knew leaving was the right thing." My voice was soft, almost wistful. I recalled those overwhelming emotions as I tried to navigate leaving Clare and what my new life might look like, but I felt none of it. There was no residual fear or anger or sadness. I'd let those feelings fall away a long time ago.

Sabine nodded, murmuring a quiet sound that I couldn't make out as a word, more just her indicating that she was listening.

I laughed softly, still unable to believe after all these years how I'd chosen to handle my breakup. "So, instead of dealing with my fears, I joined the Army. And here I am. I love my job but still, life could have been something else. The military can be difficult for those who are different."

From her expression it was clear she knew exactly what I was saying from what I *wasn't* saying—that we were both different in the same way.

I dipped my head to catch her eye. "If I may offer one piece of advice?"

Her eyes held mine, and her answer was a quiet, "Of course, ma'am."

"Don't avoid problems and don't leave things unresolved. Tell people how you feel. Go home as I've arranged for you and finalize things so you can move on with your life, Sabine." It wasn't purely selfish, though that weighed heavily on my mind. She needed to reconcile and resolve what had happened, find a way to deal with it, or it was going to eat away at her until there was nothing left of the woman I loved.

Loved.

The word stuck and refused to budge, even as I panickingly tried to put it in The Forgetting Place where it wouldn't hurt me.

"Thank you, ma'am," she murmured, her voice hitching slightly on the words. I wondered if she'd felt the movement between us as I had. We weren't going to change the paradigm, but maybe, just maybe it would change us.

I shifted, desperate to say more but knowing it was the worst thing I could possibly do. It was time for me to leave. Sabine jumped to her feet a moment before I stood, watching me carefully. I felt as if she'd run through a gamut of emotions during our short conversation, and each one had been displayed on her face. Now? She looked calm. And she looked...hopeful.

"I trust what we've spoken about will stay between us," I said quietly, aware of how much I'd left myself completely exposed and how much trust, and also burden, I'd placed on her.

"Of course, ma'am. I believe that goes without saying. I appreciate your candor, and your concern." Her face said it all. She knew everything I'd told her, knew the implications of it. But...she hadn't asked me anything and I hadn't told her. We were tiptoeing around inside the borders of the rules so clearly laid out for us. But we were still inside those borders. Just.

I smiled, feeling lighter than I had in months. "It's getting dark, Sabine. Don't stay out here for too long." I left her before she could salute, not wanting the reminder that she was my subordinate and that the one thing I wanted, I couldn't have.

* * *

The next afternoon, though I was exhausted and wanted nothing more than to skulk into my office and take a quick catnap, I dragged myself out for our weekly flag football game. Team cohesion and morale etcetera, and...it would likely be the last chance I'd have to see Sabine outside of a work setting before she flew to the States tomorrow after lunch.

Everyone was already on the field when I jogged over and slipped into the crowd. They were prepping for the game by smearing dark camo paint under their eyes, laying out the green and red team vests and flag belts, and psyching themselves up with shit-talking and show-off displays of athletic warmups. Phil grinned at me. "Just in time, Colonel Keane. Thought we'd have to sub for you."

"Wouldn't miss football day." I looked around, noting Sabine averting her eyes when mine caught hers. But I didn't sense discomfort—more like…wariness. The same wariness that I'd often felt around her. I made myself smile at the group. "Apologies for my tardiness, everyone." As I dipped my hand into the mayo bucket and pulled out a slip of paper, I didn't know if I wanted to see an S for Sabine's team, or an M for Mitch's. I'd either have to huddle in with her on my team, or risk accidentally touching something I wanted to but should not touch.

I pulled out an S.

I moved to stand beside Sabine and mustered a smile, leaning close to murmur, "Last game before you go on leave tomorrow, Captain. Let's lock it down."

"Yes, ma'am!"

I shrugged into my red vest and fastened the flag belt around my waist, keeping my eyes on the dirt beneath my feet. Bobby, captaining my team, won the coin toss and sent us on the offensive. He gestured us all in for a huddle. Sabine and I were pressed together, touching shoulder to thigh and I couldn't move because of the pressure from my other side. I was conscious of how utterly still she was, except for the movement of her deep, slow breathing.

Bobby assigned positions, keeping me, as usual, as tight end. "First play's a fake-out. Fleischer, run right, I'll hand off to Chapman left. Keane, Soldano, run left. Stevenson and me right." He peered intently at all of us. "Got it?"

I nodded and suppressed my eye roll. It's not the Super Bowl, Rodriguez. Glancing up and down the line, I found Sabine watching me, and the flutter of excitement in my stomach had nothing to do with the fact I was about to start a competitive game. Her expression was a mix of interest and amusement and I tried for a comical widening of my eyes. She grinned and rolled hers in response. Apparently we'd been thinking the same thing about Bobby's enthusiasm.

Conway blew his whistle. Sabine slipped away and began sidestepping behind the line. I could feel the rush of air as she passed me and the fresh citrus scent of her moisturizer.

"Set!" Bobby shouted before adding, "Rudolph! Polymerase! Toothpick! Angina! Hike!" The words meant absolutely nothing except for a chance to be awarded best play call of the game, and he'd have to do better than that to win.

John snapped to Bobby who feinted and passed off to Chapman as I sprinted up the field, just in front of Sabine. I made it just past the twenty-yard line when the whistle blew. Despite Bobby being flagged, Mitch wasn't happy about it. "You're guardin' your flag! Cut it out!" Mitch seemed to think Bobby trapped the flag against his hip with the ball to make it harder for someone to pull it away. Given Bobby's competitive feelings about football, he probably did exactly that.

Mitch raised both arms above his head to catch Conway's attention. "Did you see that, sir?" he choked out. Mitch wasn't quite as serious about football as Bobby, but he was pretty close.

Conway either didn't see it, or was feeling Red-Team-inclined today. Sabine said something to Mitch that warranted a middle finger as response. Bobby motioned us to huddle up and she abandoned rubbing Mitch's nose in his failed foul then skipped across the dirt and fell in beside me as Bobby gave us the play. "Same again, no fake. Keane, you run too. Sab, you're it. Count to four and take the catch."

As Sabine and I passed each other to get in line I asked, "You got it?"

Her grin was heart-melting, and her response a cocky, "Always, ma'am" that did absolutely nothing to squash my butterflies.

Bobby seemed to think volume equaled skill and practically screamed, "Set!" Everyone on my team dropped down, except for Sabine and me. She glanced over at me again and I could have sworn I saw the ghost of a wink. The woman was going to kill me.

Bobby's second call made just as much sense as his first and was just as not-winning. "Watermelon! Cookie! Puppies! Prohibition Rum! Hike!"

John snapped to Bobby and I propelled myself forward, sprinting up the line. Two of Green Team moved toward me, and in my periphery I found Sabine on the opposite side of the field, just in front of me. She turned around just as Bobby let loose with the ball, and leapt to catch it, executing a display of athleticism that would make sports scouts take note. She made seven yards before she was flagged, and we all ran up to congratulate her. But I held back a little, fearful of being close to her again. As much as I wanted to touch her, I didn't want to touch her. Not like this. Not…without being invited. And certainly not here in public, even if it was nothing more than innocently congratulating a teammate.

On the next play I caught a pass and took the opportunity of the majority of Green Team shadowing Sabine to cross the line for a touchdown. The celebration was raucous, even with Sabine and I avoiding each other like we were on opposing teams.

After holding momentum for the rest of the game, my Red Team was up 30-18 with four minutes left. Green Team had been trying to push through our defense with no luck, but they weren't letting up and had been making some bold plays. As I followed the ball from Amy's hands to Mitch's and then to Phil's after a fake pass, I saw what was about to happen. Sabine had spotted the fakeout and moved to intercept Phil when he turned to run forward, clearly not realizing she was so close.

He slammed right into Sabine, sending her flying onto her back. I heard the sound as her head cracked against the rock-hard ground and ran to David, shouting at him to stop the game. His whistle blew long and loud. Sabine rolled over and settled on the dirt, trying to roll over to get up, but the rapidly gathered crowd were all keeping her from doing just that.

And I couldn't do anything except look at her, expecting to see her flop back down to lie motionless in the dirt, not breathing. A stupid fear, because while it was a hard fall it wasn't fatal. And she'd clearly moved after she'd gone down. The noise receded to a hum of arguments—Mitch and Bobby over the foul; apologies—Phil's frantic one; and advice—pretty much everyone telling her to stay still.

I raised my voice. "Make some space!"

The crowd expanded a little to give Sabine some room to breathe. Amy's voice cut through the noise of everyone having an opinion. "Sabs?"

"Yes, Amy?" was the dry response.

"Can you hear me?"

"No, Amy, which is why I just responded to you," she said sarcastically. Sarcasm was good. Sarcasm was...Sabine. She waved everyone away and rose up onto her knees. And I stared at her, watched her moving, tried to reassure myself that she didn't have a cranial laceration, or an obvious neurological deficit.

Sabine rubbed the back of her head and when she pulled her hand away there was no blood. Still, closed skull fracture...hematoma, concussion. A cerebral bleed. The possibilities rushed at me like an out-of-control truck that I couldn't escape. She'd grazed her elbow and the blood and dirt sticking to her skin made me feel cool, sweaty. I opened my mouth to take in some more air in an attempt to calm myself. What a ridiculous reaction to a minor event, Rebecca.

Sabine grabbed Soldano's offered hand and leapt to her feet, grinning widely. "Ta-dah!"

Nearly everyone laughed. I didn't. Bobby and Mitch were still arguing over what happened, and Sabine shut them up with a cheerful, "Hey, stop it. It was an accident. Now come on, we've only got a few minutes and we need to cap our win with a penalty for Colonel Burnett's foul!" She clapped her hands and walked away as if signaling that was that, now let's move on.

I watched her gait. Normal. But she kept rolling her neck as if it were stiff, and every few steps she'd reexamine her grazed, gravel-filled elbow which was still trickling blood. I had no choice but to get in line and finish out the game, which my team won. Go us. I ran a dutiful victory lap with my teammates, holding back a little to keep an eye on Sabine who seemed fine, although perhaps a little concerned by Bobby's ridiculous winner joy-leaps every few strides. We thanked each other, stripped off our vests and belts and handed them all to Bobby.

Sabine had been nabbed by Phil, who would undoubtedly be mortified to have injured her, and the moment he left, Mitch took his place. As I walked up behind them to intercept Sabine and send her to sick bay to get checked out, I caught the end of their conversation, which was Sabine's grumpy assertion of, "I'm sure."

I quickened my stride to draw level with them. "Fleischer, meet me at sick bay immediately."

Her mouth twisted for a moment before she conceded, "Yes, ma'am." As I walked off ahead of them, I could hear her barely audible but clearly frustrated, "Fuuuuck. Seriously?"

Yes, Sabine. Seriously.

Sabine jogged up beside me. "Colonel Keane? Ma'am? I'm fine, honestly."

Though we were alone, I kept my voice low. "I watched you fall, Sabine. You hit your head. You're getting checked out and you need that elbow cleaned. Don't argue." I glanced over at her, my eyes softening the moment they made contact with hers. She was clearly resigned to being checked out—an apparent torture in Sabine Fleischer-land—but it seemed despite that resignation, she'd placed some trust in me. Maybe we were getting somewhere on the self-care thing for her.

She exhaled a sigh. "Yes, Colonel."

We walked in silence toward the main hospital building, and Sabine opened the door for me, falling in just behind. Liz Davies, the nurse on sick bay duty, looked surprised when we both walked in. "Colonel Keane. Captain Fleischer."

"Liz," I said warmly. "Sabine hit her head during a game of football and I'd like to check her. Can you grab her file for me, please?"

"Of course, ma'am." Liz rushed out of the room, leaving us alone. Alone.

I moved to the opposite side of the room, knowing if I was near Sabine, I wouldn't be able to keep from touching her. I checked the shelves for the equipment I would have had on me if I'd not just been out engaging in PT. "Take your shoes and socks off please."

She did as I'd asked and I wasted another minute looking through trays until I felt controlled enough to be beside her. I clicked on the penlight. "Any dizziness, nausea or headache?"

"A small headache, ma'am, but nothing acetaminophen won't fix. Maybe it's just from listening to Boyd complain about losing?" she wisecracked. The grimace every time she moved her head told me it was more than just a small headache.

I smiled at her mention of Boyd's whining, and brought the penlight up to examine her pupillary reflex, unsurprised when she helpfully widened her eyes for me. I inhaled slowly, and gave in, verbalizing a little of my fear. "I was worried, Sabine."

She very deliberately stared straight ahead at the light moving between her eyes, instead of looking at me. I hooked the penlight in the neckline of my sweaty tee and reached to palpate the back of her skull. As I tried to concentrate on what I felt under my fingertips, I had to ignore the sensation of my hip pressing against her knee, the sensation of her hair through my fingers. She was a statue, except for her eyes which watched my face with that intensity only she seemed able to muster.

"Any pain?" I turned to face her fully and took my hands away from her hair. Sabine's headshake was barely perceptible. I picked up her right arm to check the graze on her elbow, satisfied it was minor and would be fine once it had been cleaned up. Her skin was hot, slick with sweat and I imagined what it might feel like against mine, how it would taste if I were to slide my tongue between her breasts.

"There's some dirt and gravel in there," I said hoarsely. My throat felt so tight I didn't know how I'd even gotten the words out.

Sabine nodded and exhaled a sound that might have been a word. She leaned over, and I raised my eyes to find her face barely an inch from mine. Her eyes fell to my mouth and the anticipation of kissing her made my lips part. God, I wanted it so badly that every ounce of rationality fled. I lightly rested my hand on her thigh, felt the quick tension under my grip, and leaned in—

"I have it, ma'am." Davies's voice was both an unwelcome and welcome intrusion.

Sabine visibly startled and I stepped backward immediately. A quick glance behind me eased a tiny fraction of my panic. Davies was staring down at Sabine's file, clicking her pen in that obnoxious way she had. At that moment, I didn't care if she clicked it for the rest of the week. The trembling in my legs was so acute I felt I might wobble to the ground, and my chest was so tight I could barely draw a full breath. So close. Too close. What the fuck had I been thinking?

I cleared my throat. "Thank you. Can you scribe for me, please?" Liz noisily turned the pages of Sabine's file as I raised my index finger. "Follow it please, Captain." I kept my focus slightly to the side of her eyes, too scared to look her in the eye.

She tracked my finger and as her gaze moved back and forth, she managed to catch mine. I felt my expression mirrored in her face. She knew the truth as I did. Another heartbeat and it would have been over. I would have kissed her, and I knew nothing with more certainty than I knew that she would have kissed me back. We were a fraction of a second from risking *everything*. From having everything. I couldn't look at her anymore and forced myself to keep my eyes from hers as I moved through the rest of my exam.

Her heart rate was elevated and the raised-eyebrows look she gave me was a silent, "Can you blame me?"

I ran through a basic neurological exam—had her press her feet to my hands and do basic motor skills and cranial nerve checks—all of which she passed. I finished up by checking her patellar reflex and Sabine laughed when her knee jerked. "Sorry, ma'am." She laughed again but it sounded forced, as if she was trying to act like everything was fine and fun, not like we'd just come within a millisecond of breaking US Army regulations and being caught. "It always reminds me of the time I kicked a doctor in the groin when I was a kid."

"I think we've all done that, Captain." I smiled, though it felt so forced my cheeks ached. Adrenaline still flooded my body and made me feel simultaneously aroused and terrified. When I extended my arm, Davies dropped Sabine's file in my hand and I took my time checking Liz's notes, trying to calm the turmoil and change my expression so I was no longer afraid of giving myself away. "You can put your shoes and socks on."

"I'm cleared, ma'am?" Sabine asked.

Deliberately, I kept my eyes from her face. "Yes. All fine."

Sabine nodded. "I appreciate the confirmation, Colonel." She slid off the table and leaned against it to balance while she pulled her boots back on. I watched her double-knot the laces in her usual careful way.

When I realized how much I'd been staring, I held up Sabine's file. "Can you take this back please, Davies? Also, would you mind cleaning up the graze on her elbow, please?" I could have done it myself but was suddenly desperate to get away from Sabine. The space felt airless, too hot.

Liz nodded. "Of course, ma'am."

I let my gaze linger on Sabine for as long as I dared. "Enjoy your evening, ladies." Then I turned and left the room without another word. Another look. Another forbidden thought.

The realization of what might have happened made me feel suddenly nauseated, and I had to lean against the wall outside sick bay. But I couldn't stay there in the hallway panicking over the shambles of my life. Thankfully nobody stopped me en route to my office and once I was safe in my space, I closed the door and collapsed into my chair. My skin felt electrified at the memory of what we'd almost done. At the fact we'd almost been caught. She'd been so close I could almost taste her. I was such a goddamned hypocrite. I'd once sent two good surgeons home for having a sexual relationship, yet here I was, coming *so close* to the same thing myself, and in a far less acceptable way.

But now I was certain of two things. One, there *was* something mutual between us—chemistry, attraction, lust, love even from my side. And two, I had no idea what to do about it. We'd both climbed aboard this runaway train, and I felt utterly helpless—I couldn't stop it, and we were moving far too fast to jump off now.

CHAPTER EIGHTEEN

Sabine had left for her R&R without fanfare, leaving me at Invicta without her for eleven days. And every single one of them felt like torture. More than anything, the unresolvedness ate away at me, and not being able to talk to anyone about it left me constantly stewing, wavering between dread and excitement. The tightrope I'd been walking now felt so much narrower, and I wondered how much longer I could keep my balance on this sliver of my desire and my forbidden feelings.

If anything noteworthy happened during those eleven days, I didn't remember it. My only conscious thoughts were how stale it felt without her around, layered on top of my ever-present concern about Linda's health. It seemed I was one of the few people worried about Linda; my friend continued to act like it was nothing more than a cold which would go away soon.

When I strapped myself into the C-17 that would fly me home, the sense of relief was acute. I needed to get away. It was utterly ridiculous to feel such a sense of longing and loss—Sabine wasn't dead. I'd be seeing her again in a week when I returned. Assuming I didn't cave and call her while I was stateside to talk about this thing that was about to boil over between us.

I slept for most of the flight and let myself into my apartment just after three p.m. Right away, I noted either Linda or someone doing her bidding had done a mini-deployment-return routine on the place. There were fresh linens on my bed and the basics of coffee, fruit, milk, bread, and cereal in the kitchen. My plants were all in the start of their death throes and in a desperate attempt to break the plant deployment-death cycle, I spent fifteen minutes watering, fertilizing, removing bugs and dead leaf debris from the planters. But I had a feeling I was too late. As always. Maybe I should just scrap the planters altogether and have a garden of garden gnomes.

Linda had texted to tell me to come around if I felt up to it, which I did, and dress up for dinner so she could "have a hottie on each arm at the restaurant." I showered off my flights, and dressed in a seafoam-green silk blouse and dark-gray skirt that should suit a range of venues. It felt good to put on a skirt, and I took my time with my makeup and hair before applying perfume, transferring things into a handbag, grabbing my trench coat, and slipping into pumps.

The woman who answered Linda's door was a tall, natural redhead with laughing blue eyes. Michelle. She pulled me into a hug before I'd said anything beyond, "Hi, I'm—" and dragged me inside to the couch where Linda was reading a medical romance novel.

Michelle was the polar opposite of my friend. Where Linda was impulsive, loud, irreverence and charm galore, Michelle was quiet and watchful, gently humorous and witty. The strength of their connection was obvious, and the part of me that I allowed to think about the fact my best friend was dying was beyond grateful that she had someone like Michelle for her final months.

Once Linda and I had let go of one another after our tight reunion hug, Michelle smoothed Linda's hair behind her ears before leaning down to kiss her. "I'll leave you two to catch up before dinner." She smiled warmly at me. "We'll have plenty of time to get acquainted later."

I returned the smile. "Absolutely."

Linda patted the couch and I sat beside her, kicked off my pumps and dragged a leg up underneath myself so I could face her. She looked much the same as when I'd last video called with her, though perhaps she'd lost a little more weight. Linda looked me up and down and once she was done with her appraisal—which I'd apparently passed—said, "Fuck, you look amazing. Now, come on, let's get it out of the way."

"How're you feeling?" I asked immediately. I left it there, though it took everything I had to not push at her with questions.

"Good days, bad days. Overwhelmingly good at the moment." Her smile had a touch of weariness. "I'm not looking forward to when the bad outweighs the good." Linda glanced at the wall clock. "Come outside with me. We can talk out there. I need some air before dinner." She pulled a small box from the drawer under their coffee table. Once we'd settled on the Adirondack chairs on her rear porch, she opened the box and pulled a pre-rolled joint from a pile.

I watched her light it and take a deep drag. "Does that help?"

"A little with the pain and my appetite which are starting to increase and decrease respectively. Feels better than being doped to the gills with pills. Plus, why the hell not?" True, she'd always enjoyed a little relaxing pot here and there. She offered me the joint, along with a naughty grin. "Want some?"

"Tempting, and if I was twenty years younger, I'd be all over it." And also not employed by an institution which frowned upon such things.

She smiled around a puff and once she'd exhaled, said, "Being responsible sucks."

"Oh, I'm well aware of that."

"Mmm." After another slow puff, she asked, "How are things with your captain? Sabine." She drew the name out teasingly, apparently trying to sound sexy. Or something.

"Nuh-uh. No. We're not talking about that. This might be one of the last chances we get for some deep and meaningful in-person conversation before—"

"I croak?"

I swallowed and ran my tongue around my lips. "Right. That. I don't want to waste it talking about…that thing."

"What if I do? I want to talk about *everything*. Especially that." She fluttered her eyelashes. "You'd really deny me the chance to meddle in your love life before I die?"

"Goddammit, you're impossible." I reached out my hand and Linda took it, squeezing my fingers.

"I know. But I'm also right." She turned on the chair, hooking a leg over the arm. "And I suppose this is where I tell you that I've decided to go ahead and have treatment."

It took me a moment to process the subject change and my answer was a choked, emotional, "That's incredible. I can't tell you how… grateful I am that you even considered it, let alone have decided to take steps to prolong your time. When do you start?"

"The day after we get back from Canada."

I let out a loud, exaggerated sigh. "So, you mean to tell me you dragged me home from a deployment in Afghanistan to attend your wedding because you were about to die and *now* you're just going to go ahead and live a few more years? Geeze."

Linda laughed, wisps of smoke curling out of her mouth. "Yeah well, what can I say, seeing you on that last video call changed my mind."

"Really?"

She grinned. "No, but it did factor in very highly. Michelle and I had already been talking about it and she made me realize I was being selfish by not wanting to go through it. But we made a compromise— if my quality of life goes to utter shit then I get to call stop, no more."

"I think that sounds fair." I leaned back in the chair, trying to process the news. I'd spent weeks coming to terms with the fact she was going to die soon, and the emotion of that was still in there, but was now waiting to be turned into something less immediately devastating.

Linda fluttered her eyelashes again. "So now that I'm more or less guaranteed to live past the end of the year, let's forget about cancer and get back to your problem. Because, my darling, it's a fucking big one."

"It is," I agreed.

"So why not tell her how you feel?"

I was pretty sure Sabine already knew, especially given our almost-kiss in the sick bay. I'd thought about that moment so many times and every time, I had the same feeling. Excitement that was quickly smothered with panic at how close we'd come to breaking the rules *and* being caught. "I can't do that. It's really not allowed. I cannot stress that enough." Unease settled in the pit of my stomach.

An eyebrow slowly rose. "Yeahhh, you keep saying that and yet here you are, in love and pining over someone you say you can't be with. If you really want to be with her then you're not going to let anything stop you."

"Something *is* stopping us. Something huge and immovable. The Army. And my own morality." Which had been worn down so much that it now felt paper-thin.

"Whatever. Carpe diem and all that shit. Also, I note the absence of you refuting the *being in love*."

I chose not to acknowledge that obvious statement. "Can I just tell my bosses 'Whatever, carpe diem'? Maybe the president too? I'm sure that'll make it all right and neither of us will be kicked out of the military with a dishonorable to boot."

She flashed a facetious smile. "Sure. I'll write you a note. 'My best friend, Rebecca, is amazing and deserves happiness in her private life which will make her professional life even more productive and PS, your policies are fucking bullshit.'" Linda pinched out her joint and put the remainder back in the box. "Do you mind if we stay here and order in? Shame to waste your outfit, but suddenly I just don't feel like leaving the house."

"Of course not. Whatever you want."

"Thank you. We'll get something nice, considering you've been living on those…what are they called? Meal rations?"

"Meal, Ready-to-Eat," I supplied.

"Right. That. You've been living on those for god-knows-how-long, so it's your pick for what we have for dinner." She held out her hand.

I stood then pulled her up. "MREs are for people running field ops. We have real food either freshly made for us, or food that's prepackaged on trays and heated."

"Why you gotta burst my bubble of you being miserable over there and desperate to come home and see me?" she whined.

"I am miserable over there and do want to come home and see you," I parroted, smiling broadly at her laughing reaction. "But the food's fine, just bland, as you already know from your hot-sauce packages. Oh…I just realized I'm not going to have to find a new supplier for those as soon as I thought. Phew."

Linda wrapped an arm around my waist, leaning into me as she walked. It was a gesture of deep friendship, rather than her needing physical support. "I already told Michelle she has to be your condiment bitch when I'm gone."

"Perfect. Thanks. I think I want some amazing Thai." I paused, knowing Thai wasn't high on her list of favorites. "If you can stomach it."

"For you, I'll stomach it." She made a seesawing motion with her hand. "A little of it. I might just eat some mac 'n' cheese or something."

"You know, you'd fit right into the Army…"

Once we'd finished dinner, which was as amazing as I'd hoped for, Michelle once again melted away to let Linda and me chat. It'd begun raining, a light annoying mist, so we snuggled together inside on the couch where Linda again turned the conversation to me and Sabine. "Could you just like…be with her anyway and keep it a secret?"

"Sure we could." And we really could. "Except if it was ever found out, then see previous answers regarding career implosion. Plus, I don't want to live like that, knowing we're doing the wrong thing, hiding in the shadows and constantly worrying. I...*we* have enough of that as it is."

"Right," she mused.

Sighing, I admitted, "I hate this feeling."

"Love?" Linda squeaked out.

"God, no. I love love." Being with Linda had dragged my guard down enough that I stopped pretending. "This...weakness. It's not me. You know that. I'm not the person who just gives in to something just because I want it, especially when I know it's not reasonable for me to have it."

"Isn't admitting you're feeling weak a kind of strength?"

"Nice try. Don't go psychoanalytical on me, not now." I bumped her shoulder with mine. "I just don't know how much longer I can keep pushing this down, ignoring it, pretending like there's nothing between us. Even when I know the consequences. And thinking about it makes me feel so simultaneously excited and sick I don't know what the hell to do."

"So you're sure it's not just lust?"

I laughed dryly. "Oh, there's lust. Plenty of it. But it's more than that." I'd already given Linda my grocery list of what attracted me to Sabine, back when we'd first talked about her. "If I'd met her outside of work I would have asked her out right away."

"Are you certain there's a mutual attraction?"

I thought back to that moment in the sick bay, and all the other small moments that had passed between us. "I am. Yes, very certain. I'm also certain she's as aware of the stakes as I am." And that she would be discreet about what'd almost transpired between us. Or, my unfiltered base emotions piped up, what *might* transpire between us. We both had so much to lose professionally if we were ever found out. But what was sneaking around, hiding a relationship? Was that any better than not having a relationship at all? If we ever got to a relationship, which still felt so out of reach I wondered why I was even considering it a possibility. "So, basically I don't know what to do. Except hope I don't slip again."

Linda pounced. "Slip? There was a slip?"

Ah, goddammit. "Almost. There was a situation, it was emotionally charged, I thought she'd been hurt and we...got very close."

"Very close to what? Don't tell me you're fretting over something like standing close to her, or I swear to god I'll punch you."

"We stand close to each other all the time, it's part of the job." At Linda's withering look, I finally admitted, "We *almost* kissed. At work.

In a public place. And were almost caught." A wave of guilty nausea rolled through me.

She grinned maniacally. "Oh my fucking *god*. Why didn't you tell me sooner? Are you *serious*?"

"Deadly." I paused, and added, "Sorry."

She coughed out a laugh. "Funny." Linda grabbed my hand and squeezed it lightly. "Rebecca, this is more than just a little attraction and you need to deal with it while you have the chance. Carpe diem, remember?"

"How could I forget? You may as well have it tattooed across your forehead." She'd never been a stickler for rules, but had also never been so free and loose with doing whatever the hell she wanted—and encouraging others to do the same—either.

"I considered it. Maybe I'll get a sign I can hold up whenever I think a situation needs a little Latin action. What have you got to lose? Really? Aside from your job, let's pretend that's not an issue."

"My integrity. My reputation. My…control. You know this isn't me. I don't do things like this. I've never thought about crossing that line before. But every time I see her, all I can think about is being with her. Kissing her. Taking her to bed and—" My brain finally caught up to my runaway libido and I closed my mouth.

"Oh, go on. It was just getting interesting."

I flicked my fingertips against her arm. "Fill in the blanks yourself, you pervert."

"Already have," she assured me. "Look, I know I keep telling you to just go for it but most importantly—is this going to hurt anyone outside of you and her? Because that's a huge caveat of carpe diem, you know. What it really means is Seize The Day But Don't Be A Dick To Others While Doing That."

I took a few moments to consider it. "Given she's now single, no. And as for the work rules, I strongly believe nothing would change." I pulled myself back from where I'd jumped ahead of myself. Everything was based on a bunch of what-ifs that I wasn't even sure we would pursue. I *couldn't* pursue. But we needed to address it before we found ourselves in another situation like the one in sick bay. A situation where we weren't mercifully pulled back from the brink. I was leaning toward having an open conversation that acknowledged what felt like something simmering between us but also confirmed it could never boil.

But if it did boil… I set everything aside, and let myself pretend we were a couple, imagining how that scenario might bleed into work.

Both Sabine and I were intelligent and moral enough to recognize that in our current situation, allowing the personal and professional to blend at work was unacceptable. I simply wouldn't allow it. The principles I'd abided by for my entire career wouldn't let me treat her as anything more than a member of the unit. No special treatment.

I slumped against the back of the couch. "This is *so* unfair. To show me a woman I could see myself having a relationship with, to put her right in front of me like this, and then tell me it's not allowed. To put me in a work situation away from home, to make me lonely and longing for some companionship but to also tell me I have to remain alone, despite knowing there's someone I *could* maybe be happy and fulfilled with." I knew it was a childish and simplistic view of how things worked, but I was so fatigued from constantly censoring myself and couldn't hold back my thoughts.

"That is shit," Linda murmured. "And I know how hard this must be for you, know how much you pride yourself on following the rules. I'm sorry if me pushing is making it harder."

I laughed hollowly and leaned over to kiss her forehead. "It's okay. I know it's not intentional. And you're not saying anything I haven't thought to myself a million times."

Her eyes narrowed. "You've got The Face. What else aren't you telling me?"

"I…may have done a thing."

"Oh? Another thing that's not the thing where you almost kissed her?"

"Mhmm, yes. I may have sent her home for some rest and recreation leave. I thought about what you said about needing time to process her breakup and gave her the first available slot to come back to the States and deal with things for a few weeks."

"That's great." She gave me a double thumbs-up. "Excellent bossing."

"Yes. Excellent bossing." I cleared my throat. "She's here. In D.C., right now. Or maybe she's still with her family out of state. I don't know. But she might be here. She's going back to Invicta in a few days, so she probably is here."

Linda gaped. "What the actual fuck are you saying? Are you *kidding* me? She's in this city, and everyone you work with is overseas? It's like a movie where you've been sent on a business trip and nobody's therrrre to stop yooooou."

I shot her a withering stare. "Those are the facts, yes."

"So why, the *fuck*, aren't you with her right now?"

"Because I'm with you, for your wedding, remember?"

Linda eyed me slyly. "If you were here for just my wedding then why are you here for a week? You could have just popped over, met us in Canada and popped back again."

"I wanted to spend time with you while I could," I murmured. "And technically, it's not a whole week."

"Right." She lightly slapped her forehead. "Because I was being a dick and you thought I'd die before you left, right? Well, sorry, thanks to chemo etcetera, I'll be hanging around for a while longer yet, so consider this me kicking you out to go and see her."

"I—" That was as far as I got.

Linda reached over and gently massaged my shoulder. "What are you so afraid of?" she asked quietly. "Aside from the obvious."

"I'm afraid..." I paused, trying to get the words to come out. "I'm afraid of the hope. Because if I don't ask her, then there's no chance for her to tell me I'm out of line, that she doesn't really feel this thing the way I do. It's safe." But, I mused to myself, if I don't ask her then I'll never know for sure if we could have made something work somehow.

Linda echoed my thoughts. "And then you'll spend the rest of your life wondering." She tucked both hands behind her head. "So whatcha gonna do?"

"I guess I'll call her and then...I don't know. Fumble and panic like a teenager calling their crush to invite them to Homecoming. See if we can't reach some sort of arrangement?"

"Arrangement," she said dryly. "So sexy. An arrangement like... what?"

"Like where we agree that this thing between us can never happen." It hurt to think it, even more to say it.

"That's a shitty arrangement."

She was right, and I said nothing.

"So, are you calling her?"

"Right now?"

"Yes right now. You've wasted enough time already." She made shooing motions.

It was easier to give in than fight her on this one. The moment I went to unlock my phone, I cursed, "Goddammit, my phone's dead."

"Do you have her phone number somewhere else?"

I had all the necessary work phone numbers in the small black notebook I'd automatically tossed into my handbag. "I'm her boss, of course I do." Her boss. Those two words seemed to echo and fill my head, reminding me of why I needed to walk away.

Linda, apparently set on me seeing this through, dropped her phone on the coffee table. "Here. Go into the kitchen so I don't have to listen to you mooning at her."

Though my resolve was fairly weak at that point, I was surprised at how easily I caved. I took her phone and slipped into the kitchen with no plan except to try and clear the air. And even as I flicked through pages to find Sabine's number, I had no idea what I was going to say. Oh, hello, Sabine. Yes, it's me. Colonel Keane, your boss. I was just wondering if you wouldn't mind us trying out that kiss that was interrupted before, and perhaps something a little more intimate?

The phone rang not-quite three times before my call was cut off. The fact it happened so quickly made me suspect I'd been declined, rather than it ringing out. I'd probably decline unknown numbers during my recreation leave too.

The moment I came back, Linda's face fell. "Oh fuck, that was short. What did she say? Yes, get your ass over here right now. Or did she hang up on you?"

"There was no answer."

Linda pressed a hand to her chest. "Thank god." She took a few moments to position herself, then heaved herself up from the couch. "Now, I hate to be a downer after all that buildup, but I really need to sleep. Go see her, if you know where she lives thanks to that little book of yours, or go home and go to bed yourself. You've got bags under those baby blues and I need you looking wonderful in my wedding photos." She looked me up and down. "You look hot, you should really go see her."

I chose to skip over her *advice*. "I'll be back first thing tomorrow."

She waved dismissively. "Come back whenever. I don't mean literally, like make sure you're at the airport in two days so we can go do the married thing. Take care of what you need to." Linda hugged me, nestling her face into my shoulder. After kissing my cheek she said, "I'm not going to die before you get back. Pinky swear."

The words caught in my throat. "I don't want you to die at all. I don't know what I'm going to do without you."

She pulled back, holding me by the shoulders. "You'll move on. Or at least I hope you do. I hope you always remember me but I don't want you to let your life stall and fall apart because your best friend died. Respect my memory by living an amazing life. Hopefully with an amazing woman." Linda patted my butt.

"Is this where you tell me it'll be so much easier for you if you know I have a partner when you're gone?"

Her eyebrows shot up. "Shit, no. I hadn't even thought about using that guilt trip. But yeah, that, totally, it will be easier for me. So do something about it."

Do *what* about it?

Clearly picking up on my mood, Linda stroked the back of my neck. "I just want you to be happy. But, and I know I've said this before, I also know you need to make a decision that you can live with."

All decisions came with consequences, some more serious and far-reaching than others. Did I…*we* ignore desires, needs, wants, and break one of the most fundamental rules of the military? Or did I follow one rule of an institution that demanded everything of me while not wanting every part of me, only the bits it deemed appropriate? I'd never been a rule breaker, but if there was ever one rule I wanted to ignore, this was the one. I just had to decide if I could live with myself if I did.

CHAPTER NINETEEN

Though Sabine's house was lit up like someone was home, I had no idea if she actually *was* home or just had lights on as security. And if she was there, did she have company? The thought of her having taken a lover during her leave was unpleasant and uncomfortable. I forced that thought, and my feelings, aside. I had absolutely no claim on her and no right to any jealousy. But it was there, no matter how much I tried to stuff it down.

I took a moment to study the exterior of her house, a gray stone Tudor with blue and white contrast on the second story. I stared at the dim light emanating from two gabled dormer windows—one of my favorite architectural features—on the second story, trying to see shadows moving in the house. Nothing. Her front lawn, visible in the streetlights, was immaculately mown, and the path from the sidewalk free of debris. I strode right up to her front door and before I could second-guess myself, pressed the doorbell.

I pressed the doorbell again and heard the thud of someone running down stairs. The door flung wide open and Sabine snatched the wood just before the door hit the wall behind it, the movement jerking her almost comically off-balance.

Jesus. Christ. The sight of her, casual in jeans riding low on her hips despite her belt's best efforts and a faded Ramones T-shirt clinging to her torso made my mouth go dry. I'd seen her in uniform tees, of course, but those weren't tight like this. I really liked the tight.

She'd cut her hair, and instead of loose and layered around her face and shoulders or up in a ponytail or bun, it was now a stylish pixie cut that accentuated the strong line of her jaw and those glass-cutting cheekbones. Her expression clearly showed her thought of *What the hell is she doing here?* along with unmistakable pleasure.

My resolve for "just conversation" fell away. It didn't just fall away. It fell off a cliff into the deepest ocean, never to be seen again. And that little devilish voice in my head kept whispering that we weren't at work, we were off-base, two consenting adults, and what *might* happen was just a product of years of the Army's suppression. Blaming the institution for my weakness was wrong, but I needed something to blame other than that weakness. The urge to touch her was so overwhelming I had to clasp my hands in front of myself, holding tightly onto my fingers to keep my own body disciplined.

Her hand moved upward then dropped again. She straightened and when she spoke, the words were tight, hoarse. "Good evening, ma'am."

Certain she'd been about to reflexively salute, I dipped my head in acknowledgment. "Sabine." I felt an uncontrollable urge to fidget and gave in to it, adjusting my glasses. "May I come in?"

She moved back as if startled into action, pulling the door open with her. "Of course, yes, ma'am." As I moved inside, she asked, "May I take your coat, Colonel?"

The moment I stepped into her house all my self-doubt vanished, replaced by calmness, confidence. I knew I wasn't imagining the attraction crackling between us, and my certainty that Sabine understood what was at stake for both of us made my fear vanish. I wouldn't ask her and so she couldn't tell me. A flimsy, sneaky way to get around this but I didn't make the archaic absurd rule. I was simply forced to work within its guidelines.

"Thank you." I passed her my coat and turned on the spot to look around the open plan, modern kitchen, hardwood floors, Colonial furniture that didn't feel dated. It felt like Sabine, personal. I smiled at her. "We're not at work," I said, recognizing the impact of those words. "There's no need for *ma'am* or *Colonel*. I'd prefer it if you called me Rebecca."

She paused, and it was like all the alarm fell away from her. "Rebecca. Of course."

"You cut your hair. I like it." It was an entirely inadequate compliment, but telling her it made her look even more gorgeous was too much right now.

She reached up to push straying hair away from her eyes. "Thank you." A pink blush dusted her cheeks and neck.

"I called your cell. About forty minutes ago."

Her eye contact felt tenuous, as if she was struggling with not staring at my not-uniform. "Oh, right. Sorry. I'm just, well, I'm just sorting through some things. I didn't recognize the number, so..." Her smile was sheepish, as if conveying that she would have answered if she'd known the call was from me.

I flashed her a knowing smile. "This is a beautiful place. Have you lived here long?" I asked on my way to her kitchen. On the black granite countertop sat a bottle of 10-year-old Glenmorangie and a glass with melting ice and half an inch of scotch in it. The thought of tasting that on her lips made my throat tight.

Sabine followed me. "Almost six years." She sounded hopeful as she asked, "Can I offer you a drink, or something to eat?"

I placed my hands flat on the countertop. "Thank you, I already ate but I would like a drink." I gestured to the glass. "Whatever you're having, Sabine."

She grabbed a tumbler from the cabinet. "Ice?"

"Please."

She took her time breaking ice into the glass, then poured two fingers over it before holding the glass out to me. But she didn't let go right away and our fingers touched as the glass transferred. An innocent touch. But one that made me think of other, not-so-innocent touches. I drank a slow, careful mouthful, smiling at the welcome, familiar heat as the alcohol slid down.

And I smiled inwardly at her expression and her obvious attempts to keep her eyes north of my chest. The confirmation of her physical attraction to me, not that I really felt I needed it now, made me bold. "I'm sure you're curious about why and how I'm here."

Her grin was lopsided, perhaps a little tipsy and a little nervous. "I am, yes. Very curious actually." She crossed her arms over her breasts, tucking her hands into her armpits like she was afraid they'd give her away with their gestures.

I dipped my head, catching her eye. "Sabine, I came here because I wanted to talk to you, away from eyes and ears, and...regulations."

An eyebrow shot up as she stated, "You planned this overlap. That's why you were so specific about when I was to take my leave." She pulled a hand free to move between us, as if indicating we were somehow joined.

"Yes," I said. It obviously hadn't been my intention to start with, but when I'd realized the possibility it offered, I hadn't fought it.

"I wondered how you managed to have my R and R approved so quickly."

I smiled. "There are some benefits that come with rank, Sabine. Also, I was owed a rather large favor by someone higher up." Now my smile felt bolder, almost cheeky.

"Why?"

I decided right then to dispense with my own subterfuge. I wasn't fooling myself at all. I raised the glass halfway to my lips, murmuring, "I think you know why." I paused before adding, "I know you fly out tomorrow night."

Tomorrow she would fly back to Invicta and that would be the end of it. We would return to the dance we'd been doing ever since we met two and a half years ago. The dance where we both knew the steps but neither of us knew how to lead. The thought of returning to that unsatisfying life made my gut twist with both annoyance and longing. I swirled the glass to shake the ice free and finished the last mouthful. I'd left a small lipstick smudge on the rim of the glass, and I stared at the mark, thinking about other places I might possibly leave lipstick tonight.

Sabine's hoarse, "Another?" dragged me from my thoughts.

I held out the glass, noting how her gaze went immediately to my left hand. The left hand where my grandmother's ring usually was. Sabine refilled my glass and added another splash to her own. We both knew I was not going to be driving tonight. I wasn't going to be leaving tonight. "I'm not married, Sabine. I never have been. I thought that might have been obvious." I dragged the glass back, staring into it. The ice shifted, settling comfortably in the scotch. "I wear it at work to imply things about myself. Things which aren't true. Things to make it easier for me to do my job the way I need to, without people looking over my shoulder all the time." I drank a small mouthful. "Do you understand what I'm saying?"

"Yes," she said quietly.

"Good." I set the glass down and raised my eyes to find hers. "I'm so tired of pretending, Sabine. You have *no* idea how close I've come, so many times, to just...giving in." A sudden emotional weariness settled over me as I thought about how much I'd denied myself, and I only just held back my sigh. "In the examination room, I thought that was it and I would finally let go, rules and policies be damned."

There. I'd said it, put every one of my cards on the table. There was no turning around now, no taking it back. But there was no fear, no regret. The only sensation was one of relief, that I no longer had to hold this feeling inside myself.

Sabine inhaled shakily and dropped her free hand onto the countertop as if using it to steady herself. And I wondered if she felt the same crackling electricity as I did. The same rightness. The same almost desperate desire to touch without censure or interruption. Her expression left me with no doubt as to what she felt, what she wanted, which made all my conviction about rules and restraint float away. I pulled off my glasses and left them beside my barely touched drink, then slipped around to her side of the counter. At my approach, Sabine turned. I took the glass from her hand and placed it on the countertop.

Then I took another step toward her, conscious now of the lack of space between us. I hooked my fingers under her belt and pulled her even closer, making that space even smaller. Sabine exhaled a quiet gasp. A dozen emotions flashed over her face, but none of them settled long enough for me to decipher. What I didn't see was doubt, regret, or fear.

"What are you thinking?" I asked in a low voice, bringing my other hand up to rest against her waist. The muscle twitched under my touch.

"Nothing. Nothing important." Her teeth found the inside of her cheek.

It was a lie, or more likely her trying not to show that she was thinking the same thing as me. That I wanted to drop to my knees right where I was, drag her jeans and underwear down and bury my mouth in her heat. That visual was so arousing that I unconsciously clenched my thighs. I tilted my head, unable to stop my sly smile. "Then why are you chewing the inside of your cheek?" I touched it lightly with my fingertips before dropping my hand back to her waist. "You do it whenever you're contemplating something. You're not as good at hiding your feelings as you think you are, Sabine."

She exhaled loudly, shifting to lean back against the counter. "I'm thinking…everything. All at once."

"Do you want to know what I'm thinking?" I didn't wait for her response. "I'm thinking about how I've wanted to kiss you ever since the first time we worked together," I said, my voice rough with want.

Her fists clenched at her sides and she inhaled a slow, deep breath. With my heels on, we were almost the same height. It would take nothing to move those final inches and press my lips to hers, to taste what I'd been fantasizing about for years. Sabine was utterly still, except for the deep rise and fall of her chest. Now her expression turned almost frantic, as if she feared I might step backward, gather my things and leave. I waited, searching her eyes to see if there was the slightest hint of reluctance or hesitation. I found none. She gave the smallest, yet unmistakable, nod and lowered her eyes to my mouth as I leaned in. I paused, wanting to savor the anticipation for just a moment longer.

Then I kissed her.

As my lips touched hers, Sabine made a sound that had my stomach tightening in anticipation—a little sigh mixed with a groan, as if she'd finally been given what she'd been asking for. The kiss began slowly but built quickly, and though she was anything but tentative, Sabine let me lead. She tasted like scotch and spice, felt warm and soft under my hands and lips. The exploration, this discovery, was like nothing I'd ever experienced, and I couldn't hold back. I ran my tongue lightly along her lower lip and Sabine exhaled, her lips parting to admit me. She finally touched me, both hands cupping my face as her tongue played against mine.

I pulled back, needing a moment to reset myself. But Sabine followed, her expression hungry, lips parted as if she couldn't bear that we were no longer kissing. I placed a hand on her shoulder to give myself an inch of breathing room. "You taste exactly the way I always imagined," I murmured.

She smirked, but underneath the cockiness I caught a hint of vulnerability, as if she still wasn't entirely sure how much I really wanted her. "You thought I had a secret stash of scotch somewhere in my room?"

I laughed. "No. I may have sought you out earlier if I thought that was the case." I slid one hand up to grip the back of her neck and let my other hand roam to her ass. I kissed the base of her neck where it met her shoulder, then slowly ran my tongue up her neck, delighting in her shiver before continuing upward, licking the light tang of salt from her skin, until I'd reached her ear. "You taste like desire," I whispered.

Sabine groaned quietly, melting against me. I pressed myself firmly against her as we kissed again, aware that I was pressing her back into the hard countertop. But if she was uncomfortable, she didn't show it. The arousal I'd been trying to contain broke loose and I gripped the bottom of her tee, frantic to touch skin. Sabine maneuvered us so I could pull the shirt over her head, leaving her torso exposed except for her plain black bra.

I took a moment to indulge myself in the small swell of her breasts, before tracing my nails lightly over her belly, mapping her with my fingers. She was exactly as I'd imagined—lithe and muscular with gentle curves and dips. There was a scar over her right hip and I lightly touched the mark with my fingertips. "Appendix?"

Sabine nodded and I continued my journey upward, watching goose bumps appear where my nails had been. I wanted so desperately to have her naked on top of me, but I forced myself to keep that small distance, to be slow. The lack of body contact was necessary for what I was doing, but so unsatisfying. I reached around and unhooked her bra, tossing it away. I indulged myself and admired her breasts, her tight nipples. But as desperate as I was, I didn't touch. Instead, I teased the button of her jeans open and slid her zipper down, letting my knuckles rub against her.

I hadn't allocated much thought to the garment I'd find underneath her jeans but when I saw a scant piece of black lace—a thong—my pulse increased, thudding heavily in my ears. "That is not what I expected, Sabine." I found her eyes and slowly, lightly, brushed my hand over the lace. My voice caught. "It's incredibly hot."

Her breathing was audible as I continued my exploration of her body, leaving more goose bumps where I'd touched. Sabine let out another soft moan as my fingers traced the underside of her breasts and she pressed forward as if begging me to touch her properly. Soon… I could touch her soon. When I softly gripped her jaw and brushed a gentle thumb over her lips, she demanded hoarsely, "Kiss me again."

I didn't hesitate, and as our lips and tongues began a sensuous dance, Sabine pulled me even closer. But she left enough room to work the buttons of my blouse free so she could slide it from my shoulders. Her fingers danced over my bare collarbone in the lightest touch, almost reverently. I bit my lip on a moan as she cupped my breasts with both hands, her thumbs caressing my nipples. She inhaled sharply as I arched my back, pressing my breasts into her touch.

"Sabine…" My throat felt tight with want, my voice raspy. I was beyond rational thought, acting now on nothing but pure need. I didn't want to think, I just wanted to feel. I had never felt such desperation nestled alongside my desire, an almost panicked sensation that heightened both my arousal and the anxiety, that maybe this wouldn't happen. That she'd pull back and ask me to leave and I'd be left as I had been for the past two years. Wanting.

She became utterly still, as if hit by a wave of indecision. I knew exactly how she felt, had felt the same uncertainty where everything was too intense and my want too great. Her eyes searched mine and I could see their plea, as if she wanted me to tell her, help her. But I kept myself still, though all I wanted was to take the lead and guide her mouth to my breasts and her hands between my thighs. But more than my own want, I needed her to lead this. I was so aware of the dynamic of our relationship and the control I had over her there, that I wanted her to take control here.

I was conscious of the inequality of our relationship outside this house and would willingly give control over to Sabine. Some distant part of me wanted her to know that what we were doing right now had nothing to do with work. And perhaps I wanted to relinquish my command for the night, to let her tell me exactly how she wanted to spread me apart and fuck me, how much she wanted to make me come in her mouth.

Sabine leaned in to kiss my neck and across the curves of my breasts. I stepped out of my shoes as she began to push her jeans down, but when she saw what I was doing, she went still again. I unzipped my skirt and shucked out of it, taking my panties too. As I was removing the last of my clothing, I kept eye contact with Sabine. Her mouth fell open and she made no effort to control her focus, her gaze moving slowly down my body as if it was devouring me. When her eyes finally came back to meet mine, the heat in them made my stomach clench.

Sabine inhaled and then exhaled a shaky, "Rebecca, I...Christ."

I bit my lip on a smile. She had just verbalized my dumbstruck awe when I'd looked at her, touched her, and I hadn't even seen her fully naked yet. Twisting around, I reached behind myself and hoisted myself up onto the counter. I wanted her pressed against my intimate places. She didn't resist when I gripped her hip and pulled her forward until she was nestled between my thighs.

Sabine leaned into me, using her hipbone to grind against my clitoris. I had fistfuls of her hair, desperate for something to center myself, but it was hopeless. The sensation of her between my spread legs sent a shudder coursing through me, which intensified as her mouth closed around my nipple. Sabine's hot, wet mouth explored my breasts, lavishing each with attention as her hip kept pressing and pressing and pressing until I felt my arousal slick and hot against her skin.

I gave in to the sensation and ground against her, aware of my vocalizations and that my grip on her hair and my nails digging into her shoulder were perhaps a little rough. But I couldn't help myself. Sabine rocked her hips into me and moved that teasing mouth away from my breasts. Her lips took a leisurely path over my collarbone, detoured across my shoulder, then made their way up my neck. She licked and kissed every inch of skin she encountered until she'd found my mouth again, and I accepted her kiss hungrily.

Without breaking our kiss, Sabine wrapped her arms around my waist and lifted me down from the counter. So desperate was my need that my immediate, hopeful thought was that she would drag me to the floor and fuck me right there. Instead, she twined our fingers together and led me out of the kitchen and upstairs to her bedroom.

CHAPTER TWENTY

At another time I might have been curious about a new lover's bedroom, but the only thing on my mind when we stepped through the doorway was removing the remainder of Sabine's clothing. I'd denied myself in the kitchen, deliberately keeping my mouth from her body, knowing if I tasted her I'd have to have her and then all our delicious sensual foreplay would be over. But the small respite of our relocation from kitchen to bedroom had settled only a fraction of my desire.

Sabine pushed me against the wall just inside the doorway and kissed me with such deep ferocity that my legs trembled. The way she pressed her body against mine and the expert use of her lips and tongue had lust pulsing through me. Abruptly, Sabine pulled back, but left her forehead resting against mine. The words she whispered were unexpected. "I'm sorry."

I gently cupped her chin in both hands to raise her face, searching her eyes for answers. "For what?"

Sabine's forehead crinkled. "For being like this, so needy and overwhelmed. For wanting you so much."

A short laugh burst out my mouth. "And here I was thinking *I* was being needy and overwhelmed and wanting."

Her smile was unexpectedly shy, almost like she still couldn't believe I was so desperate to be with her, despite the fact I was naked in her bedroom. "Maybe just a little. Stripping your clothes off was kind of a giveaway." Her teeth found her lower lip. "A very hot giveaway."

"Maybe just a little," I agreed. I'd surprised myself with my boldness, but there was no regret, no self-consciousness. I gave in and nuzzled her neck, grazing my teeth over the smooth skin until an unpleasant thought intruded. This time it was me who pulled back. "Sabine?"

"Yes?"

I knew she'd obviously consumed alcohol, as had I, but I didn't sense she was incapable of making a decision or giving, or refusing, genuine consent. But I had to be sure. "Before we go further, I just…I want to be clear that you don't have to do this. I know we've established that there's an attraction between us, but I also need to be sure that you don't somehow feel obligated to be with me just because I'm your boss." The moment the words were out, I shook my head. "Sorry, that sounded a little offensive. I didn't mean—"

I saw a flash of her irresistible smile before she interjected, "I know what you meant, and I'm perfectly capable of making a decision for myself. Perfectly capable of consenting to this. And I don't feel obligated, not by a long shot." She exhaled, the sound a relieved rush of air. "Rebecca, I've been thinking about touching you, about having my mouth on you, about fucking you, almost from the moment we met. But this is more than just a crush or an attraction for me, more than just wanting something quick and easy."

"Me too," I breathed. "So much. But just because I want you so damned much doesn't mean you can't stop at any time. I mean I don't want to stop. I want to feel you coming in my mouth, around my fingers, but you're in control here. And…what happens here is totally separate from what happens at work." Work. Where this wasn't allowed. I buried the thought. I didn't want it here with me now. I wanted to savor every moment, every single tantalizing, delicious inch of her, without thinking about anything else.

Sabine's mouth quirked into a facetious grin. "Wait, hold up a minute. You mean you're not going to promote me to major in the morning if I sleep with you?"

Around my laughter I managed, "Be quiet, you." I would have kissed her to keep another cheeky remark from slipping from her mouth if she hadn't gotten in first.

I cupped her small, tight breasts and as my thumbs played over her nipples I traced a path with my tongue from her ear, down her neck and over her collarbone. Sabine inhaled a shaky breath when I sucked her shoulder before bending my head to continue my path to her breasts. She smelled citrussy, the same lotion she wore at work, and after a slow inhalation I replaced one thumb with my mouth. Sabine's hand rested on the back of my head, her fingers playing through my hair as she held me gently against her breast.

As I lightly bit her nipple, she pressed the tips of her fingers into my scalp and when I moved to give the same attention to her other nipple she tugged my hair. Her ragged breathing as my mouth and hands paid attention to enticing areas of her body sent a surge of excitement through me. She was gorgeous, intoxicating. And still far too dressed.

I hooked my fingers in the waistband of her jeans, gathered the lace of her underwear with it, and pulled the garments down. As I slid the jeans down her thighs, I knelt and helped her step out of them. She had a hand on my shoulder as if steadying herself, and I felt it mirrored in myself, her hand an anchor to keep me from floating away. I had never felt such a deep ache of want before; the years of desire and denial bubbling over to turn me into someone I didn't recognize. Someone acting on instinct. No thoughts, just actions.

I ran my hands up the back of her calves and thighs to her ass. Sabine's thighs tensed as I pulled her toward me and pressed my face against her. I kissed the smooth, tight skin of her belly, licked my way over her hipbones and down to her neatly trimmed patch of pubic hair. I could smell her arousal and the thought of tasting it made my breath catch. "May I?"

Her response was a hoarse, "God, please. Yes."

The moment she consented, I covered her labia with my mouth. Sabine sucked in a quick breath, the hand that had been on my shoulder moving up to take a light fistful of hair. After a deep breath to settle my excitement, I gently dragged my tongue through her folds. Sabine's grip in my hair tightened and I took my cue, slowly tasting her, enjoying her, until I found her clitoris.

Sabine shuddered. As I traced my tongue around her clitoris, I groaned unconsciously. It took everything I had to not devour her roughly, and I held tightly to her thighs, trying to ground myself, slow myself. But Sabine's breathing grew more ragged and my own excitement and anticipation came to the point I could no longer ignore it.

When I slid my fingers up the inside her thigh, she set her legs wider, inviting me to fuck her. And I accepted. Her arousal was thick and hot, and as I pushed my fingers slowly inside her, we both moaned.

The telltale clench and flutter around my fingers told me her climax was imminent and I sped up my thrusts, softening my tongue against her clitoris. Sabine's thigh quivered under my hand and after a sharp inhalation, she begged, "Wait. Rebecca, wait. Stop, please. I don't want to come yet. Not yet. Please."

I couldn't hold back my sound of disappointment, even as I knew the best was still to come. But I withdrew my touch, my tongue, and kissed the sweat-slick skin of her inner thigh. Sabine pulled me up and against her, cupping my face and sliding her thumbs down my cheeks. "I love these dimples," she murmured.

She kissed one cheek then the other before her mouth found mine again. This kiss was slow, sensual, and we spent long minutes languorously exploring and learning more about each other. She liked to graze her teeth lightly over my lip, but when I'd move to suck her lower lip she'd dance her mouth away for the briefest moment before coming back to acquiesce. Her hands found the places that made me want to beg and as we kissed, she softly stroked, firmly kneaded, gently caressed.

When I thought I'd collapse with desperation, she turned me away and pulled me roughly back against her. Her bare skin against my back made me shudder and I pushed into her, delighting in how she pressed herself into my ass. Sabine's hands came back to my breasts, and as she teased my nipples with her fingers, her lips and teeth traveled over my neck and shoulders. "What do you want?" she mumbled against my skin.

I didn't hesitate. "I want you to fuck me until I can't talk, until I can barely think." I turned slightly to catch her gaze, unsurprised by the heat I found there. "I want you to fuck me the way I'm going to fuck you, like I've been desperate to do it since I first saw you."

Her low groan as she turned me back toward the wall had my stomach twisting with anticipation. I'd need to brace myself against that wall pretty soon. Her right hand remained to pinch my nipples while her left moved down to rest over my belly, teasing me, until she moved lower…and lower…and lower. The movement of her fingers through my arousal was slow, teasing, and when she found my clitoris, she lingered lightly. The soft touch made me jerk in her arms, and that touch became not-so-light and not-so-lingering. I would have done anything to keep her fingers there. As she kept up that teasingly torturous motion, Sabine bit my shoulder before she kissed her way up my neck and along my jaw until I turned my head to meet her lips with mine.

"Please," I begged, kissing her again.

She dragged her hand away from my breast and I felt it cup my ass before she pressed it between my thighs. Sabine indulged herself, sliding her fingers through my labia until she found my entrance. She lightly stroked, murmuring, "Can I?"

I couldn't think, let alone speak, and I nodded for her to please, yes, enter me. Please fuck me. Please make me come. My breath caught when two fingers slid inside me with what felt like the barest pressure. Sabine paused, her mouth coming to my neck, before she began a steady rhythm. She fucked me right there, standing just inside her bedroom doorway. I pressed my palms to the wall as her confident, knowing fingers drove deep and hard inside me from behind at the same time as her gentle fingers stoked my clitoris.

The pleasure was so intense I felt like I was about to hyperventilate and had to take some deep, slow breaths. Sabine's ragged breathing was in my ear, against my neck, and I reached back with one hand to grab the back of her head to pull her closer so I could kiss her.

Sabine's tongue was surprisingly gentle considering how hard she was fucking me. When she hit a particularly sensitive spot I exhaled a moan and felt her reciprocal shudder, as if my verbalizing my pleasure gave *her* pleasure. My climax had been building steadily, but that sound undid me. The orgasm was a sudden wave of pleasure, a rush so intense I could barely think. And as that pleasure flooded my core and my legs went to jelly, she held me tight, kept kissing me, kept me from falling, kept stroking me through my climax.

Without breaking the kiss, Sabine turned me in her arms and walked me backward to the bed. Before I could think, she'd lain me down on my back, settling herself between my spread legs. Her kiss cut off my protest and the sensation of her against my already sensitive flesh sent fresh excitement through me. At my shudder, Sabine pulled away a fraction. "Can you come again?" She licked her lips. "Now?"

I cupped her ass, ran my hands lightly up and down her back. "That depends." Though my desperation to fuck her was overwhelming, the idea of her fucking me again was admittedly tempting.

"On what?"

"What you're planning…"

Her answer was a sly grin before she propped herself up to take first one then the other nipple into her mouth. She sucked and licked, lightly bit until that pleasure-pain had me squirming underneath her. Sabine held my wrists to the bed as she shifted to straddle my leg, her thigh pressed between mine. Her slick heat coated my skin and the thought of tasting that again made my clitoris throb. I lifted my hips, trying to get more friction, but Sabine refused and moved herself so she'd withdrawn all contact from between my thighs. And, heroically, from between hers as well.

Her mouth moved over my breasts, my ribs, down my belly, and as she mapped my body, little growls emanated from her as if she was having a bout of possessive lust and just couldn't help herself. She lifted her eyes to find mine. "My *plan* is for you to come in my mouth." The sound of her verbalizing her passion was *so* sexy. She roughly pushed my thighs apart and waited for me to nod my assent...my desperation...my desire, before she slowly lowered her head and put her mouth on me.

The sensation of her tongue languorously sliding through my labia was exquisite, and I gripped fistfuls of the sheets to keep myself from clamping smothering thighs around her head. I'd been excited to be with her and see how, when we were completely bared for one another, she might differ from the Sabine I already knew. Of course I'd imagined what she'd be like. But my imagination had absolutely nothing on the reality of just how sensual she was. She seemed to just... let herself go, pouring herself completely into pleasuring me. Sabine took every cue, even those I didn't realize I'd given her, adjusting her pressure, speed, tempo, until the unmistakable sensation of my second climax began to build.

I let go of the sheets, fumbling for something to grasp, *needing* something more solid to hold on to. Sabine took my hand, sliding our fingers together, then with her free hand, guided my other to my breast. She used my fingers to pinch my nipple and the sensation of her guiding me to do what she wanted, what *I* wanted, sent my excitement over the edge.

I tightened my grip on her hand until it felt white-knuckled, and was utterly unable to hold back my hoarse, "Oh my g—oh!" as I climaxed. Sabine stayed with me, her tongue lightly dancing over my clitoris, as arousal rolled through my body, leaving me squirming and unable to do anything except enjoy the intense, overwhelming pleasure.

When I had some of my faculties back, I ran my hand through her hair, trying to articulate how I felt, other than completely and utterly satisfied. I managed a weak, "I feel so greedy."

Sabine propped herself up on an elbow, the other hand playing over my thigh. She smiled that devastating smile, and this time it had a touch of coyness. "Don't worry, Rebecca. I promise, you're going to make it up to me." Sabine shifted from between my legs, moving up the bed until she lay on her back. After tugging me close for a long, heated kiss, she gently pushed me down, spreading her legs in anticipation. "Starting right now."

Her desperation was clear from the tight quiver of her muscles, the restless movement of her legs, and her tight grip on my arm. I indulged myself a little, feasting briefly on her nipples as she murmured, "Yes, just like that…yes…"

I licked a path from between her breasts right down to her pubic hair. Her glistening arousal was evidence enough that she'd enjoyed herself as much as I had. I softly dragged a finger through her labia. "You are so, so wet." I'd already tasted her, held her right on the brink, and now I was going to feel her glorious climax in my mouth.

Sabine arched an eyebrow. "Can you blame me? It's because of *you*. You're so—ahhh, fuck."

My tongue on her clitoris cut her off, and her thighs clenched around my shoulders as I lightly circled and sucked. Sabine exhaled a shaky laugh which turned to a strangled gurgle when I tongued her entrance. She fell back on the bed, bending her knees to bring her feet flat on the bed, giving me unrestrained access to what I wanted. With every stroke of my tongue, her breathing hitched higher until she was almost gasping. "I don't even…just…that, please keep doing that. Right there."

I gripped her hips harder, holding her in place as I enjoyed myself in her arousal. She was so responsive to every touch that I lost myself completely in her, and as she quivered underneath me, I had no thoughts except how utterly perfect this was, this one moment in time. And if we never had this again, then at least I would always have this memory of her completely unrestrained in her passion.

Sabine's feet moved restlessly up and down my sides and I felt the tightening in her thighs as they clamped around my shoulders. She raised herself up slightly and cupped my face, pulling me up ever so slightly so we made eye contact as I licked and sucked her toward her climax. Sabine swallowed hard. "Rebecca…" That one word, my name, was a reverent whisper. Her entire body went taut and that intense eye contact never wavered, staying with me as she rode out her orgasm. Watching her climax sent a ripple of reciprocal pleasure through me, and I barely held back my moan as I kept my mouth against her clitoris.

Eventually, her body went slack and she fell back to the bed, gulping down air. "Oh my god," Sabine murmured, her fingers slipping over my sweat-slicked shoulder as she tried to pull me closer. "Come up here." When I moved up beside her, she pulled me against her side, keeping her arm around my waist. "I feel like I should say something really profound, but I can't even think after that. That was…it was… incredible?"

"It was," I agreed, kissing her shoulder. It was an entirely inadequate description, but my capacity for allocating words to something so precious had departed me as well.

She rolled over so we were face-to-face and framed my face with her hands. "Thank you. For coming around. For trusting me." Sabine kissed me so tenderly that I almost felt I might cry. She gathered me close, stroking tenderly up and down my back as we lay silently together.

After a few minutes, she laughed, the sound coming from nowhere and incongruous with our postcoital bliss bubble. I raised myself up to look at her, both curious and amused. "What?"

Sabine's mouth twitched. "It's stupid, obviously. I was just thinking if I'd known you had this secret stash of amazing sex in your room…" Then she parroted my words back at me, barely keeping herself restrained enough to get them out. "I may have sought you out earlier if I thought that was the case."

I laughed with her. "Maybe you should have."

"Mmm," she agreed. "I think it would have made things a lot easier. And a lot harder." She settled back on the bed, mirth apparently spent for now, and resumed her light caress up and down my back.

I relaxed against her, enjoying the simple pleasure of her nearness and the residual warmth from our intimacy. I drifted on the edge of sleep, and yet… Although I felt more settled, more satisfied than I had in years, a small discomfort wormed under my skin.

Even as I'd told myself that I was coming to see her simply to clear the air between us, I'd known I wanted something more. I'd come here hoping desperately for things to be different. I'd come to her house not as her boss, but as a woman who wanted something so desperately she was willing to risk both our careers for it. And now I knew I'd risk it again and again. This tiny taste of her, of what might be, hadn't sated my appetite at all.

It had made me ravenous.

CHAPTER TWENTY-ONE

I woke to muted light peeking through Sabine's curtains, finding myself snuggled behind her with my arm around her waist and my face pressed to her shoulder. The smell of her, the sensation of her warm naked body against mine and the memory of last night launched a fresh surge of desire through me, though now it was softer, less desperate. I delicately stroked her outer thigh, up her hip, along her ribs to her breasts before my fingers trailed down her belly.

She stirred, and I continued downward, purring a little as she spread her legs for me. "I got tired of waiting for you to wake up," I whispered before running my tongue along the edge of her ear.

"I can think of worse ways to be woken up," Sabine murmured. She rolled over to face me, her arm coming around my waist to pull me closer.

Unlike last night's raw desperation, this foreplay was gentler, sweeter. But no less sensual. I didn't think I could come again so soon, but when Sabine wriggled down the bed and underneath me, settling between my thighs, my arousal peaked again. She pulled me down onto her face, then strong, knowing fingers slipped into me as she slid her tongue through my blossoming arousal. It didn't take long until the first insistent threads of my orgasm began to wind through my body. She held onto my thighs as I climaxed, and I couldn't help but think of how *knowing* she was, how intuitive and giving a lover. It almost made me laugh, as if Sabine Fleischer would be anything but a perfectionist in bed too.

As my legs stopped trembling after my climax, I carefully climbed off her face and down her body, nestling between her thighs to take her in my mouth again until she cried out a hoarse, guttural sound as she came. I kissed the silky skin inside her thighs and propped myself up to look at her. Sexy. Sensual. And so damned gorgeous my heart felt like it was fluttering out of my chest. Sabine stretched, exhaling a kittenish squeak before she raised her head a little to look down her body at me. Her mouth quirked. "Do I still taste of desire?"

I laughed, thinking of my ridiculous attempt at seduction the evening before. Though given where I was currently, perhaps it wasn't so ridiculous… "Yes. And what about me? What do I taste of?"

She moved back to sit up against the bedhead, clearly taking time to consider it. She licked her lips. "I'm not sure yet," she finally said. "Something illicit maybe?"

We held eye contact and I raised a querying eyebrow. That wasn't the answer I'd expected, but I knew why she'd said it. "You've never done anything you shouldn't have?" I sat up and swung my legs over hers, reaching for the duvet to hold back the morning chill.

"Of course not!" she exclaimed, feigning horror. She offered me a quick wink that made me laugh. Sabine shifted to face me. "So, Colonel. You've wanted me ever since the first time we operated together?" The coy question was an obvious subject change and I decided to play along.

"More or less…Captain. Do you remember? You repaired that tricky liver laceration. Then you made a stupid pun about how he was going to live-r." It still made me laugh when I thought about it, years later.

"I remember…" she deadpanned.

I laughed again, both at her expression of mortification—which told me she wished she could forget it anew—and the fresh thought of her joke. "Then you flushed and gave me that helpless look, like you couldn't believe what had just come out of your mouth."

She shook her head as if she still couldn't believe it, but thankfully was laughing with me. "You've always made me nervously verbose. At first I thought it was just a case of hero worship, then I realized it was actually the huge crush I have on you."

I smiled at that, recalling how that had been my exact thought, that she'd just had a boss crush on me. Thankfully it was so much more than that. I moved my hand under the sheet and gripped her calf, lightly raking my nails over her bare skin. "What about you?" I was about to expand my question—as in, when did she first recognize her attraction to me—but Sabine had picked up the words my post-orgasmic brain hadn't been able to formulate.

"Probably…" She dragged the word out. "Our first flag football game. You were so different, as if you had a whole new personality. Lighter somehow. It was intriguing."

Intriguing. I knew exactly what she meant, having felt that exact same thing when I'd first seen her. This attraction between us has always been there, tucked away out of sight where we both tried to keep it from harming us. I still found it hard to reconcile how something that felt so good could be so dangerous. The thought made me shiver, and I pulled the duvet up around my shoulders.

As if sensing what I was thinking, Sabine said slowly, "You know… this has changed everything."

"I'm well aware of it, Sabine," I said carefully. I was all too aware of it. *It* was never far from my thoughts. Everything I'd done to this point had consequences weighed against it. I'd thought and rethought and agonized, and in the end, had simply decided to put myself first for once and manage what happened, if it happened. She and I were two consenting adults forced into a situation under which many people would have broken. Telling myself that eased perhaps one percent of my guilt.

Sabine gently twirled some of my hair between her fingers before she let it fall back against my neck. "What are we going to do? This isn't sustainable. Not back there." Her sigh was quiet, but unmistakable.

"I know." I looked away from her and tried to unclench my jaw.

She scoffed, "So it's longing looks across the OR? Hand brushes in the hallway? Maybe we can sneak a shower together and hope nobody catches us. Otherwise, it's waiting until we can try and get on leave together. Or better yet, we can wait four years until I've finished my service obligation and hope they don't care that a lieutenant colonel is fucking a reservist. Though by then you'd probably have made colonel, which is even better." Her voice rose in pitch and indignation with every point.

"I'm not sure. I don't have an answer," I said quietly. I wanted an answer, I wanted to give all the answers as to how we could sustain what we had. But I had none. Goddammit. What was I supposed to do and say? That I'd had years of emotional buildup between us, weeks of the emotional strain of thinking my best friend was dying, and I desperately needed to feel something *good*, a connection with someone, and I just gave in to my desire?

She was clearly trying very hard to be objective, to not fall apart. Her tone suggested she was about fifty percent successful. "I can't risk it, Rebecca. Not even for you. I'm contracted to the Army. If they find us together then I'll be discharged and I'll have to repay my HPSP debt. I'll have to repay it with a job I won't be able to get because they'll probably court-martial me and then it'll be a dismissal."

Dismissal—the commissioned officer's version of a dishonorable discharge. It was highly unlikely. "I think you're being a little dramatic. They're not going to court-martial you, Sabine."

"Really?" Her voice pitched up in disbelief. "Aren't we supposed to guard and suppress all dissolute and immoral practices, Rebecca, not indulge in them? And while we're talking about rules, I'm pretty sure what we're doing is also conduct unbecoming an officer."

I pushed aside all the unhelpful emotions and focused on her, forcing myself to at least appear relaxed. Getting upset wasn't going to help anything. But watching her rising panic was increasing mine. Despite all my weak rationalizations, what we'd done *was* wrong, and there was absolutely no way I could spin that to make it seem less so. But I would do it all over again in a heartbeat. I felt vaguely sick, and more uncertain than I'd felt before I'd had sex with her. "Calm down, Sabine. You've gone straight to worst-case scenario before anything's even happened." I inhaled deeply, hoping it might calm me. It didn't. "Look, I care about you a great deal. I just don't have a solution. Not right now."

She snorted dismissively, as if it were up to me alone to figure out how we could make this work without either of us suffering. That sound snapped the last of my fraying temper. "It's my ass too! You don't think I know this isn't allowed, and it could get me severely reprimanded? You don't think I'm not..." I clutched at fistfuls of air, as if I could grab the correct answer from out of the ether, "...*disgusted* with myself for being so weak?" I rolled over, slid out of bed and stalked to the bathroom.

As I sat on the toilet, I buried my face in my hands. Oh, Rebecca, Rebecca. What the fuck have you done? From the bedroom came Sabine's, "Rebecca?" After a minute, I heard a tentative, "Bec?" Then a quieter, "I'm sorry."

I hadn't expected her to apologize so quickly, and it pulled my anger away. After I flushed and washed my hands, I studied myself in her bathroom mirror. My reflection was the same as always, if not a little disheveled, but I knew I was now a completely different person. I'd done something I'd never thought I would do, even as I was fantasizing about doing exactly this.

A decision you can live with…

I'd made my decision, and now I was going to live with it. Reconciling that fact felt surprisingly easy and I felt more of my tension ease. Perhaps I'd always been reconciling it, deep down, knowing this was where I was heading. I opened the bathroom door to find Sabine right outside. I smiled in an attempt to soften my earlier annoyance. "My aunt called me Bec." Whenever I was feeling melancholy, she used to say it in a silly clown voice to cheer me up. It was special, because it was the only time she ever did it.

She smiled apologetically. "Sorry. It just slipped out."

"Don't be. I've always liked it." Her smile was contagious and I returned it. "Is there enough food in this house for both of us to have breakfast, or do we have to go out?"

"If you're happy with booze and my sister's frozen meal, then we can stay in."

"Pass. Let's go out." I looked her up and down, noting her T-Shirt which displayed her graduating year and a shopping list of her extracurricular activities. "Nice shirt. It reminds me of how much older I am than you."

We took a shower together to wash off the sex and only just managed to avoid more sex and making ourselves even later. I borrowed a toothbrush and deodorant before securing my wet hair with one of her hairbands. It all felt so heartachingly normal, and I couldn't help wondering if we'd ever have this normality again.

It had kept raining overnight and was threatening more, but the fresh, clean smell of rain on grass and asphalt felt so foreign that I took a few moments on her front path to indulge my senses. While Sabine dealt with her garage door I grabbed my sunglasses from my Audi convertible.

Sabine's car was not what I'd expected. I'd pictured her as a hybrid car kind of person, something small and unobtrusive. But she had a very large pickup truck, complete with a trailer hitch, and English horse-and-rider stickers adorning the back tray panel. If I'd had to imagine the owner of the truck, I would have immediately pictured someone butch, which Sabine really was not. But the stickers made something click in my mind. When I'd skimmed her file and résumé, horseback riding was listed as one of her hobbies. But she'd never mentioned it in any of our conversations and with her living and working in the city or being on deployment, I got the feeling horses were in her distant past. But she still had this horse-car and despite being an older model, the car was pristine.

Apparently she'd been sizing up my car as I had hers, and after opening the passenger door of her pickup for me, she indicated my convertible with a tilt of her head. "Great car. It's very…you."

"My one luxury. A friend keeps it safe while I'm away. It's the second thing I miss while I'm deployed."

"And the first?" she asked in a tone that made me think she already knew the answer.

I smiled and ran my hand up her thigh, keeping it there as she drove into town with the same care she allocated to everything. The rain was a steady drizzle, and without umbrellas we rushed down the street and into the first café we spotted. I chose a corner booth by a full-length window and slid in beside her.

The young server who'd shown us to the booth mumbled a few things then set menus on the table. Based on the vodka seeping from his pores, he probably should have called in sick today. Watching him pour coffee with his shaky, hungover hand, I marveled that he managed to get it all into our cups. He pulled a handful of creamer packages from his apron and dumped them in the small bowl in the middle of the table.

Sabine smiled up at him. "May I please have milk? Whole."

He frowned at her. Clearly her question did not compute. "Milk?"

I turned away, pinching my lower lip to hide my smile. It was on the tip of my tongue to tell him to make sure it was powdered and lukewarm.

"Yes please. Milk," she repeated.

"Like…a glass, or…?"

"For coffee. Instead of creamer."

"Oh." He walked off without another word.

I moved closer to her and reached for the sugar to drop a spoonful into my coffee. "You and milk," I said fondly, realizing I'd given away just how much I'd watched her all this time.

"It's how my *oma* and *opa* taught me to drink coffee. I've always drunk it that way."

Always drunk it that way. I loved her for her steadfast refusal to deviate from *her* things. All of these parts of her, these funny little quirks, added to the things I already knew about her and just made me love her more. I tilted my head. "You call them by their German names?"

"Mhmm."

I watched her, waiting to see if she was going to elaborate. When she didn't I flipped open the menu, aware of her gaze as I read. Our server returned with Sabine's milk and seemed in even worse shape than before, if that were possible. We ordered breakfast and once we were alone again, I turned back to her. "Tell me more about your grandparents. You speak German with them?"

"*Ja, natürlich.*"

"What's it like?"

She arched an eyebrow, barely holding on to her facetious smile. "Speaking German?"

I softly pinched her thigh. I probably should have elaborated, but assumed she'd get that I'd meant, "Your family."

Her smile was sad, and I thought I knew why. She was about to go away again and wouldn't see them for another three months, which made me glad that I'd sent her home so she could spend time with them. Eventually she described them as, "Loud. Crazy. Wonderful."

"Tell me about them?"

"Of course." Sabine blew out a breath. "Where to start? Uh, my grandparents moved here from Germany after the Second World War and built a whole new life for themselves. They worked really hard to overcome anti-German prejudice, to integrate into the community, to help their community. They're my role models." She smiled sheepishly at that, and was suddenly intent on the contents of her coffee mug. "They're fun and funny, creative, clever, upstanding." We both raised our mugs to drink at the same time and her left elbow bumped my right. Sabine offered an automatic, "Sorry," and began to slide away from me.

"It's fine." Still, she tried to move away and I placed a hand on her leg to stop her. I wanted her right next to me. "I said it's fine. Really. Stay here with me."

She bit her lower lip. "Okay."

I turned slightly sideways to avoid clashing elbows. "What about your parents?"

"After Vietnam, Dad took over the dairy farm from his father, my *opa*. Mom is a high school teacher. They've got the best marriage, just always seem to be in sync. I mean, they fight, but I never feel like they're angry with each other."

I smiled. "Role models too?"

"Absolutely. I know a lot of people say it, but I have the best parents. Supportive without being overbearing, loving without being stifling. Both Jana and I grew up thinking we could do whatever we wanted."

"And is *this* really what you wanted?" I asked.

"Mostly, yes. I love my family, Bec, they're the most important thing in the world to me. If spending seven years of my life in the Army, where I'm becoming a better surgeon, a better person, will make them happy then I'll wear it gladly." She laughed. "God knows Jana wouldn't join the military if she was paid a million bucks a day."

"Jana's your younger sister?"

"Mhmm. Only sibling. A divorce lawyer. My best friend." Again, that sheepish smile.

"And what's she like?"

Sabine laughed. "Like a less mentally disheveled version of me." She held her thumb and forefinger close together. "Only just. She's more adventurous, less neurotic."

"I don't think you're neurotic. Just…careful and thorough."

"You're very diplomatic," she drawled.

I winked. "Part of the job. Is she married?"

Sabine choked on the mouthful of coffee she'd just swallowed. "Oh, hell no! She will *never* settle down. Think of the pickiest person you know, then multiply it by a hundred thousand. She's been on more dates than I've had cups of coffee. She once left a date because she didn't like the way the guy ate the bread as soon as it came out instead of waiting. Oh, and the one where she didn't like how he pronounced *species*. Oh, oh, oh! And the one where he didn't wear matching belt and shoes." She raised both hands, palms up, as if indicating she was completely lost as to why her sister thought these things dealbreakers.

And I almost choked on my laughter. "Oh my god. Really?"

"Mhmm, really. I think she's just a huge commitment-phobe, but hey, who am I to tell her that."

These details probably seemed like nothing to her but were like oxygen for someone like me, who grew up with an aunt and no other family. I could have listened to her tell me about her family for hours, but the server returned with our breakfast, refilled our coffee and placed another small jug of milk in front of Sabine. She cut her pancakes. "What about you? Parents? Siblings?"

I shook a disgraceful amount of salt over my plate. "No, I'm an only child."

She hastily swallowed her mouthful. "Where do your parents live?"

"They don't." I probably would have been less blunt if I wasn't so desperate to eat. Unsurprisingly, after last night and this morning, I was ravenous.

Sabine paused, her expression softening. "I'm really sorry."

Smiling, I assured her, "Don't be. I was only five. I've got very few memories of them, honestly."

Her teeth grazed her lower lip. "Where did you grow up? Who raised you?"

"My aunt. In a one-bedroom in New York." I speared another forkful of French toast and bacon.

"New York? I never would have picked that."

My eyebrows shot up. "No? You know, for a while I wanted to do musical theater. Broadway and all that stuff."

Her mouth twitched like she wanted to smile but was holding it back. I knew why—I do not project an image of a theater nerd. "Why didn't you?"

"Turns out, I can't sing," I said dryly.

She coughed out an amused laugh.

We dug back into our food until Sabine asked out of the blue, "What were your parents' names?"

"Hélène and Matthew."

Sabine's forehead wrinkled. "Your…mom was French? Or French grandparents?"

"Mhmm, she was born in Saint-Étienne. She came over here with my grandparents and her twin sister when they were sixteen."

"Do you speak French?"

"Yes, I do. My aunt, Thérèse, kept me fluent." I smiled at the memory. "She deemed it one of her duties as my guardian."

"Oh. That explains it…" she murmured.

I quickly swallowed my mouthful. "Explains what?"

Sabine flushed, obviously having been caught in something she didn't expect to have to tell me. After a few moments, she made eye contact. "The way you say my name. Like it's French, not German."

"Ah." I hadn't even realized I did that. "Then perhaps I'll have to learn German so I can get it right."

Sabine fiddled with her fork, turning the handle around and around in her hand. "Or…you could just keep saying it the way you do. I kind of like it." She laughed. "And it's close enough to the German, which is more than I get from everyone else."

I dipped my head. "French it is."

"Good." Her eyes sparkled. "Speaking of French, why don't we talk about all that French kissing we did last night."

"Oh, you're so smooth…"

* * *

Breakfast turned into lunch and even more conversation. I wanted to tell her why I was here in D.C., to let her in on my life. But sharing Linda and everything that came along with that felt almost too personal for this…whatever this was. A new relationship? Despite the intimacy of last night and this morning, something still held me back from giving everything to her.

I'd learned so much about her in these past few hours and still didn't feel satisfied. We talked about college and med school and I opened up about why I'd joined the Army. "She wanted white picket fences and this big American dream. I got scared, thinking eventually she'd maneuver me into being a housewife who gave up her career to bake or something. I didn't want that, so I broke up with her and ran to hide in the Army." Laughing, I said, "I admit, it was a little extreme." I'd often wondered what my life might have looked like if I hadn't done that. But if I hadn't run away, I would never have met Sabine.

She kept stirring her coffee, almost as if on autopilot, while she thought. After a full, quiet minute, she asked a tentative, "Are you still hiding?"

"No." I clasped her hand. "After so many years in the service my perspective seems to have changed." Completely flipped more like it. Three years ago, the thought of a relationship filled me with dread. Now the prospect of it, even with its issues, filled me with joy.

"Anyone you've considered testing this change of perspective with?" she asked cheekily.

"I've had my eye on someone." I paused, frowning. "Do you think it's too soon, Sabine?" The thought had been niggling for some time now, wondering if maybe I pushed too far too fast after her breakup. I knew the attraction that lingered between us wasn't new, but everything moved so quickly and I just moved along with it.

"No, I don't," she said carefully. "Now, I feel like this was always going to happen. We aren't strangers, Rebecca. This is just another layer." Our eyes met and I read everything in hers. This thing between us, with everything that's wrong, is right.

Wrong, but right. "I struggled with this, with wanting you," I admitted quietly. "So much, every single day. Wanting you turned me into someone I didn't recognize, because there was nothing tangible between us, just a *feeling* and I don't usually deal in feelings. It was exhausting."

Sabine's forkful of salad paused on its way to her mouth. "Me too." She quickly ate the mouthful then set her fork down. "I'm glad it wasn't just me."

"Me too." I laughed. "That would have made last night far more awkward."

Her nose wrinkled. "Maybe just a little." After a pause, she confirmed what I'd suspected. "I tried to squash it when we came home from Atlantis, tried to pretend that I didn't have a massive physical and emotional crush on you, tried to pretend that my relationship wasn't being held together with frayed string and tape."

"Did that help?"

"Not at all. I was miserable at work, being around you and having to always be on guard so I didn't slip up. I felt kind of like I'd lost a friend as well as a mentor, even though it was my own choice. And I was miserable at home too."

I took her hand, squeezing her fingers gently. "I'm sorry you felt you had to do that."

She smiled, her thumb caressing the back of my hand. "I'm not. It got us here, didn't it?"

Got us here… I leaned back against the booth. "I didn't make this decision lightly, Sabine. I just want you to know that, and that I realize the implications of what we've done. Maybe things will be easier for us now, or maybe they'll be harder. I don't know. But I know that I don't want you to get hurt because of this. Because of us."

"Then don't hurt me," she said seriously. I caught the nuance of the fear she carried from her previous relationship, but she was also smiling as she said it, as if it was the simplest thing. It was, really.

Because along with her fear, I recognized the trust she was placing in me both personally and professionally. Even though I would *never* knowingly let *us* affect our working relationship or her career, the undeniable fact was that I held all the power at work. I pulled her hand to my mouth and kissed her knuckles. "I won't. I promise."

Once our lunch dishes had been cleared, Sabine said, "I need to leave and get everything organized to go back. I don't want to risk missing my flight and getting into trouble with the boss." There was a hint of genuine regret and sadness mixed with the teasing.

I chuckled. "I'm quite certain she won't mind."

She held my gaze. "If we leave now, then we might have time for a proper goodbye."

I raised my eyebrows and Sabine raised a lightning-fast hand to catch the attention of our poor, hungover server. Before I could reach my purse, she'd already left some cash to cover our meals and a generous tip. I slipped into my trench coat and then through the door she held open for me. The rain had eased back to annoying drizzle and we made our way to her truck, ducking under awnings and avoiding small puddles.

I thought about taking her hand but that old worry of being seen stopped me for a moment. But our unit was thousands of miles away and the risk of anyone seeing us who might know who we were, out of uniform and here away from base, was miniscule. As we waited for the crossing light, I slipped my hand into hers, interlacing our fingers. Sabine's grip tightened on mine and we held hands as we walked back to her truck.

The drive home was quiet, but there was no tension between us. I kept my hand in hers, and lightly played my thumb over her skin, thinking about her *proper goodbye* comment. We had so little time left and I needed to make the most of every second. I slipped out of the truck and around to her door, unsurprised when she met me with a heated kiss.

We'd barely made it out of the laundry before we were pulling at each other's clothing as we kissed our way through the house. I was too hungry for her and dragged her down to the floor near the stairs, and straddled her. She sat up, and with our breasts pressed together I rode her hard and rough to my climax, well aware that it would be the last time I would be with her like this for months. If ever again.

I held her against me and kissed her through her climax, enjoying the fresh rush of heat her pleasure brought me. I kissed her again, sweetly, and was surprised by her barely stifled sob. I pulled back in concern. She'd just verbalized my exact feeling in one quiet syllable and I had to swallow my own sadness.

I cupped her face, kissed her forehead, lightly stroked her cheekbones with my thumbs as I soothed, "It's okay, it's okay."

Sabine reached up to hold my wrist, keeping my hand against her face. "This is so fucking unfair, to give you to me for less than twenty-four hours and then take you away again."

"I know," I murmured, kissing her again before carefully releasing my grip. Sabine lay back down and I slid off her lap to lie beside her, hooking my leg over her thigh. She was trembling, and I gently stroked the smooth skin of her abdomen, trying to soothe her.

She turned to face me. "We could always go AWOL together."

"We could," I agreed slowly, tracing my fingers over her skin, memorizing every landmark. "This is almost worth it." The corner of my mouth twitched at my gross understatement.

"Almost?" Sabine almost choked on her mock-indignation.

Laughing, I leaned over to kiss her. I wanted as many kisses as I could take before I left her. I lingered as long as I dared before pulling back. "How would we pay our bills while we're running from a court-martial, Sabine?"

She grinned, affecting nonchalance. "A minor detail."

I laughed again. Minor detail, sure, along with every other *minor detail* we had to think about. Kissing her properly was too tempting, so I placed a soft kiss on her nose then disentangled myself. If I didn't move, I wasn't going to. Sabine had a flight to catch, and I had a friend to spend time with. Linda. Shit. She was going to die when I told her. Metaphorically.

When I returned—now dressed—from the laundry, she'd pulled on underwear and jeans and was hunting for the remainder of her clothes. I held up her bra and shirt which I'd hastily removed on our trek through the house. "I found these on top of your dryer."

As I watched her dressing, I wondered what to say. Nothing adequately conveyed what I felt, the sense of relief and complete satisfaction that being with her had given me. So I pulled her into a hug, burying my face in her neck, absorbing the feel of her in my arms, the scent and feel of her skin. "If you want it to, it'll all work out. We don't need to decide anything right now, Sabine."

She made a quiet, ambivalent sound and pressed her face to my hair. I felt her nod. Reluctantly, I relaxed my grip and stood on tiptoes to kiss her. "I'll see you when I get back in five days. Have a safe trip." I almost said *I love you* but caught myself. It was far too soon for such declarations, even if I knew it to be true. I forced myself to let go completely and stepped back.

Then I took another step back, and another and another toward her front door. We said nothing more as she opened the door for me. I walked along the pathway with my head ducked down against the now pouring rain. Safe inside my car I took a few deep breaths to settle the threatening tears. Aware she was watching me, I couldn't linger too long. I waved goodbye and started the engine.

And Sabine stood in her doorway with a carefully blanked expression and watched me drive away.

CHAPTER TWENTY-TWO

Though I knew that Sabine going back to Afghanistan would be hard, I wasn't prepared for just *how* hard. Being without her at Invicta had felt undeniably dull—not having her by my side during work, not hearing her voice, not having her laughter echoing through the buildings. But now it felt like a fresh torture.

Thankfully, I had why I'd really come home to distract me from that torment. Linda's wedding. The event held both an abundance of happiness and grief, and I probably would have been overcome by the latter if not for my friend's excitement and optimism. Linda had always tended toward glass-half-full, but since her diagnosis she'd really adopted carpe diem to the extreme. She'd taken the news of my time with Sabine with more manic glee than I'd ever seen from her, but aside from her expected excitement, she was unusually subdued. I'd expected the glee, but I'd also expected her to pick at me about it and for us to have yet another conversation that went around in a circle.

Worried she wasn't feeling well, I'd asked if she was okay and received a quiet, "There's nothing more to say, Rebecca. You did it and I'm proud of you. Now you need to figure out what you're going to do from here…"

Tell me about it, friend.

Michelle and I had taken her to her first chemotherapy session and while Linda was in treatment, we sat together in a café getting to know one another better. And when the time came for me to board my flight back to Afghanistan, I knew I was leaving my best friend in the most loving, supportive hands possible.

I barely slept on the flight back to Bagram, jolted out of my fatigue when we came in for our almost dive-bomb landing to avoid surface-to-air missiles. The familiar sights brought a sense of peace and resolve. Though there were still mountainous obstacles to overcome, I'd found what I'd been searching for—hope. There was hope for us, small as it may be, that we could work things out. The alternative was unthinkable now and it was on me to behave professionally and fairly at all times. Until we came home again and were alone and could shed that work relationship...

After unpacking, I made a lap of the barracks, hospital, chow hall and rec room but didn't find Sabine. That would have made me uneasy before, thinking she might have been avoiding me, but now I took it for what it was. She was obviously busy somewhere, and I would see her eventually. I caught up with a few of the team members, had a late lunch, then took a shower. On my way back from dumping my toiletries in my room, I spotted a familiar figure running alone on the track. Pleasure at seeing her was joined by a rush of heat down my spine.

Sabine slowed to a walk then stopped at my approach, standing at attention in front of me. Her face telegraphed her joy at seeing me, and her greeting was a calm, respectful, "Colonel Keane." She *almost* managed to hide the quick flick of her gaze to my breasts.

I smiled, dipping my head. "Captain Fleischer, good afternoon. May I join you?"

"Of course, ma'am, but I'm afraid I was just going to start a cooldown lap."

"That's fine, Sabine. Honestly, I'm a little jet-lagged," I admitted, not bothering to disguise my fatigue. She fell in beside me as I began to walk, desperate to stretch the flights from my body. She was careful to keep a good distance between us, and my immediate thought was that we could totally do this, be together while staying apart.

Being with her again was indescribable. As clichéd as it sounded, I suddenly felt like I'd come home and found something I'd been missing, right there waiting for me, found again. My head swam with thoughts, questions, things I wanted to tell her. But this wasn't the time. I flashed a cheeky grin. "How was your leave, Captain? Did you manage to resolve anything?"

Her response was a broad smile, and an almost sly, "Yes, ma'am, as a matter of fact I did." She held my eyes, arching an eyebrow. "May I inquire about yours? I heard you took a break. Did you enjoy your time away?"

"Indeed, thank you." I adopted a musing tone. "It was very relaxing and also *quite* informative."

We laughed at our ridiculous jokes as we strolled around the track. At the farthest corner from the buildings where it was most private and I knew nobody could ever hear us, I turned to her. The admission made my throat tight, but I had to say it. "I missed you, Sabine."

Her response was an equally quiet, but no less emotional, "I've missed you too."

We exchanged a knowing, tender look and in that instant, I knew I was exactly where I was meant to be—emotionally, personally—and felt the rightness of that as a lightness in my body. Professionally, alas, I had somewhere else to be. "I do have to get in. I've got a meeting with Burnett, but I just needed to see you. In case I don't talk to you during work tomorrow, I'll meet you here at the same time and we'll talk?"

"Yes, ma'am."

"As you were, Captain." I winked at her and left her to finish her cooldown. The whole walk back to my office, I had to stop myself from shouting with delight, jumping in the air and clicking my heels together like some ridiculous Vaudevillian.

* * *

Sabine and I managed to sneak a handful of moments together to talk, though they were few and far between. And all too public. I'd called her in for a faux-meeting almost every day and was starting to wonder if people were becoming curious about what we could be talking about behind closed doors.

But that's all we were doing. Talking. We didn't touch, though we could have easily done so or even kissed in the closed safety of my office. There seemed to be an unspoken understanding between us that a touch, a kiss, would send us down a slippery slope until we were sneaking around and sleeping together on deployment. Despite every line I'd already crossed, I refused to cross that one. We both had much to lose, her more so than me, and regardless of the desperate ache of want, I wouldn't risk our careers any more than I already had.

We'd found time to run together, jogging around the dirt track while we talked, using that time as well to catch up. She'd tell me about her family goings-on—including Jana's latest hilarious dating story—and then we'd separate, and I felt like I was leaving part of myself with her. I made sure to meet up with some other unit members for a workout and chat, just "checking in" as I told them, so it didn't seem so odd that I was doing the same with Sabine.

When Phil queried why I was running so much with Fleischer, I told him I'd decided to work on my fitness with one of the best motivators on base. He laughed and patted me on the back, then wished me luck. It felt almost too easy, these lies.

Most nights, alone in my room, I relived those precious hours I'd had with her. Remembered her kisses, our touches, the whispered words and desperate pleas. And I had to stifle the sound of my solo pleasure as I recalled our shared pleasure.

When we worked together, I made sure to be as cool as I could, scared that someone might somehow pick up on something. In my head, I pretended I was annoyed with her for some imagined action, because that was the only way I could keep my mask in place. These mental gymnastics were another reminder of how it would be until she left the Army.

I finally told Sabine about Linda, and with Linda's ecstatic permission—because sharing meant Sabine and I were obviously getting "super serious"—filled her in on Linda's treatments, which were going as expected. Sabine's sweet and unwavering support made it easier to deal with watching my friend go through a health crisis from afar. Most hilarious was Sabine's incredulity that I'd taken my friend's pushy advice and come to see her.

Laughing, I told her, "I wasn't really given an option." Then quietly added, "And I wanted to see you." Having that brief respite where I could focus on nothing but mutual pleasure had been a true gift.

But now it was time to tackle the consequences, aside from the obvious ones—the rules around fraternization and also the fact *Don't Ask, Don't Tell* was still in effect. I almost brought up the Army Command Policy for a long, slow read through the section that dealt with fraternization, but decided against it, not wanting that search history to be traceable. Geeze, Rebecca, almost sounds like you're sneaking around, circumventing the rules.

Oddly enough, I felt less worried about consequences—aside from moral ones which really did eat away at me—than I did about the fact that being together really wasn't an option, not openly. Because if it came down to it, we could easily argue that because we were both commissioned officers that our offense was lesser than say if Sabine were an enlisted rank. Sure, we had that chain-of-command issue, but given I'd never shown any preferential treatment toward her, and never would, that aspect was flimsy. Plus there was that old saying, "No proof, no problem," and even if they *did* find proof, they would find no evidence that what we'd done, what we might do, was to the detriment of order and discipline or had brought discredit to the Army.

So I decided to set aside that issue and focus more on the personal aspect. We'd spent hours discussing our feelings about it—our shared guilt, and Sabine's concerns about her family finding out, especially her Vietnam Veteran father and his inevitable disappointment in her—and spitballing solutions.

But we found none. We discussed being discreet and only being intimate off-base which still risked being caught, applying for a unit transfer for either of us—though it would likely be for her rather than me—waiting out the rest of Sabine's four-and-a-bit years contracted to the Army, and then what felt like a million other options in between.

The end of DADT was in sight but even if the repeal was enacted before Sabine finished her service obligation, we would still have the issue of me being her direct superior. Unless she applied for a unit transfer, in which case we would be separated every time we were deployed. So our options were: Be together and pretend we weren't—miserable. Be apart for deployments and miss one another like crazy—miserable.

I knew military families, including spouses who were both active-duty, dealt with deployments all the time. We weren't special snowflakes and it felt wrong to add "being apart because of deployments" as one of our cons. Sabine had mentioned offhandedly that she *could* extend her contract, but all that would mean was the same thing, just for longer. And I knew how she felt about serving in the Army.

Every way I looked at it, I felt that even if we managed to make it work, it would feel a little pyrrhic. And I knew she thought the same thing as I did. *Is it worth it?* Was it too soon to make such important decisions based on a relationship that was so fresh, and being overshadowed by so many things? It was hard to separate the wrong from everything that felt *so* right. All I knew was that being with her made me feel more like myself than I had in a very, very long time.

As we strolled around the track late one afternoon, Sabine exclaimed, "Maybe I should just stand on the table at breakfast and shout 'I'm gay!' Problem solved."

I laughed, imagining her doing just that. "I'm sure that will end well." I paused, mulling over the idea that'd just come to me. "You know, I could leave the Army. My obligation is long over." I hadn't thought before saying it, and the moment the words were out, a wave of panic hit me. I knew I was in love with her, and could see a future for us, but leaving the one solid thing in my life was beyond frightening. The Army had been the thing I'd run to, the thing I'd buried myself in when my first serious relationship fell apart, and perhaps I still equated the Army with a sense of safety and security.

She stumbled, just catching herself before she hit the deck. "Really?"

"Yes, really. I'm not sure it's the best solution, but it's another option."

Sabine nodded slowly. "I think…maybe we shouldn't make huge decisions about our careers right now." She smiled. "We've only just started dating or sexing or whatever we're doing and it's all still so new and unsure. Plus with the repeal looming…" Sabine trailed off, looking over to me as if expecting me to finish the thought for her.

"Right. It's all up in the air."

Sabine huffed out a breath. "I think I just have to stick with it, because finishing my contract will clear my college debt. I mean, it's not a dealbreaker, but it *is* something to consider. Because if I get dismissed because we're found out then it's just another thing on my plate that I don't want to have to deal with."

She seemed a lot calmer about this now than when we'd argued that morning in her bed. But there was something about her tone that made me think there was something she wasn't saying. So I came right out and asked, "Are you saying you don't want to continue this?" Even thinking about it made me feel like I had my chest in a vise.

"Not at all," she said immediately. "But we'll have to be ultra-discreet, especially on deployments. Even now I'm worried people think we're spending too much time together. When we're home and off-base it'll be easier, but not easy."

"No, never easy," I agreed. I took a few moments to consider what she'd said. "I think you're right."

She flashed me a charming smile. "Of course I am."

It was so hard not to take her hand there and then, and I sidestepped to put more distance between us to push aside that temptation. This would be our lives until she left the Army—years of pretense and subterfuge and denial.

I groaned, feeling like screaming. "I just cannot think of a way around it. Not one which won't risk our jobs and reputations, or disappoint your family."

"I know," she whispered.

"Maybe when we get back home we can sit down and talk about it, away from the stress of being on deployment and the stress of worrying about being overheard all the time."

"Okay. I just, I think that continuing as we are now feels like the best option for me. The best of a bunch of bad options," she added dryly.

"I agree…"

As if by unspoken agreement, we began spending less time together on the running track or in our "meetings," and other than a few brief mentions of our predicament, we chose to focus on more personal conversations. And with every conversation, I found myself falling deeper for her. I'd almost forgotten what being in love felt like, the way it permeated everything, made hard things feel easy, dark things seem light.

After barely speaking for two days, I decided to meet her for a late afternoon run. I was desperate to loosen some of the tension from my body and I could think of no better way than with a little exercise and her company. Sabine was inside the track, stretching, and the moment I came over she jumped up. "Come to help me with my hamstrings, Colonel?"

I could just imagine helping her with that stretch, full body contact of course. I smiled wistfully at the thought. "If only. Are you ready to go?"

"Always."

As we settled into a steady running rhythm around the track, the repetitive sound of my footfalls on the firm dirt ground lulled me into a thought pattern I'd been over and over for weeks now. How could we make this work? After almost four laps alone with my thoughts, I couldn't hold them in anymore. "I wish I could make this work. I'm so sorry. I've tried. We've both tried. I've barely thought of anything else, Sabine."

Aside from the steady sound of her breathing, she was silent, watching the ground as she ran.

My voice cracked as I tried desperately to hold on to my emotions. "I hate it," I spat out. "I hate not touching you, and pretending I'm annoyed with you, because if I don't do it this way, then I'm scared

I might slip up." I had to pause to suck in some air. "Every night I go to bed thinking about you, Sabine. The way you taste and feel. Every look and every touch. It's driving me fucking crazy." My legs felt wobbly, and I let myself fall back to a walk. Sabine stopped running right away, but still kept her distance.

She ran her palm up and down her sternum as if trying to ease discomfort in her chest. She quietly echoed a question I'd already asked her days before. "Do you want to forget it altogether?" Her gaze was everywhere but on me, and I felt like she feared I might say something she didn't want to hear.

"No," I said immediately. That was the last thing I wanted to do.

Sabine exhaled audibly. "Me either."

"I just want it to be different. The way we know it can be. The way it will be." I peered over at her in the darkening light and just caught her eyes, but I was unable to read the expression in them. "It *can* be, Sabine, but we just have to wait and try to find some way to make it through together."

She said nothing, just kept staring at the ground as we made our way back inside. When we were almost to the barracks, she coughed out a hiccupping sob, swiping both palms across her eyes. And I couldn't comfort her.

CHAPTER TWENTY-THREE

The tentative knock on my partially closed office door was an unwelcome distraction from reading reports, until I glanced up to see Sabine. A very welcome distraction. She seemed as delighted to see me as always, and that delight, in turn, filled me with warmth. Waiting things out thankfully hadn't broken anything between us, and strangely enough I felt we were stronger for having to endure this thing together. Her eyes widened hopefully. "Colonel Keane, do you have a moment for me?"

"Sabine, of course. Come in."

She closed the door without me asking and moved to stand in front of my desk. Now we were away from public eyes, I indulged myself with a long look. I took in all of her, letting my gaze sweep the length of her, down and up, until I was back at her face. Sabine's expression was knowing and she stood without moving, letting me enjoy this moment. My stomach twisted with familiar desire, which I acknowledged before pushing it down. I gestured across my desk. "Take a seat."

Despite everything that had passed between us, our shared intimacy, she still sat as ramrod straight in the chair as she had that first day. I rested clasped hands on top of my blotter. "What can I help you with, Sabine?"

"I was just talking to Liz and she said she's going over to Fermo tomorrow to give flu vaccinations to the company stationed there."

"That's correct."

She raised her chin and her eye contact felt even more intense than usual, as if she thought she could convey what she wanted with just a look. After a long pause, she said, "I'd like to go in her place if I could, please, ma'am."

I was about to say no, because sending a surgeon to another FOB to administer flu vaccinations was ludicrous. But as if she knew my thought process, Sabine's expression softened to something that looked like pleading before she repeated, "Please."

I should have asked her why she wanted to go so badly, what was so important about being at Fermo for the day. But her reason didn't really matter. I trusted that if she'd asked me for something—which she'd never done in our relationship as commanding officer and subordinate—then she had a good reason and it was nothing to do with nepotism. Sabine's face still wore an expression like she was on the verge of really begging.

Begging.

It'd been thirteen days since we'd been together, thirteen days since she'd begged me for other things—to touch her there, to keep my mouth on her breasts, for me to come in her mouth. Thirteen days since I'd touched her, *really* touched her instead of accidentally brushing against her during surgery. I thought about when I'd first touched her, first kissed her, that sound she'd made which had sent a thrill through me, still thrilled me when I recalled it.

I remembered how perfectly her breasts fit in my hands, how responsive her nipples were to my touch. I remembered the taste of her skin, of her arousal. I remembered the smell of her hair, lemony and clean. And I remembered how perfect those hours were and how they were exactly as I'd always imagined they'd be. Thinking about it now, I wanted nothing more than to lock my office door, drag her to the floor behind my desk and fuck her right there, over and over again. And I realized in those few seconds that I was so helplessly in love with her. Being intimate with her had cemented those feelings into an immovable mass. But I had no idea how to tell her.

A far more uncomfortable thought came to mind. This was why fraternization wasn't allowed—it could lead to favoritism. But was this favoritism? Was she going to gain something by me letting her go do something she was overqualified to do? No, she wasn't. Was someone else going to be denied an opportunity if I let her go? No, nobody liked going off-base to give vaccinations. And, it was something she, a member of the team, wanted to do and I'd always tried to accommodate requests as best I could.

"Yes. Okay. You can go instead of Liz."

Her exhalation was a relieved rush of air. "Thank you, ma'am."

"You're welcome. Please find Liz and tell her to come see me immediately so I can tell her she can sleep in tomorrow. And I know you're more than capable of poking needles into arms, but have her run you through the procedures so you're up to speed. Dismissed." I smiled to soften the harshness of that final word.

"Yes, ma'am. I'll do that right away." Sabine stood slowly, reluctantly, and I felt that reluctance mirrored through myself. I knew that this was the best way, the only way, but damn if us separating after such a brief time together wasn't the hardest thing.

The desire to get up, go to her and touch her was so strong that I gripped the arms of my chair until my knuckles hurt. "I'll see you when you get home tomorrow evening."

She flashed me an easy grin. "That you will, ma'am. I—" Sabine paused, her tongue quickly swiping over her lower lip. "Never mind. Sleep well." Her voice lowered to a whisper. "I...miss you."

"Me too, Sabine." More than I could ever express to her in the confines of this place. I made myself smile. "Have a good day tomorrow."

* * *

Despite Sabine's wish, I didn't sleep well. I was awake to hear the rumbling diesel engine of a Humvee coming through the checkpoint a little before dawn. As I heard Sabine's light footsteps past my door, I almost raced out of bed to see her, but instead I rolled over and closed my eyes, thinking about what it would be like to wake up next to her again. The noisy barracks door opened and then I heard the Humvee leaving. I slipped out to catch the end of the sunrise.

Without Sabine around during the day, I felt less like I was missing part of myself and more like I was just waiting for part of myself to return. We had a trauma midmorning, and I rushed a late lunch before settling in for an afternoon of paperwork and the background pleasure of Sabine being in my thoughts.

Linda had sent me her semiregular hair update photo during which she also dutifully told me how she was doing. "Feeling crap. Tired, so much nausea, can't shit. Shaved my head to get it over with, and think

I actually look kind of hot?" was this week's update accompanying the photo in which she was now completely bald. She actually did look kind of hot. And aside from a little more weight loss and pallor, she was smiling and seemed in reasonable spirits, all things considered.

I wrote a quick email agreeing she did indeed look hot, reminded her of some things that could help with her chemo side effects, told her I loved her and missed her and asked her to give Michelle my love too. I'd just finished post-op checks and rounds when the incoming phoneline blared obnoxiously in my ear as I walked past it. I snatched it up, pulling the small notepad and pen from my breast pocket as I answered, "LTC Rebecca Keane. Available for intake."

The steady male voice relayed, "Three on their way, ma'am. Two with GSW and blast trauma, both conscious. And one DOA."

DOA. Dammit. "Copy. What's the ETA?"

"Nine minutes." A pause. Awkward throat clearing. "One of them's yours, ma'am."

His words made my breath catch. "Repeat, we have bad comms." There was only one person in the unit who was outside the wire and there was no way, it…no, it wasn't…no. Oh no. Please no. The unease that had welled up when I'd heard *yours* turned to sharp, raw fear. I knew it wasn't bad comms, I just didn't want to hear it. Didn't want what I knew was true to be true.

He slowed to enunciate, "One of them's yours, Doc. Fle…Flee… Fleischer? Sabine. Captain. Do you copy, ma'am?"

The sound of my pen hitting the floor was like an explosion. I swallowed thickly, trying to find the words I needed. "Yes. Copy." I was so afraid to ask, but I had to. "Who is the DOA?"

"I don't have that information, ma'am."

"Thank you." I swallowed bile. "We'll be ready." Those words almost choked me. After signing off, I carefully replaced the phone in its cradle, then slammed my fist against the call button on the wall.

"Attention on the FOB!" reverberated throughout the building and across the base, the message repeating, echoing, taunting.

I leaned against the wall and stared at my intake notes. The last line was just three letters—FLE then a scrawled line where I'd faltered and dropped my pen. My legs carried my unwilling body to the muster area where the team was assembling. I stared at faces holding the usual mix of emotions about an incoming trauma. Excited. Apprehensive. Annoyed. Tired. But every eye was on me as they waited for me to tell them what to expect. I didn't want to tell them. I didn't want to verbalize this thing that made me feel like I was about to vomit. I swallowed hard and rushed out, "We have three incoming, one is DOA. And one of them is Sabine."

There was no clichéd collective gasp of disbelief. No shocked "NO!" screamed and echoing through the room. No falling to the floor. Zero histrionics. They all stood completely and utterly still, unnaturally so, eyes locked onto me as if they expected me to fix everything for them. I couldn't fix anything. I could barely move, barely breathe. It was like when I'd heard my parents weren't coming home. Not numb—I felt every single emotion, every ounce of pain. Deep, crushing pain.

Amy was the only one who spoke up, quietly asking the question I saw on all their faces. "Is the DOA Sabine?"

"I don't know." It was like I was standing beside myself, watching myself calmly telling everyone that their friend, their colleague, my lover and the woman I felt could be my soulmate might be arriving in a bag.

Mitch Boyd's face was blank and the only reason I knew he'd heard what I'd said was that the color had slid from his skin. I felt the same, like I'd been drained until there was nothing left. Seeing Sabine's best friend processing the information snapped me out of my daze. "Enough standing around like idiots. We have a job to do. We'll need to go meet them. This isn't a Pararescue unit and they won't know protocol." I turned away. "Let's go. Bring full resus gear and hemorrhage control kits."

I hated asking this of them, but Sabine was a professional conflict for everyone, and even if Phil had offered to pull his team in to keep mine from seeing this, I would have declined. She was mine. This mistake, this…consequence, was mine. It was my burden alone.

The sound of speeding diesel engines echoed through the valley, along with something I couldn't place. Metallic, coarse, uncooperative. The moment I saw the convoy I realized what it was. Three Humvees rushed through the checkpoint, the last one lagging behind as it dragged a ruined, uncooperative vehicle behind it like a macabre "Just Married" string-of-cans. I stared as long as I dared before mentally snapping myself to attention.

"Mitch, Amy, Bobby, with me for Trauma A. John, Nate, Rachael, Stephen, on Trauma B. Peta, please confirm Trauma C, the DOA. Nurse teams A and B, your assignments are with your casualty designations." That's all Sabine was now. A designation, not a person.

No no no. She *was* a person. She was *my* person, not just someone I was responsible for, but—

Everything happened so fast I could barely process it. Two fabric stretchers were rushed through the doors, one with an alert young man. The other stretcher was—

Sabine. It was Sabine. The moment I saw her, I felt like someone had given my brain an electric shock. Somewhere between the call and now she'd lost consciousness. So pale. So much blood. It seeped through a rough field dressing on her thigh and the pads a young man held under her armpit. Alive. She was alive.

I pointed at the casualty I didn't know. "Trauma B team, go. Trauma A team, here with Sabine."

Sabine.

Sabine.

Sabine.

No. It was not Sabine. It was just a patient. This is Trauma A who is nothing more than a body full of systems that needed us to fix them. I forced my brain to shut down that part that kept chanting "This is Sabine, *my* Sabine" and put myself into medical autopilot. I gathered everything up and stuffed it into The Forgetting Place, then slammed and locked the door on it all. Vitals assessment, listen to what these people I didn't know were telling me.

"Why isn't there a chest tube?" I asked. It'd taken me about five seconds to determine that she was bleeding into her thorax. When there was no answer, I looked around. "Anyone? Why isn't there a chest tube? Who's the damned medic here?"

A tall young man with striking blue eyes spoke up. "I am, ma'am."

"Why didn't you insert a chest tube into a patient with a penetrating chest wound and a chest full of blood? Do you make a habit of compromising patient care in the field?" It was unfair to snap at him, but also a fair assessment of his incompetence.

His mouth fell open and he straightened himself to attention as if bracing himself for more of my criticism. "I…she said not to, ma'am. Only if she went blue. I, she said something about wanting someone here to do it." His nervous tongue slid along his lips. "This is my first—"

"I don't care if you only learned how to do a chest tube yesterday and she said she wanted the president himself to tube her," I snarled. "Get out of my sight. It's possible you've killed her with your stupidity. Fucking useless idiot. Get out!" My fury was uncaged, and I couldn't drag it back, even as I knew I shouldn't be letting myself go. I shouldn't be allowing them to see me like this. I needed to be strong and calm. I needed to remember the most important rule of leadership.

Never let them see you sweat.

But I couldn't stop myself. I had to shift this blame, just a little, so I could function. I had to unburden myself of some of my emotion or I was going to smother myself. If I was smothered, then I couldn't save her. I had to break it down into tiny manageable steps. Little pieces I could chew then digest, one horrifying bite at a time.

I'm scrubbing. I forgot to put on PPE for assessments and there's blood on my scrubs. Sabine's blood, though it might as well be my own.

She's screaming.

I'm in the OR.

She's moving, squirming, mumbling. Fluid gurgles in her throat.

I can't get my fingers to seat themselves properly in my gloves.

She's choking, crying.

I'm yelling at Amy.

There's so much blood.

I look at her face. A mistake.

I'm snapping at Bobby.

She's unconscious.

I'm cutting her. Cutting *her*…

I'm shouting at Mitch.

And I don't know what to do.

She's still alive, I haven't killed her.

I'm deep inside her chest. There's so much blood. I'm inside her body, touching things I should never have needed to touch. Is this the thing that makes her *her*? Or is this the piece? What about this one? What if I screw this up? Am I going to ruin everything that makes Sabine *Sabine*, even if she lives?

I spent far longer with her than I needed to, checking over every single cell inside her until I was satisfied there was nothing left to hurt her. And when I stepped away from the table, my legs wobbled so much they barely held me upright, and I almost grabbed her limp, unconscious hand to steady myself. I couldn't look at her.

There was…so much blood. Clumps of bloody lap pads all over the floor, smeared where they'd been stepped on. Sabine's blood. It was on my shoes. I took a step backward, stepped in more of her blood. I couldn't get out of it. I spoke to the room. "Get her to recovery and keep me updated. I want to know everything. Every breath. Every heartbeat. Every BP change. Every milliliter of fluid output."

Someone answered, "Yes, ma'am."

Once I'd peeled off my gown and gloves, I stared at the board handed to me and began to write. I wrote so I didn't have to watch her being taken away. I didn't know for how long I wrote and had no conscious idea of what I was writing but when I clipped the pen to the board and stared at the words, it was like reading a summary of my worst nightmare. "Mitch? Amy?" I murmured, not even sure if they heard me—my words felt like I was shouting down a wind tunnel. "Confirm these op notes for me. Please. Bring them to my office when you're done. I…need to write the report."

When I held out the clipboard, Mitch took it with a quiet, "Yes, ma'am."

Sabine's uniform lay discarded and tattered on the floor where it'd been cut off her. I bent and retrieved her jacket, and carefully peeled every one of her Velcro patches from it. If…*when* she woke up, I knew she would want them. And if she didn't, then they'd be mine forever. I put them in my pocket and pushed out of the room.

As I washed my hands, I tried to recount the surgery. But there was nothing. Blank space. I knew what I'd done, I'd just written op notes for Christ's sake. But now there was nothing but a dark screen with small flashes of disjointed memory. I didn't know if it was better or worse that I couldn't recall the procedure.

Amy stepped in beside me at the sink to wash up. She had never been this quiet and that alone unnerved me even more. I knew I should ask her how she was, should chase after Mitch who'd washed his hands like someone had poured a burning chemical on them before he charged out of the room. But I couldn't. I could barely breathe. I felt like I was choking, like I couldn't get air down into my lungs.

"Amy," I said without looking at her.

"Yes, ma'am?"

"I…I need to take care of something. Call me immediately if her status changes *at all*." Without waiting for a response, I shoved out of the room and raced along the corridor. The nausea I'd been suppressing for hours rose swiftly and I clapped a hand over my mouth, breaking into a jog as I rushed toward the door and the promise of fresh air. I only just made it outside before I vomited.

CHAPTER TWENTY-FOUR

The rancid hot air outside somehow felt better than the cool, clean air inside. Inside was Sabine and my remorse. Out here, there was nothing that could hurt me.

Except maybe one thing.

With every step away from her, my panic and anxiety and fear and guilt rose until I wanted to scream—the only way I felt I could rid myself of it. But I couldn't scream. So I stuffed it down where it couldn't touch me. But no matter how I tried to push it all into The Forgetting Place, it kept welling up, like trying to sit on a bulging suitcase while the contents spilled from the sides.

I had to see that one thing that could hurt me. I had to see where Sabine had been when it happened. As I approached the innocuous garage-sized building I could hear voices from inside, laughing and cracking morbid jokes about the opposition forces. Macho, ridiculous, and nothing I'd ever heard from my Med Corps, or ever wanted to hear again. But I wouldn't berate them. If this was what they needed to process what had happened then I wouldn't begrudge them that.

I dragged the full-length sliding door open, and a dozen bodies came to attention. It would have been laughable if I wasn't so utterly broken. Me in sweaty, bloodstained scrubs and this ridiculous show of respect at such a time. I didn't want it. I didn't want them looking to me for guidance. I wanted to run away, sprint into the mountains and hide from everything here that made me feel like my insides had been ripped out.

"At ease," I said, surprised by the steadiness in my voice, when I felt like I was breaking apart inside. The Forgetting Place was threatening to crack open and I hastily ordered them to, "Leave me, please. Wait outside if you must but I want this space cleared in thirty seconds."

The chorus of, "Yes, ma'am!" echoed through the garage before the group filed silently from the shed. Someone pulled the door closed, coating the space in darkness. I stood utterly still, staring at the ground. I knew what was in here, saw the vague, mangled shape. But I couldn't look at the vehicle just yet. Not yet. I took in a slow breath. Then another. In the closed-in space, the mess of odors was overwhelming.

Dried blood and viscera. Shit and urine. Vomit. Sweat. Dust and diesel fuel. They mingled together so nauseatingly that I had to breathe through my mouth. I wanted so much to turn and walk out, to walk away from this thing for which I was responsible. But I needed to see it before they came to collect the wreck. I didn't want to see, but I owed it to Sabine and to myself to see it and own what I'd done.

Someone had discarded a flashlight near the deflated left rear tire. It shook in my hand as I turned it on, the loud click startling me in the quiet space. I slowly dragged the beam of light along every inch of the vehicle. The Humvee was upright on its tires but the left two were completely flat, which made it tilt perilously to the side. The driver's door had been wrenched off its hinges and leaned against the crumpled hood. Broken windshield glass littered the interior, and most of the armored metal was dented. Bullet holes were sprayed everywhere. But the thing that made me pause, the thing that made my legs tremble, were the two gaping holes—one on each side—from whatever had punched through the armor. I could have easily crawled through either of them.

I sagged against the vehicle, felt the ragged edge of torn metal scrape my arm, and tried to push down my panic. I needed to focus on the information in front of me. I knew that it was the gunner who had been killed, and I also knew that Sabine would have been sitting in the rear of the vehicle. The rear of the vehicle with that massive hole through it. There was little space back there, and I had no idea how the projectile hadn't launched through her body to split her in half like the poor Specialist who'd arrived in pieces. The driver would be okay. As would Sabine. She would live. She was going to be okay.

I'd never found much comfort in any spiritual belief system, but as I leaned against the mangled metal and plastic and glass and rubber, I sent up gratitude to anything or anyone that might be listening for letting her come home alive to me. Alive. Somehow, that didn't ease the gut-wrenching guilt nestled alongside a sick sense of satisfaction. Satisfaction that I'd gotten what I deserved.

I also didn't believe in karma, but I truly felt as if I deserved this, this…torment. I'd broken one of the most fundamental and unbreakable rules of the military. I'd struggled with my decision, sure, but I'd still broken the rule and this was my punishment, to come so close to losing her. To have her blame me for not protecting her. And now I'd have to live with it for the rest of my life.

The scream I'd been holding back built in my chest, choking me, bubbling up and demanding to be let out. I pressed my hand hard over my mouth to keep it from escaping. But, god, I wanted to scream it all out. I had never wanted to scream as much as I did in that moment. But I couldn't. I couldn't do anything about the crushing weight of my guilt and regret.

My despair scratched at me like coarse fabric. I couldn't let anyone outside hear me lose it because I knew it would be clear that I wasn't crying for a subordinate. I was crying for love. The sound that managed to escape was a sob, thankfully muffled by my hand. It didn't match the sickening feeling inside and the disconnect was disorienting.

My breathing caught, refused to slow. I cupped both hands around my mouth to try and stem my hyperventilation. It took a few minutes for the feeling to ebb enough so I could breathe without feeling as if I were about to pass out, and another few for my legs to stop shaking enough so that I could walk.

I glanced one final time at the Humvee then left the shed, murmuring, "Thank you" to the assembled group outside. I rushed away as quickly as I could on adrenaline-weakened legs. I had an important phone call to make, one I should have made before, but I hadn't been able to find the words I needed to tell the Fleischers that Sabine had been wounded in action. After stopping in to check on Sabine—still alive, still unconscious, still wounded because of me—I locked myself in my office and brought up her file. But every time I went to pick up the phone, my hands refused to cooperate.

Closing my eyes, I shook out some of the emotion clouding every thought. I could do this, even though I'd never personally had to call a subordinate's family to convey news like this. But this was part of my job. My job was second nature. Don't think about it, just do it. This is Sabine's family. I already knew the names of her parents and sister, but still I stared at them on her next-of-kin listings. Father, Gerhardt. Mother, Carolyn. Sister, Jana.

I'd let myself dream of meeting all of them, but not like this. The call seemed to ring for an eternity and with each one of those tones I wanted to slam the receiver down and flee my office. Eventually, a cheerful female answered with a simple, "Hello."

"Hello. Is this Carolyn Fleischer?"

A no-less-cheerful, "Yes, speaking."

I exhaled slowly and put on my pleasant-but-no-nonsense voice. "Mrs. Fleischer, I'm Lieutenant Colonel Rebecca Keane. I'm calling from Forward Operating Base Invicta about your daughter Sabine Fleischer. I'm—"

Before I could say anything more, she cut me off with a wavering, "Wait. Oh god, wait, please. Just wait." The sound of her covering the phone wasn't enough to muffle her panicked screaming. "Gerhardt! Gerhardt! Please, *please* come to the phone! Please come now. Hurry. Oh god, please *hurry*. It's about Sabine. God, no. Please no, please."

I clenched my molars in a desperate attempt to not cry. The raw fear in her voice was gut-wrenching, and knowing this was Sabine's mother made it even harder to keep myself under control. I swallowed hard, took a deep breath, anything to maintain my composure. I had to press my knees together to stop my legs from shaking. Sounds of a male voice, again muffled. Carolyn again, crying. Sounds of a phone being passed. A throat clearing.

I didn't know why—because Sabine had said her father and his late brothers had been born in the States—but I'd expected him to have a German accent, and the blandly American, "Gerhardt Fleischer" startled me.

"Mr. Fleischer. I'm Lieutenant Colonel Rebecca Keane, your daughter Sabine's commanding officer. I'd—"

He cut me off to get right to the important question, the answer to which I'd been trying to tell them both. "Is she alive?"

"Yes, sir, she is. Currently she's in recovery after emergency surgery for trauma sustained in an operation. I'm sorry to inform you that she...she was injured on her way back to Invicta from another FOB." There. Just the facts.

"What the hell was she doing outside the wire? Ma'am," he added in a softer tone.

Excellent question. Go on, Rebecca. Tell this man why you let his daughter leave the relative safety of her FOB and travel to and from another FOB where she was totally exposed. My response was impressively neutral. "A medical operation, sir."

"What about Mitch Boyd?" Gerhardt cleared his throat. "He's like a son to us. I, is he…" His voice broke and then broke off.

"Mitch Boyd was not involved and is fine, Mr. Fleischer."

Gerhardt's shaky exhalation came down the line. "Thank you. Now, can you tell me about her injuries? I don't understand a damned word of that medical talk but I know my wife and other daughter will want to know." He paused, and I only just caught his whispered, "Oh god, I have to tell Jana."

I quietly cleared my throat. "Of course, sir. She has a penetrating ballistic wound in her torso as well as some shrapnel wounds, which are mostly superficial. Her status is serious but stable. Currently, she's in post-surgical recovery and still unconscious but I expect her to recover fully. We're taking excellent care of her." I knew how bland I sounded, calmly telling this man his daughter had been wounded. Just the facts, no emotion. I held all my emotion deep down where it couldn't come out during this conversation. I couldn't let it come out.

"Penetrating ballistic wound. Fancy words for she was shot," he said bluntly.

"Yes, sir."

I told him more, went into detail about her status and the surgery and my more in-depth thoughts about her prognosis, but it felt like I was standing next to myself listening in, not actually having this conversation with the father of the woman I was in love with.

"Ma'am, thanks for calling and notifying us. Could I ask a favor? Could you please ask Mitch Boyd to call us right away?"

"I will. And I'll be in touch as soon as I have a medical update for Sabine."

I hung up the receiver, pushed my chair back and melted to the floor. Leaning against the desk, I wrapped my arms around my knees and cried and cried until my throat felt raw and my eyes swollen shut. I couldn't remember the last time I'd ever cried like this. I didn't think I ever had.

It took a little time until I felt both controlled enough and also presentable enough to leave my office. Amy had been sending me half-hourly status updates on Sabine and I'd accepted the post-op notes from her and Mitch, and also asked Mitch to call the Fleischers as I'd promised Gerhardt I would. At least Mitch would be able to provide some comfort in the wake of my stale presentation of facts.

While I waited for the evidence of my grief to recede, I typed out my surgical report on autopilot before shoving it in a folder where I knew I'd never look at it again. Phil had popped his head in to check

214 E. J. Noyes

that I was okay and tell me he was here if I needed to unpack. I smiled, lied, and thanked him for his concern.

I needed to unpack, sure. But what I *really* needed now was to shower and scrub away every trace of these awful hours. Before I went out, I sent a message asking the team to meet me in the briefing room after dinner. As I showered a fragment of my grief away, I couldn't stop staring at my hands, certain somehow that her blood had managed to seep through my gloves to stain my skin. It was such a ridiculous thought, and if I'd told Sabine about it, she would probably have laughed and made a Lady Macbeth joke. *Out, damned spot! Out, I say!*

Sabine.

Don't cry. No more crying. I'd already cried so much that my eyes felt like they would barely open, and crying more wasn't going to help Sabine at all. The last update told me she was still stable, and though I would have loved to drop everything and be there with her every minute, I couldn't. Not only would it look suspicious, but I still had work to do. I still had a unit to lead.

But first… I needed to do something else. The buildings' lights dotted around the base were enough for me to see where I was going without spotlights. At the farthest fence from the checkpoint gate were our burn pits. They would throw Sabine's ruined uniform into the medical waste pit and that's where I threw the wadded-up scrubs and the shoes I'd been wearing during her surgery. I flung them as far as I could, watched the bundle separate—my shoes thudded to earth, but my scrubs fluttered for a few moments, fanning out in the breeze until they too dropped out of sight.

Then I slipped around the back of some buildings, creeping like a thief, until I'd reached the bench where I'd bared a little of my soul to Sabine. I dropped onto the bench and leaned forward to rest my elbows on my knees. A little of that sick adrenaline feeling had gone, but in its wake, the crushing guilt had expanded to take over. It had just been an ordinary day. Like we were two ordinary people at work. An ordinary day for me while she was perhaps enduring one of the most horrifying things she ever would.

I had no idea how I was ever going to get past my role in what had happened to her, even as I knew that holding on to all this guilt and grief would only eat away at me until something broke. I couldn't break. I needed to be there for Sabine during her recovery and rehabilitation and then beyond when we were building our life together. I needed to be whole for her.

I couldn't stomach dinner, and just sat on that bench staring into the darkness until it was time to meet everyone to give a speech that

I did not want to give. Instead of standing behind the table I used to hold assorted meeting paraphernalia, I stood in front of it, hands loosely clasped in front of me, and took a few moments to gauge the mood.

Overall they seemed okay, perhaps a little flat, shell-shocked maybe. It was clear some had been crying, but they seemed solid and supportive as a team and the sight of them together made me realize that we would be okay. "Team, thank you for giving me some of your free time, especially in the evening." I hadn't really thought about what I was going to say to them, and dove right in. "Today was rough. You were put in an awful position, but you all rose to the challenge and I was glad for your support during the…trauma." Trauma A. Just a designation. Not a person. Not Sabine.

I glanced around to see that I still had their attention. "I'm proud of you, and for those not present, I'm proud of you for supporting your teammates who were." I paused and inhaled deeply. Now it was time to admit my weakness. "And, I would also like to apologize deeply, sincerely, for my poor leadership during our trauma involving Sabine." There, I'd said it.

Sabine.

Sabine.

Sabine.

"My behavior was disrespectful to all of you, and unacceptable and unbecoming of a team leader. I should have set a better example. I should have been supporting all of you through such a difficult time, and I'm sorry that I wasn't the leader you needed and deserved."

There were nods and murmurs all around which made me feel marginally better. They all seemed accepting of my apology and likely understood my lapse of control. On a surface level at least. I cleared my throat, suddenly so ashamed that I could barely get the words out. "If you'd like to talk to me about it, I'm always available for you, or you can schedule a psych session. Otherwise, I hope we can all support each other as a team during this unusual and difficult time."

I wished I could ask them for the support I really needed, support so I could talk through my feelings without anyone judging me. I wished I didn't have to offer my open door because I had no idea where I was going to put those feelings while helping them with theirs. What I really needed was a friend to hold me and let me cry. What I really needed was Sabine. But Sabine was in recovery on a ventilator. Because of me.

CHAPTER TWENTY-FIVE

Sabine had come through post-op without complication, but we were keeping her sedated and ventilated until we were certain her respiratory function was uncompromised. Perhaps overkill, but I was leading the Overly Cautious Crew. Instead of keeping her in the recovery ward, we'd moved her into an empty office beside the ward—partly because she deserved privacy, and partly because I wanted her as close as possible to an OR if anything happened.

After downing what felt like my hundredth cup of coffee for the day, I squished myself into an uncomfortable plastic chair by her bed so I could watch her overnight. I *needed* to watch her, to make sure she kept breathing. My paranoia was irrational but my personal fears seemed helpless against the calm logic of my years of medical experience. I had never watched monitors as closely as I watched hers; memorizing the progress of every line, every number. The regular pump and hiss of the ventilator was both a comfort and a taunt.

My stomach felt sour and acidic from too much coffee and not enough food. I took her limp hand in both of mine and lowered my voice. "Sabine? I feel ridiculous talking to you while you're unconscious but I really want to talk to you, so…I guess I'll wear the ridiculousness." My voice cracked. "I'm sorry. Please be okay. *Please.*"

I obviously hadn't expected a response, but was disappointed all the same that there wasn't even a movie-clichéd squeezing of my fingers. I couldn't risk telling her out loud that I loved her, not with ears everywhere. But I thought it, over and over. And I felt that somehow, she knew.

I woke with a stiff neck and back, chastising myself for falling asleep. Someone had obviously done regular checks on Sabine and I'd had a hospital blanket thrown over me. A quick, frantic look at her—sleeping; and the numbers on her monitors—normal, eased my dread. Busy sounds around the hospital told me I didn't have much time before someone would be in again. The door was partially closed and I couldn't hear anyone nearby. I'd risk it.

After another quick glance at the door, I leaned over and kissed her forehead. Then moved back before anyone caught me. She smelled like surgical prep overlaid with the coppery tang of dried blood that hadn't been washed off her face and body. I'd get someone to clean her up. I could have done it myself but again, considered how that might look, and was again reminded that this was my life, our life, now. Forever looking over our shoulders.

The morning was free of traumas and I spent my time trading Sabine-watch shifts with Mitch and Amy around doing my actual job, until it was time to see if we could bring her off mechanical ventilation. We'd been gradually easing the ventilation flow rate, and Sabine had been showing good signs of being able to maintain her O_2 sats. I almost laughed. Of course Sabine would be doing everything perfectly.

I put out a page for Mitch and Bobby, and both arrived within minutes of my call, offering an almost simultaneous, "Yes, ma'am?"

"Gentlemen, it's time to do a spontaneous breathing trial on Sabine. Bobby, I need you to manage her sedation. Mitch, I want you to confirm stats for me."

Bobby, the anesthesiologist, nodded, his face a mask of not-gonna-screw-this-up determination. "Of course, ma'am."

Mitch cleared his throat. His mouth opened and closed before he finally asked, "Isn't it too soon, Colonel Keane?"

Apparently Mitch was struck with the same irrational panic as I was. "I don't think so, no. Chest tube output looks good. All her vitals are stable within acceptable range. There's no medical reason to keep her ventilated." Unless she wasn't ready to be weaned and extubated. Unless I'd screwed up.

As Mitch and I stared each other down Bobby took a slow step backward, as if backing away from a couple's argument he'd just run into. "I'll just get some drugs."

Mitch turned to me. He crossed his arms over his chest. "I don't want to step outta line here, Colonel Keane, but are you absolutely certain this is the right call? Are you sure she's ready?"

I knew he was only challenging me as her best friend, but the implication that I would recklessly endanger any of my patients, let alone a member of the unit, made my annoyance flare. After a slow breath to calm myself, I assured him, "Yes, I'm sure."

He said nothing more and we kept staring at each other, broken only by mutual reassuring glances at Sabine, until Bobby stole back into the room and cut in with a quick, "Ready when you are, ma'am."

"Good." After a final, thorough check that everything was as it should be, that Sabine was as she should be, I steeled myself. "Okay, then. Bobby, lighten her sedation, please. But be ready to bring it back up if she doesn't respond as we want."

I watched the administration of the reversal agent like I was watching winning lottery numbers come up. As Sabine came out of the heavier sedation her eyelids fluttered, fingertips and toes twitching until the movement seemed to crawl up her limbs. So far, so good. But I knew what was to come and hated that I was about to cause her such grief.

She came awake suddenly, as if jerking from a nightmare. Her eyes opened fully, and she reached up with her left hand, clumsily swiping her hand in front of her face until she managed to touch the endotracheal tube. It was frightening her. This was what I wanted, spontaneous inspiratory efforts, but fuck it was heartbreaking to watch her panic.

Sabine gripped the plastic and managed a weak tug on the tube. Dammit, she was determined. I grabbed her left hand and gently pushed it back to the bed. The vent hissed and her arm jerked underneath my hand. I tried as hard as I could to keep my voice calm and quiet, focusing on her eyes, not allowing myself to look at the tube. "Sabine, it's Rebecca...Keane."

Her unfocused eyes stopped moving around the room and finally settled on me. They were wide, as if she was trying to communicate without her voice. Panic. Fear. Confusion. Accusation. Seeing her like this was almost worse than when she'd first arrived bloodied and pale and unmoving.

Tears leaked from the corners of her eyes, sliding down her cheeks to her neck. Her eyes were locked with mine as she tried to wrench her wrist free from my grasp. And over the top of it, all I could hear was the ventilator and her obvious attempts to breathe over it. I kept stroking her hand with my fingers, even as she dug her nails painfully into the back of my hand, scratching my skin. "Everything's fine. Relax, relax," I soothed her. "We're just checking functions. You're fine. I know you're scared but we're going to sedate you now. Sabine, I need you to stop trying to breathe over the vent."

She didn't seem to hear me, but more likely was she couldn't help her autonomic reflexes. Good, but horrible to watch. I glanced over my shoulder at Bobby and nodded, hoping he'd hurry up and increase the sedation again and relax her. Sabine's nails scraped over my hand, pressing hard into my skin. She blinked a few times before her eyelids slid closed again.

I blinked hard to stop my tears from falling and as subtly as I could, wiped my eyes. Mitch wasn't subtle at all, and had pulled a handkerchief out to mop at his face. Even Bobby, whose default state was stoic with a tinge of loveable asshole, looked like he was struggling. Their obvious distress made me even more determined to hold on to my own. "Okay. We'll wean her slowly and then we'll extubate."

Bobby nodded. Mitch did not. "Are you absolutely sure, ma'am?" he asked tightly.

"Yes, of course I am. She fits every criteria and she's been comfortable on lower vent settings. We can safely extubate," I asserted. "FiO2, PEEP, H_2O, all within limits. Cap refill normal. O_2 sats looks great."

Mitch rolled his shoulders as if something in his uniform chafed. "She was agitated when we brought her out of sedation, ma'am."

"I think I'd be agitated too if I woke up on a ventilator after experiencing a frightening attack." I looked to Rodriguez. "What's your assessment, Bobby?"

"I agree with you, ma'am." He shrugged at Mitch. "Sorry, dude, but you know Colonel Keane is right. You're being tentative because you're worried about her. I get it. We're all worried. But she's ready. And if anything goes south I'll have a tube back down her throat faster than you can say *You're an asshole, Rodriguez.*"

Mitch's jaw bunched. "I'll be doin' more than just sayin' it, Bobby."

I ignored their mild bickering and checked my watch. "Good. It's settled then. Give her steroids for laryngeal edema, and we'll extubate early this evening."

After a quick check that she was indeed stable and would remain so until I returned, I left the smothering confines of the room. As much as it killed me to leave her, I had paperwork and rounds. But everything felt out-of-body. Part of me felt like I was still sitting beside

Sabine, willing her to be okay as if I was simply her girlfriend and she'd had an accident. I wanted someone who knew more than I did to come out and tell me they'd fixed her, that she would be totally fine.

But *I* was that someone. There was nobody here to comfort me. And I wished someone would take my place and that I could throw off the heavy weight of leadership, because I didn't want to be responsible for this. I desperately needed to stop, step back, and process everything that had happened, why and how it had happened, my role in it, what I might do about it. But I could barely even allocate five minutes to those thoughts because Sabine needed me. The team needed me. There was no room or time to spare.

Amy lingered at the door as Mitch and Bobby handled the procedure, while I watched them like they were first-day interns. The procedure was textbook and as Sabine was extubated, I held my breath. Sabine didn't. She breathed in and then out. Then she did it again. And again. And again. And she kept doing it. Breathing. On her own.

I took a few breaths myself, feeling a fraction of my stress release as this hurdle was cleared. "Thank you, both of you." My smile felt weary, my eyes teary. "I'll stay with her for now." I desperately wanted to touch her, to stroke the stubborn line of her jaw and kiss the faint frown line between her eyebrows. But even if we were alone, I couldn't do that.

Bobby nodded his agreement, checked her vitals again and after a thumbs-up and a solid man-pat on Mitch's shoulder, left the small room. Amy peered in and after a tearfully happy smile for both of us, followed Bobby.

"I'll stay," I repeated when Mitch remained rooted in place.

He looked set to argue with me but at my look he backed down. "Yes, ma'am."

I softened my tone. "Go rest, Mitch, then come back fresh to relieve me so I can get some sleep tonight."

He nodded. "Yes, ma'am. Fine idea. I'll do that." He moved forward a few steps, then back again and I realized he'd been about to hug me. His blinking was rapid and his usually deep, confident voice was quiet and hoarse when he said, "Thank you."

Mitch closed the door behind him, leaving me alone with Sabine. She lay quietly, eyes closed, and for a minute I just stared at the placid lines of her face before wiping away some of the crud from the corner of her mouth. I pulled up a chair and sat to her left, ready to take her hand if she tried to meddle with her oxygen mask.

Given the injuries on her right side, I doubted she'd be able to move that arm with any real purpose yet. But she *would* be able to eventually, there was nothing about any of her injuries that would affect mobility and dexterity of her arm or hand. Sabine could do anything she wanted to, but I knew what she wanted was the thing she'd been working toward ever since she was a teenager. Being a surgeon. And she could still do that.

I couldn't kiss her, but I could hold her hand and I did just that. Though only lightly sedated, she was still sleeping and I slid my hand under hers and entwined our fingers. When I placed my other hand on top of our joined ones, her fingers twitched against mine. A perfect movie-clichéd hand twitch.

I couldn't say what I wanted to aloud, so I let the thoughts rush around inside my head. You scared the shit out of me. I shouldn't have let you go. I should have said no. I'm scared I fucked something up and you're going to be compromised. I love you.

Her legs squirmed and she made a small sound that seemed like discomfort. She shouldn't have any pain, but something was bothering her. There was a laundry list of what could be annoying her. I knew she'd hate lying on her back, preferring to sleep on her stomach or side. When we'd woken up the morning after our night together, I'd been spooning her as she lay curled on her side, and had been unable to resist kissing the smooth skin of her shoulders. Been unable to resist sliding my hand over the warm skin of her breasts and stomach until it found the warmer flesh between her thighs.

Over breakfast and lunch, preferred side of the bed and sleeping positions had come up as one of the many topics we'd touched on during our frenzied attempt to absorb as much about each other as we could in the brief time we had. "I hate the beds on deployment because they're so narrow. I'm a side or stomach sleeper, sprawled, for sure," she'd said after swallowing a mouthful of coffee. Then she'd added a cheeky, "Or now…in front or behind you." The memory of those hours before had come rushing back to me as a flood of heat.

I studied her face now, slack and serene with sleep. It was such an odd look on her, usually so animated, to be so still. Though it felt like an inappropriate indulgence, I let myself stare at her. Those long, dark eyelashes. The straight line of her nose. Strong jaw. Full, kissable mouth. I'd thought her attractive the moment I'd first seen that picture of her and that feeling had only grown with each day past that point. But now it was so much more than the physical aspects of her, though the sight of her made my pulse quicken. It was the sum of all her parts.

I closed my eyes and let myself relax, trying to blank my mind. The sensation of Sabine's hand pulling free from mine startled me, and I pushed myself groggily upright in time to see her hand move to her face, her fingers brushing over the plastic mask administering oxygen.

My voice was barely audible, rough from exhaustion. "Leave it alone, Sabine."

She turned her head toward me and the moment we made eye contact, hers softened. I sat up and slid forward in the chair. Sabine reached up again, fingers slipping on the plastic as she tried to pull the mask away from her face. She didn't resist when I gently took her hand and put it back down on the bed. "I said leave it."

I adjusted the mask from where it was riding up her nose. Sabine opened her mouth a few times, tongue flashing out as if she was rubbing it between her front teeth. Carefully, I pulled bangs away from her sweat-damp forehead, smoothing them back. "Do you need anything? Do you have any pain?"

She shook her head then made a clumsy action with her hand, a loose-wristed cocktail-shaking action. I suppressed a smile at her unusual awkwardness. "You're thirsty?"

She raised both eyebrows and made a sound like a weak foghorn. I twisted my watch from where it'd slipped to the underside of my wrist. "You've been off ventilation for three hours. You may have ice in twenty minutes." I felt like an ogre, but I also needed to be sure she was swallowing normally. Aspiration would only add to the nightmare.

Sabine glared, or tried to, but she looked more like a kitten pretending to be a lion. I smiled at the thought until she started squirming on the bed, finally managing to raise her hand an inch. I slid to the edge of the chair and faced her, resting my elbows on the mattress. "Stop it. You have a chest tube in. Do I need to sedate you again?"

Her headshake was emphatic and after a few attempts, she exhaled a hoarse and breathy, "Whaaat..."

I tilted my head to catch her eyes, pushing away my disheveled hair. A sudden anvil of fatigue had landed on my head. "I'd always heard doctors make the worst patients, but I never believed it. Until now." Or, more likely, it was just Sabine Fleischer. I took her left hand and cradled it between mine, bringing it to my lips. As I kissed her palm, Sabine's fingertips lightly stroked my cheek.

A gentle knock on the closed door behind me made me abruptly drop her hand. I moved back in the chair and turned in time to see Mitch wander into the room. Of all the people who might potentially catch us, I supposed he was probably the one about whom I was least concerned. He paused then dipped his head. "Colonel Keane, ma'am."

Like his best friend, Mitch Boyd was guileless, and though I could tell he knew something was going on, he didn't seem overly concerned. Or he was doing a very good job of hiding it.

I smiled. "Boyd."

Mitch leaned over to fetch Sabine's chart from the end of the bed. I watched her watching him, her eyes wide and her expression one of expectancy. But he deliberately kept her chart held up as he wrote so she couldn't see it. She glared. Mitch chuckled and dropped the chart back into the holder. "How would you rate your pain, Sabine?"

She slowly lifted her middle finger. I suppressed a laugh. I guessed that meant one out of ten?

His mouth turned up into a teasing smile. "Any difficulties breathing?"

Sabine shrugged.

"I think perhaps you need to rest a little longer. I'll send someone in with somethin' to help you sleep."

Good plan.

Sabine turned her head toward me as if hoping I'd overrule Mitch. No chance. She needed to rest and she was just going to keep herself awake and keep trying to get information when she needed to be healing. I shook my head and reached to take her hand again, remembering at the last moment that we weren't alone. I tried to hide what I'd almost done by resting two fingers on the underside of her wrist. Her pulse was racing.

CHAPTER TWENTY-SIX

With Sabine sedative-assisted sleeping and in the capable hands of her colleagues, I felt comfortable enough leaving her to take a shower and eat. Food first, shower second otherwise I wasn't going to make it to the shower block. My stomach had a familiar empty, acidic sensation from living on basically nothing but coffee for the last few days, which made the thought of food almost nauseating. But I needed to eat something solid.

The chow hall was empty except for a small group of weary-looking nurses cradling cups of coffee and eating cupcakes. My options were leftover pizza and soggy lunch salad, or all the bad sandwiches like the bland egg salad that were usually only consumed by people like me who'd missed the main lunch round and didn't want to wait for the kitchen to make something for them. Jenny, one of the kitchen staff who was often on duty at the random times I found to eat, leaned over the serving counter. "Can I make you something, Colonel Keane? We're just preparing for dinner service, but I'd be happy to whip something up for you."

I could have just put something in my stomach for sustenance and been done with it, but the thought of comfort food was too good to pass up. "I would really *really* love a waffle, if it's not too much trouble to make one."

Jenny laughed. "Ma'am, you should know by now that they're all frozen. Couldn't be easier." She raised both eyebrows questioningly. "Bacon and syrup?"

"You know me too well. Yes, please."

"I'll make some fresh coffee for you and bring all that right over."

After thanking her for her usual motherly I'll-feed-my-troops-no-matter-what care, I slid into a seat away from the food stations so if anyone came in to eat, they wouldn't feel like they had to pass me and make small talk on their way to food, and also so I didn't have to talk to anyone. I was all talked out. In less than ten minutes, Jenny brought a steaming plate and mug over and set them in front of me. "Let me know if there's anything else you need, ma'am."

"Thanks, Jenny. I appreciate the special meal."

Though my stomach turned at the thought of eating, I carefully cut up a small portion and stuffed it into my mouth before my brain realized what I was doing. That made me think of Sabine right after her breakup with Victoria when I'd watched her eating or rather, trying to eat and obviously having to fight her reluctant stomach with every mouthful. It'd made me both sad and amused to watch her, as if she was giving herself a pep talk with every mouthful and then arguing with her pep-talking self. She tried so hard to get everything right and I loved her for it, for not just rolling over and giving up when things were hard.

Loved.

I didn't need to mull over that thought. Didn't need to talk it back. Didn't need or want to deny it. I knew, with as much certainty as I knew my own name, that I loved her. Was in love with her. I had been for years and had hidden that love away and kept it as my own personal battery for when I felt low. Battery. Recharging, but could also be acidic and corrosive. An apt way to think of how it had been before I'd visited her house.

I thought about eating breakfast with Sabine that morning. How we'd talked about our lives which, until that point, had felt so disparate. And then we'd both realized how alike we actually were, how suited we could be, and how our lives could come together and would remain together. And then I'd gone and almost jeopardized that one thing in my life that was more important to me than anything else.

Sabine was the only person who made me feel so un-alone, so needed, so desired, so…enough as I was with all my flaws. And if I wanted to have her in my life for as long as it lasted, then something had to change, because the current situation was unworkable. I knew, and I was sure she did too, that despite agreeing to it, we'd never be able to work so closely together, live so closely together on deployment, and pretend that we were nothing more than commanding officer and subordinate. It would slowly chip away at both of us.

There was only one thing that *could* change. Me and my job. I knew what I had to do and knew now I was strong enough to do it. I now had the support I needed if I left the military. I had something to leave the military for. Some*one*. We'd talked about this exact thing: me resigning. I'd resisted because I'd been so afraid. A stupid and pointless fear. The fear of thinking she might be dead, of seeing her injured, far outweighed my fear of leaving the only life I'd known for almost two decades.

There was only one real, right solution. I needed to be with her, and the only way we could do that openly, honorably, was for me to resign. There was no anxiety, no fear, just relief which strengthened my resolve. This was the right thing for us. I almost went to speak with her about it, to confirm this was what she wanted, when I realized I already knew it was. We'd shown each other that repeatedly, now all that was left was for me to take this step for us.

But first, I needed to regroup and recharge before I crashed. I took a shower and a nap, and woke feeling slightly more human. Shut away in my office, I called HR to confirm that what I thought I could do actually was something I could do, then logged into the online portal and made a few calculations before I wrote my letter and dragged out the relevant forms. I could have just sent them through without comment, but Donna was not only my boss but also a friend and she deserved an explanation. She answered on the second ring.

"Donna, it's Rebecca Keane."

"Rebecca." She sounded pleased to hear from me. "How are you? How's your friend? How was the wedding?"

"She's responding well to treatment, prognosis is as good as can be expected, which of course, isn't great. It was a beautiful wedding, and I was so glad I could be there for her."

"I'm very pleased to hear that," she said warmly, genuinely.

A sudden surge of nervousness made me second-guess myself, and the words caught in my throat. Until I thought of the woman that was more important to me than what I was doing here. I cleared my throat. "I wanted to call you to tell you in person that I'm relinquishing my command and retiring from the Army. Effective end of this deployment. You'll have my official letter and forms within the hour."

There was a long pause before she calmly said, "I see. That is not what I thought you were calling to tell me, Rebecca. May I ask why? I assume you've confirmed your eligibility."

I had to smile at her last statement, which sounded like she was grasping at straws to keep me here. "I have, and yes of course I'm eligible. And as to why? I...I found something that's more important to me than the Army. Something personal."

"Personal," she mused.

I kept my tone light. "You're not asking?"

She chuckled. "No, I'm not. But you do know *Don't Ask, Don't Tell* will be a thing of the past, right? Just a few more years and it'll be that monster under the bed that we all talk about."

"I know. But there are other factors at play here," I said carefully.

There was a pause. "Then I think I'm better off not knowing the reason..."

"I think that's wise."

Donna puffed out a long breath. "Goddammit, Rebecca. You're one of my great ones. Now I have to put up with someone under my command who I bet I'll hate."

"You know, Henry Collings is a good guy. And a good leader. If I had to recommend anyone, it'd be him. I'm sure you'll be able to whip him into a shape you like in no time."

"I suppose." I could almost hear the despondent rock-kick in her voice.

"I really am sorry to do it like this but...there's no other way forward for me."

"I understand. And I'm proud of you. It takes courage to grab what you want when there's dozens of forces trying to hold you back."

My throat felt tight. "Thank you for everything, you've been a true friend for over half my military career. I don't think I would have known what to do without you to lean on. I don't even know how to thank you."

Donna laughed. "That one's easy. Invite me to your wedding."

I sent my letter and forms through to Donna, along with a personal note thanking her again for her years of friendship and promising me retiring wouldn't mean the end of it. The moment I'd hit Send, I felt a hundred emotions rush over me, but the overwhelming one was relief. That alone told me I was doing the right thing. After a quick stop to freshen up—hair, face, teeth—it was time to see Sabine.

Unsurprisingly, Mitch was there, and Sabine glanced up as I knocked on the doorframe. Her color was good, and the moment she spotted me, her expression brightened. Mitch pulled his feet away from where he had them resting on the bed frame and stood to greet me with a polite, deferential, "Ma'am." Since his questioning my postoperative plan, he'd dialed up his already high polite-to-my-boss, which I hoped meant he recognized that I'd made the right calls.

I felt like I was interrupting an important conversation, and my smile was tentative. "May I come in?"

Sabine nodded, then kept nodding like she'd found some momentum and couldn't quite stop herself. "Of course, Colonel."

I stopped at the end of the bed, trying to figure out the looks I'd seen passing between the pair of them. Clearly a silent conversation.

"I'll leave y'all to it." Mitch collected a chocolate-bar wrapper from the tray beside the bed, and left us with a quiet, "Colonel."

"Mitchell," I said warmly.

Mitch closed the door behind him. Interesting. My gut feeling was that he now knew about us. Though I was itching to talk to Sabine about stepping onto the path to—hopefully only a brief—unemployment, I had a more pressing need. Checking she was okay. Sabine watched me intently as I collected her chart and skimmed through details. There were a lot, even more than our usual thorough charting.

She hadn't needed any supplemental oxygen since yesterday. Good. But she was still having pain. I shifted to her shoulder and slid the chart onto her bedside table, nudging it so she wouldn't be able to reach it. Her eyes narrowed, and I could tell she was having a hard time holding back her exasperation. I tugged the stethoscope from around my neck. "How are you feeling?" I only just held on to my *darling*.

"Annoyed."

My mouth twitched at her obvious frustration but I held back my smile as I rubbed the diaphragm on my sleeve to remove some of the chill. Being in this bed probably ranked high on her list of tortures, as did not being told the minutiae of her recovery. She was being told what she needed to be told. "Why is that, Sabine?" I shifted her gown to the side, exposing the smooth skin of her chest, careful to keep her breasts covered.

"Because nobody will tell me anything!" she croaked, looking up at me. It was a microsecond from being a pout.

"You don't need to know. You need to concentrate on recuperating." I placed the diaphragm on the left side of her chest and when she shuddered, I murmured an apology. As the edge of my hand unintentionally brushed the exquisitely soft skin on her breast, her heart rate increased.

Sabine muttered, "I don't feel any fluid." I recognized her adorable petulance as an attempt to cover her embarrassment at the fact there was no way I would have missed her reaction to my innocent touch.

I raised a finger. "Be quiet, please." I moved around, listening intently and thankfully hearing nothing I shouldn't and everything I should. "Breathe in."

She inhaled slowly. Good.

"And again."

She did so again.

"Can you sit up for me?"

"I'll need some help, please," she said.

I helped her sit forward, keeping my hand on her shoulder for support. "How'd you sleep?" As I slid the stethoscope through the gap in her gown I saw the dressing covering the exit wound along her right scapular. Bruising had spread out past the dressing in an angry purple-black-green. I shifted my focus to the wall.

"Okay."

Now she kept quiet as I listened, using my thumb to massage the tight tense muscle of her neck. "Any pain around the dressings or chest tube?" Carefully, I pulled her back to the pillow, fluffing it behind her.

She bounced her shoulders. "A little. And some stiffness and weirdness."

What a perfectly Sabine answer. As I wrote my notes, I asked, "Stiffness and…weirdness you said? Is there a rating scale for those?" I let my grin free.

"Don't tease."

I laughed, finished my notes and set the chart back. Relief at the steadiness of her recovery made me feel light. "I think the chest tube can come out this afternoon. We'll move you to Germany in the next day or two, then we can start thinking about recovery. It'll be months. You'll go back to the States." I pulled the chair closer and dropped into it, crossing my legs.

"Wonderful." Sarcasm dripped from this one word. I could just tell she was going to be an absolute pain. And I looked forward to every one of those pain-in-my-ass minutes with her.

She cleared her throat and fumbled for the PCA button and after pressing it twice with no response from the machine, I glanced at her. After checking the settings and dosage rates for the last 24 hours, I made an adjustment to allow her a little more pain relief. There was no need for me to ask if she was sure—I knew her and I trusted her. "Try now, Sabine."

"Thank you." She pressed the PCA again and exhaled a quiet sigh when the machine acquiesced with a beep. "Why haven't you moved me on to Landstuhl yet?"

Because I can't let you go. Because I want you with me forever. Because I'm scared. I softened my expression, hoping she hadn't caught my fear. "Because I want you here where I can make sure you're all right. I need you near me until I know…until I know you're really safe."

She smiled, and singsonged, "You're going to get in trouble."

"Yes, I know. And I don't care." She looked worried, that telltale movement of her teeth in her lower lip and the creasing of her eyebrows, and I wasn't sure if she was worried about me getting into trouble or because she sensed I was about to drop something big on her. I caressed her face before settling back into the chair. "I thought I might come with you."

The PCA controller fell to the bed. "What do you mean? Come where? Germany?" Her voice pitched up on that last question.

Despite my certainty, I still felt a flutter of anxiety at what I was about to tell her. "Home," I whispered. "I've spoken to HR and handed in my letter of resignation."

"Really?" she squeaked out. "Why now?"

"Because…" I blinked to catch tears before they fell. "I want to come home with you and help you recover. I want us to be settled when it's time for you to leave the Army and come back home for good. We can deal with you finishing your contract, deployments and the distance later."

"Is that what you want?" Her words were starting to slur ever so slightly.

I lightly held her forearm. "It is. I told you that you'd changed my perspective but if I can be honest, I wasn't totally certain before. I wanted it and I wanted you, but I was scared to make such a drastic change to my life."

"I get it," she said quietly.

"Sabine, I cannot even begin to tell you the terror I felt when I heard your name on the incoming call. That fear is a million times worse than fearing a life change."

Sabine took my hand, interlacing our fingers and pulling my hand closer to her. Her fingertips slid back and forth over my knuckles. I tilted my head to the ceiling, not wanting to cry right now. If I cried, I didn't think I'd be able to stop. But the tears came anyway and I gave in, letting them dribble down my cheeks. "I felt so…" I struggled to find the words to articulate my emotion. "*Helpless*. I was paralyzed by fear, Sabine. There aren't words to describe it. I knew right then it was because I love you. I love you so much and I want to be with you, and this can work." I wiped my eyes with the side of my hand. "It seems so simple now, why didn't I see it?"

Sabine choked, and I immediately moved forward to assist.

"No, no," she wheezed out. "I'm fine. I'm just…I don't know. Relieved? Happy?" Her forehead wrinkled as her mouth worked open and closed. She looked like she was just making her mouth move in the hope words would come out of it. Eventually, she managed to blurt, "Full of opiates and unable to find a word? I love you. I love you too."

Laughing, I adjusted her gown that had slipped from her shoulder. The love I felt for her, feeling that reflected back at me was unlike anything I'd ever experienced. But even as I felt cocooned by it, utterly absorbed in it, I wondered if it was yet strong enough to withstand her blame and my guilt over what had happened. She'd said nothing yet, but I was sure when she stopped to think about it, that feeling would come.

"I'll be deployed again after I've finished my medical leave." She glanced down the right side of her body. "Assuming this arm works properly. It feels like it will, but…it's so *weak*."

"You know this injury isn't one that will affect your surgical career," I assured her, hoping with everything I had that I wasn't lying. I knew it rationally, but that fear I'd screwed up was an almost constant companion now.

"What will happen? You'll be back in the States and I could still be away on deployments or working in Germany until I'm out." She raised her chin and found my eyes with hers, and the fear in her gaze made my stomach clench. "Are you sure you can wait for me back home?" she quietly asked.

I knew exactly what lingered under the surface, the question she couldn't bring herself to ask me outright. Again, she was asking me not to hurt her, and I knew without hesitation that I would never do what her ex had. "You know I will." I felt my gaze soften as I studied the face of the woman I loved so deeply that she made me feel like I'd finally found my place in the world, despite me having thought for decades that I was already there. "I've already waited most of my adult life for you, Sabine. I'm not letting a few more deployments or some distance come between us now that I know you're really mine."

CHAPTER TWENTY-SEVEN

I tilted the laptop screen back and tried to not be too obvious as I gauged whether or not Linda had lost more weight or seemed more tired than the last time I'd seen her. Maybe a little of both, but not enough to worry me under the circumstances. Cancer treatments were a bitch. "Hey, how are you?"

"Marvelous. Can't you tell?" Linda squinted, eyeing me speculatively. "You have news."

She seemed happy and reasonably comfortable so I let her facetious *marvelous* go. "How do you know that?"

"Because you have the I-have-news face. Wait, wait, let me guess. You have terminal cancer and you're getting married." She tried for dry and deadpan, but the smile twitching at the corners of her mouth ruined the effect.

"Oh, good guess. So close. But not quite."

"Damn. I could really go for another round of wedding cake." Linda squirmed against her pile of pillows. "Well? Don't leave me hanging. I'm literally running out of time and you're wasting it with your dramatic pause."

I bit down hard on my lip to keep my tears from spilling. She didn't want pity and sadness. She wanted joy and friendship. I knew Linda intimately—we'd been friends for as long as I could remember—and I still had no idea how she just laughed her way through a terminal cancer diagnosis. "Sorry. Habit. You know I like the suspense. And you're not running out of time *that* quickly." I wasn't immune to death, faced it nearly every day and had lost people close to me, including my whole family. But losing Linda was going to sting. Luckily we still had a little time. "I decided to take your advice. I am carpe diem-ing."

"If the next words out of your mouth aren't 'I'm going to do everything I can so I can be with Sabine,' I'm ending this call right now." Though I'd felt horrible for adding to her burden, I'd emailed Linda—not wanting to risk breaking down during a call—with details of Sabine's incident. And she and Michelle had taken a little of that load and carried it for me. Taken enough so that it didn't feel *quite* so choking.

"I'm going to do everything I can so I can be with her," I repeated back.

"Heyyy! That wasn't so hard, was it? Now tell me everything."

"You were right. Life's too short to prioritize things like working for an institution that doesn't support who I truly am. I've relinquished my command, and I'm going to find a job in a civilian hospital and spend the rest of my days with an incredible woman." Or that was the plan.

Her face lit up immediately and she fumbled her words in her excitement. "That's fucking fantastic! When are you coming home?"

"Same as before. I'll finish up this deployment, and I've put in for terminal leave. So, after we do all our debriefings and whatnot, I'll be done with actual work and will finish up my career by being on vacation."

"Terminal leave. Ha!" It was a laugh and cough all in one. "I know you're not doing it on purpose but fuck me, your accidental dying puns are hilarious. How're feeling about the whole thing?"

"Relieved. Happy. Excited." I paused. "But I do wish it'd happened differently, that we hadn't broken rules."

"Isn't the alternative that you'd never have been together?"

"Likely, yes."

"Then I say you did what you had to do. Nobody got hurt." Linda's mouth fell open and she hastened to amend, "I mean, aside from that thing, which had absolutely nothing to do with you two. It didn't bring the Army crashing down, did it?"

"No, it didn't," I agreed. "But Sabine *was* wounded." Unwanted tears built and I had to bite my lower lip to stop the tremble. "Badly, and I let that happen."

"No, the bad guys did it to her, not you," she said firmly. "Rebecca, nobody could have known something like that would happen. And if you hold on to that guilt, it's going to eat you up. So find a way to let it go." She leaned a little closer to the screen, voice softening. "Do you want to actually talk about it instead of just spilling the story in an email?"

"I will, yes. But not right now." I made myself smile. "I need a little time to figure out my feelings about it."

"Fair. But do try to figure them out."

"I will."

Linda took a long drink of whatever was in her mug before asking, "How is she?"

"She'll be going to Germany soon." Too soon, I thought. "And then on to Walter Reed for about another two weeks, assuming no complications." A cautious amount of hospital time, but I wasn't leaving anything to chance, even though I was sure her medical recovery would continue as smoothly as it had been.

Linda rolled her eyes. "That's not really how she is, Rebecca. That's what she's been doing and what she will do."

I rolled my eyes right back at her. "Fine. She's medically stable and comfortable. Annoying as hell about being a patient. So amazing she terrifies me." I frowned and rephrased what I'd just said. "*This* terrifies me."

"What's that saying?" Her face wrinkled in thought. "If what you want doesn't scare you, you're not aiming high enough."

"I think that applies more to life and career goals as opposed to a relationship."

Linda scoffed. "Why the hell shouldn't it be about a relationship? It scares you because feeling this way is new to you. It scares you because it's so damned important."

She was right, of course, and I told her so, much to her delight. I absorbed her expression, putting it into a safe place for when I wouldn't see it in person anymore. "Please don't have some horrible reaction to your chemo and die before I get home. Or like…trip over the curb and get hit by a bus. I've had a horrible week and that would ice the cake. And also, Sabine really wants to meet you and Michelle and dying would make her sad."

"Fuck me. It's all about you and your feelings, isn't it," Linda drawled. "Typical." She exhaled a teasing *tsk*. "I'll try my best. Now, tell me, how are you? You've just made a *huge* life change."

"It is a huge change, isn't it? But I don't feel anxious about that side of it at all, which means it's the right thing."

"Sounds like it."

"So, I think…apprehensive but excited would sum it up." I shifted slightly so I could lean closer. "Are we going to talk about you at all?"

"We can, but all I'm doing is having treatment for cancer, working when I can, which isn't much, watching bad television, and being doted on by my gorgeous, wonderful wife. All pretty boring. And yes, before you ask, I'm doing okay. Maybe getting tired more easily but other than that, same-same."

"Mmm. Can I just say, that ever since your diagnosis this friendship has felt seriously lopsided. And not toward the person with terminal cancer."

Linda laughed. "Friendships aren't a tennis match, where we do one support from me and one support from you, back and forth."

"I know that, but…it feels odd."

The laughter faded, replaced by gravity. "Do you remember when my mom died and you *literally* kept me alive and helped me function for months?"

"Yes," I said quietly.

"If you're worried about lopsidedness, you're good, we're even. But, Rebecca, please rest assured I am getting everything I need from this friendship right now. I know you care about my health stuff and that you're worried and supportive of all that. It's there in the background all the time. But you're giving me something so important. Normality." She raised both eyebrows. "Or kind of, I mean this is some pretty new and exciting shit you've got going on."

"That it is."

"Right. So unless you're sick and tired of talking about yourself, I'm good. For real."

I took a few moments to compose myself. "I don't know what I did to have you pop up in my life, but I'm glad I did it."

"You were hot in a bar. Not hard. But speaking of getting tired." She stifled a yawn. "Now that I've heard your fabulous news and confirmed you're good and Sabine's good and you know I'm good, I'm pulling the cancer card and signing off to sleep."

"I need to think of a card I can pull whenever I need to leave."

"Oh you have one." She grinned. "Your job. But not for long…"

* * *

Four days after the attack on Sabine's Humvee, I found myself wandering around the recovery wards yet again. It'd become my default when I couldn't sleep—standard situation for me since her incident—but couldn't be by her side yet again for fear of how it looked. I'd passed by the darkened room and peeked in, saw nothing but shapes, and continued on my way.

"Colonel Keane," came Amy's quiet call from behind. She'd just slipped out of Sabine's room where she'd been on night watch.

I forced a smile. "Time for a leg stretch?"

"Something like that. She's sleeping right now, seems comfortable and stable. Vitals and fluid outputs are all spot-on."

My eyes strayed to the door before I could catch them. "Excellent."

Amy stared intently at me. "If I may speak freely, ma'am, you look like you could use some sleep yourself."

She looked much the same, and it reminded me of how this was affecting all of us. "You're probably right. If only my brain would cooperate," I said wryly.

She kept studying me, and an odd look passed over her face. If I didn't know better, I would have said she had a suspicion about why I was there, but there was no disgust or anger alongside that smiling, knowing expression. If I had to put a name to what I was seeing, I'd call it *pleased*.

"I'm taking very good care of her," she said quietly. "I promise."

"I know you are," I answered before I could stop myself.

Sabine mumbled something in her sleep, before the sound of thrashing sheets and the clink of something against the metal bed frame. Another nightmare. She'd been having them intermittently at all times of day and night, and usually managed to soothe herself. But not this time. An alarm I recognized blared from the monitors. Heart rate outside normal range, likely due to her dream.

Amy lightly touched my forearm. "I've got it, ma'am. It's just HR, she's okay." Before I could even open my mouth or move in my dull and fatigued state, Amy had slipped back in and flipped on the light. And I hung back, leaning against the wall out of sight but not out of earshot.

I stood outside, utterly helpless, while Sabine's friend helped her. While Sabine's friend soothed her. While Sabine's friend assisted when she was so upset that she vomited. While she cried out her fear. And even as my gratitude for Amy welled up, my own jealousy pushed to the forefront. Jealousy and guilt and gratitude and an unnamable feeling all fought for front row seats.

Sabine began sobbing, and I had to press my hands against the wall to stop myself from rushing in there to comfort her. I knew she had Amy, but I wanted it to be *me* even as I knew it couldn't be. My legs suddenly gave way, and I lowered myself to the floor, leaning against the wall. I could hear them talking quietly, but couldn't quite make out the words.

Kathy, one of our nurses, approached from the end of the hall, looking vaguely confused when she spotted me sitting outside the room. I nodded and indicated that she should attend to Sabine. Kathy leaned her head in the door. "Everything okay?"

Amy's cheerful voice answered, "Peachy. Thanks, Kath. Can you get me alprazolam, point five milligram please?"

Xanax. Good call. Sabine had it available as-needed, but rarely asked for any to help with her obvious anxiety. After a pause, Amy murmured, "Actually, make that one milligram."

Kathy slipped out of the room, and came back a short while later not only with Sabine's medication but a blanket and pillow for me, which she offered without a word.

"Thank you." I dragged my legs up and wrapped myself in the blanket. And I sat outside that room for hours, semi-aware of people moving around me, until the sound of Sabine and Amy conversing had long died away and the only thing I could hear in there was the quiet, regular sound of Sabine's monitors.

CHAPTER TWENTY-EIGHT

Though I knew it was inevitable, I'd still tried to delay Sabine's transfer to Landstuhl and subsequently on to Walter Reed in D.C. for as long as I could. And I'd been successful for a few precious extra days until I couldn't lie my way out of it anymore. With no medical reason to hold her at Invicta, her transfer was arranged for late afternoon, seven days post-op.

There was no time or privacy for anything more than a basic goodbye, a mouthed, "I love you," and promises that I'd call and email and that she'd try not to be a pain in everyone's ass about her recovery. I stood outside and watched the helo take her from me, then turned away. I knew she would be in safe hands until I saw her again in a little over seven weeks when I left Afghanistan for the last time. And as she'd pointed out, I would be up to my "beautiful eyes" in paperwork, and having her at Invicta would just be a distraction, plus she would be surrounded by doctorly types, as she was here, and would be fine.

Her jaw had set into the stubborn line I was coming to know so well, so I smiled and agreed with her that yes, I'd be busy, but she was always my priority. And she'd laughed at me then pulled me down for a sneaky kiss and murmured that she knew that, but she also knew how my job worked and that once I came home, we'd have all the time in the world.

All the time in the world.

I knew while she was at Landstuhl I wouldn't have much communication with her, and after speaking to a counterpart in Germany about Sabine's stubborn refusal to rest so she could recover, they agreed a little chemically assisted sleep might be beneficial. As much as I wanted to check in with her every single day, I also didn't want to smother her, and as such, had yet to find a balance. Consequently, by the time she'd spent almost a week at Walter Reed after moving from Germany, I still hadn't actually spoken to her, but we'd emailed every few days.

There was really no easy way to tell the unit that I was leaving them, so I went with quick and truthful during a meeting I'd called for this exact purpose. I wasn't surprised at the tightness in my voice, and fought to moderate myself. "Team, I'm saddened to tell you that this deployment will be my last with you. Due to some unexpected personal circumstances, I am relinquishing my command. Once we've completed our post-deployment briefings after our block leave, I will no longer be your commanding officer."

Everyone except Mitch looked as if they'd just been slapped. None of them said anything. So I spoke instead, desperately trying not to sound like I wanted to cry. "I'm assuming everyone's too shocked to say anything, or you don't know if you're allowed to comment. Please, if you have something to say, I would love to hear it."

Amy spoke up first. "Ma'am, I sincerely hope you find every happiness in your…unexpected personal circumstances." She winked.

I held on to my smile. The smile that would give me away. "Thank you, Amy."

Nobody else seemed to have anything to add, so I continued, "Lieutenant Colonel Henry Collings will be taking over my command, and I hope that you'll show him the same respect, trust, loyalty and best of yourselves that you've shown me. I say without reservation that it's been an honor to be your commanding officer."

The quiet murmurs of assent, nods, and even a little silent applause made my chest feel so tight that I had to concentrate on breathing before I hyperventilated from emotional overload. Because that's what it was—I was overloaded. Sabine aside, this had been my job for almost half my life and I'd invested all of myself into it, and not just the surgical side. I'd not only saved countless lives but I'd also mentored dozens of surgeons.

"I—" I cleared my throat in a futile attempt to clear the emotion. "I'll leave my personal email address with all of you, so that if any of you require references in the future you'll know where to contact me. And…I'd like to know how you're all doing from time to time."

Mercifully, the ring of an incoming trauma saved me from baring any more of my soul, and we all rushed out of the meeting room after my blurted, "Dismissed."

* * *

I spent every spare moment ensuring everything was in order for the handover, and the endless paperwork felt mountainous. With Sabine gone, time passed much as it had when she'd gone for her R&R—non-linearly, blurrily, stagnant. Being busier than I had ever been helped with the loneliness and also the guilt and worry that was a now-permanent fixture. I had no time to sit and dwell on how much I missed her, until I fell into bed and it all came crashing down, leaving me lying awake for most of the night.

I knew she had excellent medical care, and being back in D.C. she would also have her family, but I wanted it to be me. I wanted to come by during my lunch breaks, before and after work, bring her books and the cheese I knew she loved. But I was stuck in another country and still pretending I was nobody more than her boss.

I'd tried to find space to call Sabine at reasonable times for both of us, and failed. But two weeks after she'd left Invicta, I was still in my office at 9 p.m. when I was struck with a sudden desperate urge to talk to her. Some mental math told me it was after midday in D.C. To hell with it. I missed her, and I wanted to talk to her. The teetering stack of reports I was checking was ignored in favor of the phone.

After being routed to her room, I waited for an eternity until I heard the familiar husky voice, perhaps a little rougher than usual. So she wasn't sleeping well. Hmmph. Sabine's, "Hello?" almost made me burst into tears.

The line crackled before settling with a low, background hum. "Sabine? It's Rebecca."

Her tone brightened instantly. "Hey!"

"Were you sleeping?"

"No, just watching TV and trying not to go insane with boredom."

Laughing, I told her, "Well, be glad. It's a madhouse here."

"Mmm." The tone conveyed she'd rather be at Invicta than at Walter Reed.

"How are you feeling?"

"Just a sec, I'll get my chart."

I should have been more specific. "Sabi—"

But there was no response, just some muffled conversation with someone who I assumed was her mom, given the pitch of the voice.

After another few moments I heard paper rustling then a bright, "Okay." Sabine sounded like she was about to give me a verbal post-op report.

Thoroughly exasperated with her inability to switch off, while simultaneously loving that about her, I said, "Sabine. I asked how you were feeling. Not what your status is."

She deflated. "Oh. Well...I'm feeling like I'm in the hospital recovering from an explosion and a gunshot wound."

I bit my lip. I would have laughed at her dry joke if the reality of it wasn't so smothering. "You're such a smartass. And your mom's there."

"Yes, and I know." A pause, then a quiet conversation that sounded like Sabine asking her mother to get her some food. Another pause, then Sabine came back. "Sorry about that. I just...I need some privacy."

"You're terrible. She's going to be trying to find someone for half an hour." If she was lucky.

Sabine made a musing sound of agreement. "I miss you, Bec." Those four words were so soft, almost desperate.

"I miss you too. It's dark without you here." I'd said it without thinking, but I knew it was true. She was light. I cleared my throat and grabbed a pen to make notes. "Okay. Let's start with pain score. Don't lie..."

* * *

A little over two weeks before we were all due to fly home, Mitch appeared in my open doorway, tapping lightly on the interior wall. "Ma'am? May I come in?"

"Afternoon, Mitch. You beat me to it. I was just thinking I needed to come talk with you." I gestured across my desk, which was slowly clearing of paperwork. Happy days. "Have a seat."

He carefully closed the door and sat with surprising grace for a man so tall and well-built. I closed my laptop and pushed it aside. "How can I help you?"

Mitch paused, seeming to stumble over his thoughts. "Colonel Keane, this is awkward as heck for me so please excuse me, but I needed to come talk to you about Sabine."

My panic spiked. "What about her? Has something happened?" I'd spoken to her a few more times before she'd been discharged from Walter Reed last week, and I was now in regular contact with her. But I wasn't her next of kin, and our relationship wasn't public, so I wouldn't be the first to know if there'd been a complication.

His eyes widened and he laughed. "No, oh hell, no. She's fine, I had an email from her this mornin'. Sorry, I didn't mean to scare you, ma'am."

I relaxed back into my seat. "Okay, good. What can I help you with? You can talk to me about anything, Mitch."

"Thank you." He leaned forward. "Ma'am, she's been my best friend since we met our first day of premed and I'd taken the seat she wanted. Course I had to move to the next seat over, 'cause you know when she gets *that look* you just have to do what she wants. Her whole family took me in when my own family pushed me out and I love her as if she were my flesh-and-blood sister."

Smiling, I gestured to him. "Sabine told me that her parents call you Mitchell Boyd-Fleischer."

Laughing he agreed, "Right." The laughter faded and his posture stiffened slightly. "May I speak freely for a moment, ma'am? Or a few moments more accurately."

"Of course."

"I'm six and a half weeks older than her which technically makes me her big brother. Part of a big brother's job is keepin' his younger siblings safe. Now I'm sure you've no intention of acting in any way that's not honorable, but if I could just have a quiet word, said with utmost respect of course, that if you hurt her then you'll have me to answer to." He smiled broadly. "Ma'am."

He'd said it so steadily and earnestly and with not an ounce of malice at all, just like he was stating his plans during an ordinary conversation, that I took it as he'd intended. "So noted. And thank you for your concern about Sabine. I would hope you'd know that I would never intentionally do anything to hurt her." I debated whether or not I should elaborate and decided that as Sabine's best friend, Mitch and I would be spending time together and would likely become friends ourselves. And he would see how I felt anyway. Lowering my voice, I told him the truth. "I care about her, Mitch, and speaking freely myself, whether it's right or wrong to do so at this point, I love her."

"I can see that, ma'am."

I thought carefully about how to word what I wanted to say, because while I knew he was a man of solid moral integrity and also

Sabine's best friend, I didn't want to admit what we'd done outright. And I also didn't want to burden him with it because if anything came of it while Sabine was still commissioned and contracted to finish her time, he might have to testify under oath about what he'd known. It was paranoid and unlikely, but it was on me to protect the unit. Even after I'd left.

I exhaled slowly. "I know what we did wasn't exactly right, but—"

Smiling, he interrupted me. "But nothin'. You don't have to explain yourself to me, ma'am. The heart wants what it wants, and I for one don't honestly give a fuck, excuse my French, about stupid rules like those ones." Mitch slapped the arms of the chair as if indicating that was that. "Now when we get home I've got a little catchin' up with a sweetie of my own to attend to but once y'all are settled, expect an invitation for a barbeque."

"I can't wait. I make an amazing potato salad. Or so I've been told."

"I look forward to eating that, ma'am." He smiled a contented smile. "Have you told her our exact homecoming date?"

"Not yet. I've been so busy trying to make sure everything's sorted here and ready there that it's falling farther down my to-do list."

Mitch leaned back, the chair creaking under the movement. "Might I suggest you keep it a secret, ma'am. She'd never admit it, but Sabine sure does love a surprise."

Smiling, I asked, "Is this one of those things between you two where you're just trying to get at one another, so you're telling me she loves surprises when in reality she hates them?"

His eyes widened. "Absolutely not. I'd never do something like that in these circumstances. That darn attack ruined all my pranks and now I gotta behave myself till she's feelin' better. Might even have to let her throw some jibes my way when we're back to playing football."

I tried to keep the sadness from my response. "I admit I'm going to miss that."

"We can start up a few games during social events. It doesn't get any friendlier outside of work."

Laughing, I said, "Noted. Thank you, Mitch. For coming to see me, for your honesty, your discretion and for your trust. I look forward to your friendship."

"My pleasure, ma'am. I trust you'll treat her right and that's good enough for me. She needs someone unlike her ex, who understands who she is, why she acts the way she does and doesn't try to force her to be something she's not."

"She's incredible just as she is," I murmured.

He smiled, nodding as if I'd just given the correct answer to a *Jeopardy* question. "Indeed she is." Mitch eyed me. "Given I've already crossed one line, what's another one? If you don't mind my saying, ma'am, you look like hell crammed into a handbasket."

I laughed at his expression. "You know, I feel a little like that too."

He hmmed. "You also look like you could really use a good hug."

Biting my lower lip didn't help stifle my tears, but I managed to stop them before they spilled over into a torrent. My voice cracked with my admission. "It sure has been a shitty few weeks."

"It has," he agreed, his voice just as tight. "Sabine calls me her teddy bear, and given you and I are gonna be friends and all…" The implication hung between us.

I would have loved a hug, but quietly declined with, "I'm still your boss, Mitch, but thank you for the offer."

He stood and flashed me a grin. "Not for long, ma'am. Not for long." After a quick glance down at the pile of papers on my desk, he backed up. "I'll leave you to it."

After he'd closed the door, I stared at the eight-inch-high stack of folders, allowing myself a few moments of reflection before I dove back in. Though I'd joined the Army in a feeble attempt to flee from my problems, as I'd moved through the institution, and learned about leadership, humanity and more importantly—about myself—I'd come to love my job and my role.

I'd found my niche. I loved leading a team and it was probably the main reason I hadn't left sooner. I could ignore *Don't Ask, Don't Tell* because I could pretend it didn't affect me as deeply as it did those in relationships. The toll DADT took had always felt small for me. Until Sabine. But now I knew out of all the things in my life, she was the most important thing, the thing I needed to prioritize.

I could apply for civilian jobs running trauma units in hospitals and I would still lead a team. I could find teaching hospitals or implement training programs and ensure a steady flow of interns and residents through my trauma unit. And I could see my girlfriend after work, or at my workplace, and kiss her in the open without fear.

I huffed out a quiet laugh. I'd come to the Army to run away, and it'd given me something to run toward. Typical. When I'd joined the military, my CO had told me the same thing I'd once told Sabine— the Army will always give you something, whether it's something you thought you needed or not.

I'd finally found exactly what I needed.

CHAPTER TWENTY-NINE

As I boarded the C-17 with a mass of adults who were acting like squirming, excitable puppies, I mentally ticked it off the "Never Going To Do This Again" list. It was quite a long list. Some things I was grateful to tick off—no more bland food while deployed. Some of the things I knew I'd miss—FOB haircuts, which, surprisingly, were some of the best I'd ever had. I'd snuck one in that morning before I left Invicta.

The flight was unremarkable, though remarkably, given my excitement, I slept for most of it. When we were boots-on-ground, I wished everyone a relaxing two and a half weeks of post-deployment leave, and reminded the team I'd see them after our leave for briefings and evaluations. After which, I would be officially separated from the Army. I would have preferred to get everything out of the way directly after returning instead of dragging out my retirement, but what I wanted and how the Army did things rarely intersected.

I left my unpacked bags on the floor near my kitchen, took a quick shower, said hi to plants that were surprisingly alive—Michelle's influence—and tried to decide what one wore to see the woman they loved after seven weeks' absence. Eventually I went with a blouse, jeans, and loafers, with a few spare sets of clothes as well as toiletries in an overnight bag.

Unexpected nervousness snaked through my body as I drove to Sabine's, part of it second-guessing my decision to just show up on her doorstep and part of it expected anxiety about the change I'd made to my life for us. Then there was the part of me that still worried I'd panic and feel trapped as I had with Clare, and be unable to maintain this relationship. I pushed away those thoughts, not into The Forgetting Place, but gone forever.

Clare and Sabine were polar opposites—not only in appearance and personality, but how I felt about them. Everything with Sabine felt right, natural, with the only conflicts in our relationship coming from external sources. I'd never felt so immediately attracted, comfortable or certain with any other woman as I did with her.

I knew I'd made the right choice for us. I knew she was waiting for me, and as excited as I was about beginning this new life together. I also knew that changing our dynamic from what we had to what would be was a big turnabout. But… I loved her. She loved me. We had the foundations to build something great and lasting.

I pulled up in front of her house, checked my reflection in the rearview mirror and touched up my lipstick. The overnight bag stayed in the trunk for now. Almost a minute after I'd rung the doorbell, nobody had answered. I knew Jana was staying with Sabine, helping with household chores and keeping her company. Maybe they were out on a walk? Fetching groceries? Or even better—at PT for Sabine.

I'd almost decided to give up and just call Sabine when I heard footsteps on the other side of the door before it was violently flung open. Instead of Sabine, it was someone who looked just like her, staring at me like I was trying to sell her a vacuum cleaner or religion. I offered my best disarming smile. "You must be Jana."

Her eyebrow quirked but she said nothing. I extended my hand. "I'm Rebecca Keane."

Those words gave her an instant attitude change. She gaped. "You have got to be fucking kidding me." I'd expected her to sound like her older sister, given looked so alike, but Jana's voice was higher-pitched and without the huskiness of Sabine's. I did recognize Sabine's almost-manic excitement in Jana's tone, as if her brain also ran at a million miles a minute. She ignored my hand and threw herself at me for a hug. It was warm and genuine, not a polite-acquaintances hug.

Once she'd released me, Jana ushered me inside. "Jesus Christ. You know, I asked her 'Is she pretty?', with *she* being *you*, a million times, and Sabine wouldn't say. You'd think she would have told me her girlfriend looked like a blue-eyed Elisabeth Shue with dimples, right? But she's told me absolutely nothing about you. It's infuriating."

I wasn't sure which of those things to respond to first. "Well…I'm sure we'll be getting to know each other, and I'll be happy to tell you anything that you want to know to make up for Sabine's reluctance to share."

Jana nodded slowly, feigning thoughtfulness. "I like you, Rebecca Keane. And I'll be happy to share every embarrassing story about Sabine I can think of. She deserves it after being such a deliberately evasive shit about you."

"I look forward to hearing them. Is she awake?" My hopefulness made the question come out as a whisper. I desperately wanted to see Sabine, but I also didn't want to interrupt her rest.

"Yeah, just woke up from a nap. I was just grabbing her a pain pill." She reached both arms up and stretched, twisting side to side. "And taking a break from a ridiculously lopsided pre-nup."

I had to bite my tongue on the next question that nearly shot out. Asking Sabine's sister about Sabine's pain wasn't the best way to approach it, though I was sure Sabine would answer evasively as she had done during our calls. I watched as Jana used a pill splitter to carefully break a pill in half and once she'd placed it into a small pill box she turned to me. "So. Given I've been with her since she came home, I know she has absolutely no idea that you're even in the States instead of over there."

"That's right."

"Then I guess it's time you learned how to play nurse." After a quick inspection of my outfit, she smiled. "Not quite a nurse's costume, but I'm sure she won't care." Jana extracted a small yogurt tub from the refrigerator. "She likes a yogurt with her pain pills. I don't know why, it's just a Sabine thing."

I suppressed a smile at her description. There were a lot of things that were just Sabine things. "How many times a day is she taking pain relief?"

"As of two days ago, every six hours."

"What was it three days ago?"

"Every four hours. And she's just asked me to halve the dosage." Jana rummaged in a drawer for a spoon which she passed to me along with the yogurt and pill box. "Okay. You're up." She flashed a grin identical to Sabine's. "Ohhh she is going to shit when she sees you."

"I was hoping for just excitement, not excrement," I deadpanned.

Jana exhaled a *heh*. "She also never said you were funny. I sure hope she marries you." She gave me another impromptu hug. "And if she doesn't, I might just do it myself." After checking I had everything, Jana drawled, "I guess you already know where the master bedroom is? Or did you guys not even make it that far?"

Smiling, I assured her, "I know where it is, thanks."

Upstairs, Sabine's bedroom was empty, bedsheets and cover pushed back haphazardly, and the door to the master bathroom closed. From behind that closed door was the sound of Sabine moving about, muttering to herself. Jana called out, "Sabs? Everything okay in there?"

The toilet flushed. "Yes!" came the indignant response over water running in the sink. "I've been peeing for thirty-five years, Jana." As the door opened, the indignancy rose. "I'm sure I can—" Sabine's mouth fell open before she snapped it closed, finishing her sentence with a choked, "Manage." A squeaked-out sob escaped her mouth along with that one word.

"I brought you a gift," Jana said dryly. "Are you going to thank me?"

"Thank you, Jana," Sabine said immediately. She finally made eye contact with me and the naked emotion in her eyes made my throat tighten.

Jana let out an exaggerated sigh. "Nonreturnable, I'm afraid." She glanced at me, gave me a sneaky wink, then crossed the room to collect her laptop from the bedside table.

In utter delight, I studied Sabine. Though her movements were a little guarded, she was clear-eyed and looked healthy. An overwhelming sensation of rightness washed over me. Seeing her in person instead of just stuttery, pixelated video calls made me realize just how lonely and sad I'd been while separated from her.

Jana paused in front of Sabine and whispered something I didn't catch but that made Sabine grin. Jana yanked the cord from the socket and balanced the laptop on her palm. "I'll be downstairs in the den. Holler if you need me."

"I won't," Sabine assured her.

Jana stopped next to me and placed her free hand on my arm. Her fingers squeezed reassuringly. "I've been replaced. Devastated."

I smiled and turned to watch her leave, then closed the door partway. I moved forward a few steps, but still not close enough to touch Sabine. "Your sister looks just like you." An inane statement but I needed a moment to control myself before I dissolved into a puddle of tears.

Sabine glanced at the doorway behind me. "She's shorter." The way she said it was like it was an important aspect of their sibling relationship.

I moved even closer. "I've been given a detailed rundown of your pain pill routine and I think she *might* trust me enough to give you this dose." Holding up the yogurt I asked, "Do I have to feed you this beforehand?"

She wiped her eyes with the sleeve of her hoodie. "Yes. Yes, you do."

"That's what I thought."

Sabine's voice broke when she said, "You're here."

"I'm here. Thought I'd surprise you." I took the final step toward her. "Say please."

Sabine's eyes were wide and full of emotion as they searched mine. Her answer was a hoarse, "Please."

I held her hip and leaned forward to kiss her. The kiss was gentle and unhurried, sweet and soft, and I felt her raw emotion—love, relief, trust. I gathered her into a hug and Sabine wrapped her arms tightly around me, sending all of that emotion into me. I buried my face in the smooth, warm skin of her neck and tried not to burst into tears. She kissed the top of my head, and we stood like that for a while, just hugging, reconnecting. Once I'd finally let her go, I guided her back to the bed and though it wasn't necessary, helped her get settled again.

She shuffled sideways to make room for me to sit beside her. "You don't really have to feed me."

I smiled. "What if I want to?" But I passed the things to her because I knew despite her agreement to the joke I'd made before, she didn't like feeling babied.

Sabine peeled back the lid on her yogurt. "I can't believe you're really here."

"Me neither." I exhaled slowly. "It's been so horrible without you. I don't think I really realized *how* horrible until just now, seeing you again."

"Same. I've missed you, so much. I love you." She cupped my cheek, her thumb sliding along my cheekbone. "Give me a minute to get this pill down then we can get all caught up." Sabine leaned forward to kiss my forehead, then both cheeks. "And then you can check your handiwork because I can tell by your expression that you're dying to look."

I indicated my face. "Maybe this expression is that I just want to see you naked." Which I did, but that want was a lesser want than needing to be sure she really was healing as she should. Despite Sabine good-naturedly complying with my request and sending me pictures of her wounds turning into scars, I wanted to see them in person. Wanted to see what I'd done to her.

Grinning, Sabine bounced her eyebrows. "It has been far too long since we were naked together."

I noticed the careful wording. Not "too long since you've seen me naked" because I had seen her laid out bare in front of me. On a surgical table. "It has," I agreed, careful to keep my tone neutral.

She took her time eating the yogurt, pausing here and there to ask how my trip home was, how Linda was doing, if I'd left a sneaky RK & SF 4 EVA inside a heart written on the plywood wall under her bed at Invicta like she'd asked (yes), and how hard was it to convince Mitch to not come charging around the moment he landed. And as I answered her questions, I watched her, absorbing all that I hadn't seen for far too long.

She'd let her fingernails grow out, which drew my gaze to the shape and taper of her hands, her slender fingers and square knuckles. Unconsciously, my thoughts slipped to what those fingers were capable of and I had to consciously try not to think about the weight of her on top of me and the way those fingers felt gliding in and out of me. I knew why she'd let her nails grow—it'd be a little while before she came back to work, and there was no point keeping her nails short when she didn't have to worry about sterile scrub practices or tearing surgical gloves.

That thought morphed into an unpleasant and unexpectedly upsetting one. She and I would never work together again. Intellectually, I'd known this when I'd made that choice for us but now, thinking about it, about never having her as a surgical partner, made me feel tight-chested. And we were going to be apart when she deployed again. I'd done it before, been away from close friends, Linda, lovers I'd discarded. But none of those people felt like part of my soul the way Sabine did. I took a slow breath. Sure, I'd lost her in a work setting but what I'd gained was priceless.

Once she'd swallowed her pill I asked, "How's your pain?"

"Manageable." She gave me an easy smile. "I'm sure Jana told you everything, from my pain management to my bathroom routines, but I've just started weaning off the pain meds today."

"Did you discuss it with your physician?"

"Mhmm. He agrees if I'm comfortable then I should start to decrease the dose. It feels okay, hence the lower dose."

"Make sure you do it gradu—"

She squeezed my hand. "Bec. Babe. I know. I'm a doctor too, remember?" The rebuff would have been brittle if not for the singsonginess and her grin as she said it.

I wilted. "I know. I'm sorry. I'm being that overbearing annoying girlfriend, aren't I?"

"More caring than overbearing." Her mouth quirked. "And... girlfriend?"

"Mmm. Jana said it downstairs and it's stuck in my head ever since. I know we haven't discussed what we are exactly, except dating and learning how to be in a relationship, but I like the way it sounds. Or partner, whatever you want," I hastened to add when she simply sat there, silent, her eyebrows working in thought.

"I like the way it sounds too." She leaned in for a kiss. This kiss was intense and needy, and I sensed her desire even as I sensed her reluctance. Sabine pulled away, brushing her nose against mine. "Okay, let's get it over and done with."

It was said lightly, but there was undeniable tension in her expression and I wondered if she was just sick of being examined, or if there was something deeper. Something deeper like she didn't want me, with all the background stuff, seeing and touching those parts of her. But I knew if I asked why, she would brush it off in typical Sabine fashion. I made a note that we should have a discussion about the attack. Maybe even go to therapy together. I almost laughed at that, and wondered how much convincing it would take, given how resistant she'd been to this point.

After I examined where a large piece of shrapnel had penetrated her thigh, Sabine dragged her tee up over her breasts and turned her back to me. She shivered as I lightly touched the new scar tissue of the exit wound on her right scapular. Once I'd checked it to my satisfaction, Sabine shuffled to lie on her back. She had her arms flat along her sides, hands balled into loose fists, and the tension in her abdominals made me pause. I kept my eyes from the smattering of small scars made by pieces of explosive shrapnel, and found her watching me. I held her gaze. "I don't have to continue if you don't want me to."

"You're technically my surgeon, Bec. You should check it all out." She turned on a smile, but it was tight at the edges of her usually soft, sensuous mouth. "Sorry. I'm just being a weird-brain."

I stroked her thigh absently. "Do you want to tell me about it? Talk about how you're feeling?" I doubted she'd acquiesce.

She shook her head and kept chewing the inside of her cheek. After a few long moments she quietly said, "Maybe later? I don't want to ruin our first time being together in ages with…this."

"Sure, darling." I held up my hands, twinkling my fingers. "May I? I'll be quick and gentle."

She bounced her eyebrows. "Normally I wouldn't enjoy those two things, but in this case, I'm all for it."

I bit back my response to the innuendo.

The scar tissue of the bullet entry wound under her right armpit was healthily pink, not swollen or tender, and the scar from my clumsy surgical incision looked just as good. All in all, everything was healing exactly as I would have hoped. But the scars were there. And I hated that. I had to keep myself from examining her more thoroughly and let myself trust that she and her physicians knew what they were doing. I had a sudden urge to kiss her belly, like I could somehow kiss the scars and make them better, and had to forcibly keep myself from doing just that.

Jana knocked then pushed the door open without waiting for Sabine to call for her to come in. She was one of those people, so noted. Luckily, Sabine had kept her shirt on, and she hastily pulled it down to cover herself. Not hastily enough. Jana snorted out her laugh. "You two could have at least waited until I left the house before jumping on each other."

Sabine threw a pillow at her. "Bec was checking my ouchies, thank you very much, Gutter Brain."

"Ohhh. Is that what lesbians call it?" Jana bent to retrieve the pillow she hadn't caught, then came over to toss it onto the bed. "How's it all looking, Rebecca?"

"Really good," I said automatically. It was the truth, but I didn't think I'd ever get over the fact I'd left such a clumsy, ragged mark on Sabine's skin. She'd wear it for the rest of her life, a reminder that I'd let her down. I made myself smile. "You've been taking great care of her. Thank you."

Jana shrugged, her smile barely contained. "I know. I'm great."

Sabine grunted in disbelief, and I covered her hand with mine. Partly for support. Partly to stop more pillows flying across the room. Jana stood beside the bed, resting her butt against the bedside table. "Just came up to tell you I'm going home. Now Rebecca's here, I'm superfluous to requirements and I think I might go insane if I have to watch any more women's soccer with you, Sabs. So, I'm out. I'll come round in a few days for a visit." She kissed Sabine's forehead then leaned down for a tight hug, and I heard the murmured, "Love you" from each of them. Jana hugged me too and once she'd straightened up again, offered a casual, "Just hit her with a pillow if she gets annoying. Always worked for me."

Laughing, I agreed, "Will do." Once Jana had left, I spun on the bed to face Sabine. "She's really great. Exactly like you described."

Sabine smiled fondly. "She really is. Best sister ever." She pushed herself into a more upright position. "Looks like she's going to attach herself to you pretty fast too. Ready for a sister?"

A sister. Hmm. Having a sibling, even a non-blood one, was an interesting, yet undeniably appealing thought. "I look forward to it."

"Me too." She traced her fingertips from my temple, over my cheekbones and along my jaw as if she wanted her fingers to relearn my face. "Will you stay for dinner?"

"I'll go one better. I'll make dinner. And...stay the night?" My voice caught. "If that's what you want." More than needing to be with her, I wanted to be sure she had someone close by, even as I knew she was long past complications in her recovery.

"Yes, that's what I want." She reached for me and when I moved closer, she took my face in her hands and kissed me. When she pulled back, she still lingered close. "I love you, Bec. So much. And I can't wait for us to start our life together without all this other shit in the way."

Her mouth was so close and so tempting that I couldn't help but kiss her again. "Me too, darling."

Sabine dragged me into a hug, pressing her face into my shoulder. "Thank you."

"For what?"

Both hands came back to my face, and her expression was so open and raw that I felt every ounce of that love from her deep in my core. "For choosing me."

CHAPTER THIRTY

I found enough ingredients for dinner and while Sabine set the table, I cooked in her modern, well-appointed kitchen. I tried not to think of what we'd done the last time I was in this kitchen, and instead focused on cooking. It was such a normal couple thing, something we'd never done, and a small thrill shot through me at the thought that we'd have this routine tomorrow and all the days after.

After one mouthful, Sabine looked over at me. "This is really tasty."

It was just a simple chicken puttanesca, but her food delight made me smile. "Thank you."

Sabine tore her slice of bread in half but it seemed more a thing to buy herself some time. "I was thinking. I really want you to stay here tonight, honestly I do, but maybe we shouldn't sleep in the same bed right now?" She hastened to add, "It's not that I don't want to share a bed with you, Bec, it's just...I think I'd like to take things slow and if you're next to me then I'm probably going to find it hard to control myself."

"Whatever you want. I don't want to push or make things harder for you. Do you want to talk about why you're worried about sex?" Though I would have loved to spend the night by her side, I respected her need to work through her feelings, not only about what had happened, but about us and our new dynamic. I didn't want to tell her that even though I was desperate to be intimate with her, I couldn't deny I also felt anxious.

She took a minute to verbalize her thoughts, still tearing her bread into tinier and tinier pieces. "I guess I'm just worried about damaging something that's healing, even though I know how unlikely that is because I'm basically healed and that I'm just being stupid."

"You're not being stupid at all. You suffered a serious trauma, darling, and that's going to affect how you feel about things, even everyday things from before."

She bit her lower lip. "You're not mad?"

The quiet, tentative question pulled me up. "Of course I'm not mad. Why would I be mad?"

"Well maybe not mad but, you know, annoyed or whatever that we're not having sex."

I took her hand, squeezing gently. "Sabine, I'm not mad or annoyed or anything like that. I *promise*. I'm not saying I don't want us to be intimate, but sex is only part of what we share and if you're not fully comfortable and ready and engaged then it's absolutely not something I want to force upon you just so I can have an orgasm. That's not us, darling."

The corners of her mouth twitched until frown turned to smile. But she didn't say anything, prompting me to ask, "What is it?"

"Nothing. Just the way you call me darling. I used to hate it when Victoria did, but I love the way you say it."

"Ah. It just slips out."

"Like when I called you Bec that first time by accident?"

I smiled. "Something like that."

As we talked after dinner, we agreed that as well as keeping separate bedrooms for now, that we'd take our time before making any big decisions about living arrangements, though it seemed inevitable we'd cohabitate. And given the size of my rented apartment, it made the most sense for me to move into Sabine's house that she owned. Moving in together wasn't just us adhering to lesbian clichés, it was a genuine desire to share our lives fully. "I want that, Bec," she assured me. "But I don't want us to rush just for the sake of rushing. Know what I mean?"

"I do."

Her mouth quirked into an inscrutable expression, but she didn't elaborate on what she was thinking. We did the normal couple thing of watching a little television, and it was Sabine who pointed out around

9 p.m. that I was basically asleep sitting up on the couch. One point to long hauls and jet lag. She wrapped her arm around my waist and took me upstairs to her guest room.

Sabine kissed me, lingering long enough to make the kiss meaningful without it being teasing. "This is just like being on deployment with you down the hall."

"It is," I agreed. "Less snoring though."

"Mmm. That's true." She hugged me long and tight with her face against my hair, and I felt her relax into the embrace. "G'night."

I held on to her, absorbing her. "Good night. I love you. You know where I am if you need anything."

"I do. Love you too." She took my face in her hands and kissed me again before leaving me. I waited until she'd left, listening to the sound of her walking down the hall, before I readied for bed with the slow, clumsy movements of the sleep-deprived.

I fell asleep quickly, and most surprisingly for me, slept almost without waking until morning. We spent a quiet day together talking about the time we'd been apart, watching a movie, taking a relaxing walk, and making plans for some short hikes before it turned too cold and skiing when it turned cold enough. And when it was time for bed, we repeated the same routine from the night before where she kissed me at the guest room door and then left me.

I came instantly awake as I usually did at any interruption, unsure of the time. It took me a moment to realize what had woken me wasn't the sound of an incoming alarm or being paged. It was noise from the other side of the wall—something I was well used to, but not in this context. A thud. Sabine crying out something unintelligible. I paused and waited for a few moments and when I heard her call out again, I swung out of bed and rushed into her room.

She was clearly having a thrashing nightmare, fighting with the sheets tangled around her. "Sabine?" She didn't respond, but instead choked out another panicked cry. I gripped her shoulders, trying to steady her as she jostled and fought with imaginary terrors. It took a few shakes and another, louder, "Sabine!" to wake her.

Her eyes opened suddenly, saw me, and she went completely still. Her chest heaved, sweat glistened on her skin. She swallowed convulsively a few times before she managed a hoarse, "Bec?"

I kept hold of her, gently rubbing my thumbs into the tight muscles cording her shoulders. "It's just me, darling. That's right, it's Bec. You're okay, just had a bad dream."

Sabine wrestled with the sheets until she freed herself enough to sit up. "Fuck. I...I..." She held trembling arms out to me as if begging me for comfort.

I knelt on the bed and pressed myself to her, wrapped her tightly in my embrace, tried to chase away the nightmare. I kissed her sweat-damp temple and hair, rocked her gently, rhythmically, and tried to calm her with what felt like ineffectual words.

Her fingertips dug into my back as if she was trying to ground herself with this touch. "I'm sorry," she mumbled against my shoulder. "I didn't mean to wake you."

"It's okay, sweetheart," I soothed her, stroking her back which was tight with tension. "Good times and bad, right?"

Sabine eased back slightly, and I noted a hint of mirth in her tear-filled eyes. "Are you proposing?"

The light teasing was so like her that a fraction of the emotion in the room eased. I kissed her forehead, my thumbs smoothing the tears from her face. "If I did, you'd know about it."

"Mmm." She shuddered, pulling me closer like she wanted to wrap herself up safely in me. "It was just a nightmare about Richards. The guy who died," she added as if I wouldn't remember. I remembered, even as I wished I could forget. Sabine's inhalation stuttered. "I hate it. And I always remember the nightmares when I wake up so it's like it's always there. Did you see him? Richards?"

I thought carefully about my answer. She was hinting she wanted to talk but I still wasn't sure how to approach her trauma. I went with honesty, but didn't elaborate. "Yes, I did." Specialist Richards had suffered a traumatic hemicorporectomy when the projectile hit him directly, and had arrived at Invicta in two very messy halves contained in a body bag. I'd seen him before his remains were repatriated because I owed it to the man who'd died in service of his country.

"Mmm. I dream that even though he's missing everything below his chest, he climbs down from the turret and drags himself over to me and he's begging me to do something, to stop the bleeding and he's trailing all his internal organs and I just keep thinking how contaminated they're getting and he's ruining his chances of us attaching his bottom half even though it's completely mangled and his injuries are incompatible with life and I know he's going to die."

She paused to take a few deep, heaving breaths. "And *every time*, he manages to reach me and he grabs me by the shoulders but it's like he's got his hands around my neck and he's choking me, and he's just repeating 'Help me, Captain. Help me, Doc' over and over and over. But I can't help him because he won't let me."

After a few steadying breaths, I managed, "I'm so sorry, Sabine. I'm so sorry that it happened to you. It must have been indescribably horrific and frightening. And such an awful, terrifying dream. How can I help you?"

"I don't know." Sabine inhaled slowly, deeply and then burst into heart-wrenching sobs. I bit down hard on my lower lip, holding back my own tears. When I wrapped my arms around her and pulled her close to me, she buried her face in my neck and bawled. There was nothing else I could do or say. So I just held her, rocked her, murmured over and over that she was safe and I loved her and she would be okay.

It took almost half an hour, but eventually her breathing slowed and she relaxed into my embrace. "Can you stay?" she mumbled against my shoulder.

"Of course. Do you want me to leave the light on?"

She huffed out a hoarse laugh. "No. I'm not afraid of the dark."

After slipping out of bed to plunge the room back into darkness, I slid into the bed behind her and spooned her tightly. I held onto her and hoped that my being with her might help. When she woke again a little before three a.m. it was less violent but not less tearful. I wasn't sure what had woken me exactly—the movement or the sound but as I took a moment to sort through everything, I realized she'd squirmed out of my embrace and was sitting on the edge of the bed.

"Sabine?" I ran my hand down her back.

"Bec…" It was so quiet, I wasn't even sure I'd heard her until she said it again. She turned and lay back down, facing me. The half-awake moon shone a little light through the curtains, but she was cast mostly in shadows.

I traced my fingers over the familiar shape of her face. "Yes, darling?"

Again, that quietness. Then, eventually, "Can we talk about it?"

"Yes. Of course we can." I agreed to her request, even as I feared I might not be able to stand the onslaught of emotion.

After turning on the bedside lamp, she reached between us and took my hand, gripping it tightly as she slid her fingers over mine. I waited silently until she finally spoke.

"I'd actually had a really good day doing those vaccinations, you know? Stale donuts and all. It was just nice to have some space and talk to some new people. And the guys who'd driven me there were so sweet and friendly and helpful. They, uh, Elliot the driver, and

Richards the gunner, they were already waiting when I was done that afternoon and they were so funny and teasing about the fact they'd had to have their flu vaccine.

"Elliot looks like he's still too young to even shave and he was just this cheerful, goofy kid. Is…he is. And Richards. He was so funny, the *worst* singing voice. Just two normal people on what should have been a normal day at work."

She swallowed audibly. "We got this call on the radio that there'd been insurgents spotted along our route and I wondered how they knew and where they were because we hadn't seen them that morning. I remember Elliot's voice squeaked like it'd just broken and it was kind of funny but not funny. And Richards had popped down for a moment, I don't think he thought we could hear him properly even with comms. And he looked at me with these bright brown eyes and he asked me 'Are you dressed, Captain?'" She imitated him in a deep voice. "Like he was checking on me, the highest-ranking person in the vehicle. The person who should have been checking on him and Elliot. And he wriggled back up into the turret and then it just—it just exploded." Her voice cracked on that last word, and she began crying again as everything streamed from her like a faucet left full-open.

"Bec, it just happened so fast that I didn't realize at first that what was happening was actually happening. It was so loud and so *so* fucking hot I can't even describe it. Then we were spinning and the seat belt bit me so hard it took my breath. I hit my head. Something hit me in the shoulder and it was Richards's legs, I think." She shuddered, a deep, full body shudder instead of just a little one like she was chilled. "And the smell and taste of it, I don't think I'll ever forget it, it was like this mix of fireworks and gas, and it was horrible, like in my eyes and nose and mouth, it was like I was choking on it."

I'd smelled a little of that, mixed with everything else when I saw the Humvee in the shed, and couldn't imagine being trapped in that small space with it.

Her free hand moved over my thigh, making tiny circles on the outside. "My leg hurt and my first thought was that I couldn't stand if it'd been blown off, like this disgusting selfish thought in that moment that I didn't want to be like those people we saw nearly every day." She blinked hard a few times. "How gross is that?"

I wasn't sure if it was a rhetorical question, but decided to answer anyway. "I don't think it's gross, I think it's a normal response to a traumatic event the consequences of which you understood."

"Maybe? I just…I didn't know what to do and I felt like I couldn't settle and think, there was no calm brain zone like I always have during traumas. And then there was gunfire but I couldn't figure out its origin and I moved up beside the driver to kind of hide. I didn't know what to do," she repeated tearfully.

I pulled her hand more tightly against my breasts, waiting silently until she could continue.

After a little while she did, swiping at her eyes. "When I'd first buckled myself in, I'd loosened my vest a little because you know how those fucking things dig into your boobs and armpits and sit hard on your hips and it didn't even occur to me to tighten it up again. Like, what kind of a fucking idiot am I to not utilize one thing that might have helped? They were shooting and I don't know how but it got me. Got Elliot too. And I was so fucking scared and I couldn't do anything, not even return fire. All I could think was that I'm not a real soldier, I'm just a physician and I didn't want to be here in the Army. And then I got stuck in a loop about how my right hand, my shooting hand, was nonfunctional, but my dominant hand wasn't, so why not just shoot southpaw, right? But my dad only had right-handed firearms so that's how I learned and that's my muscle memory and I panicked, thinking I wouldn't be able to do it perfectly with my left right when I *really* needed to shoot perfectly. Just so many stupid fucking thoughts taking up the space so there was no room for helpful thoughts."

She bent forward to wipe her face against my shoulder and when she pulled back again, her expression was one of confusion, devastation, like her whole world was crumbling and she had no idea what to do. "And now? I still have nothing but stupid fucking thoughts and I don't know where to put them. I mean, fuck, Bec, you know how much I hate talking about my feelings. I don't even know how to articulate when I'm not feeling right, like it's just a feeling that something isn't as it should be. And I don't even know how to tell Psych because these feelings still don't feel real. But it *was* real."

"Yes," I murmured tightly. "It was." It was so hard to keep my own reactions out of the equation because this was her trauma. But her trauma was tied to my trauma and would forever be. Sabine withdrew her hand held between us and swiped softly under my eyes. I'd been distantly aware that I was crying while she'd been pouring her emotions out to me, but maybe in some warped way I'd thought if I didn't acknowledge it then it wasn't real, that the tears would miraculously go away.

But when she lovingly wiped away my tears even as her own spilled, I lost the battle I'd been fighting for two months. We lay there together in the semi-darkness, clinging to each other, and cried until we both fell asleep.

CHAPTER THIRTY-ONE

It took me exactly three days to cancel the lease on my studio apartment, and borrow Mitch and his new boyfriend, Mike, to help me move all my stuff to Sabine's. Inevitable, really, and me "U-Hauling without a U-Haul" had become Linda's new favorite catch cry, thankfully less prevalent than the still oft-blurted "carpe diem!"

Since moving in, I learned things about Sabine that I wouldn't have thought possible, like her lack of patience for nearly empty toothpaste tubes—she'd just get a new tube instead of trying to squeeze the last bits out of the old one—and her hatred of doing laundry which oddly enough, butted against her love of wearing freshly laundered clothes.

I'd tried not to push her to keep talking about things, but every now and then I'd catch a hint of something on her face, and "Do you want to talk about anything, darling?" would just fall out of my mouth. Every now and then she'd share something small with me, and I wondered if she felt that same small easing of pain I had by letting a little of the past go.

I marveled at the normality of partnership again, how easily we fit together, how easily I'd adapted to sharing myself with someone after so long alone. The prospect of years with her—cooking, housework, making love, collecting mail, vacations—gave me a deep satisfaction

I'd never felt before. The complete lack of anxiety about leaving the Army was a welcome relief, but job-searching after so long was less so.

When Sabine had caught me grumbling, she'd offered a tongue-in-cheek, "Can't you just say 'I know my shit and I'm a fabulous surgeon and I wrangled people in the Army for a hundred years, so you'd be dumbasses not to hire me'?"

"I could," I'd agreed. "But I'm not sure that's going to get me through the door. Processes, you know?" The problem wasn't that there were no suitable jobs, but that there were two Head of Trauma positions at teaching hospitals, both within a good commute and both with very attractive salary packages.

I'd been working on one of the job applications for most of the afternoon, and when Sabine declared she was going to bed I decided to join her. With my laptop. Being with her was always preferable to not, even if I was technically fiddling with words that had probably been fiddled with enough.

Though I was trying hard to concentrate, I became suddenly all too aware of Sabine reading beside me. She wasn't doing anything to draw my attention but as I edited, I started thinking about things irrelevant to what I was doing—like how she'd stand behind me in the kitchen while I was cooking, giving my shoulders a silent massage. I thought about how much I loved her concentration face, the exacting way she folded laundry, her grumbling about her PT exercises, and her careful pour of my nightcap. I thought about how if she saw an insect freshly trapped in a spider's web, she'd liberate it then spend ages with a pair of tweezers lovingly removing every bit of web from wings and legs before releasing it safely away from more webs. She was the kindest, gentlest, most thoughtful person, and she showed me more and more of that every single day.

And though I was already half-thinking about her, she startled me when she put her book down then carefully extracted the laptop from my lap and set it on her bedside table. I was even more startled when without warning, she straddled me and leaned forward to kiss me. The kiss began tentatively but quickly grew hard and needy, dragging a groan from my throat. "You're sure?" I murmured.

Her answer was to slide my glasses carefully from my face and place them on the bedside table, then to not-so-carefully pull my tank top off. Her gaze remained intently on my face and I saw the honesty there, nestled right alongside her desire and trust. Sabine's knees tightened on the outside of my thighs. "I'm sure. I want you, honey. I *need* you so badly."

I pushed my hands under her tee, indulging in the feeling of smooth, warm skin before I pulled the garment over her head. I slipped my hands around the back of her neck, pulling her down to me for a kiss, this one slow and tender. The undercurrent of desperation built through the kiss as we struggled with the last few pieces of clothing keeping our skin apart. My fingers fumbled, useless in the wake of my desperation but eventually I was naked except for my panties, and Sabine…Sabine was caught up in her pajama bottoms.

Our shared laughter broke a little of the underlying tension. As my hands slid over her back I wondered if it was the tension of expectation, excitement, or something less pleasurable. I realized then that I hadn't fully let go of my own anxiety about intimacy and could finally pinpoint its origin.

My guilt.

Being with her intimately required trust between us, but hadn't I jeopardized that trust, put her at risk by sending her to Fermo? Hadn't I scarred her emotionally and physically? Did she know how I felt? If she did, she wasn't showing it. I brought myself back to the present where Sabine felt fully engaged with me on all levels. I kept myself in the space where her body told me that she trusted me, that she wanted me. I gripped her thigh to stop her wriggling. "Let me help."

Sliding down the bed, I let my lips guide me down her body until I could free her from her pants. Her abdominals tensed as I licked below her belly button. But this was good tension, the kind that came with anticipation. I paused momentarily, trying to decide my next move, but in the end my need to feel full skin-on-skin contact won out. I dragged her panties down and threw them aside before kneeling to wriggle out of my own underwear.

Her eyes wandered, languorously surveying my body. The naked want in her expression made desire curl through my stomach, and the familiar heat spread through me. Sabine reached out a hand to me, murmuring, "Come back."

I crawled back up the bed, unable to stop myself from exploring her skin with my fingertips, until I settled against her uninjured left side, lying half-on and half-off her. Her hair had grown, the shaggy bangs sweeping across her forehead, and I brushed them from her eyes. There were no adequate words for what I felt, how much I'd been wanting this since that first night, how much I loved her. "I've missed you, Sabine."

"I'm sorry," she whispered.

Her misunderstanding me made my throat ache. "That's not what I meant. Don't apologize. Ever." I gripped the back of her neck, holding her in place as I kissed her. My tongue slid along her lower lip and she made that sound I loved before her lips parted and her tongue met mine.

My arousal was soft, sensual, but no less insistent as Sabine cupped my breasts, shifting as though she was going to roll me onto my back. I wanted that, wanted everything she would do to me, but alongside that was the almost desperate need to taste her again. I wanted soft and slow before our hard and fast. So I held firm and pushed her onto her back. Sabine looked up at me, mouth twisting devilishly. "Really?"

I bent to suck a nipple, mumbling, "Yes, really."

With every rediscovered place, Sabine grew more relaxed under my hands and mouth, as if she'd just been waiting for permission to release her tension. Her hands moved over my shoulders, stroked my neck, my back, but she was soft and responsive under my touch, letting me make love to her. And though we were frantic, we weren't rough.

Shifting on the bed, I murmured, "Wait. Let me…" I settled between her spread thighs, hands and mouth sliding along smooth skin until I found what I'd been wanting. That first touch, first taste, made my arousal flare and I rolled my hips, seeking friction that I didn't find. "You taste exactly the way I remember," I said hoarsely.

Sabine's moan followed a rush of arousal against my mouth and I dove in again before her murmured, "No" and restless hands on my shoulders pulled me reluctantly away.

I moved back up beside her, my hand playing lightly over her belly. "No?" It wasn't a "No, please don't touch me" but rather a "No, I want something else."

She held my face in both hands, and kissed me, murmuring against my lips, "I want you up here. Here with me." She pressed my hand downward, guiding me toward what she wanted and when I penetrated her, her moan of assent was all I needed to press inside with a second finger.

I hooked a leg over hers, holding us together and selfishly pressing my clitoris against her sweat-slick skin. With every thrust and stroke, Sabine's breathing grew more ragged, her body more taut with anticipation. Her hand slid between my thighs and I parted my legs for her, begging her to touch me. She lightly circled my clitoris and I bucked underneath her hand, pressing my hips forward in silent assent. My arousal was so abundant that she pressed inside with no resistance, her thumb moving over my clitoris. I bit her neck, sucked gently and tried desperately not to come undone as she fucked me. There were no words, other than my mumbled, "I love you, I love you…" against her neck as we drove each other closer and closer to release.

She came with a hoarse cry, her back arched and her fingers still driving against me even as she climaxed, sending me tumbling after her. We lay like that, tangled together, breathing hard, sweating and trembling with the aftermath of our love. I drew my hand upward over her belly and breasts, lingering to brush her nipples before moving downward again. When I paused near the scars over her ribs, she shivered. I propped myself up on my elbows. "Are you okay?"

She raised herself up slightly to look at me. Her mouth twitched into a smile and I saw nothing but honesty. "Yes. Perfect."

I bent down and slowly, lightly, kissed the uneven new pink skin. I stared as long as I dared, and finally felt some peace in my ownership of those scars. My voice caught on my agreement of, "Me too."

* * *

I had another eight days to enjoy my technical unemployment before starting my new job which was almost exactly midway between our house and our…*her* duty station at Walter Reed. Sabine and I had talked about the timing of my new job with her returning to work, and I'd declined the other job because they wouldn't give me the leeway to start after Thanksgiving. I knew she was perfectly capable of being home by herself and was all but healed, but I didn't want to leave her home alone.

I wanted to enjoy this free time together while I could, these full days and nights, which would dwindle to erratic hours with both of us working on-calls and eventually be me left here alone when she inevitably deployed again. We hadn't talked about that yet, still trying to wrap ourselves around The Incident—as Jana and I had begun referring to it—and the massive shift in our relationship away from any work interference.

We'd become nauseatingly domesticated and after cleaning up after our lunch, I finally decided to move some clothes into the spare room closet while she went to talk to the neighbors about taking care of their pets while they were out of town for Thanksgiving the following week. Something that had made Sabine laugh, because she'd deemed it something she would do rather than me, was that I didn't like keeping out-of-season clothes in the regular closet, preferring to move them to the guest room out of the way until they were needed.

I'd also hung all my well-worn ACUs, and the more formal Army Service Uniforms in that closet, unsure exactly what to do with them. I could have donated all my uniforms to an Army surplus store, but they represented so many years of my life. They represented years of repression, of growth, of realization, and then of finding something I never thought I would. I ran my fingertips over the lieutenant colonel's silver oak leaves, and the service ribbons for my ASU jacket. In a small cloth bag hanging from the rack were all the Velcro patches, like my name, my US ARMY patch, rank insignia and service branch.

I swung open both closet doors to give myself extra maneuvering space to put my clothes away and noticed, tucked into the corner, tins of paint, paintbrushes, rollers, trays and drop sheets. I'd completely forgotten that Sabine had sanded down the walls of our bedroom and painted a coat of primer when she'd been home on leave. The uneven not-really-painted off-white of our bedroom had been the last thing on my mind since I'd come home, as if my brain had just accepted our bedroom was a kind of transparent primer color.

A new life deserved a new bedroom color.

Tilting one of the cans told me I'd soon be sleeping in a mid-blue bedroom. I chuckled. The color didn't surprise me one bit, given how much blue was scattered throughout the house already, from Sabine's clothing to appliances to the color of her truck—which she'd sold a few weeks ago, citing she wanted to put the past aside—and now her new Honda.

There was still no sign of Sabine, and when I opened the window I could hear her continued laughing with the neighbor, so I decided to just get started. Linda would be proud of me. Carpe diem.

Thinking about Linda made me desperate to hear her voice, and after a quick catch up with Michelle, she put Linda on the phone.

"Still here," she said dryly.

"So I noticed. Unless you recorded yourself saying thousands of phrases and Michelle is just pressing buttons to play each one."

"Oh, clever. I'm going to write that down."

"Credit me with the idea, please. Quick question. I'm about to paint our bedroom. Roller or brush?"

"Roller," she said immediately. "And take your time or you're going to have uneven patches. Nobody wants to see unevenly painted walls when they're fucking. It's distracting."

"Have you slept with a lot of women in badly painted bedrooms?"

Linda's laugh was sunshine. "Too many. So use the roller. Cut in the corners and edges with a brush first. I'll see you two on Thursday for dinner?"

"Absolutely."

"Great. Love you, miss you."

We'd never actually said it, only the acronym. My voice caught on my response. "Love you, miss you too."

Those words echoed about the room and I hastily put them aside. Not now, not now. It was too soon to be thinking about that. Busying myself in repainting the bedroom was exactly what I needed to take my mind off Linda. Sabine had bought everything and I transferred it all to the bedroom next door. Changing into an old pair of cut-off jeans and a tank top that should have gone in the trash years ago but was so comfortable I kept justifying keeping it, and moving and draping furniture and the floor around the baseboards only took fifteen minutes. I'd just stirred the paint back into a shade resembling blue and made my first few swipes over a wall when I heard the front door.

"Bec?"

"Yep, I'm in here," I called back.

Sabine appeared in the doorway, leaning against the frame as she watched me. I didn't know why, but even though I knew it was something she'd planned I suddenly felt as if I should have asked her if I could paint the room. "I hope you don't mind. I found all this in the spare room closet while I was putting some out-of-season clothes away." I held out my hand to her as she took a step into the room.

"It looks great." She captured my hand and traced circles on my palm before bending forward to kiss me. We were both careful of the paint roller, but not with each other, and I felt the familiar stirring of longing. Sabine lingered close then softly rubbed the tip of her nose against mine. I loved how she did that. "You know," she said, "I think I finally figured it out."

I stared at her in confusion, trying to connect the dots of her subject shift. "What exactly have you figured out?"

Sabine inhaled slowly. "I figured out what you taste like."

It took me a few seconds to drag my mind back to that night. To the first night of the rest of our lives together. "And what's that?" I asked quietly, studying her.

"Home." The word had caught, and she tried again. "You taste like home."

"Oh…" I blinked hard to chase away the threat of tears, and set the roller down. "I, uh…" I cleared my throat. "I think I might have figured something out too."

She smiled a knowing smile. "And what's that?"

"That you're more than my desire, Sabine." I watched understanding dawn on her face as she too connected my dots from that night. "If I'm your home, then you're my safe harbor. The sanctuary where I can finally rest. You're my everything—my truth, my strength, my trust, my hope, and all my love." I shrugged and gave in to my tears. "You're the rest of my life."

Bella Books, Inc.

Women. Books. Even Better Together.

P.O. Box 10543
Tallahassee, FL 32302

Phone: 800-729-4992
www.bellabooks.com

CPSIA information can be obtained
at www.ICGtesting.com
Printed in the USA
JSHW052309230422
25147JS00002B/2